THE PREGNANT MAN

Social Orders

A series of monographs and tracts
Edited by Jacques Revel and Marc Augé
Ecole des Hautes Etudes en Sciences Sociales, Paris, France

THE PREGNANT MAN

Revised and Updated Fourth Edition

by

Roberto Zapperi

Istituto Enciclopedia Italiana, Rome, Italy

Translated from the Italian by
Brian Williams

harwood academic publishers
chur · london · paris · new york · melbourne

Harwood Academic Publishers

Post Office Box 197
London WC2E 9PX
United Kingdom

58, rue Lhomond
75005 Paris
France

Post Office Box 786
Cooper Station
New York, New York 10276
United States of America

Private Bag 8
Camberwell, Victoria 3124
Australia

Library of Congress Cataloging-in-Publication Data

Zapperi, Roberto.
    [Uomo incinto. English]
    The pregnant man / Roberto Zapperi; translated from the Italian
by Brian Williams. — Rev. and updated 4th ed.
        p. cm. — (Social orders, ISSN 0275-7524; v. 3)
    Translation of: L'uomo incinto.
    Includes bibliographical references.
    ISBN 3-7186-5033-9.
    1. Pregnant man (Tale)   2. Interpersonal relations in literature.
I. Title. II. Series.
GR75. P73Z3713 1990
398'.353—dc20   90-4198
                                                                      CIP

CONTENTS

v

PART III
Section I

Section II

Preface to the English Edition

This book, first published in Italian in Rome in 1979, was subsequently entirely rewritten and published in French in 1983, and in German in 1984. The two translations have led to some criticism and debate, and at least one contribution to this deserves special mention. This is by F. Delpech: "Culture folklorique et rapports de pouvoir—R. Zapperi: Le folklore et l'ordré tabli", in *Annales: Economie, Sociétés, Civilisations*, May–June 1987, pp. 687–703; it deserves mention because it introduced new elements, with the result that this English translation contains important variants (including one new chapter) and thus represents the latest state of development of the work.

List of Illustrations

1. Eve emerging from the side of Adam, and the Church from the side of Christ. A detail from the *Bible moraliste* (13th century). Paris. Courtesy of the Bibliothéque Nationale (Ms Lat. 11560, folio 186 r).
2. Birth of Eve and marriage of Adam and Eve. Wall painting (beginning of the 16th century). Church of Lohja, Helsinki. Courtesy of the National Museum of Finland, Helsinki.
3. The Fourth Commandment. Part of the *Ten Commandments*, Woodcut (15th century), Strasbourg.
4. Birth of Eve. Mosaic from the Cathedral of Monreale (12th century). Courtesy of Guidotti, Rome.
5. Birth of Eve and Expulsion from Eden. Reliefs from the Cathedral of Worms (14th century). Bildarchiv. *Photo Marburg*.
6. Birth of Eve (14th century). Cathedral in Freiburg in Br.
7. Birth of Eve, Sin, and Expulsion from Eden. Embroidery (1813). Stockholm. Courtesy of Musée du Nord.
8. History of the Creation of the World. Woodcut, (1849) Naples. Museum of Popular Traditions, Rome. *Photo Guidotti*.
9. The Miracle of the Healing of the Man with Dropsy. Mosaic (12th century) from the Cathedral of Monreale. *Photo Guidotti*.
10. Heinrich Douvermann: Altar of the Seven Sorrows of Mary. Detail from the *Flight into Egypt*. Wood carving (1521), Church of Saint Nicholas, Kalkar, Germany. *Photo Michael Jeiter*.
11. Battle of St Michael and the Dragon. Reverse side of copper-plated wooden cross (11th century). The National Museum of Denmark, Copenhagen.
12. The Last Judgement. Anonymous painting (Early 19th century). Courtesy of the National Museum of Finland, Helsinki.
13 Plan of Rome. Detail (13th century). Vatican Library. After G.B. de Rossi: *Piante iconografiche e prospettiche di Roma*, Rome (1879), Table 1. *Photo Guidotti*.
14 Urs Graf: Two Women brawling with a Monk. Drawing (1521) Basel, Kupferstichkabinet *Photo Kupferstichkabinet*.
15 The Doctor tells Calandrino of his Pregnancy. Wood engraving (1492). German translation of the *Decameron*, Staats- und Stadtbibliothek, Ausburg.
16 Gravelot: Calandrino's Abortion. Engraving (1761). *Decameron*, London (but actually Paris). *Photo Guidotti*.
17 Scenes of the Life of Witches. Woodcut (1511). Ulrich Tengler, Layenspiegel, Ausburg. *Photo Staats- und Stadtbibliothek, Augsburg*.
18 Linda Maestra. Francisco Goya. Etching from the *Caprichos* (1799).
19 Lucas Cranach: The Calf-Monk. Woodcut (1523). Martin Luther, *Deutung des Münchkalbs zu Freyberg*. August Bibliothek, Wolfenbüttel. *Photo Herzog*.
20 Domestic Harmony ensured by the Rule of the Husband. Woodcut (17th century). Courtesy of the Germanisches National Museum, Nuremberg.

PART I

Chapter 1
The Christian Myth: The Birth of Eve

Towards the end of the eleventh century, a strange hieroglyph began a slow but steady conquest of the cathedrals of Europe. It represented three figures in relation to one another—two men and a woman, or rather a half-woman, since all that one could see of her was the upper half emerging from the body of one of the men, within which (we are meant to understand) the remainder of her is contained. In some cases a scroll tells us that the scene refers to the creation of Eve; more often, however, the clue to understanding it for the unlettered (who were after all the majority of the faithful in this period) is provided by the context of the other Biblical scenes in which it is included.

The departure point for this voyage of conquest was the city of Augsburg in southern Germany, where the scene made its first appearance in a panel of the bronze doors of the cathedral. From the doors it climbed like a creeper into the reliefs which often provide a frame for them: in the lateral reliefs at San Zeno in Verona, but also in the frieze surmounting the architrave which we find in Andlau in Alsace. This brings us to the twelfth century, during which it headed off towards more distant horizons; in the north it reached Novgorod in Russia, and in the south, Monreale in Sicily. From the thirteenth to the fifteenth centuries it remained largely in the doorways, such as those of the cathedrals of Amiens and Auxerre in France, and the Sainte-Chapelle in Paris. In Germany we find it in the cathedrals of Freiburg in Breisgau, Ulm and Worms, and, in Italy in the Cathedral of Bologna and the Baptistery of Florence. However, even in the twelfth century, the doorways were not enough for it, and at Elne in Roussignol it can be found in a capital in the cloister. Later on, in the fourteenth century, it has reached the facade of the Cathedral of Orvieto, while in Florence it has found its way into the reliefs on Giotto's campanile. In all cases it obtains its objective of presenting its theme plainly to the eyes of the faithful, which accounts for the preference for the doorway, obviously the obligatory point of passage for all those who wanted to enter the church. This concern to transmit a message which was clearly felt to be of maximum importance was thus very evident, and it could not be allowed to remain merely outside the church. It thus passed through the doorways, to occupy walls and windows, altars, chapels and even holy-water stoups. Mosaics and frescos, windows, reliefs, ivories, arrases, altar-pieces and paintings representing the creation of Eve can be found in dozens of churches all over Europe, and not only in the cities, great and small, but in the countryside, in churches annexed to monasteries, or in tiny towns and villages lost in the mountains.

When the Reformation later banned all kinds of images from the new Protestant churches, the invention of the printing press made the diffusion of the images easier, and it was decided to accompany the faithful into their homes by regular illustrations in vivid images along with the Bible, in the vulgar tongue now being read daily by all the literate people of God.

Before beginning this conquest of the churches, the iconographical pattern of the creation of Eve had been through a long period of incubation, which reached maturity in the second half of the eleventh century; it remains obscure which routes actually brought it to that point. It is also surprising, for in the Biblical text, Eve does not emerge from Adam's side, but is created by God from one of his ribs. The text of Genesis is quite specific on this point (*Genesis* 2: 21–23):

> "So the Lord God caused a deep sleep to fall upon the man,
> and while he slept, took one of his ribs and closed up the
> place with flesh; and the rib which the Lord God had taken
> from the man he made into a woman and brought her to the
> man. Then the man said: "This at last is bone of my bones
> and flesh of my flesh, and she shall be called
> Woman because she was taken out of Man"."

The iconographical tradition which illustrates this Biblical account initially adhered to the letter of the text, beginning with a sarcophagus at Saint Paul's-without-the-Walls in Rome, dating from the fourth century. This shows two distinct and successive scenes, dedicated in the first case to the extraction of the rib, and in the second case to the creation of Eve from it. The two scenes appear, always distinct from each other, in the Carolingian miniatures, and they are again found on the bronze doors of the Cathedral of Hildesheim, dating from the early years of the eleventh century. However, when we come to the bronze doors of the Cathedral at Augsburg, which date from the second half of the same century, the scenes have already been fused into one: God extracts the whole body of Eve from the body of Adam, drawing it out with his left hand while he makes a gesture of benediction with his right.

Thus a new intention has been substituted for the original one; the creation of Eve is transmuted into an actual birth. The creation, in fact, becomes a procreation, and the role of the Creator himself passes to the agent of procreation: it is no longer God who creates Eve from Adam's rib, but Adam himself who procreates her, as an effect of the will of God. And so the gesture of benediction becomes a specific gesture of command, since Adam, as a mere man, can certainly not procreate—it must be that he does so by divine intervention. An act of procreation, with the role of man and woman inverted, is presented as a scene of creation, with a most important transition, mediated by divine will, of the feminine act of procreation into a masculine faculty of creation. While woman procreates children, it is man who in fact creates works and produces objects.

This is the obvious content of the image. But as we have seen, it no longer coincides with the Biblical text, of which it also claims to be a visual representation. The role of the male rib in the birth of Eve as found in *Genesis*, is not present here, and this is to be put down to the artist's own initiative—which, incidentally, enjoyed the full blessing of the ecclesiastical hierarchy, and could thus be adopted in churches all over Europe. The innovation was judged to be highly effective in terms of communication with the mass of illiterate faithful who filled the churches, but it was also seen as strictly orthodox on the doctrinal level, because otherwise such a wide diffusion of the image would never have been possible. There can be no doubt on this point; churchmen were agreed on the extraordinary effectiveness of visual representation, and it was certainly not just for aesthetic reasons that they allowed artists to introduce this novelty. Moreover, the artists were technicians in communication, enjoying an even higher degree of credibility in a society where the level of literacy was as low as it was in medieval Europe.

The fiction of this 'male parturition' acquired a new element of the greatest importance, introduced by the Fathers of the Church. Adam, explained St Augustine in his *Commentary on the Gospel of John*, "while he slept, was found worthy to receive the wife whom God had formed from his side, because the Church was to be born from Christ as he lay asleep on the Cross, so that from the rib of him who hung upon the Cross pierced by the lance, would flow the Sacraments of the Church." (15: 8)

Figure 1   Eve emerging from the side of Adam, and the Church from the side of Christ.

The artist, then, limited himself to a visual representation of the creation of Eve, as he would have represented the birth of the Church. The most convincing evidence of this assimilation on the visual level is found in a miniature in a *Bible Moralisée*, dating from the thirteenth century, which represents the birth of the Church above and the birth of Eve below, with one and the same image of a woman emerging from the side of a man (Figure 1).

It proved possible to superimpose the two myths on each other, and thus they converged in the same visual representation of Eve, for they are concerned with the same things, and in the first case with matrimony. For this reason the murals painted at the beginning of the sixteenth century in the little Finnish church of Lohja explicitly link the birth of Eve to her marriage with Adam. The same wall as surrounds the earthly paradise encloses the two scenes: above is the scene of the birth, and below, that of the marriage, celebrated by the Heavenly

Figure 2 Birth of Eve and marriage of Adam and Eve.

Father in the presence of two prelates who represent the church, which will continue His ministry through the centuries (Figure 2). The natural order of generation is overturned by Divine Command, in the context of the union between the man and the woman. The passage from *Genesis* (2: 24) ends with the well-known conclusion: "For this reason a man leaves his father and mother and cleaves to his wife, and they become one flesh". St Paul refers to this passage, which he reproduces verbatim, in order to sketch out the first rudiments of Christian matrimonial doctrine (*Ephesians* 5: 31). He also states: "Be subject to one another, out of reverence to Christ. Wives, be subject to your husbands, as to the Lord. For the husband is the head of the wife, as Christ is the head of the Church, his body." (*Ephesians* 5: 21–23). Christian matrimonial teaching is here presented with its essential connotations—defining the relationship of woman to man as one of subordination. But why was there the need to convey this traditional doctrine by making use of the fiction of a birth out of the man's side? And why did this need exist particularly in the latter half of the eleventh century?

We know that the Church itself was conquered in this period by a widespread movement of hierarchical and disciplinary reconstruction, which goes by the name of the 'Gregorian Reformation' Strengthened in its autonomy, the episcopate launched a violent offensive against the lay power in order to reverse the traditional relationship of strength, and to subjugate christian society to its own total control. As Georges Duby has recently reminded us, this struggle took place with particular tenacity in the field of matrimony—the institution stressed above all by St Paul, presented even as the image of the union between God and His creatures, and between Christ and His Church. The episcopate sought to impose its own rules on a society which professed christianity, but which governed itself in family matters and sexual issues on the basis of an ethic which was not yet christianised at all. This concept could be summed up in one fundamental point: sexuality is a foul and wretched thing, from which God's favoured children must know how to distance themselves. It may be permitted to those who are not called to special grace, in order to ensure the preservation of the species, but even then only within the context of monogamous marriage, and under the rigorous control of the Church—the sole source of authority for laying down times and modes. It was not easy to get people to submit to such harsh rules, even less in the top ranks of society, where the power to dispose of others and to take advantage of them for one's own pleasure found widespread response in the field of sexuality. In order to win, the Church had to offer substantial counter-concessions. The doctrine of subordination as defined by Paul was the most important of these; it was repeated and proclaimed as widely as possible, and in the end it would produce the clear consequence that it was the Church which came to offer the greatest guarantee of power. This guarantee was all the more necessary in that the Church's matrimonial teaching included an element which might well appear dangerous to the preservation of order. This was the clause of 'mutual consent' which matrimonial theology was not, at this time, able to avoid defining as an essential prerequisite to legitimate matrimony. In a society which reserved for the head of the family—the father or whoever was his delegate—the prerogative of deciding on the marital choice for his children, this principle of consent could even appear subversive. However, the Apostle had spoken clearly, and there could be no mistake: the great Christian conjugal mystery, the *Sacramentum Magnum*, in fact assumed not only that the wife would love the husband, but also that she would honour him (*Ephesians* 5: 33). It also assumed the obedience of children to their parents, which is enjoined in the subsequent chapter (6: 5-9). Obedience thus formed the bond between liberty and authority, and linked the free consent of the spouses to the will of their parents. Good and obedient children must consent freely to their parents' marital choice for them, and there should be no need for them to be constrained.

Georges Duby has singled out Bishop Ivo of Chartres as one of the greatest champions of the struggle in which the Church was engaged in the second half of the eleventh century to bend the practice of matrimony to the imperious demands of its own doctrine. Two of the most important canonical compilations of the western church can be traced back to him, and they too were concerned with matrimonial matters. "It is according to the natural order of the human race that women should be subject to men, and that children should submit to their parents, for in the human race justice demands that the lesser should serve the greater." (P.L.161: 603). Thus, an article in his *Decretum*, which reproduces a passage from St Augustine, links the doctrine of the family to the concept of the relationship of servitude. The formula was extremely effective: it passed into the *Decretum* of Gratian and remained in the *Corpus Juris Canonici* for centuries to come as a law of the Church. It also received the seal of approval of 'The Bride of Christ': as Hildegard of Bingen said to his scribe: "The woman is under the power of the man just as the servant is under that of his master". The basis of this close association was still that of the Pauline doctrine expounded in the Epistle to the Ephesians, which closes with a peremptory exhortation to servants to obey their masters. (*Ephesians* 6: 5–9).

Ivo of Chartres himself refers in a sermon (P.L.162: 506) to the close connection between the birth of the Church and the creation of Eve. According to Duby, it is from his influence that the *Glossa Ordinaria* of Anselm of Laon is derived. This was the most widespread of all the commentaries on the Bible, and in it the birth of Eve is explained in terms of a relationship of subordination. In a gloss on a passage from *Genesis* borrowed from Gregory the Great, Eve is said to have "come out of the side of Adam so that it may be made clear that one must command (i.e. the man) and one must be commanded (i.e. the woman)". (P.L.113: 90). Our iconographical scheme, therefore, was designed to show that Eve was symbolically born from the side of Adam because woman is in reality dependent on man. The choice of parturition was dictated by the conviction that giving birth, generation, implies domination by the generator over the generated.

In a letter of 1373/74 to her brother Benincasa, in which she reproves him for his neglect of their mother, St Catherine of Siena writes: "You have not taken account of the exhaustion that comes from giving birth, nor of the milk which she drew for you from her own breast, nor of the many wearinesses which she had to endure for you and for all her children. And if you tell me that she had no pity for you, I say that it is not so, for she had great compassion for you, and for all her other beloved children. But even if by any chance it were true, you would still be obliged to her and not she to you. She did not take her flesh from you, but on the contrary, she gave you of her own flesh". There could hardly be a more specific statement that the son is subject to his mother because she gave him being. Here, giving birth is adopted as the supreme title which legitimises power over one's children. The obvious and elementary contention that the mother makes the child and not vice-versa is linked to the power relationship within the family, in terms which recall the passage from *Genesis* (2: 23). If the birth of Eve from Adam was understood to legitimise the power of man over woman in terms of the power of the father over his child, its reversal signifies exactly the opposite—i.e. that the power of woman over man is seen to be lodged in the power of a mother over her child.

However, the implications of this reversal also involved an issue which was no less alarming in its own way. The myth of the birth of Eve had a preeminently matrimonial significance, because Eve was the bride of Adam. But if creation is converted in this way into procreation as happens constantly in the iconographical scheme which we are examining—then Eve becomes the daughter of Adam, and in the marriage of father and daughter there is an inescapable implication of incest. St Thomas Aquinas, the greatest of all the Doctors of the Church, is in a great hurry to free himself from this awkward dilemma. He must have seen various visual representations of the Birth of Eve, and he would have been struck by that particular element in the birth. In *Quaestio* No.1.92.2 of the *Summa Theologiae*, dedicated to the creation of woman, he effectively raises the question of incest, and provides it with a clever resolution: "Natural generation causes a "contraction" of an affinity which is in effect an impediment to marriage. But it is not by natural generation that the woman was produced by birth from man; it is by Divine Virtue alone. Thus Eve may not be called the daughter of Adam". Saint Thomas concludes then that Eve was not in a true sense Adam's daughter, and St Catherine would have agreed with this, because in her view Eve was Adam's mother! We should stress that she does not state this explicitly—indeed, how could she have done so? However, when she puts the question of the mother-child relationship in the terms which she uses in the letter to her brother, she does in fact end up by asserting this, even though she may not have intended to, or even realised that she was doing it.

It was not only to St Catherine that a mishap of this kind occurred in the Italy of the fourteenth century. A famous ascetic preacher and writer—one of the most widely read of his time—Jacopo Passavanti, slipped up in the same way, though for very different reasons, on the question of the incest of our primal forebears. He was a rigorist who pushed the Christian sexual phobia to its furthest limits, and he was not totally orthodox, in the sense that he even included (in his overall condemnation of sexuality) marital sex aimed at the procreation of children. Because of this, he makes one reference in his *Specchio di Vera Penitenza* to original sin as the sin of incest rather than that of pride. The reference is allegorical, but nonetheless unmistakable. For him, it was obviously a matter of incest between father and daughter, because Pride, of which Eve was the incarnation, led her to "marry herself to her father, most illegitimately, for it was from him that she was born." Thus she provoked divine punishment, and banishment from Eden. At the very origin of the family, therefore, he placed incest between father and daughter, thus departing radically from the letter of *Genesis*, which does not declare it specifically in the case of the first parents of the race, though it is admitted to have occurred in later generations in the story of Lot's daughters (*Gen.* 19: 31–38). In any case the whole of *Genesis*, according to a famous essay by Edmund Leach, tends in fact to absorb incest into the story of the family, and render it functional.

From ethological as well as anthropological research, we know that incest taboos have the purpose of allowing the permanent insertion of the male into the primary biological nucleus of mother/children. The family is constituted at the moment when the male is added to this nucleus and becomes its head. As the first rule of co-existence, the banning of other males from the nucleus is then established, to prevent them from having access to the women. It is on this ban, which neutralises the sexual initiative of the male children (his most powerful competitors) and directs their sexual drive outwards, that the power of the father is founded—and it manifests itself first of all as a sexual privilege over the women in the nucleus. But the incest taboo, instituted to safeguard this privilege, has fatal repercussions, and becomes in itself a natural limitation on it. For the father's privilege can only remain such with regard to his wife; in the case of his daughters it is forced to convert itself into a simple power of control over their sexual behaviour. The definition of the crimes of adultery and fornication, therefore, seems to be an automatic corollary of this incest taboo, as indeed does the father's prerogative of selecting his children's spouses, with the difference that for the females, the matrimonial choice must correspond with the sexual, while this is not so in the case of the males. The father only reserves to himself the choice of their marriage partner, without claiming to intervene in their sexual activities outside marriage. According to this scheme, which is still provisional and needs more historical and anthropological verification, the incest taboo structures the family into a hierarchical system, rooted in the inequalities of sex and age, and centring on the power of the father. Its important social consequences, perfectly identified by Levi-Strauss, have this rather disconcerting family hinterland which cannot be easily eliminated, and it is to this hinterland that the representation of the birth of Eve refers. With its inversion of the mother-child relationship into that of the father-child, it ends up by invoking the most dreaded incest of all—and the one that is most dangerous for the father, as the psychoanalyst Theodor Reik has pointed out.

This justification of the mother's claim to power menaced the family order which had been built up over more than a thousand years, and it could not be followed through to its conclusion. However, it reappeared sporadically, in isolated episodes and sudden unexpected flashes which for a moment light up the eternal struggle of the sexes for mastery over the family. The letter of St Catherine of Siena to her brother is one of these episodes; the case recorded in 1502 by the Bolognese chronicler, Gaspare Nadi, is another. On this occasion, the conflict put the mother in opposition to her daughter and to the father, for the latter were agreed on the choice of a husband whom the mother disliked. The mother claimed the power over her daughter, and in the father's absence she used extreme means of correction against her, even to the point of beating her to death.

But these were exceptions: the rule was quite different. The place of the mother in the family was certainly not that of the head, and even St Catherine of Siena acknowledged this. So while in the private letter to her brother she asserts the mother's power, in a public letter of 1376 (to Nicolo Soderini, one of the Priori, or governing council, of Florence), she transfers this power to the father, with a similar argument: "even though the father may offend, the son is never justified in taking revenge on him. He cannot and must not offend in his turn, or he will run the risk of death and damnation. He is always in debt to the father for his existence, which his father bestowed on him. The son must never ask his father to give him something of the substance of his flesh, and yet the father—moved by love for his son—may nevertheless make such a gift before he even thinks of asking." Here Catherine is obviously not talking about giving birth, but she does return to the argument about 'the flesh', and in place of parturition she mentions the 'substance of the flesh', evidently referring to the well-known Aristotelian/Thomist teaching about the predominance of the male seed in human generation.

This was the official view, as found in the *Ricordi* of a fifteenth century father, the Florentine Giovanni Morelli. On the occasion of the death of his greatly-loved son, he writes that he remembers "the hour and the place and manner in which he was generated by me, and what a consolation he was to me and to his mother." For him the mother had a purely subsidiary function in the process of generation: the decisive act of conception seems to him to belong primarily if not exclusively to the male. Gestation, birth and breast-feeding were absorbed in the initial moment of fertilisation, which occupied the principal place in the father's memory.

Every male-dominated society has a need to distort the biological fact of generation, and sometimes even to ignore its most obvious elements in order to claim a necessary primacy for paternity. This is clear from the exhaustive research by the anthropologist J.A. Barnes. In the place of parturition, in Morelli's *Ricordi*, fertilisation appears, for the obvious reason that in the natural order of generation the only clear contribution of the father is in his semen. But the importance of this is emphasised only to reach the conclusion that the son belongs to the father rather than to the mother. *Filium enim naturaliter aliquid est patris* (The son is naturally something belonging to the father), pronounced St Thomas (S.T.II.11.10.12). What mattered, therefore, was to clarify who had authority over the son, and it was only to legitimise this authority that it was necessary to know who had made him. The recourse to masculine parturition was thus an artifice of symbolic representation, in which the natural order of generation was overturned in conformity with the then prevailing pattern of authority.

While in the family it was the man and not the woman who commanded, one can easily see that in order to represent this relationship in symbolic terms with the greatest immediacy it might prove necessary to resort to portraying the man giving birth in one way or another to the woman. This was in fact the easiest and most direct way of representing what was merely a social relationship as both natural and even biological. But apart from this, what else was the laconic definition in the *Decretum* of Gratian actually saying? It is clear that the iconographical scheme of the birth of Eve was intended to convey a conception of the family based on a hierarchical organisation and dominated by the father. Symbolically he gave birth to the daughter-wife in order to assert his power over both of them. The child is of the female sex, since her image must also remind us of the wife. But in that she is a child, she also stands apart from her own sex so as to represent the simple filial relationship—a reference to her derivation from the father who procreates her. This means that the representation seeks to tell us that children—all children, whether male or female—are symbolically born from their father, because in social terms they depend on him and not on their mother, as they would do if the merely biological order of birth were to apply.

What dependence on the father could mean in specific terms, in the reality of family relationships, can be deduced clearly from an episode in the biography of St Francis of Assisi. When he fulfilled his religious vocation in 1207, he found himself in open conflict with his family. His father, a rich merchant, accused him of wasting his patrimony in almsgiving, and making a display of unwarranted extravagance. By virtue of the Statute of Assisi, which gave him the right to do so, he chained him for punishment in a sort of family prison, from which his mother released him a little later, profiting from his father's absence on a business journey. But it was he who gave the orders, not she, and in order to reassert the principle, the merchant appealed to the public authorities as soon as he returned from his journey. He called his son to judgment, and demanded justice against his wicked deeds and insubordination. He wished him to be exiled and reduced to the level of a pariah, as the law in fact provided. The saint saved himself by declaring his status to be that of a *conversus*, which automatically transferred him to the jurisdiction of the episcopal court. When his father summoned him before the bishop, he was able to make a speedy return of everything he possessed, and even handed over all his clothes. Thus he withdrew himself from the power of his earthly father, but only to pass under that of a heavenly father who was in fact far more stern and demanding.

We now come to one of the most difficult chapters in the whole of this already complex story. The clear subordination of woman to man involved in practice a drastic limitation of the mother's power over her children. But in the last analysis this risked compromising the whole family hierarchy and the principle of authority on which it was based. Though inferior to her husband, the wife nevertheless remained his companion, and could not lose the power over their children to the extent of joining them on a lower step of the family hierarchy. The hierarchical system of the sexes had to be reconciled with that of the generations.

The problem had already presented itself in the 12th century, in the theological reflections of Hugh of St Victor, which was then the highest point of artifice reached in the definition of Christian marriage teaching. Hugh sketched out a solution of great boldness: the woman, he wrote, "was made from the side of man so that it should be clear that she was intended for a union of love, and so that it should not be thought by any chance that—if she had been made from the head—she was intended to command, or—if she were made from the feet—she would have been subject to servitude. For in fact man was given neither a mistress nor a servant, but a companion; neither from the head nor from the feet was she to be drawn, but from the side, so that she would know that it was at his side that she must place herself." In St Thomas' *Summa*, however, the Victorine text is eliminated, and a note (I: 92.3) is added which deprives it of its most significant element—that which associates woman with her husband as a companion.

And yet, the fifth commandment had enjoined that we should honour both our parents, not the father only, but the mother too; and St Paul had certainly not overlooked this in the Epistle to the Ephesians. In fact no-one actually forgot it, but everyone was anxious to insist on the father's power, and preferred not even to hear mention of the power of the mother. In the *Book of Good Manners*, the fourteenth century manual of good behaviour by the Tuscan, Paolo da Certaldo, it is said that the good son "loves, esteems and honours his father" because he has brought him into the world, albeit with the aid of his mother. To the mother, on the other hand, love and honour only belong within certain limits, and in a totally subordinate fashion. Thus the father, when making his will, was to make sure he avoided committing the safe-keeping of his children to her, and the government of his house and patrimony, because "women are almost all vain and frivolous".

In the following century the position of the theologians is very different. Antoninus, Archbishop of Florence, writing a manual of behaviour for one of his devotees, referred to a specific widow who was to be "father and mother to her children: father to castigate and teach them, even when they reached sixty years of age, and mother to nourish them". The same position is to be found with even greater emphasis in the preachings of St Bernardino of Siena. Now it is a fact that both these saints—the first a Dominican and the second a Franciscan—took down and dusted off the ancient Victorine texts on the birth of Eve out of Adam's side, because she was meant to be his companion and neither his slave nor his mistress. For these two saints, the mother is the supplement and the helpmeet of the husband; she derives all her power from him, but she exercises it in her own right, and with the full necessary authority. The contradiction with the demands of the fifth commandment which might seem to arise from the myth of the birth of Eve was thus resolved by an implicit solution found within the myth itself. The visual representation had always stressed that Eve was born from the actual side of Adam, and the reason had to be that she must then place herself by his side. The woman was thus perfectly integrated as wife, mother and daughter, in that complex power-structure which is the family. "It is fitting that a father and mother should keep their children as servants" wrote St Bernadino: "bring yourselves to serve, from small things to great; make yourself pick up their shoes, wash their feet, massage and bathe them..." and again, "you, mother, have your daughter wash your hair and do you all other services." A Strasbourg print of around 1460 (Figure 3) illustrating the Ten Commandments, shows at the Fifth Commandment (Honour your father and mother), the

Figure 3   The Fourth Commandment.

father on his knees washing his son's feet in a bowl, while the mother is combing her daughter's hair, with the daughter holding her hands in an eloquent gesture. The woodcut gave examples, in a series of ten scenes, of the sins which observance of the Ten Commandments helped to avoid. In each scene a diabolical tempter appears, but in the fifth one he is missing; in his place we find this perfect inversion of roles which the scene represents as a sin in itself, evidently the work of the devil.

The family hierarchy, with its complex articulated structure of grades of power, emerges clearly in an episode from the trial of Joan of Arc, also in the fifteenth century. The Maid tells her judges that her parents "took great pains to watch over her and kept her in great subjection". When her father began to suspect that she wanted to go away with the soldiers, he said to her brothers (as her mother recounts) that if she did, they would have to drown her, or otherwise he would do so himself. To the question of whether she thought she had done right in running away from home without her parents' permission, since "one should honour one's father and mother", she answered that "she had truly obeyed her mother and father in all other things", but this time she had had to disobey because it was the will of God. However, the judges were unwilling to take this Will into account, and among the reasons for which they condemned Joan was the fact that she had "left the home of her parents against their will". "You were impious towards your parents", they said, "and you have transgressed the commandment of God to honour them". The power of controlling the sexual behaviour of the daughter—and this after all is what it was really all about—was recognised as belonging to parents, but in fact it was the father who exercised it, and delegated it to his male children, exactly as in the case of the incest taboo. The hierarchy is complex, but it is also quite specific and precise: the father stands at the head, then comes the mother, after her the male children, and finally the female children.

The moment has come to make a direct analysis of at least one of the visual representations of the birth of Eve, which play such a large role in creating the meaning of the myth. We shall choose one from the cathedral of Monreale in Sicily (Figure 4)—a twelfth century portrayal which is one of the most complete in all its details. Here we find the three figures with whom we have already met: on the left, the Eternal Father who is seated on a globe and is making an imperious gesture with his right hand while he holds a scroll of parchment in his left. He is clad in a stately tunic over which is a full-sized cloak, in contrast to the figures of Adam and Eve who are naked. Not only naked: they are also castrated, for the two bodies only show sexual characteristics in the man's beard and the woman's long hair. Adam is sleeping, resting on a contour of the land, while Eve is emerging half-length from his side,

Figure 4 Birth of Eve.

and stretching out her hand towards God.

The detail of the birth from Adam's rib occurs with greater or lesser emphasis. In some cases great stress is laid on it, as in the cathedral of Worms (14th century), but in all cases the creation is turned into a procreation which appears possible only through direct divine intervention. Of the two male figures, one is actually carrying out the act of procreation at the command of the other, who makes it possible through his omnipotence. The relationship between the two constrains one of them to passivity, but this passivity is recognised as such only in terms of the command, not in terms of the act itself. The act which is commanded, that of bringing forth the woman, is carried out by the sleeping man; he procreates while he sleeps. This means that he is acting because he submits to the will of the other. One commands and the other fulfils the command, but the representation of this particular mosaic presents the one who commands as active and the one who carries out the command as passive. The paradox of this visual representation faithfully reproduces the social relationship between the master who commands and does not work, and the serf who obeys and does work.

The serf, wrote St Thomas, differs from the irrational and inanimate beings in that he is "moved to action by the command of his master". And while such beings "do not have free mastery of their actions", man, on the other hand, "even when he is subject or subordinate, may certainly bow to the commands of others, but does so freely consenting" (II.II.50.2). The relationship of servitude, Thomas states, "being a punishment for sin, deprives man of rights which otherwise belong to him. The result is that the serf cannot any longer dispose of his own person" (II.II.189.6). He is "moved by his master's command because he is obliged to work for him." Elsewhere Thomas explains that the preservation of human life necessitates the support of serfs and women (I.II.105.4); without the labour of serfs, human life would be very much harder, and without the reproduction of the species ensured by woman, it would cease altogether.

Thus an equivalence is introduced between the production of goods and services and the reproduction of the species—an equivalence regulated by the principle of alienation which was introduced by original sin. Man is constrained by God's punishment to work for a master, just as woman is constrained by the same punishment to bear children for him. The children and the goods alike are produced by the woman and the serfs, but they belong to the husband and the master, because it is they who possess the command over those who produce them. The equivalence between creating and procreating is referred back to original sin, and is restored to the consciousness of society as the specific condemnation of mankind. We may be quite certain that this does not owe its origin merely to the thought of St Thomas, who in this (as in many other cases) simply limits himself to systemising one of the fundamental principles of the christian religion according to the dictates of the philosophical tenets of the time. "Religion", Marx wrote to Ruge in 1842, "does not live in the sky but on the earth". The relation of servitude which Thomistic doctrine defined was a human relationship, historically determined within the social framework, as we find it recorded in the evolution of language. In French (and the same applies to other neo-Latin languages) travailler means, from the Middle Ages onward, "to perform a work or a labour", but it also means "to suffer the pains of childbirth", and more generally, "to torment, or cause suffering". Its etymology takes us back to the Low Latin term *tripalium*, which an eleventh century gloss described as "the place where the guilty were whipped". From *tripalium* we move on to *tripaliare*, meaning to torture, and finally from there to *travailler*.

Thus, in the act of the birth of the woman from the man by divine commandment, the symbolic representation of the birth of Eve both includes and foreshadows the successive events of sin and punishment. We can find this represented in many illustrated cycles of the Genesis story, in the scenes of the temptation and of condemnation to labour (on the part of the man) and to childbearing (on the part of the woman). This means that the symbol of birth links production and appropriation to the biological means of procreation in the presentation of the myth. While in the natural order of the generation of children, the son is 'made' by the mother, in the social order the mother depends on her husband, who, as a consequence, controls the process of procreation and appropriates its fruits to himself. It is thus the father who commands, and who can dispose of both the mother and the children. In just the same way, in the social order of production, the master who has control appropriates the produce and proclaims himself to be the symbolic producer because it is he who commands, and imposes his will, thus becoming the effective producer.

In the fifteenth century tract, *Della Famiglia*, by the architect Leon Battista Alberti, there is a reference to a commonly-held opinion in his words: "It is always said that the villa is the work of true gentlemen and well-ordered husbandmen". According to this view, then it is the masters, the owners, who initiate agricultural enterprises, take care of them and maintain their productivity by their efforts. The farm is theirs, as are its products, because both belong to those who 'make' them—in symbolic terms, of course. The symbolic substitution of the proprietor for the peasant who does the actual work is carried to such a point that Alberti can say that it is the proprietor who "cultivates and takes care of his fields". This same proprietor (an architect and a town-dweller) had been praising the country a little earlier on because one could live peacefully and calmly there and enjoy the fruits of the labours of others. ("You may retire to the farm and live there in tranquillity, providing nourishment for your family"). Needless to say, the praise of the country involved the use of the metaphor of the farm being fertile just as the wife is fertile. It must be cared for and governed, just like a wife, so that precious fruit can be obtained from it. The idyll was interrupted only by the unavoidable presence of villeins—i.e. of the effective working force, who are thieves by definition, because "they always seek to possess, and to appropriate by any available means, what is truly yours".

The appropriation of children has as little legitimacy as that of produce, and the axiom of "he who makes, appropriates" is not even valid; firstly because he does not 'make' alone, and also because it should follow that the actual producer should also be able to appropriate his produce. But the child is not an object of produce, he or she is a human being, and as such cannot belong to others but only to himself or herself.

The rule of appropriation/expropriation is a rule of violence, which presupposes a coercive capacity in order for it to be effective. But St Thomas always has a formula to hand: the orderly development of human life demands a precise division of tasks between those who command and those who must, of necessity, obey. Since "according to the order established by God in nature, it is a necessity for inferior beings to submit to the impulses which are given to them, so in the same way, by natural and divine right, it is a duty for men to obey their superiors." (II.II.104.1).

In this way we have reached the roots of public authority, and its divine legitimisation. "Christianity does not decide to what measure constitutions are good, for it knows no difference between constitutions; it teaches (as all religion should teach): submit to authority, for all authority comes from God". Thus Marx wrote in 1842. The symbolic representation of the Birth of Eve also teaches the same notion. The male figure seated on the globe commands and disposes of the lives of the other two figures, and for this very reason represents power at its highest level. The globe on which he is seated obviously represents the world, and the power which he exercises over it. The roll of parchment held in his hand symbolises the law, on the basis of which judgment and condemnation are executed. But this 'man' in the representation is in fact God himself, because the relationship of submission which exists between God and man repeats and amplifies the one which subordinates the serf to his master. The relationship of servitude is sublimated by religious sentiment, and it re-enters the life of society as a relationship of subjection. At the end of this process of doctrinal distillation, the master finds himself sovereign, and the slave subjected. To govern is only a more general mode of commanding, and it involves the exercise of the reason and the will, reserved exclusively for a small élite, because it is clear that "the subordinate and the serf, as such, do not have to govern but rather to be governed and directed" (II.II.47.12). The myth of the birth of Eve thus gathers together the whole of the Christian philosophy of power, with its roots based in the family and its disciplinary effect on all social relationships, into one comprehensive and representative image.

Towards the end of the 11th century, Bishop Ivo of Chartres had preached that at the marriage of Christ with his church, the invited guests were "all mankind, whether noble or non-noble, rich or poor: all conditions, all sexes, all ages." (P.L.162: 607). Generous though it may have seemed, this invitation concealed an intimation and concluded with a threat: to the "multitude of reprobates who preferred the Lordship of the Devil to that of Christ", he recalled the Gospel parable of the marriage feast and its sinister conclusion: "Many are called but few chosen" (*Matthew* 22: 14). The marriage to which St Ivo invited his listeners was the mystical one which sealed the entry of the faithful into the Christian community, but it was also a real one, which rested on the family and its basic support. The ideology of the family and the relations which regulated it must therefore proceed step by step with christianisation itself, and involve all the levels of society, including the lowest level, which of course included the overwhelming majority of the population. The penetration of the christian family ethic was slow and laborious, but it continued progressively over the centuries, and eventually conquered the whole of society.

The traces of this slow conquest can even be found in proverbs. This ancient fount of popular wisdom is in fact widely affected by biblical and scriptural quotation. Armed with the strength which enabled the Church to bombard its people from the pulpit and dominate them from the privacy of the confessional, it succeeded in converting its precepts into popular sentiments:

> "he who beats his wife with a stick is a holy
> angel in the sight of God",

says one German proverb, present in a collection published as early as 1630, and this is perfectly in harmony with a French proverb of the 16th century:

> "Good horse and bad horse both need the spur;
> Good wife and bad wife both need the stick"

"A man may correct his wife not only with words but, when the occasion arises, also with the rod"—so we find in the *Summa Sacrae Theologiae* of St Antoninus, Bishop of Florence (III.XIII.IX.4). Three centuries later, in the middle of the eighteenth century, and almost on the eve of the French Revolution, we find the same sentiment in the *Theologia Moralis* of Alfonso Maria di Liguori (also a saint, naturally) (III.III.II.V) Here there is a slight modification, in that the beatings should be 'moderate', and the cause must be quite serious. But Christian pedagogy of the rod has a much wider application, as we all know, in the education of children. St Antoninus (IV.II.V.6) recommended it warmly, and St Alfonso (III.III.II.1) also expected to see it used—though with the usual moderation, of course.

"Spare the rod and spoil the child", runs a proverb which occurs in England and Germany in all ages, and a lapidary Italian proverb responds to this in just two words: Padre padrone (father/master). There is an ancient French saying which goes:

"Very justly is he punished,
When his boss he disobeys..."

The primal parents, Adam and Eve, are also present in the proverbs, taken as the prototypes of the sexual role in the family, in faithful conformity to the Christian doctrine which we have already encountered:

"When Eve commands, Adam sins"

An Italian proverbial saying merely reproduces a gloss by St Augustine on the passage from *Genesis* which we have already met with frequently (II: 21–24): "What can be worse than a house in which the wife rules the husband?" he asks in his *Commentary on the Gospel according to St John* (2: 14). Among the proverbs we also find a flourishing but unacknowledged echo of the Victorine teaching on the creation of Eve from Adam's rib, even though the Thomist version has softened it so as to deprive it of some of its more important implications:

"Eve was made from the Rib,
For she must neither grow above the head of her
husband,
nor lie between his feet."

Thus proclaims a German proverb which appears for the first time in a collection printed in 1605. The Victorine text must surely have made its appearance by this time through preaching, in which it had a widespread currency. The theologians had discovered its importance for the purpose of better integration of women into the family scheme of government. The old text met up with another motif from folklore, this time a visual one, and thus we return to the figurative representations of Eve, as they were seen by the illiterate faithful in German churches. The proverb literally states that "Eve must not grow above the head of her husband", and there is an obvious reference to the fact that in Germany Eve was often represented as a baby emerging from Adam's side. The baby would obviously have to grow to become his wife, but according to the proverb, she must not grow to the extent that she would exceed him in height. If she were to become taller than him, she might feel entitled to command him, and this absolutely must not happen. "Take a wife smaller than yourself if you want to be master" is the recommendation of an Italian proverb. Eve appears as a child in the reliefs which decorate the main doorways of the Cathedrals in Worms and Freiburg (Figures 5 and 6). The carvings make a discreet reference to her future growth and to the conjugal destiny which is to crown her existence—by providing the child with the breasts of an adult woman. The gesture of her hands, which seek to cover them in modesty, takes on a greater significance in terms of Eve's matrimonial destiny, since it obviously cannot avoid reference to sexuality altogether. In the upper image of the relief in Worms, which represents the scene of the expulsion from the Garden, we can see that Eve has grown and has already enacted the sexual sin, but her height is slightly less than Adam's, as the proverb demands that it should be.

There is also a little German riddle which refers to the same myth, with its deliberate confusion between creation and procreation, and its inevitably incestuous outcome:

"I am dead and not born
I married my father at the age of one day,
and I had no mother..."

In order to propagate its own ideology of family relationships, the Church made extensive use of the means of communication then available through the visual arts, as we have already seen. In fact, the myth of the birth of Eve as a figurative representation was widespread all over Europe and it was not limited to the churches. From them it passed into printed Bibles by the second half of the fifteenth century, and in this way it also penetrated into the intimate life of the family; it also came to adorn all sorts of domestic furniture. Alone, or in company with other scenes from the Genesis Cycle, it appeared on carved wooden furnishings, copper and brass plates, majolica and other domestic fittings. These objects of domestic use take us into quite different social environments, though to judge from the quality and the provenance of

Figure 5 Birth of Eve and Expulsion from Eden.

the artefacts these environments were almost invariably well-off. Moreover the manufacture of these objects corresponds perfectly to their destination, since it follows the path of what came to be called the 'Major Arts'.

The iconographical scheme of the Birth of Eve had a complex role in the history of the visual arts in western Europe, a role involving innovations, regressions and resistances, which are all accurately reflected in these objects. The most important innovations, introduced by Lorenzo Maitani at the beginning of the fourteenth century into the reliefs on the facade of Orvieto Cathedral, concern the replacement of the birth of Eve from Adam's rib by a kind of euphemism: Eve no

Figure 6   Birth of Eve.

longer emerges at half length from the sleeping Adam's side, but appears with almost all her body outside, leaving only the feet and ankles within his side, or perhaps hidden behind him. This innovation, which tended to camouflage the crude representation of male parturition by a characteristic euphemistic device, was widespread in Renaissance Italy, and it even appeared, by the hand of Michelangelo, on the ceiling of the Sistine Chapel in the Vatican. In the rest of Europe it met with much more gradual acceptance, for reasons both of taste and culture. In 1530, for instance, Lucas Cranach remained faithful to the older medieval scheme in his painting *Das Paradies* which is now in the Vienna Kunsthistorisches Museum. In the course of the sixteenth century, however, the Italian innovation began to make headway north of the Alps, and slowly gained favour among painters.

A subsequent innovation which took place in the eighteenth century probably originated in France, though I do not know of any single direct attestation of this. However, it is obviously merely a matter of the iconographical representation of the new creed of Deism spread by the philosophers. To Voltaire, for instance, it seemed absurd that "the unengendered, immutable nature of Almighty God should take the form of a man." The Eternal Father exits from the scene of the Birth of Eve, as far as I have been able to ascertain, in an eighteenth century print by the Augsburg artist, Martin Tyroff. A Delft majolica, also from the eighteenth century, and a Swedish embroidery dated 1813, also leave out the Eternal Father, and are thus fully aware of this innovation, and they also show awareness of the previous one, by which the euphemism was introduced. Eve, who is in fact standing upright, has her feet and ankles hidden behind Adam's side as he sleeps, stretched out on the ground. In the Dutch majolica, Eve is thoughtfully holding in her hand the rib of Adam from which she has been 'made', with a gesture which in itself contradicts the idea of parturition from the side of man, though she continues to suggest that allusion, on the other hand, by the fact that her feet and ankles are hidden by the sleeping man. Here Eve is pointing a finger towards Adam's side, which shows a scar at the point from which she emerged. The two gestures are as unusual as they are irreverent; they have a doubtful significance, which gives every sign of seeking to contradict the role which ancient tradition had given to Eve. The submissive woman of former times—even after her body had been restored to wholeness by the use of the euphemism, made only gestures of recognition and adoration. Now, however, she is clearly taking on the mastery (or mistressry) of herself, and controlling the situation. While Adam sleeps, she shows an obvious scepticism about the alleged circumstances of her birth. The times were a-changing, and at Versailles it was now Madame de Pompadour who was in command—not merely of matters of taste, but also in matters of much greater significance. She had a heavy influence on Rococo taste, including the choice of subjects and the symbolic meanings which they were chosen to represent. Both the print and the majolica, therefore, belong to the vogue for that kind of aristocratic feminism which spread all over Europe from Versailles in the course of the century of the Enlightenment. This feminism was aristocratic in that it concerned itself with the inequalities of the sexes only within that narrow upper class, and showed no interest in the more general inequality which prevailed in all other areas of society.

The 1813 Swedish embroidery is in fact intended to be a decisive counter-statement to that vogue of aristocratic feminism (Figure 7). Here Adam appears clothed, and this detail must be seen in relation to the disappearance from the scene of the Eternal Father. We know that his full-length stately outer garment regularly appeared as a symbol of power, contraposed to the nakedness of his defenceless creatures. When Adam appears clothed in the scene of the Birth of Eve, it means that in visual terms he has taken on one of the fundamental attributes of the Eternal Father; the power of the Creator is transformed into that of the procreator, and procreation takes on the role of creation itself. Thus, even though he is asleep, Adam controls the situation, and once again

Figure 7   Birth of Eve, Sin, and Expulsion from Eden.

Figure 8 History of the Creation of the World.

assumes his ancient role of husband/father/master. In 1813, only two years before the opening of the Congress of Vienna which ushered in the Restoration, this idea had every attribute necessary for it to be in keeping with the times; this was even more the case because it used typical modes of popular art for its figurative representations. The European reaction to Napoleonic despotism, the legitimate child of the Enlightenment and the French Revolution which crowned it, must surely make use of popular garb for some purpose? After the Second Empire had seemingly wiped out the last remaining nineteenth century illusions of revolution in Europe, Adam reappears naked, and the Eternal Father is able to resume his place of command, clad in the sumptuous garment of former times. Only Eve continued to hide her feet and ankles behind Adam's flank, as we can see in Gustav Doré's print dedicated to the Birth of Eve, and used in his Illustrations to the Bible published in 1864.

The three scenes of the Birth of Eve, the Temptation, and the Expulsion from the Garden, can also be found in the woodcut which provides the frontispiece for a little book of eight pages—the *Istoria della Creazione del Mondo*, printed by Avallone in Naples in 1849 (Figure 8). Avallone was noted for his vast production of tracts; in this

Italian text, a version of the Bible story which remains faithful to the original is presented. But the woodcut makes no reference to the rib, and in fact the visual representation of the birth of Eve is shown according to the medieval scheme. On the right, the familiar trio appears: Adam stretched out in sleep on the ground, Eve emerging from his side as in the past, and the Eternal Father bending over him, holding him beneath the arm with his own hand, and drawing him towards himself. All we can see of Eve is her head with its long hair, and a hand resting trustingly on the Eternal Father's shoulder. All the innovations introduced into the iconographical scheme over so many years of the history of European art are cancelled in one moment. The same iconographical conservatism is characteristic of other aspects of the woodcut also; for instance the serpent with the head of a woman twisted round the tree of the knowledge of good and evil, and other animals of a vaguely medieval appearance, among which we can even distinguish a unicorn. The archaism, however, is associated with the inclusion of typically naive elements which refer to the popular art of the centuries which followed the middle ages. This applies to the Eternal Father's crown, the sun and moon, and indeed to the Eternal Father himself in the foreground. This woodcut contains one of the last representations to have come to light of the story of the Birth. But by a curious coincidence, not entirely without significance, its composition recalls the first representation of all—the eleventh century one adorning the bronze doors of the Cathedral in Augsburg. Eight centuries have passed, and have not passed in vain. The ancient christian message continues its subtle penetration of society, moving downward through the classes until it finally reaches the lowest steps in the social scale.

Around 1883, the Italian folklore expert Serafino Amabile Guastella gathered from an illiterate peasant that he was in the habit of beating his wife, and he asked him why this was so. "Neither God nor the Law bestows any such unjust right on you", he said. The peasant was astonished at his indignant tone, and he told him the following tale to illustrate his motives.

When the Lord God made Adam, he led him first to the earthly paradise, to show him all the animals which would be useful to him, and those which would be harmful. The first animal was the ox: Adam sees him and the Lord says: "This one is called the ox, and he will serve you to till the soil." Then they see the ass, and the Lord says: "See, Adam, this is the ass, and he will serve you by carrying you on his back. This one is called dog, and he will serve you by guarding your house against thieves, and here is the cat and she will keep all the rats and mice away. And this is the cock, he will warn you when to expect bad weather." Now while they were talking, Eve came up—she whom the Lord had created a little earlier from Adam's rib—and up she came with swaying hips, all decorated with flowers. And this animal—what is she called?" Adam asked the Lord, who replied "This is not an animal, but your companion, the one who must bear your children—but make sure that you are the master, and that she is your servant, and must obey you in all things." "And what if she isn't willing to obey, Lord?" And the Lord turned round and showed him the rod of oak, and asked him: "What is this called?" "It is called an oak rod", he answered. "No", replied the Lord, "You're wrong, Adam. When it serves to minister justice to your wife, it isn't called a rod; it's called reason. Lay it across her and you'll find she'll become as mild as a sheep."

The peasant who told this tale was called Mariano, and he lived in Chiaramonte, a village in Sicily. The leader of the Church in Sicily, Cardinal Michelangelo Celesia, had declared only a few years earlier: "Every power comes from God", and in his Pastoral Letter of 1879 he added: "since it is in accordance with the Gospels that authority is grounded in parents as in masters, and in the right of the heavenly Father and Master". It was this divine investiture which Mariano meant to refer to in his story, because this investiture also included authority to beat one's wife! Even if Cardinal Celesia happened to omit it in his pastoral letter (a moment of distraction, perhaps?) another and more authoritative Cardinal, Giuseppe D'Annibale, left no doubt about it when he wrote in his very polished Latin in the *Summula Theologiae Moralis* (XI.1.561), which we quote here in the 3rd edition of Rome, 1891: "since the man is the head of the conjugal society... the woman must be submissive to him, but as a companion rather than as a slave, even though she owes him obedience. From this it derives that if she does not obey him in serious matters she is guilty of a moral lapse, and the man may administer the appropriate chastisement". Certainly Mariano knew no Latin —in fact he did not even speak Italian, knowing only the Sicilian dialect—but he came straight to the point nevertheless. For him the *coercitio* of which the learned Cardinal, was speaking in 1891 meant nothing other than those beatings which until recently the theologians had been quite specific about: had not St Alfonso of Liguori spoken of *moderatis verberibus* (moderate beatings)? The great folklore collector, who was incidentally himself a baron and a rich landowner, was thus making a great mistake when he denied the peasant's right to beat his wife, and he was even more mistaken when he claimed that the law did not recognise that right.

Article 131 of the Civil Code then prevailing in Italy laid down that the husband is head of the family, while Article 515 of the Penal Code provided for the punishment of "Ill-treatment of one spouse by the other", but only when this was serious and frequent. The law of the

State was thus in perfect harmony with the teaching of the Church, since juridical doctrine coincided with theological. According to both jurisprudence and doctrine, the intention was only to punish "the excessive use of an action which, when used appropriately, is recognised as legitimate by every law", since the person who exercises authority—whether of father or tutor or instructor or manager or master—has the right to correct those placed under him by manual and moral means... the crime thus consists not in the use of that right, but in its abuse." We can see a confirmation of this in the article "Maltrattamento in famiglia, o verso fanciulli", in the *Digesto italiano*, the great juridical encyclopedia published over a twenty-year period, which summarised the juridical thought and practice of the time. It is worth noting that the powers of the husband were again confused with those of the father, instructor, manager and master. Authoritarian morality was always the same, and remained unaltered as the basis of the Civil Code. With his Biblical tale, the Sicilian peasant limited himself to referring it back to its original source. The ambitious programme for the conquest of society begun by Bishop Ivo of Chartres long ago at the end of the eleventh century had thus reached its fulfilment: now Europe could call itself truly Christian, at all levels and in every class of society.

Chapter 2
The Theme in Folklore

a) *The Pregnant Man of Monreale*

In the Cathedral of Monreale in Sicily, built by the Norman kings towards the end of the twelfth century, the Birth of Eve appears twice: in a panel on the bronze doors and in the mosaics of the inner facade, which we have already mentioned. It is given great prominence in both presentations, precisely at points where the eye of the faithful was bound to be caught just before they entered and left the church.

The eye of the faithful was certainly meant to stop there; this is what both the clergy and the monarch intended. But it would not be likely to remain fixed there for long; it might well prefer to wander elsewhere, in which case, thanks to a trick of fate and the influence of the folklore tradition, it might come to rest on a quite different scene. This time it is one from the New Testament, but as it is a subject of minor doctrinal importance, it has been relegated to one of the lateral mosaics, in the left hand side aisle of the nave (Figure 9). Two male figures stand in the foreground, in front of a building which looks like a Christian church. The first of them, dressed in a tunic and cloak, bearded and with a halo, is making the right-handed gesture of omnipotence with which we are already familiar; with his left hand he holds the wrist of the other man, who is, contrastingly, naked, or rather wearing only a girdle covering his genitalia and leaving his belly exposed. This is swollen and elongated, in the shape of a pear. Two groups of men with an air of authority about them are standing behind the two main figures, and form a kind of train in the background.

The Latin inscription above the scene cites a passage from the Gospel according to St Luke (Ch.14: 1–6), and it states specifically that the scene represents the miracle of the healing of the man suffering from

33

Figure 9 The Miracle of the Healing of the Man with Dropsy.

dropsy, on the Sabbath. In the Gospel passage, after he has cured the dropsy victim, Jesus says that despite the Jewish custom, it was legitimate to heal on the Sabbath, in case of need. "If one of you has a son, or even an ox, and it falls into a well, will you hesitate to haul it out on the Sabbath?" he asks. This is what we read in some current versions of the Gospel. But in the Latin translation of St Jerome—the famous Vulgate, which was widely recognised and exclusively used in the western Catholic tradition until quite recently—we find the word 'donkey' instead of the word 'son' This reading—of donkey—is also quite well-attested in the manuscript tradition of the Greek version of St Luke's Gospel. It appears for the first time in the *Codex Sinaiaticus* of the first half of the fourth century—i.e. well before St Jerome undertook his translation into Latin, and it became the accepted reading in later versions, probably because of the influence of that translation. The preference for the term 'donkey' may possibly be due to the fact that in Greek manuscript writing the two words are quite similar in appearance, and could easily be confounded (the Greek uios and onos, meaning son and donkey respectively). The error (always assuming that it is an error and not a Freudian slip) was later given credence, almost certainly, because of association of ideas: the ox could easily be associated with that other beast of the stall which recurs so often in the gospels. Moreover, in St Luke's Gospel itself (13: 15), the ox and the ass had already been associated with each other in another incident which occurred a little earlier. This referred to the healing of a woman bent double, and it also took place on the Sabbath. The genuine text of the passage on the healing of the man with dropsy undoubtedly speaks of a son, not of a donkey; it is the word which we find in the most ancient and authoritative sources, like the third-century papyri and the fourth century *Codex Vaticanus*. This reading is also found in several later but equally authoritative manuscripts which reject the reading 'donkey', at least until the eleventh century. The word 'son' returned to usage with the rise of protestant philology in the eighteenth century, which culminated in the famous Berlin Edition of the Greek text, first published by Lachmann in 1831.

Lachmann's philological researches, however, took some time to penetrate through to Monreale. The Italian clergy of the last century, after all, were obliged to use the Vulgate; they knew little or no Greek, and had never heard the name of Lachmann. 'Donkey' was what they read in all the Italian translations I have been able to find, and it was only at the beginning of the present century that the reading 'son' began to reappear—evidently through the influence of modernism, which introduced the Italian clergy (amid a flurry of excommunications and purges) to the study of Biblical philology.

The 'son' whom the Catholic Church had ignored for so many centuries was reintroduced unexpectedly at Monreale, but not as a result of philological research! He came back to life through folklore, on the basis of a visual representation of the miracle, which can be seen in the mosaic of the cathedral there: the swollen belly of the dropsy victim, which fatally recalled the 'son' buried by the Vulgate beneath the word 'donkey'.

In the Sicily of the nineteenth century, there was still a proverb in current use which ran: "Anything can happen except a pregnant man:

and even then, there's the pregnant man of Monreale!''. The historian of popular tradition, Giuseppe Pitré, commented in 1875: "The people say that in the Cathedral of Monreale there is an image of this pregnant man, and they point it out as being in one of the mosaics representing the miracle of Jesus Christ healing the man suffering from dropsy". Other evidence from folk tradition may be added to the visual representation of the miracle, such as the tale told in the village of Borghetto, not far from Monreale. "A man from Monreale is taken ill and calls in the doctor. The doctor asks for a sample of his urine. The wife accidentally throws the sample away, and in order to escape reproach, she gives the doctor her own urine instead. By chance she happens to be pregnant; the doctor, thinking that there is no doubt that the urine is her husband's, declares that the man must be pregnant. This is the origin of the story of "the pregnant man of Monreale".

The series concludes with a story told to Pitré by a woman of the people—the Palermitan Rosa Brusca: "This pregnant man of Monreale was a fellow whose belly and thighs were swelling up, and they swelled so much that he was on the point of death. The barber-surgeons came and bled him, but when they cut him open instead of water or pus, a baby came out. It was a great sensation and even today they still talk of the pregnant man of Monreale."

In one of his collections of unpublished proverbs, the eighteenth century scholar the Marquis of Villabianca explains the proverb connected with the pregnant man of Monreale (which was evidently well-known in his day) by a local event which had happened in his own lifetime. According to him, it was a question of a hermaphrodite in a noble family of Palermo—the Abbé Corvino. "Since the female sex was predominant in his youth, he was made pregnant by a certain Commendatore Carlo Castelli, to whom he bore a girl in Monreale. This girl, Girolama Castelli, later married a certain Leonardo Cadelo, a nobleman of Trapani. After the birth, the female Corvino became a male, and setting aside the woman's attire, he donned the monastic habit instead and became an abbé". From the genealogical records of the Sicilian nobility, it emerges that at least three of the people in this story really did exist. A certain Salvatore Corvino was Vicar-General of the Archdiocese of Monreale at the end of the eighteenth century and he could easily have been the hermaphrodite referred to by Villabianca. There have always been hermaphrodites who have opted during the course of their lives to abandon the female role for that of the male. However it seems to be a strange coincidence that Corvino, who was a Palermitan in every sense, should have allowed him/herself to be made pregnant by another Palermitan—and should have done so at Monreale of all places, and borne the child there. There is also the fact that the historical figure of the Abbé Corvino can only be found in the sources kept at Monreale under the title of Vicar-General—a post he only held in old age. The location where the incident is said to have taken place (if it really did happen at all) can easily be explained by a mere reflection of this position. Moreover, according to Villabianca's explanation, the pregnant man of Monreale was only recognised as such afterwards—i.e. as a consequence of his decision to change from the female to the male role. This local event was thus reabsorbed into the folklore tradition linked to the mosaic in the cathedral, like the Borghetto story which can be found in one form or another all over Europe from the middle ages onwards—though obviously with no reference to Monreale.

The folklore tradition of the Pregnant Man of Monreale gathers certain significant elements together, and blends them into a comprehensive context. These elements make it possible for us to establish a direct connection between the folklore motif of the pregnant man and the Christian myth of the Birth of Eve. The visual representation of the healing of the man suffering from dropsy presents us with an image of two principal characters—both of them male— which recall certain aspects of the Birth of Eve. Christ reminds us— almost too obviously—of the figure of the Eternal Father in that earlier scene by the power which he is exercising: this is made clear by his clothing, his halo and his gesture. It is the same gesture of command as we saw previously, and in the gesture of contact, by which he takes hold of the wrist of the dropsy victim, as if to draw him to himself, we find an echo of the gesture of extraction which is often to be found in the medieval iconography of the Birth of Eve. (In Monreale it is absent from the mosaic, but present in the panel on the door). In common with Adam, the man with dropsy has the characteristic of passivity, and submission with head bowed to sickness and nakedness. In this scene too, the clothed man is active and potent while the naked man is passive and impotent. Eve, of course, does not appear here, but her place is taken by the swollen belly of the dropsy victim, from whose misery Christ must free him. According to the folk interpretation mentioned by Pitré, the miracle of the healing of the man with dropsy was nothing else than the pregnancy of man, willed by God. In other words, instead of healing the victim of his disease, Christ would allow him to give birth, exactly as happens in the visual representation of the Birth of Eve. The symbolic logic which governs the representation of this scene was thus transferred by an exact parallel to that of the miracle of the healing of the dropsy victim. This was not just a natural transposition, however; it was aimed at contesting the doctrinal message which the representation of the Birth of Eve was meant to convey.

The first little folk-tale introduces us to intimate family life, presenting us with the couple's relationship as it was regulated by the unwritten laws of matrimony. The exchange of the urine stresses the contradiction in the marital relationship between the real and the symbolic roles of the two partners. The husband, weakened by his illness, is *de facto passive*, even though he is *de jure active* (because as the husband he is in command). The wife, who is healthy even though she is pregnant, is *de facto active*, even though *de jure* she must be passive, in obedience to her husband. The rule of married life thus demands that the merit of the pregnancy belongs to the husband and not to the wife. The proverb confirms this contradiction, since it says: a male pregnancy, impossible in the natural order, becomes possible in the symbolic order. The anecdote seems to confirm this—not only is it possible, but actual. "It's incredible but true", Rosa Brusca tells Pitré: the son was born to his father and not to his mother. The symbolic order thus imposes itself on the biological order, and takes its place in the consciousness of society. And not just of any society, but of that society which is historically described as "Christian society". The mention of Monreale, constant in all these testimonies from folklore, has the effect of a specific historical reference. Monreale means the visual representation of the two scenes, from the Old and New Testaments, present in the Cathedral there—the Birth of Eve and the Healing of the Man with dropsy. The first scene provided the key to the reading of the second, and the dropsy victim was identified with the pregnant man. This tendentious reading of the healing miracle was far from being arbitrary; indeed it revealed a profound understanding of the message which it was intended to convey. So profound, in fact, that it managed to effect a perfect restoration of the Gospel text without the aid of philology!

In the Gospels the miracles of Jesus are always witnesses and previews of the redemption of man through the work of the Saviour. The salvation of the body from sickness and death thus always symbolises that of the soul from sin and damnation: the remission of sins which has been merited by faith. Now in the Gospel according to St Luke, this complex doctrine of salvation is gradually expounded with the example of many miracles, which from time to time lay special stress on one or other of its elements. This is due to one of the concerns of proselytism, which made frequent use of metaphor derived from the experience of everyday life, for this could be brought into play in order to aid the understanding of the message transmitted by the miracle.

There is more to this, however. Intervention, even if it involved violation of the Sabbath rest, to extract a son or an ox who had fallen into a pit, was already provided for by Hebrew tradition. It was in fact the Pharisees who specifically prescribed it (*Baba Qamma*, V.6, and

Joma 84b), as against the rigorous prohibition enjoined by the Sadducees. In St Luke's Gospel this intervention is adopted, however, against the Pharisees themselves, as a metaphor of salvation, used in connection with the miracle of the man with dropsy. Jesus saves the dropsy victim not only in a bodily sense. He also saves his soul. The healing miracle thus redeems him from sin, and regenerates him to the new life. This new motive for salvation, seen in terms of regeneration, explains the fact that the donkey, which had appeared alongside the ox in the previous story of the healing of the woman bent double, is here substituted by the son. On the previous occasion, in order to justify the healing of the woman which had also taken place on the Sabbath, Jesus had said: "Is there anyone among you who would not turn his ox or his ass loose from the manger on the Sabbath and take him to drink?" (*Luke* 13: 15). The two miracles, which are intended to bear witness to the same doctrine of salvation, are arranged in a particular order for teaching purposes. The first presents the need to break any prohibition when the issue of the salvation of the soul is in question. The second restates this need, but adds the idea of regeneration as the specific task of salvation. In the metaphor, the son replaces the donkey, because his image obviously recalls the image of birth. The ox then comes to represent the physical, or purely animal, side of the body, while the son represents that aspect of the soul which is born again with new life. The message of salvation, therefore, now uses pregnancy and parturition as a real term of comparison for its symbolic structure. It connects the image of extracting a son or an ox from the well with that of the swollen body of the dropsical, and it does so by a metonymical concatenation, in which the naming of the thing contained is effected through the naming of the thing which contains it, while the naming of the thing which contains is effected through the naming of its contents. In other words, the son recalls the spiritual father from whom he was born, as the swollen belly of the dropsy victim recalls the son who is spiritually reborn. The semantic function of connection is performed by the water, which functions both as the thing which contains (in the sense of the water in the well where the son and the ox risk being drowned), and as that which is contained (in the sense of the water in the belly of the dropsical, who may die because of it).

The water also fulfils another semantic function of basic importance, because it is converted from being a negative element, bearing death, to a positive one, pregnant with new life.

As we know, in Christian mysticism, one of the most fundamental cornerstones of which is the Baptismal Rite, immersion in water symbolises death, and emergence from the water symbolises resurrection and rebirth. Birth from water to eternal life was proclaimed in unmistakable terms in St John's Gospel, which was clearly being kept in mind when the final version of St Luke's Gospel was being drawn up. To Nicodemus, who did not understand how a man could be 'born again' ("can he enter a second time into his mother's womb and be born?") Christ replied: "I tell you truly that unless a man be born from water and the Spirit, he cannot enter the kingdom of God (*John* 3: 4–5). But in the Christian economy of salvation, rebirth to eternal life is a symbolical birth from the father, not from the mother: "Whoever is born of God does not commit sin..." as the first Epistle of St John puts it (3: 9) For this reason, the woman bent double in the first miracle is replaced in St Luke's second story by the man, suffering from dropsy, just as the donkey is replaced by the son in the metaphor which both defines the miracle and gives it its meaning. The mother—i.e. Holy Mother Church, as we already know—is symbolically born from the body of Christ on the Cross, just as Eve was born from the body of the sleeping Adam—and in each case the birth was the result of the power of God the Father. "Adam prefigures Christ, and Eve the Church", wrote St Jerome (P.L.XXVI: 59). The man with dropsy, replies the folk-tale, represents Adam redeemed by Christ, as Christ represents his heavenly Father on earth. But the Christian economy of salvation masks the servile role of subordination, because the dropsical with his swollen belly symbolises the power which the Father exercises over the wife and children by virtue of investiture by the Lord and Master above.

The explanation provided by the Marquis of Villabianca is completely at odds with this interpretation. He sought to bring the folklore motif back to the original meaning of the christian myth, but in fact it is quite opposed to it. Moreover there is a specific reference to the social hierarchy which then prevailed. If the claim of a male pregnancy corresponded to a demand for power, it was logical that it should then be attributed in the first place to the nobles, who then stood at the head of the hierarchy. Nor was an anti-clerical bias entirely absent; the pregnant man gives birth as a nobleman, and in order not to fail to keep faith with the example of Old Father Adam, he gives birth to a girl, who will then go on to marry another nobleman. But the nobleman only assumes the female role temporarily, so as to assert his claim to the paternal power represented by procreation; once the child is born, he takes off the female attire, and dons that of the priest. The compromising figure of the hermaphrodite, needed to provide a rational explanation of the 'pregnant man' has now become an embarrassment. It involves the permanent assumption of female roles, which are seen to be degrading for a man, and especially so for a nobleman. Thus the androgyne is jettisoned in favour of the priest. As we shall see, the pregnant man is nearly always a priest in folklore too, but there the priest mainly features as Lord and Master. The Marquis' little game with the story, therefore, met with no success.

b) The Pregnant Lieutenant

In Palermo, where the proverb about the pregnant man was repeated for centuries along with the story which explained it, Pitré also found, in the same period, this other fable which again involves confusion between pregnancy and dropsy.

"It is said that there once lived a merchant who had a daughter. Every day a woman with a little boy would come to them for alms. The merchant grew fond of this child, and one day he said to the woman: "My good woman, would you be prepared to give me the child for a large sum of money?" She went and asked her husband, and the man said yes, especially because the merchant had promised her that she would be able to go and see him every week. So she brought the boy to him.

This boy grew up in the merchant's store, and believed that he and the merchant's daughter were brother and sister. She was very fond of him; he was the apple of her eye, in fact. Time passed, and Peppino— that was his name—grew up. One day a message came to his father that the king wanted to see him. The merchant said to Peppino: "I have to go off; you stay here and look after my affairs and take special care of your sister".

The merchant left, and went to the king, while Peppino stayed with his sister, and every day they hugged and kissed each other so much that it was something out of the ordinary. One Sunday, while they were embracing, a princess, who had called suddenly and unexpectedly, happened to notice them, and thought the worst. She said: "As soon as the merchant comes back, I must tell him about this". When he arrived she sent for him and told him everything. Because he had been reproved by the princess, the merchant returned to his home in a furious temper, found an excuse, and chased Peppino out of the store. When she learnt that her father had sent her brother away, the girl turned his house into a hell.

So what happened to Peppino? After he was thrown out, he went off to join the army. The merchant's daughter got to know about this, took a large sum of gold, dressed as a man and left her father's house. She went straight off to enrol as a soldier in the same regiment as Peppino. She spread a bit of money around and claimed to have done great deeds of prowess, killing some thieves who had attacked her, and she was promoted to corporal. After a few months' more valorous deeds: she put down a pledge and was promoted to sergeant. Having become a sergeant, she got it into her head that she must be promoted to lieutenant—more money was pledged, and promoted she was. When she got to the rank of lieutenant, she was given a room in the actual palace of the king, and was made one of his personal attendants. She began to look around the regiment, and chose Peppino as her batman. Would he recognise her, perhaps?

In her room, she began giving him instructions about what had to be done, and she said: "You see these boots? You polish one and I'll polish the other". Lunchtime arrived and the lieutenant made him sit down to eat with him, though it seemed odd to Peppino that his officer should show him these favours. When they had finished eating, she gave him twelve tari—"Take this, Peppino, and go off and amuse yourself", she said. And Peppino was glad to do just that.

In the evening, Peppino went off to bed, and the next day the same thing happened. Then she said to him "Peppino—who are you? How did you come to be a soldier? Tell me all about your life". When he began talking about her, the lieutenant said: "...and did you love her?" "Well, of course I loved her, but then I loved her as a sister, because I didn't know that she wasn't". She gave him another twelve tari, and sent him off to amuse himself again. That night: "Peppino, instead of making up your bed all alone, why don't you make it next to mine?" The batman did as he was ordered. That night she made herself known to him, and things ended as they were meant to end.

After a while, the lieutenant became ill. 'His' belly swelled up, and the joke went around: "The lieutenant's pregnant! He's got a bun in the oven!". But they were only joking, of course. Round about the seventh month, the sickness was continuing, and his belly swelled more and more. The doctors said: "It's dropsy". When nine months were up, the lieutenant felt the pains coming on. The doctors said: "What's to be done? We daren't puncture him, in case he dies". But while the doctors gave up hope for him, the lieutenant gave birth to a fine baby boy. The news got out, and they said, around the Palace: "Boys—the lieutenant's given birth: he's had a baby!" The rumour reached the ears of the king, who sent someone to call his attendant to him. How could he/she hide it? She told him everything; the king wrote to the girl's father and ordered him to come. When he arrived, the girl married Peppino, and took him back to her home, along with the baby and a big present from the king.

They lived on as man and wife, and here we are like a lot of jackasses.

c) Man and Woman in Folklore

As we can see, the confusion between pregnancy and dropsy in this story recalls the proverb of the pregnant man of Monreale and its explanation, in the same context of folklore as the mosaic in the cathedral and the folk-tales collected by Pitré. In both cases, the responsibility for the confusion is attributed to the doctors and surgeons, possessors of a professional claim to positive observation which is revealed as a fraud by the fragile experimental basis on which it rests. The rejection of the symbolic plane in favour of the real one takes both stories out of the normal line, because it is in each case reality which takes on the responsibility of giving the lie to the diagnosis which they had claimed to be the realistic one. The dropsy is in fact revealed to be pregnancy, and the pregnancy, diagnosed on the basis of the urine examination, to be merely an illness, which in the case of the pregnant man of Monreale could not be anything other than dropsy. Popular suspicion of academic medicine is added to the accusation of inability to assess the importance of the symbolic plane in relation to the real, while the folk-tale never loses sight of the latter. Doctors and surgeons who diagnose dropsy judge the patient to be in grave danger of death. Only in the anecdote they deal with it by puncturing the belly and discovering the baby instead of the water, while in the fable they hesitate until the baby is born of its own accord, by natural parturition. In both cases, the test of reality reveals that behind the supposed dropsy there hides a real pregnancy. But in the anecdote the dropsy victim remains a man, and the symbolic plane dominates the real, while in the fable, the victim is exposed as being a woman, and the realm of reality returns all her rights to her. The two planes, which in the proverb remain linked, even though distinct, are separated in the fable and carefully confined to the spheres to which each of them belongs. This operation, which recalls the one performed by the Marquis of Villabianca in the eighteenth century, is of the greatest interest, because it now takes place in the popular context, and entirely within the folk-tale itself.

The dominant motif of the fable of the pregnant lieutenant concerns the definition of sexual roles in relation to the social hierarchy, and it is significant that in the crucial point of its narrative it runs into both the story of the dropsy victim and the theme of the pregnancy of a man. Man, says the fable, is superior to woman, and because of this rules over her, despite any social conditions which may impose exceptions, without ever breaching the rule. The hierarchy is precise: the merchant commands his daughter, Peppino's mother does not have authority over him, and in order to hand him over to the merchant she must first get the authorization of her husband. The king commands the merchant, but the princess does not. She denounces the incest, but cannot in fact order him to punish it. The superior social position of the girl does not, in the end, authorise her to take the initiative in rejoining her supposed brother who has been sent away by her father. She can only escape from his tutelage by flight. She can only seek out her lover and bring him back to her by dressing up as a man. Under this guise she can insert herself into the military hierarchy, rise up through it by means of the money stolen from her father, as far as the rank of an officer—as superior to that of a common soldier as that of the king is to that of the merchant. The man's subordination to the woman becomes even more binding when the lieutenant chooses the soldier as her batman and binds him to herself according to a real relationship of servitude. The adoption of male dress and the assumption of rank in fact allow her to overthrow the sexual roles both on the working plane and on the level of amorous relations. Orderlies have to carry out the domestic tasks normally reserved for women, while the female lieutenant commands the amorous approach normally reserved to the male. The reversal of roles, however, leads to resistance, which tells us in advance that the roles will shortly be restored. The girl hesitates to make her lover clean her boots, and seeks to polish at least one herself. The boy is reluctant to accept the favours which the lieutenant insists on bestowing on him. The amorous relationship which in the end arises between them, and even the pregnancy of the lieutenant do not prejudice the overthrow of the roles, which only giving birth can finally restore to the norm. The birth of a baby in fact exposes the lieutenant as a woman, and brings about the king's intervention which restores authority to the father. The reparatory marriage reestablishes order, and puts them all back in their places: the girl will go back to the authority of her father and that of her husband, who remains poor as before, and hence once again dependent on the merchant, even though this time as his son-in-law not as his adopted son.

All the transgressions of the social rules, as well as those of sexual propriety, are promptly cancelled out: the incest is shown to be non-existent because the boy and girl are not in fact brother and sister; their illicit sexual relationship is put right by marriage, the male pregnancy is shown to be a fiction; the woman returns under the authority of the man, and the poor under that of the rich. But if everything was going to end up as it had been previously, what need was there to bring about such transgressions? In order, of course, to reassert the definition of the roles within the context of the established social order. The moral is simple: it is the man's place to command, not the woman's, and the very privilege of procreation which nature has bestowed on women does not permit them to abrogate this right, however powerful and prestigious this faculty may be. The lieutenant commands because of what he is, not because 'he' is a pregnant woman. The pregnancy which counts is the symbolic one which allows the woman to assure the continuity of the species. So beware, says the fable: The pregnancy of the man is only a fiction, and pursues the aim of symbolically representing, as effectively as possible, the male assumption of those powers which real pregnancy involves. It is only these powers which pass to the man, and certainly not the biological faculty, which belongs strictly to womankind. The mocking reaction to the lieutenant's pregnancy means just that. In other words, the fable takes on a role of counterpart to the proverb, which in fact sets aside the mockery, and places the stress on the "and yet..."— the conflicting conjunction which expresses reproof and bitterness. We know very well, says the proverb, that male pregnancy is only a fiction, but this is what it is really about: symbolic, not real, pregnancy. While nature has assigned to women the task of bearing children, it isn't obvious why the powers which derive from this have to belong to man. The fable thus contradicts the proverb, just as it is contradicted by the proverb. The contradiction is even clearer if we consider the sex of the narrator, and his individual repertory in relation to tradition.

The fable of the pregnant lieutenant was in fact recounted to Pitré by a man, Luigi Patuano, who, all the evidence suggests, must have been the same Giovanni Patuano, a blind man of Palermo, who told him a number of other stories. It clearly derives from the traditional motif of the girl dressed up as a boy, widely diffused in the folklore of all countries since time immemorial, and often inspired by a strongly feminine standpoint. In the majority of versions known to us, the motif seeks to stress the capacity of women to undertake the most difficult tasks, on the sole condition that they could enjoy the benefit of dressing in male clothing. The girl dressed as a man only rarely becomes pregnant, and almost exclusively in the tradition of songs about the girl soldier. In the case of our fable, the theme of pregnancy only appears in the tale of the pregnant lieutenant, and in another version closely linked to it, which was found, again by Pitré at the same period, in a mountain village in the province of Palermo, Polizzi-Generosa. Patuano's chosen version thus seems fairly typical, and fits perfectly into his repertoire, which has a strong anti-feminine streak. At least four of the other seven tales which he recounted to Pitré are unmistakably misogynistic: the first (no.18) deplores the abominable curiosity of women; the second (no.54), the real archetype of misogyny for all ages and places, states that not even the devil is able to satisfy their insatiable vanity; the third (no.72) punishes the queen's adultery with her death at the hand of another woman, who as a reward is married by the king, and the fourth (no.252) counsels us not to trust them because they are too inclined to gossip and can't keep secrets.

Read in the context of this repertoire, the fable of the pregnant lieutenant seems to be linked to the folklore motif of the girl dressed as a man, but by a relationship which overturns it in the direction required by anti-feminine polemic. Clearly, this purpose was also served by the alien introduction of the theme of the pregnant man which Pitré's blind narrator must have already found existing in complete form in tradition. The only thing which is probably owed to him alone is the location of the story, with the reference to the victim of dropsy, recalling the theme of the pregnant man of Monreale.

We are already aware of this, in fact. The proverb and the anecdote which explains it were also recounted in Palermo, by a woman who, like Patuano, was blind, and was known as one of Pitré's principal story-tellers. The Sicilian scholar has also left us a rapid sketch of her, which gives us an idea of the features of this ex-seamstress in middle age, intelligent and humorous despite her blindness, very industrious with her hands, and always busy with her knitting as well as with her tongue. Rosa Brusca had a baker husband, a drunken good-for-nothing, and this fact must have had some bearing on her repertoire, which lies at the opposite pole to that of Patuano. The former seems to favour women to the same extent as the latter appears hostile to them. In her fables, the themes of the feminine condition are handled with unusual open-mindedness and precise awareness of the power-relationships. At the heart of them lies sexual liberty, which finds a limit in adultery, though the latter is punished only with a hiding, and certainly not with death (no.170). It also leaves to women the initiative of choosing their own partner, and the right to entertain premarital sexual relations (no.13). The interweaving of the social hierarchy with that of the sexes is rejected: the Empress Trebisonna (no.31) recognises no male superior, buys her husband for cash down, imposes obedience and marital fidelity on him, and checkmates the king himself. The daughter of the merchant, on the other hand, (no.9 in Fiabe e leggende) claims the King of Portugal, bends his pride, and succeeds in making him marry her.

This reversal of sexual roles is also accompanied by irreverent irony towards the custodians of morality—the priest (nos.172 and 173) and the doctor (no.251)—and goes so far as to challenge the healing power of relics (no.140 in Fiabe e leggende). Like Patuano, Rosa Brusca didn't invent her stories, and only adapted them to her personal needs as a woman. Like Patuano, she drew from the great reserve of folklore tales, though from an opposing standpoint which favoured feminine interests as against those of the male. With their respective repertoires, these two narrators of Pitré thus record the existence within folklore of two contrasting poles, without either of them ever being able to touch the other, as became virtually the rule in the systems of expression aimed at damaging the weaker party—i.e., the female. The presence of a feminine standpoint in the folklore tradition of all countries is not something new. It has been known to folklore collectors since the days of Asadowsky, and it was recently given even more convincing confirmation in the researches of scholars such as Rudolf Schenda, who tried to return fables to their social context, removing the private interests of the narrators and their particular environments.

Chapter 3
Two Italian Folk-tales

a) The Beetle

Once upon a time there was a priest who had two servants, a man and a woman. He was a real fusspot, and the servants were at a loss as to how to keep him happy. One day the maid said to the manservant: "I can't stand this master of ours any longer; what do you say if we find a beetle and put it in his bed? Then the beetle might crawl up his behind and perhaps we'd get a bit of peace!" "Yes, yes, a great idea!", the man said. So off the priest went to bed that evening, and the beetle roamed round and round until he finally found the little hole and crept up it. On the next day, the priest, poor fellow, felt a persistent tickle in the gut. "What on earth can it be?" he asked himself... "Oh, no... I must be pregnant! Yes, that's what it is—I'm going to have a baby!" And he really believed it.

A day went by and he went to one of his penitents. "Tell me the truth, dear child, have you ever had an abortion?" "Well, yes, Father, I did have just one". "And what did you use?", the priest asked. "I used a cassata". So the poor priest went home and called his manservant—let's call him Peppi—"Here are twelve pence, Peppi; go and get me a cassata". Peppi went off and brought the cassata in no time at all. "Now Peppi", the priest said, "you eat the cassata with Vanna" (that was how the priest thought he could have his abortion!). The servants didn't want to, but in the end they were prevailed on after a lot of yes-ing and no-ing, and the priest got his own way. They had to eat the cake.

What pains the priest had to suffer. His stomach swelled and swelled, but no more came of this would-be abortion. So one day he went to another of his penitents: "Dear child, have you ever had an abortion?" "Yes, Father, it did happen to me once". "And how did you do it?"

"Why, I fell downstairs, and only about an hour later I lost the baby!".
Back home went the priest and called: "Peppi, Vanna, come here". He
was standing on the landing. "Give me a kick and a push so that I end
up at the bottom of the stairs." "Your Reverence, what can you be
thinking of?" they asked. "We'd never even think of doing such a thing,
now or at any other time". "But you MUST!", the priest cried, and
they said "No, no, we won't"—in the end the poor servants had
perforce to do what they were told, and Peppi gave him a hefty kick in
the behind and Vanna a good shove, and off he went, all the way down
the stairs. "Ohh! Aaah! Help, I'm dying... aaaah, the pain" he yelled,
thinking that he was aborting. The servants ran and picked him up and
carried him off to bed; he lay there for a couple of days, flat out; but
nothing happened, there was no sign of an abortion. So after a couple
more days he went off once again to yet another of his parishioners:
"Dear child, have you ever had an abortion?" Well, yes, Reverend
Father, I have had one". "And what did you use?" "Three ounces of
English salts". So off he went home again and drank it all down with a
great deal of water; after two hours he felt a tremendous pain in the gut,
and seemed to be dying once again. He felt a great need to go and
empty his bowel, sat on the stool and felt as if his insides were falling
out. When he got up he looked into the cesspit and there he saw
something black; he turned round and said "Ah! my little son; I've
given birth to you with your cassock ready-made! And how I've suffered
for you." The servants came running in—"Is anything wrong, your
Reverence?" "Can't you see? I've given birth, and produced a baby
wearing a cassock!" "But your Reverence, that's a BEETLE!" "What
are you talking about—a beetle? A beetle, indeed!"

It was no use their insisting that it was a beetle—the priest was still
convinced that he had given birth to a baby with a cassock—and I'm
sure he still believes it to this day.

b) *The Pregnant Priest*

Once upon a time there was a country parson, who suffered from body
pains. The doctor was a long way away, it was necessary to go off to the
city to find him. So he sent his peasant servant off to get a medical
opinion. "Tell him", the priest said, "that I have pains all over my
body, and ask him what his advice is." The peasant went off to the
doctor, who told him "I must have a sample of his urine". "Very well",
the man said, "I'll tell him". He went back to the priest and said: "The
Doctor says you have to send him a urine specimen". "Very well; I'll
put it in a bottle and you take it to him". And that's what he did.

The city was a long way off, and the peasant was overtaken by a storm while he was en route, and had to shelter in an inn. The storm didn't abate, so he was forced to stay the night in the inn. He left the bottle on a table, and said to the hostess: "Mind you take great care that no-one breaks this, because it's the vicar's pee, which I have to take to the doctor". "Don't worry, my good friend, just leave it here and you go off to bed; I'll see it's safe."

But the hostess didn't mention it to her husband, and while he was stomping around the house, he knocked into the bottle and spilled it. The hostess saw what had happened and cried: "Now what have you done? The poor fellow warned me to be especially careful with that bottle because it's his master's urine, and he was taking it to the doctor for examination!". "Aw, never mind that" the husband said—"just fill it up yourself". So the wife took the bottle and peed into it. Now it so happened that the woman was pregnant at that time...

The next morning the peasant got up and asked for his bottle. "Here it is, sir". He thanked her and off he went on his way. He reached the Doctor's house, and gave him the bottle. The doctor began his examination and shook his head, because he hardly knew what to say. "Are you sure that it's your master's urine in this bottle?" he asked. "But certainly, Doctor". "Well, what can I say? This is the urine of someone who is pregnant! If it's really his, then he must be pregnant".

The peasant came back in a great state of shock. "Master, I'm almost ashamed to tell you", he said. "But what did he say?" asked the priest. "He said you must be pregnant!" "Pregnant? Me!!" The poor priest began at once to despair: "What a scandal for my bishop to discover that I'm pregnant. What can I do? Tell me what medicine I have to take to get myself an abortion!" "Oh, you'll have to see to it yourself... I don't know what to suggest". The priest tried every way he could, but he couldn't get an abortion. Then he thought: "I'll have to try falling down" He threw himself out of bed; he caused himself a lot of pain and was covered with bruises, but there was no sign of an abortion. In his desperation the poor priest thought: "There's only one remedy; I'll have to fall down the stairs". And so he did, breaking his pate and doing himself a lot of harm—but even so he couldn't get rid of that baby.

Finally, when the months were well on, he had the idea of climbing a tree. He climbed as high as he could, then threw himself down. Underneath there was a hare which had given birth to a litter of leverets; when he fell, he landed on the little den, and he saw a leveret bounding off. He said "God be thanked! But may He save your soul, with those great ears I've made for you!"

Chapter 4
Priest and Master

The first of these two tales, published by Pitré in 1888, was recorded orally from a townswoman, Loreta Zangara, at Terrasini, a small town of peasants and fishermen in the province of Palermo, on the state road to Trapani. Three years earlier, Pitré had also published the Tuscan variant, which was likewise recorded from the oral version given to him by a milliner named Nunziatina, who was of advanced years by the time he heard her story.

The first thing that the Sicilian tale confronts us with is the picture of the priest duly superimposed on that of the Master. With his two servants in attendance, the priest clearly has substantial means. As well as being rich and owning servants, he also has the arrogant and unpredictable way of giving orders which belongs essentially to the Master. It is easy enough to confirm whether the portrait corresponds to reality: all we need to do is to open Volume XIII of the *Inchiesta Agraria* relating to Sicily, published in 1885, three years earlier than the collection by Pitré which includes our story. Here, then, is a description of the clergy of Calascibetta: "Numerous, ignorant, corrupt, backward and bigoted. The leading adulterers, usurers and libertines are all to be found among them", Things were no different in San Fratello: "He is ignorant, corrupt, and immoral; his education is limited, superstitious and over-pedantic". The same again at Santo Stefano di Camastra: "They are extremely ignorant, they live by idleness, sluggishness and lechery, and cases of priests living openly in concubinage are frequent". In Palermo, the priests live "a completely bourgeois existence". And we could go on multiplying instances *ad infinitum*.

The second matter which the tale brings to light is the issue of abortion. Again it does so in complete conformity with the real situation. In 1878, a strange book was published in Palermo: *Le cronache*

51

delle assise di Palermo. The author, hiding his identity in anonymity, must have been a judicial recorder, one of those who until a few years ago gained a reading public among the semi-educated by publishing stories of famous trials. The style is tear-jerking, and not without some signs of literary pretension, but it may be just as well to pass over these signs and come straight to the facts. The first story, which begins the book, deals in fact with a case of an abortion carried out at lethal cost to the woman concerned. It is the story of Marianna, a young peasant girl from the village of Ventimiglia in the hinterland of Palermo, about twenty miles from the capital. Seduced and made pregnant by some minor nobleman, she decided to have an abortion to save her honour. She went to the family barber for help—an unscrupulous rogue with previous convictions—and he squeezed some of her savings out of her, giving her a dose of deadly powder which in a couple of days had killed both her and her unborn child. There was a scandal—the doctor, the priest, the mayor and the Sergeant of the Carabinieri all intervened. The barber was arrested, and the Court of Assize sentenced him to seven years' imprisonment. He had given the girl a powder made out of rue and sabina, traditional abortives in popular medicine, but he had made a mistake with the dosage. The barber, the herbs and the question of honour are all typical ingredients of a popular abortion story; only the death of the girl makes this into a special case, which ended in the courts and passed into the written records. By far the greater part of all abortions in all classes did not end up in court; according to the jurist, R. Balestrini, the author of a monograph on the subject, in 1881 only thirteen cases came to court in the whole of Italy, and in four of these the accusations were not upheld. The penal code punished the procurement of an abortion by a penalty of from five to ten years in prison, and a 'question of honour' could always reduce the matter to a year or two. The Church, which has always considered abortion as a simple homicide, was much more severe. The seventeenth century manual of St Alfonso of Liguori, which laid down the rules for confessors until the last century, reminded them that abortion came into the category of special cases, and this meant that only the bishop could absolve the woman concerned from the penalty of excommunication which it incurred *ipso facto*.

Our tale thus speaks the language of the people, and it tells the priest: your practice is even worse than your preaching. What other meaning can there be in the fiction of presenting him as faced with the necessity of having to abort in order to undo an illicit and unwanted pregnancy? The polemic of women against the priests derives from the inversion of roles which prevails even in the search for the means to carry out the abortion. It also lays stress on the Confessional—the place chosen by the

Church for the investigation and prohibition of abortion. The three women to whom the priest has recourse are presented as penitents: i.e. people who as a rule make their confession to him. From them he comes to learn first of all that abortion is a popular current practice, only the distant echo of which ever reaches the confessional. In fact the priest always begins by asking his penitents whether they have ever had an abortion, and thus makes it clear that they have never mentioned the fact in their confessions. The three women, for their part, show themselves to be very prudent, making it clear that they do know about abortive methods, but only revealing this gradually and with evident anxiety about incurring ecclesiastical sanctions and penalties. Above all, they only admit having had one abortion. The first two then try to lay stress on the ingredients of natural abortion agents, which are those of typical folklore beliefs (unsatisfied envy and an accidental fall) and they leave the priest with the full responsibility of making himself an agent for the procurement of the abortion. Now the understanding between the confessor and his penitents is fully realised, and the reversal of roles is complete.

But why does the fable associate women so closely with servitude—to the extent that it reserves the initiative for the trick played on the priest to his servants—or more precisely, to the maid assisted by the manservant? Was it not perhaps that servants, according to the saying in the Gospel, were the 'preferred of the Lord', creatures predestined by their lowly status for the Kingdom of Heaven. Without having to go back a long way in time, we can find a complete answer in a strange hagiographic collection printed in Rome in 1866 with the title. *The Lives of the Saints who served in the rank of family servants, recounted for the benefit of those who find themselves in the same condition and office.* The author is an obscure writer, Constantino Zanzarri—not very well-equipped as far as hagiographical information goes, in fact, but in compensation well-versed in Holy Scripture. No-one would have suspected that there could be so many domestic servants among the saints in Paradise, but if we are to believe him they are indeed legion— so many as to fill a huge volume of 500 pages with their edifying works. Servants, then, did not lack good examples; it was only necessary to follow them and the game was won... Paradise was assured. Do you want to know what you need to do? It is summed up in a few words by Zanzarri himself: "The whole point lies in the precise fulfilment of the obligations attaching to the servile state, according to the rules prescribed by the Law of God. There are four of these obligations: (1) Respect and obey your masters in all things which are not contrary to the Law of God; (2) be faithful in all things concerning the master's property or his affairs and interests; (3) with patience and forbearance put up not only with the labours and sufferings connected with your estate, but also with the capricious and extravagant temper of your masters, with unjust reproofs and with other wrongs which may come your way, and finally (4) have no other aim but to please God and to reflect in your own persons that of Jesus himself, from whom (and from no-one else) you are to hope for reward for your services—not in this world but in the glory of heaven"

Zanzarri did not need to make any great effort to define his four golden rules, because all he had to do was to paraphrase well-known passages from the letters of the Apostles, Peter (I *Peter* 2: 18–25) and Paul (I *Corinthians* 7: 20–24, *Colossians* 3: 22–25 and *Titus* 2: 9–10).

If this is the Christian teaching about servitude, it is easy to understand why the fable institutes a relationship of equivalence between the two couples, the woman and the priest and the servant and the master—for the woman is to the priest as the servant is to his master. The christian ideal of the family, in which wife, children and servants were all subject to the same authority (paternal) was being called into question all over Europe, but in Sicily it still persisted strongly. And even though it was beginning to lose its hold over the servant class in general, it still maintained it in regard to women, as the German Consul in Messina discovered in 1886: "subordinated in everything to the omnipotent will of their husbands and relegated to mere domestic labour". Thus domestic servitude was seen as co-natural to the female condition; women and servants were seen as essentially the same thing.

As we can see, the conformity of the fable to the most burning problems of the moment is quite beyond question. However, its most surprising trait is in its ability to express such a sad and even tragic content in the cheerful, easy-going form of a witticism. The light, jokey tone, the sharp irony of the allusions which characterise the form of its expression produce a frankly merry effect which is even more remarkable if we read the fable in its own counter-light, and relate it to its underlying assumptions. Its narrative scheme is in fact the same as the one identified by Propp as that of the fairy story. On the basis of the syntax of the narrative function, the hero here is the priest, the antagonists his servants, the donor the three penitents, and the Princess the Church. The definition of the personages in conformity to the narrative function which they fulfil makes it possible to reconstruct the scheme of the composition as follows: The hero runs up against a ban (i.e. the priest is forbidden sexual behaviour), the infraction of which (the notorious practice of clerical concubinage in Sicily) sets the action in motion, and allows the antagonists to lay a trap for the hero. He falls into it, suffers great harm, and finds himself in a situation of loss (the pregnancy could cost him exclusion from the Church—i.e. loss of his mystic bride), and this transforms him into a hero/seeker (the quest is concerned with the means of abortion), and forces him to leave. The hero leaves and meets the donor, who puts him to the test three times, and only on the third attempt hands over the magic remedy (the English salts). The hero then returns to the point of departure (his home), engages in a struggle with the antagonist (the servants who deny the abortion right up to the end), and he wins. He eliminates the misfortune, the initial loss, and wins the prize—the hand of the Mystic Bride, i.e. the Church, to which the false abortion, under the form of a very real and malodorous intestinal discharge, reunites him. From the comparison of its narrative scheme, the ironic and derisory intent of the story thus comes across with even greater force, and it resolves a bitter and distressing conflict in humorous fashion.

The free and uncontrollable laughter which makes a figure of power look ridiculous has quite a different function, we should stress, from the mocking laughter of the powerful at the oppressed. The first sets free from violence, and anticipates liberation; the second reinforces the violence and confirms oppression. The mechanism of violence which rules the relations of man and woman, the fable is saying, boomerangs fatally on man, and recalls the similar relationship which man establishes with the animals. Because of this, the beetle, the most despised and repellent of all creatures, the nauseating insect who gives the title to the tale, becomes in popular thinking a symbol of the priest. The Sicilian proverb says "Cops, garlic and priests—don't touch them unless it's to beat them into the ground".

In the Sicilian fable the priest behaves like a master, a 'padrone'. In the Tuscan story, he is stated specifically to be one—first when the hostess tells her husband that the peasant has been so insistent on looking after "his master's pee", and then when the peasant returns from the town and tells the priest the dreadful news of his supposed pregnancy with this preamble: "Master, I'm ashamed to tell you". Thus the priest once again appears as a master, and again in relation to a servant, who in this case is a peasant. Right from the start the story makes it clear that the priest sends 'his peasant' into the town to consult the doctor—i.e. the peasant who took orders from him as a result of a relationship of personal dependence; in practice a working relationship. Since the servant is referred to as a peasant and the priest as a country cleric, it is clear that this relationship has something to do with the soil. But even though a country clergyman was concerned with souls because of his vocation, it is more difficult to see what connection he can have had with the *land* in the context of 19th century Tuscany.

From the information available from the agrarian registers of that time, we learn that in Tuscany the majority of the country parishes had at least one farm as their property, and sometimes more than one. This means that one or more families of peasants worked the land, in almost every parish, as direct dependents of the parish priest. Ecclesiastical property, as is well known, did not come under the same juridical regime as private property. For instance, it was not alienable; however, in compensation it could easily be expropriated by state law, because its exorbitant quantity had always excited the formidable greed of the secular rulers. In the history of Europe, provisions for the expropriation of church goods recur with regular frequency, and a short time after the unification of Italy, Parliament passed a law in 1867 to incorporate them into the royal demesne. There was one exception, however—the property of parish churches, which was respected and confirmed in its inalienability. Thus a royal decree of 1871 equalised the administration of such property with that of private property, and recognised rights of fruition and full powers of management to the parish clergy.

So according to the laws of the state, the parish priest of our fable was a master, as far as 'his peasant' was concerned, in all important respects. This implied anything but an easy life for our peasant. The form of agrarian management most common in Tuscany in the nineteenth century was that of share-cropping, founded on the supposition of a perfect division in half of the produce between the owner and the peasant. In the agricultural inquiry which we have already mentioned in connection with Sicily, (the volume concerning Tuscany is Volume III and was published in 1881), this system was stated to be most advantageous to the proprietors. In effect share-cropping placed no limit on the working day, nor on the work due from the share-croppers, and the proprietor could always demand more from them, virtually at pleasure. The coefficient of exploitation was therefore very high, and it involved all the members of a share-cropper's family, who were equally bound to labour on the farm. It thus gained a "free addition of minimum but constantly active forces", such as the old, the infirm, and the children. Proprietorial control of production thus extended to family life, and subjected it to heavy limitations on personal liberty. None of the members of the family could leave the estate, nor could they marry without the consent of the master, and every one owed blind obedience to the head of the family, who was personally answerable to the master for any absence (or shortcoming) on their part. Sacred respect for paternal authority was thus placed at the basis of the needs of production, just as morality and the sense of duty served as its guarantee. This was the rule, and there was no getting around it: the contracts, of which several examples are provided by the agricultural inquiry report, regularly provided for on-the-spot sacking of those who did not scrupulously maintain the agreements.

The best-known, most enterprising and enlightened of Tuscan landowners of that time, Bettino Ricasoli, known as the Iron Baron— who became Prime Minister of the new Kingdom of Italy, for very good reason—wrote to his daughter about the case of an 'insubordinate' share cropper, and made it clear that if he did not apologise he was to be dismissed without mercy. At the root of this elementary ethic of subordination to the master in the view of Ricasoli, a fervent Catholic despite his 'liberalism', was the 'evangelically Christian religion'.

Canon Lambruschini, a patriot like Ricasoli and his intimate friend, praised this religious virtue in a prayer to God which he composed to be recited by the peasants: "Bless above all the master whom You have bestowed upon us, and who helps us as a father, shows us our duty, and speaks to us of You". Thus in an odd reversal of roles, the Master told the peasants about God while the canon instructed them about their Master! There was perfect harmony between them, and this was completed by the intervention of another Canon, Ignazio Malenotti, who wrote manuals instead of prayers: *Il Padrone Contadino*—i.e. the Master who remains in the country and personally supervises his share-croppers—was the most fortunate of all. He gave valuable advice to proprietors as to how to get "even more" out of their holdings, and how to prevent the peasants from robbing them. There were counsels of all kinds, but the most important was this: "I advise the Master to dismiss at once any peasant who shows himself to be incapable of inducing good behaviour in his family". And at this point another figure enters the scene, who is the natural antagonist of the priest in our fable, just as the peasant is the natural antagonist of the Master: the Host. The place which Christian morality designated as the home of the consummation of the vices of the peasantry was, in fact, the inn. There they drank, gambled and swore. Malenotti thundered against the taverns, and the agrarian reports also commented unfavourably on them.

Like the Sicilian fable, the Tuscan one thus appears rooted in the reality of current social relationships. The interest in social conflicts in this tale is so strong that it even surpasses that of the sexes—even though this was what the folklore motif of the pregnant man had originally conveyed. There is only one female personage here—the hostess—who always leaves the initiative to her husband; it is he who causes the bottle containing the priest's urine to fall, and he who tells his wife to replace it with her own. Pregnancy, the fable is telling us, is something which concerns women, and without their consent there is no way in which it can be achieved. Its polemical use against the priest, however, is handed over to the male initiative: to the peasant who takes the bottle to the hostess, and from the hostess to the doctor, from whom he then brings back the diagnosis of pregnancy. And then it passes to the host himself, who induces his wife to substitute her own urine for the priest's. The host is never described as such, and is merely referred to as the hostess' husband, thus clearly stressing his family rather than his professional role. The same consideration applies to the abortion: when the priest asks his peasant what to do about the abortion, he answers that he hasn't the faintest idea. Female concerns were thus recognised as possessing their own autonomy; however they were integrated into a broader social context which may seem to have been animated by essentially male conflicts.

In Tuscan peasant society, the woman was an integral part of a complex family organisation, programmed and directed from above in relation to productive needs. The head of the family, known as the *capoccio*, exercised power over it, as we have seen, by the express delegation of his master, and in his master's interest. He was helped by the *massaia*—usually his wife—to whom a substantial share of the power belonged; that part of it which related to the control of the household and the threshing-floor, an essential part of the family concern. The subordinate relationships which governed the life of the family thus always referred back to those which governed work, just as religion and morality, which gave them their sanction of legitimacy, also referred back to the same relationships. Everything was directed towards the interests of the master—even sexuality, only allowed if it assured him the abundant supply of peasant children which he needed to improve the returns from his land. Since this was the way things were, it is easy to understand that hostility towards the master and the priest who backed him up was widespread. All the other conflicts to be found in peasant society could effectively be summed up in this one, and found their rightful place there.

After the priest has failed in his first two attempts to bring about an abortion, he decides to throw himself down from high up in the tree. He falls on to a hare's den and causes a leveret to bolt. Symbolically, he falls from the height of his social position into the depths of degradation which the procured abortion incurred. But his fall also involves the symbolic order, to bring about the return of the natural order. According to the natural order of generation, polemically exemplified here in animal nature, it is the woman who, fertilised by the man, undergoes pregnancy and parturition, not the man himself. Moreover, pregnancy and parturition do not confer any powers on the father over his child, who runs freely away, master of himself, and of his own actions. Nature does not attribute any power to the mother, but even less so does it attribute anything to the father; in the animal world, often we do not even know who he is. The fable confronts the priest and the master with this check; the claim that power over children should be attributed to the father, it says, has no basis in nature, and serves only to safeguard the interests of the master. The only thing left to the unmasked priest/master is the wretched consolation of despising his offspring for his long ears!

PART II

Section I

Chapter 1
Two Aesopian Fables

The folklore motif of the pregnant priest, in both the basic variants illustrated by the two Italian tales collected during the last century, has a long history with roots in the distant past of Europe. The most ancient source of which I am aware is an anonymous Latin collection of Aesopian fables, which the philologists trace back to its earliest known edition in the ninth century. The two variants of our theme, however, appear only in two German manuscripts of the collection, which show signs of subsequent and much later editing, though they are certainly earlier than the translation into old French which dates from the second half of the twelfth century. The collection is undoubtedly monastic in origin, and enjoyed great success in north-western Europe, from where it originally spread abroad. It was progressively enriched with new fables, and was translated into English, into more modern French, and later into a number of Italian dialects, most notably Tuscan.

a) The Thief and the Beetle

There was a famous thief who made good use of the silent hours of the night. Once, tired of his night wanderings, he came to a meadow; it was summer and the meadow was covered in flowers and grass, with a stream murmuring gently through it. All this led the tired thief to thoughts of rest. Delighted by the charms of the place and the season, he lay down and stretched out his weary limbs to sleep. He had hardly dozed off when a beetle crept inside him. If you are wondering where he did this, well—remember his murky nature—he naturally came in through the back passage. The thief became aware of the presence of his unwelcome guest; he woke up suddenly and felt a sharp pain in the

63

place where the beetle had entered. Eventually he went off to see the doctors and consult them about this strange matter. But they told him that he must be pregnant, and he believed that they must really have diagnosed the cause of his trouble, because the same idea had also occurred to him. The news of this unheard-of and amazing event spread all over the countryside and those who got to know about it were astonished—and frightened too because, they said, the thing must be a prelude to some disaster. Gathered around the thief, they watched him writhing and crying out in pain, waiting to see how it would all end, and what event it might presage. But even while he was groaning and moaning, as if about to give birth, the beetle, tired by his long efforts, came back out from the same hole by which he had entered. And this creature, which usually pricked horses, found itself instead goading a thief and being 'given birth' by him.

Moral: This is the wretched way with mankind: always to take advantage of every novelty and desire it, even when it brings danger in its wake.

b) *The Doctor, the Rich Man and His Daughter*

A rich gentleman had himself bled, and gave the blood sample to his daughter to take to the doctor so that he could examine it as quickly as possible and see whether there were any unmistakable signs of what was the matter with him. However, the negligent girl didn't take proper care of the blood sample, and in fact tripped over a dog, which caused her to spill half of it; the dog then licked up the rest. When the girl saw what had happened, she was afraid that her father would be furious, and she was very upset. So she told one of her friends immediately what had happened, and the friend, to cheer her up, said: "I know what you should do: put some of your own blood in the jar, and take that to the doctor when your father tells you; who's going to know the difference?" She was pleased with this advice and decided to act on it straight away. But the doctor, who was skilled in his art, noted the unmistakable signs of pregnancy in the blood as soon as he examined it, and said: "I'm quite sure, on the basis of the rules of my art, that in this blood there are the clear signs of the pregnancy of the donor". The gentleman never ceased to proclaim his amazement and wonder at such an unheard-of event, for which he could find no explanation—and he was filled with dread about his approaching parturition. The whole household was astonished, in fact, and filled with concern for the pregnant father. Not knowing what to do, they decided that the doctor must be a liar and a trickster. While they were all worked up and full of apprehension about the future, they began to enquire more closely into how it had come about, and then they discovered that the blood had been spilled. They questioned the daughter and put pressure on her to find out the truth. Realising that she had not been able to deceive the doctor, the girl explained what had happened, and went to confess her shameful deed to her father.

Moral: This is how dishonest things done by unfaithful and negligent persons usually come to light in the end.

Chapter 2
Christianity versus Folklore

There can be little doubt about the intention of these two stories; they are intended to cast ridicule on the superstitious credulity of the peasants, always ready to mistake common, everyday events for prodigies and wonders. But why should this objective be pursued by insisting on the story of the pregnant man—and in both fables? There can only be one answer: the theme was very widespread, and the monks who were the authors of *Romulus* judged it to be so dangerous that they decided to combat it. This is shown by the actual literary form of the Aesopian fable, which is always quite close to the oral tradition, even in its content. But while the presence of the motif of the pregnant man in folklore seems unquestionable, our information for the High Middle Ages is all derived from literary sources which aimed to dispute it, and which twisted its meaning for polemical purposes. We may try and draw closer to it by using mythology: i.e. remembering the meaning that this same motif has in various religious environments, particularly those of ethological interest.

In the essay "Structure and dialectic" contained in his volume *Structural Anthropology*, Claude Levi-Strauss has studied the actual motif of the pregnant man as it is found in the mythology of the Pawnee Indians of North America. Here it is the story of a boy who discovers extraordinary powers of healing, arousing the envy of an old wizard who visits him several times in the company of his wife, to try to steal the secret of his success. He fails, and in vengeance he offers his pipe, full of magic herbs, to the boy who smokes it and then finds that he is pregnant. Desperate with shame, he escapes from the village into the forest in search of death. But the wild animals from which he requests death take pity on his misfortune instead; they help him to have an abortion, and they confer new powers of magic on him. Fortified with these, the boy returns to his village, brings about the death of the old wizard, and becomes a famous healer.

The American myth stresses a series of oppositions, particularly the one dividing the generations. In fact, it opposes the ritual which forces a son, if he wishes to be great, to submit to his father and be symbolically fertilised by him. According to Levi-Strauss' analysis, the myth revolves around certain oppositions which were dialectically related to a ritual opposed to their own, but practised by other neighbouring and closely related tribes. The theoretical scheme constructed by the French anthropologist provides a model which it is possible to verify in our texts—on condition, however, that we consider it in the social and religious context from which these texts come.

The opposition between confusion of the sexes and distinction of the sexes is one of those which Levi-Strauss points out as most important in the American myth, and it also dominates the two Aesopian fables. They are in fact intended to refute belief in the pregnancy of a man, which they attribute to popular credulity. However, they do not hide the fact that in this prodigious event, the announcement of misfortunes yet to come is feared. And in this way they bring us to understand that according to the actual convictions of the monks, the folklore motif of the pregnant man was directed against the confusion of the sexes which the idea of a pregnant man implied. It was against it, because overturning the distinction of the sexes pushed man back into the primeval chaos from which he had emerged with such difficulty. The punitive character which the event assumed is explained in this way.

This is confirmed by German mythology, where the myth of the pregnant man is also present, but always with a strictly negative connotation, which reaffirms the distinction of the sexes as an irreversible advance. The main actor in the myth, on a number of occasions, is Loki—a malevolent personage whom Dumezil describes as the "real demon element" in the German pantheon. He is reproached with the perverse predilection for transforming himself into a woman, in order to give birth to hideous and harmful monsters. But there is more than this: according to the Swedish mythologist, F. Ström, reproaches directed at Loki came within the more general accusation of *ergi*—i.e. homosexuality—generally levelled at those men who dared to practise the *seidr*, a divinatory act reserved by ancient tradition for women alone. The accusation of *ergi* had a quite disgraceful significance, and may be explained as a reaction against male incursion into an exclusively female sphere, which was viewed with hostility by the common consciousness and was thus rejected as totally improper. In the first place it was the women who were hostile to it, because the male practice of *seidr* threatened to deprive them of one of the last incontestably prestigious roles which society still recognised as theirs. It is no accident that the retaliation makes use of this same negative value which the female condition already involved, for if it had all the connotations of undeniable inferiority in the common consciousness, it was logical that it should reappear in the retaliation as a degradation of the feminised man; i.e. the man who seeks to usurp the female role. German religion, however, reserved vitally important roles for women in the priesthood right up to the last, and only Christianity removed these finally from them, thus reintroducing strong elements of the confusion of the sexes. We should make it clear that this confusion did not involve any idea of liberation from the old preconstituted roles of society, because Christianity introduced into the antique hierarchy of superior and inferior a new element of imbalance in favour of man, taking some of their specific attributes away from women without any compensation.

If, then, it is Christianity which reintroduced the confusion of the sexes with a sharply anti-feminine undertone, it is clear that our two Latin fables, under the guise of the attack on the superstitious beliefs of the folklore tradition, mask the defence of retaliation against the priest because he is a man-woman. The retaliation is distinctly portrayed as one of the functions performed by the motif of the pregnant man in the context of the folklore of Christian Europe.

Monastic polemic against the folklore motif of the pregnant man was thus founded on a subtle interplay between the symbolic and the real. It was the monks who attributed belief in the prodigy of male pregnancy to the common people; it was an easy way of accusing them of superstition and gaining dominance over them. The underlying element in the story was that prodigies could only be recognised as such if they were actually miraculous, and the intervention of the divine will in them was clearly observable. This was the case with the birth of Eve from Adam's rib, of course. But there is nothing which entitles us to think that anyone actually believed in the 'prodigious' reality of a male pregnancy. The people were in fact opposed to the symbolic function fulfilled by the Christian myth, as it was exemplified in the churches from the end of the eleventh century onwards in the visible representation of the birth of Eve. They were opposed to it because they suffered the consequences, at the level of social relationships and power relationships.

The Christian myth was the simple ideological projection of the ritual which was carried out in the sacrament of marriage. The folklore motif stood in opposition to this ritual, and to the myth which represented it, and above all to the power relationship which was sanctioned both by the myth and the ritual. It stated that the master-servant opposition had no foundation in the natural order, but rested simply on oppression by the strongest. In doing so, it also regulated two other oppositions: that of man/woman and that of father/son. The two Aesopian fables should therefore be viewed in relation to their opposition to the folklore theme, just as that theme itself was in opposition to the Christian myth of the birth of Eve and the matrimonial ritual which it represented in visual terms.

Chapter 3
Father versus Son

Since in the figurative representation it was only divine intervention which made the male pregnancy possible, it was logical that in folklore the symbolic father should be substituted for the real father, the direct descendant of Adam, in its polemical struggle. In folklore all over Europe, the pregnant man was the priest—i.e. God's representative on earth, who legitimised the power-relationship sanctified by the sacrament of matrimony and visibly represented by the images of the birth of Eve. It was equally logical that in the Aesopian fables, aimed at contesting the folklore motif, the real father should return, in place of the symbolic father. In effect, real pregnancy was restored to the girl, but the father retained his symbolic pregnancy in the form of the paternal power which he exercised over his daughter. The father punishes the girl who is surprised in an illicit pregnancy. The thief, guilty in turn of an equally illicit activity, occupies a position which is symmetrical to that of the daughter. A particularly interesting point: the father is portrayed in the second of these two fables as rich (*dives*) and as lord (*dominus*), in the sense of the owner of the house and the head of the family, who also exercises dominion over his servants. The first condition, that of being a rich man, shows him as a privileged victim of the activities of thieves; the second, that of being a 'lord', stresses his authority as *pater familias*, though the judicial institutions which bestow this power on him are not exactly those provided for in Roman law. Thus the father appears as a doubly vulnerable figure, the guardian of his riches and the guardian of his daughter's chastity—a real father/ master, in fact. Thus the two fables associate theft and sexual behaviour in a negative way, while property and chastity are given positive connotations. The renunciation of sexual behaviour is presented symmetrically with respect for property: two exquisitely Christian

70

virtues which celebrate submission to the Father/Master as a perfect viaticum for salvation.

The punishment of the two transgressors reaches the height of perfidy in the first fable, where the thief who allows himself to be too easily convinced that he is pregnant is reduced to ridicule by the fantasy of male omnipotence which lurks beneath his facile acceptance of the illusory pregnancy. The polemical revenge reaches the point of parody with the two journeys, in and out, made by the beetle (a typically faecal insect, which was widely believed to be born from dung as well as living on it): penetration and expulsion are of course the two acts which begin and end the process of generation. Fertilisation and parturition, in other words, assume a sharply negative and denigratory connotation by the mere circumstance that they both take place in this case through the anal passage.

The monastic version, then, ends by involving sexuality itself in denigration by associating it closely with defecation. If we consider that the monasteries in which these fables originated were then the most important centres of economic life, we can understand that social concerns were as strong as religious ones. The feudalisation of the Church was already a fait-accompli: clergy and lords, more and more closely associated, were often embodied in the same person. Resistance to the confusion of the sexes could not be dissociated from resistance to the exploitation and subordination which ecclesiastical as well as lay feudalism imposed on both men and women.

Into the two Aesopian fables there then enters the figure of the Doctor, well-established in his professional role and in his rationalistic type of knowledge, which is polemically contraposed to popular superstition. In the context of these superstitions, traditional medicine still enjoyed a high degree of credit, as it was well-known to subordinate therapeutic practice to the possession of innate powers. In fact, not everyone was capable of exercising magic medicine, but only those who showed themselves to be possessed of a particular vocation, and hence of powers which were vaguely Shamanic in character. The exercise of professional medicine, on the other hand, required only the frequenting of approved schools, which would later become the recognised faculties of Medicine, and did not demand any form of psychological predisposition. It is a fact that there has always been a place for women in magico-popular medicine, and almost none, until quite recent times, in professional and academic medicine. Thus as the second has gradually come to assert its dominance over the first, they have found themselves excluded from an activity of extremely high social importance, for which, in fact, they have always displayed a particular aptitude.

The figure of the doctor appears in the two fables fresh with rediscovered social prestige, like a *deus ex machina* to chase away the folklore enigma of the pregnant man with rational explanations. This means that the doctor represents the monk, who in the text never appears in person, but who directs the course of the story from the outside. Science and religion are thus found closely allied in the struggle against women and folklore.

As we already know, in European, as opposed to North American folklore, the pregnant man was always the father and never the son—the symbolic father and not the real one. This symbolic pregnancy of the father represented in the Christian myth of the Birth of Eve showed the power of the father over the wife and her children, and it was against this that the folklore motif was directed. The contents of the American myth and the European folklore motif thus differ in relation to the profound diversity of the two historical and religious environments which they reflect. But over and beyond specific content, the formal scheme constructed by Levi-Strauss is shown to be valid for the study of the European folklore motif. In effect it is shown to be similarly structured according to a system of oppositions and contradictions, and in a dialectical relationship to a ritual perceived as external and oppressive.

Chapter 4
Excursus: Christianity and Castration

We can hardly say that we know a great deal about the specific character of Christian misogyny and its most deeply rooted motives. The doctrinal notion of original sin adopted by St Paul still remains obscure, even though psychoanalytical investigation has opened up prospects of great scientific importance for further research. Ernest Jones has plunged the lancet deeply and courageously into the dogma of the Trinity, and produced scientific hypotheses worthy of the greatest respect, but they need to be carefully and closely reviewed and verified by reference to the New Testament and Patristic sources. While it is not possible to carry out such extensive research here, it nevertheless seems indispensable to trace at least its main lines.

The first fact which struck Jones about the Christian conception of the Trinity was the lack of any feminine element in it. There is the Father and the Son, but the Mother "has been replaced by the mysterious figure of the Holy Spirit". The mother-goddess, who in pre-Christian religions (including the Jewish faith, though in veiled form) had a place of primary importance, is transformed into the Holy Spirit and changes sex, for within the Trinity, He occupies the place of the Mother, alongside the Father and the Son. However, in occupying this place he shows unmistakable masculine attributes, which are revealed unambiguously in the mystery of the incarnation of the Messiah. The human birth of the Son, in fact, comes about in the Gospel according to St Matthew (1: 1.) "by virtue of the Holy Spirit". "You shall conceive, and bear a son, whom you will call Jesus", the Angel announces to Mary in the Gospel according to St Luke (1: 31) and to her bafflement as to how she is to conceive without having 'known' a man, he answers:

"The Holy Spirit shall come upon you, and the power of the Most High shall overshadow you" (1: 35).

More particular details of the conceptual intervention of the Holy Spirit are provided by the Armenian redaction of the apocryphal *Gospel of the Infancy* (ed. Peeters, p.97), according to which the "Word of God penetrated her through the ear". As the readers of Jones' essay, "The conception of the Madonna through the Ear" will already know, this version was accredited by the Fathers of the Church, and by St Augustine in particular. Later on, St Thomas (*Summa contra Gentiles*, IV.46) comes to ascribe to the Holy Spirit that same active virtue which is to be found in human seed. The Church has never expressed any doubts on the conceptional intervention of the Holy Spirit, and it has always defended his fundamentally masculine character against anyone who challenged it.

Excluded from the Trinity itself, the Mother returns, in the mystery of the Incarnation, as a simple woman, unadorned with grandeur or divine attributes. In relation to the pagan religions which honoured a mother goddess, the exclusion of the Mother from the Trinity thus took on the significance of a real dethronement. And this is how it was understood in the actual Christian environment of the first centuries by all those heterodox theological currents which in one way or another sought to reestablish the feminine element in the divinity. For instance, it is significant that Christian texts such as the Apocrypha of John (mid-2nd century) and the Acts of Thomas, (mid-3rd century) claim a feminine character for the Holy Spirit. Even more significant seems to be the later heresy (4th century) of the Colliridians, who actually worshipped the Virgin Mary as a Goddess. According to St Epiphanius it was an exclusively female sect, which spread from Scythia across Thrace and as far as Arabia. The cult was centred on the sacrifice of bread, which was symbolically eaten by the women in imitation of the sacrifice of the Eucharist. St Epiphanius' refutation follows the lines, laid down by St Paul, of anti-feminine discrimination: no ritual sacrifice to women is permitted, particularly to the Madonna, who is a mere mortal and cannot in any way share honours with God.

But while the Mother of God is denied divinity, perfection is conceded to her, and the special sign of this is declared to be her virginity before, during and after parturition. The dogma of the Virgin Birth introduces us to the great Christian theme of castration. Virginity is in fact conceived merely as the privileged vehicle of perfection, because it excludes totally all forms of sexuality.

Man is thus involved to the same extent as woman in this symbolic construction, and pays no less a price for redemption. Jones' analysis on this point is particularly perspicacious. It is a fact, he observes, that in the conception of Christ, God the Father does not appear. The fertilisation is carried out mysteriously by the Holy Spirit, which intervenes by means of a breath, and takes on the semblance of an angel—or if we look to the iconographical tradition, of a dove. "The achievement of long-distance fertilisation by agency of a messenger, and the choice of an 'airy' way of conception reveal the idea of a tremendous power to which the son is completely subject. The instrument used to translate the fertilisation into action is, however, far from being characteristically virile. Though the dove is obviously a phallic image, it owes its association with love to its gentle and caressing manner of paying court. It must be said, therefore, that this is one of the more effeminate of phallic images! It is thus clear that the power of the Father is only manifested if it is associated with a considerable degree of effeminacy. The same theme is even more evident in the case of the son. He attains grandeur only after having suffered the most profound humiliation, accompanied by a symbolic castration and death. A similar road awaits the followers of Jesus, in the sense that salvation is attained by meekness, humility and submission to the will of the Father."

Exclusion of women from the priesthood is the most obvious aspect of a complex symbolic construction which associates the renunciation of virile powers in the male figure of the priest with the assumption of specifically feminine attributes. Jones notes: "thus obligatory celibacy, the tonsure, and so on, clearly express the deprivation of masculine attributes, and amount to a symbolic self-castration". A specific reference to self-castration can actually be found in the passage from St Matthew (19: 11–12) in which Jesus, talking about the theme of voluntary celibacy, actually says: "Not everyone understands this saying, but only those to whom it has been given. There are eunuchs who have been such since their mothers' breasts, and there are eunuchs who have been made such by other men, but there are also eunuchs who have made themselves such for the sake of the Kingdom of Heaven. Let him who can understand, do so". As we know, there was no lack of cases of all-too-literal interpretation of this passage from the Gospel in the early years of Christianity. The case of Origen is the best-known, but he was certainly not the only one, if we note that the Council of Nicaea concerned itself in 325 with devoting the first of its canons to the subject of self-castration, to exclude from the priesthood those who had had recourse to it in a fit of excessive and misunderstood ascetic zeal. The canon was repeated in various successive Councils, and incorporated into the *Corpus juris canonici*. Self-castration, therefore, was meant to remain purely symbolic, and to be given concrete expression in the ascetic practice of continence, which the Church did not find easy to impose on its clergy. It was only after a good thousand years of permissiveness and tolerance of married priests that the obligation of perpetual continence was definitively imposed by the Second Lateran Council of 1130, as an irrevocable condition of the priesthood. The results were none too satisfactory, for 'right-thinking' people in all times were to protest at the scandal (which lasted about a thousand years and continued until the dawn of our own century) of the obstinate and invincible resistance of a good part of the clergy, in the practice of clerical concubinage.

Literal self-castration—however cruel and barbarous it might appear—at least had the undeniable advantage of resolving a rather difficult and tortuous aspect of asceticism in one neat cut. There can be no doubt whatsoever as to the symbolic significance of continence. A confirmation of Jones' interpretation can in any case be found, clearly stated, in the Jesuit *Dictionnaire de Spiritualité* (II, Paris, 1953, col. 780), which lauds chastity as "the most beautiful of the virtues, because it harmonises in one the most exquisite delicacy which is feminine par excellence, with the energetic mastery of man. To be chaste requires the most uncompromisingly brave efforts by the strongest male forces".

As we can see, we are led inexorably from misogyny to sexophobia; to the rejection of sexuality which is one of the fundamental characteristics of the Christian religion. The rejection of sexuality lays the foundation for an entire hierarchy: the highest crown belongs to virgins who have never practised sex and will never do so—they are the purest and the best. They must act as guides to the others; i.e. the impure who do indulge in sexual practice and thus easily lose the way which leads to the Kingdom of Heaven. In the Christian religion, the rejection of sexuality thus provides its practitioners with a counterbalancing reward—power. On the basis of the distinction between pure and impure, medieval Christianity built the whole model of society which has recently been studied by Georges Duby. The superiority of the clergy, based on their virginity, obviously did not fail to provoke fierce opposition from the powerful laity, and for this very reason they were even less inclined to renounce sexual behaviour. But at the same time it did provide an opening for their womenfolk to seize a small portion of that power which, to their despair, the society of the 'three orders' denied them.

The primacy of continence, and the androgynous compromise which underlies it, was to remain one of the fundamental pillars of christian doctrine in all its forms for many centuries. The Protestant Reformation did not introduce any substantially new element on this point. We can take Luther as typical: the great Rebel of Christendom never at any stage sought to bring the androgynous compromise into his critique of the Catholic tradition. And while he allows the marriage of the clergy, he by no means denigrates chastity; on the contrary, he consistently recognises its absolute perfection, which makes it difficult for the majority of Christians, including the clergy, to practise. In his tract 'On Good Works' (1520), he restates the ancient Christian doctrine of the primacy of chastity. "Repressing impurity", too, remains for him a primary duty of every good Christian. But he has learnt from St Augustine that "of all the struggles of Christians, that for chastity is the bitterest, simply because it recurs every day". The difficulty must not be underestimated; faith must be "the guardian of chastity", which is a gift of God, and is observed only by those on whom the gift has been bestowed. Others may marry and live out their struggle against concupiscence within the state of matrimony, because—let us be quite clear—"no-one, single or married, is without concupiscence, but all must battle against it every day". Even on this point, then, the real novelty lies in the doctrine of salvation by faith alone: "Marriage is good; virginity is better; liberty of faith is best of all", he writes in his tract "On the vows of Monks" (1521). If we rule out the merit of good works, in other words, the ancient excellence of chastity remains beyond discussion, like the dogma of the Trinity and the mystery of the Incarnation of the Son. Luther is even less willing to acknowledge any form of relief of the inferiority of woman. No matter how reduced the gap between the evangelical doctor and the simple Christian may seem, it was still sufficient to exclude women from the sacred ministry.

None of this escaped the notice of Ernest Jones, who took the Reformed variant of the androgynous compromise into account in order to demonstrate its more rigid adherence to the original pattern of Christian thought. The malaise at the dethroning of the Mother, and the consequent need to follow through with some form of restoration of her position had in fact infiltrated the heart of catholic orthodoxy for some centuries. The Marian cult and the various forms of Mariology only concern Roman Catholicism. The proclamation of the dogmas of the Immaculate Conception and the Assumption into Heaven of the Blessed Virgin Mary sanctioned by the first and second Vatican Councils are the basic steps in this ascent, which, however, does not make an iota of difference to the substance of the original Christian doctrine. That is to say, Mary does not acquire any divine attribute; she remains a simple human creature, though one with a privileged role in the economy of salvation. "In Mary, the redemption in the fullness of its effects is realised", the most recent Marian theologians maintain— but virtually the same was stated by Irenaeus of Lyon in the second century—one of the earliest of the Church Fathers. "The virgin Eve disobeyed, and became for herself and for the whole human race the cause of death. The Virgin Mary obeyed and became for herself and the whole human race the cause of salvation". (Adv.haeres. III.22.4). If disobedience is the sin of sins, which brought Adam and Eve their expulsion from Eden, then obedience is the essential prerequisite of salvation.

Christianity is the religion of castration above all for this very reason: submission and obedience are its virtues. It is no accident that the greatest political theorist of modern times began his research with the study of the Christian religion. In order to understand how authority may be based on consent, Hegel begins with the hypothesis of a popular religion as "a system of religious and moral truths, which can have the free consent of all, or at least of the many". He even wrote a *Life of Jesus*. Nietzsche, who knew a great deal about them both, put forward the ingenious notion that: "A doctrine and a religion of 'love'; of the repression of self-affirmation, of tolerance, long-suffering, help and reciprocity in deed and in word, may also be of great value from the point of view of those who wield power, because it puts a brake on the all-too-natural sentiments of the disinherited: indeed it divinises for them the fact of being dominated and enslaved, in the ideals of humility and obedience—legitimising poverty, sickness and subjugation. On the basis of this it is clear why the dominant classes and races and individuals have always maintained the cult of the disinterested, the Gospel of the Humble; the 'Crucified God'".

Chapter 5
How the Fox Got His Name: A Danish Folk-tale

Once upon a time there was a monk whose name was Master Michael. In former days he had been as thin as a rake, but all of a sudden he began to grow more and more gross, until eventually he became so fat that it was a scandal. Everyone was talking about fat Master Michael— and everyone was saying that it had all happened too quickly to be from natural causes. There's something fishy going on, they said. Something strange must be behind it; perhaps the worthy monk had been wandering from the straight and narrow in some way? But how unfortunate—and he a holy man too...

Master Michael heard the gossip from morning till night; people were pointing fingers at him, and the boys made fun of him openly. He couldn't find anywhere where he could be private and calm any longer—even his own brothers in the monastery despised him for his huge bulk, and in the end his situation there became intolerable too. He ended up even convincing himself that there really must be something behind it all. He was overwhelmed by shame, and felt compelled to run away into the forest like an outlaw. He ate wild fruit and roots, and quite a lot of time passed in this way.

One day, however, he was particularly restless; he feared what would become of him, and wandered about from here to there without pausing or resting. In the end he was quite exhausted, and felt the need to sit down on the top of a little hillock—quite a comfortable place to sit. There was a little gulley on one side of the hillock, and while he was sitting there, a fox popped out of the gulley all of a sudden, and ran right between his legs.

"God be praised!", the monk cried. "I'm delivered!" But when he

70

tried to examine more closely what had happened, he exclaimed: "But just look what a horrible red beast has got mixed up with my family! Wait!", he shouted to the fox; "Wait—I must baptise you and give you a name". But the fox ran off; he didn't want to know about names and baptisms. "Whatever you are, since I can't give you any other name, I'll at least give you my own: you shall be called Michael, like your father". And to this very day, the fox has kept this name.

When the monk looked down at himself, he realised that there really had been a miracle, because he had become thin again. Happy and contented, he returned to his monastery.

Chapter 6
Folklore versus Christianity

This folk story was collected by the Danish folklorist, Jens Kamp, towards the end of the last century, on the island of Seeland, and more precisely in the province of Holbaek. On this same island, before the Reformation, there were various visual representations of the Birth of Eve; at least two of these, dating from the fifteenth century, were in the province of Sorö; one frescoed in the Church of Vigersted, and the other carved in the wooden choir of the Church at Ringsted.

What strikes us most in the fable is the main character, the monk. The story, therefore, must go back to Denmark's Catholic past—i.e. to the period of the Middle Ages before the Reformation, which abolished monks and monasteries wherever it took hold. Why then was the figure of the monk retained as the protagonist after three centuries of Lutheranism, and not replaced by the figure of the Protestant pastor? The most obvious answer is that the Lutheran pastor was normally married, and not bound by the vows of chastity—thus he did not lend himself as well as the monk to the old anti-Christian polemic. Once the vow of chastity had been eliminated, the protestant church was out of the line of fire, immune to the popular reprisal which the theme of the pregnant man conveyed.

But a substantial body of unpublished tales, both German and Finnish, collected in the latter part of the last century and the first part of the present one, do in fact make the Protestant pastor their main character; and they often present him with his wife alongside him—as in the Russian tale of the pregnant man which features the Orthodox 'pope' or papas. Being married, then, does not exempt the priest from the shame of being declared pregnant, and indeed in some of these tales it is even his own wife who willingly and knowingly makes herself the instrument of the popular vendetta. If the various christian denominations remained faithful to the same concept of power, what reason was there to introduce innovations in the main figure of the story? The Catholic monk of the Danish medieval past was no different in substance from the protestant pastor of the present epoch. "The existence of a work of folklore", note Jacobson and Bogatyrev in their basic article on *Folklore as a form of autonomous creation*, "presupposes a social group which welcomes and sanctions it". And it is precisely this kind of "preventive censure by the community" which presides over the transformation of folklore texts. "In folklore", conclude the two scholars, "only those forms are preserved which have a function for a particular community". The monk therefore remains protagonist of the story because he represents perfectly, and contemporaneously, the christian androgynous compromise.

When compared to the two Aesopian fables, our Danish story reveals further elements which link it to the original German medieval version whose existence we have assumed. The responsibility for the confusion of the sexes here lies with the monk himself. Because he has pushed it as far as the idea of a male pregnancy, he falls into female shame and degradation, and provokes the contempt of his brothers and the ridicule of the ordinary people. The relationship of the monk with his peer-group and with society as a whole is thus the same as the girl-mother suffers with her unwanted pregnancy; the transgressor is in fact shown to be literally alienated from his own monastic community and from normal society as a whole, which drives him into a ghetto of contempt and ridicule. The only recourse left to him is flight to the woods— recourse to nature which nourishes him and releases him from his shameful 'pregnancy'.

At this point, however, the recourse to nature enters into a conflict which cannot be resolved with the return to civilisation. The flight of the fox prolongs that of the monk, but takes it across boundaries which the monk cannot transgress. Freed now from his weighty burden, he takes a good look at himself after pursuing the fox, and then returns happy and contented to his monastery. He imposes his own name, Michael, on the fox (who, incidentally, wants nothing to do with it). 'Michael' was the name by which the fox is commonly called in the Danish countryside, even today. To follow the fox in his flight would evidently have been too dangerous.

In a Swedish variant of this story, we find the hare taking the place of the fox; he also flees into the forest rejecting the receipt of a name or baptism. Fox and hare both had strong magical connotations in European folklore. Because of this, Luther noted in his *Tischreden*

(4: 4040) that these animals are habitually incarnations of the devil. The animal which refuses name and baptism is thus associated with the Devil. But baptism itself is also linked to the Devil in an ancient formula for abjuration and faith, which was used in the eighth century for administration to German converts: "Do you renounce the Devil?" "I renounce the Devil". "And all society with the Devil?" "I renounce all society with the Devil", "And all the works of the Devil?" "I renounce all the works of the Devil and all his words, and Thunaer and Woden and Saxnote, and all other evildoers who are their equals". It is very likely that this formula or one very like it was used in later centuries in Scandinavia for the conversion of the Vikings. Through the mediation of the Devil, we have thus gone from the fox to the gods of the Germans and the ancient Scandinavian religion.

The Christian metamorphosis of the ancient gods into demons (Heine called them 'Gods in exile') was visually represented in the *Altar of the Seven Sorrows of Mary*, which Heinrich Douvermann carved in wood between 1518 and 1521 for the Church of St Nicholas in Kalkar, in the Lower Rhineland (Figure 10). On one of the columns, which was in all probability intended to represent the Irminsul, the sacred column of the Saxons overturned by Charlemagne, a male figure holds a pointed stave in his hand; the upper part of his body bends backward as a little devil pops out of his belly, grimacing and showing two long, sharp teeth. The figure is also to be found elsewhere on the column, enthroned in the midst of a scene from the Flight into Egypt, and here it recalls the short biblical verse: "The idols of Egypt tremble before him" (*Isaiah* 19: 1). The birth of Christ thus proclaimed the defeat of the ancient gods, who, in the process of christianisation, became devils. The birth of Christ from the Virgin parallels that of the devils from the idols, in a way that was far from the process of nature. The artist used this image of unnatural birth to represent the christian transformation of idols into devils in order to reveal the mystificatory intentions of the theologians: they saw in it the ruin of the ancient religion. We can probably see the influence of the folklore motif of the pregnant man here: just as the monk in the fable 'gives birth' to the fox, so the overturned idol gives birth to a daemon. In both cases the result is the same: the fox rejects baptism just as the devil does.

By a different route, though still through the mediation of the Devil, the name Michael which the monk bestows on the fox again brings us to the same religious issue. The name in fact derives from the Archangel, Michael, who enjoyed enormous honour and popularity throughout Europe in the Middle Ages, and especially in Scandinavia. His cult was widespread there, and before the Reformation, at least twenty Churches were dedicated to him in Denmark alone. The first was built at the end

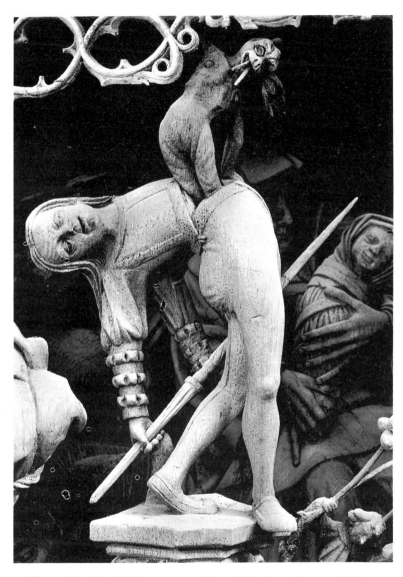

Figure 10 Heinrich Douvermann: Altar of the Seven Sorrows of Mary.

of the eleventh century, and on the very same island of Seeland, at Slagelse. The saint's cult was even more widespread in pious iconography, which often represented him with a lance or sword, victorious in battle with the Dragon. It is well known that the Dragon represented the Devil, but perhaps less well-known that Michael himself represented Christ—this has only become apparent through recent iconographical studies. The victory of the archangel over the Dragon in effect symbolised the victory which Christ won over the Devil by his sacrifice on the Cross for the salvation of the human race.

A wooden cross of the eleventh century preserved in the National Museum in Copenhagen carries the scene of the Crucifixion on one face and on the other the scene of the battle with the Dragon (Figure 11). In the Scandinavian countries where the Devil was identified by the Church itself with the ancient gods, the victory of the Archangel Michael over the dragon became a sort of symbol of the Church's victory over the pagan religions. The christian interpretation of the symbolism of the dragon and the battle against him had, moreover, been in vogue since the first stages of the christianisation of Europe. As Jacques Le Goff noted in a famous essay, it was already present in France in the sixth century, underlining the triumph of christianity over paganism. For this reason the battle of St Michael with the dragon was also taken as a symbol of baptism, and frequently reproduced on the baptismal fonts of Danish churches. The defeat of the Dragon was meant to evoke the death of the old man, and his rebirth—the victory of Christ over the Devil, of which the Sacrament of Baptism is a symbolic repetition. The connection of the cult of the Archangel Michael with the Christian conquest of Denmark is thus very close. This was a historic as well as a symbolic connection, because the cult of St Michael is effectively the first cult of a Christian saint attested in these countries, recorded as early as the sagas of the tenth century. There is nothing surprising in this: St Michael is in fact a warrior saint, defender of the Church and protector of Christian Denmark. In figurative representations he bears the lance or the sword in his hand, and recalls that in Denmark and the other Scandinavian countries, Christianity had won by the power of these arms, and was defended and preserved by them.

The story of the conversion of Scandinavia to Christianity has always been told from the point of view of the victors, and it is certainly not possible here to try and retell it from the standpoint of the losers. Like all the stories of conversion to christianity, it has its supply of victims and illustrious martyrs, raised to honour at the altar. It will suffice for us to remember that a fair number of the martyrs and saints of the age of christianisation of Scandinavia were kings: the three most famous are

Figure 11 Battle of St Michael and the Dragon.

Cnut of Denmark, Olaf of Norway and Eric of Sweden, but they are certainly not the only ones. We know that they burned with the holy zeal of missionaries and spared no efforts to christianise their peoples, not without resort to some suitable crusades against the more recalcitrant resisters. Cnut of Denmark was killed in the course of a popular uprising which broke out against the excesses of his policy of forced conversion. Olaf of Norway was killed by some of his Danophile opponents who had chased him from his realm, but nevertheless, he passed for a martyr of the faith. Eric of Sweden enjoyed the same honour, though he was killed by the Danes, and not for any reason of faith. Sanctity, therefore, was a kind of court apanage. The kings were useful to the Church in death as well as in life, and though they were by no means saints during their lives, they became so after their deaths. The fact that the saints had to be kings meant that christianisation, in the plans of the Church, must come from above, must be imposed on the rest of society by the key centres of power. Pagan resistance was, however, very strong indeed, and prayer was not enough to overcome it: the sword was also needed. This is attested by well-known episodes like the rebellion against Cnut of Denmark, and that against Olaf Skötkung of Sweden, driven out because of their attempts to convert their realms to Christianity. The policy of *compelle intrare*, i.e. forced christianisation, was a necessity. The historians say that for the Scandinavian countries the most important consequence of christianisation was the introduction of the monarchical institutions and feudal system of Christian Europe. And for once they are right.

As we can see, the Danish tale of the pregnant man brings us back to the tragedy of christianisation, revealing the hidden violence which ruled it then, and which remains apparent in the rite of baptism. Christianity, the fable seeks to remind us, was imposed on Denmark with the same violence by which it is imposed on the newly-born all over the Christian world in baptism. No-one asks the children if they wish to become Christians, any more than the monk asked the fox in the fable. No-one is concerned to take account of their wishes; children have no will, just as the fox has none. They become Christian by the will of their parents, just as the fox was christened Michael by the monk's decision. But the symbolism of the battle with the dragon, as Jacques Le Goff saw clearly, had a different connotation from the Christian one in folklore. While in the Christian interpretation the dragon was regularly killed or beaten and tamed by the saint's lance, in folklore things were otherwise. In our fable, the fox is neither killed nor tamed; instead he flees into the forest, refusing both name and baptism. We should point out at this stage that in the Swedish variant of the same tale, the name which the hare refuses is not that of Michael, but in fact

Jösse, which in Swedish means Jesus.

The fox's flight matters very little to the monk. What matters to him is being freed from the presumed pregnancy, which is such an inconvenient and oppressive burden. The miracle—and this is precisely what he calls it—of his recovered thinness seals the tale, and ends it with an edifying return to the ranks. The ancient miracle of a male birth, which at the origin of the race permitted Eve to be born from the rib of Adam, is renewed with all the strength of its well-known ideological implications. Happy to have overcome the transitory stage of his female identification, the monk restores full value to the ancient hierarchy: first the father, then the mother; finally the son. That ugly red beast which had dared to associate with his family is worthy only of contempt or commiseration.

Chapter 7
The Master Who Went Looking for a Servant: A Finnish Fable

Once upon a time there was a master who went searching high and low for a servant. One day he chanced to meet a stranger on his travels, and asked him where he came from and where he was going. "I'm Tappola's seventh son, and I'm looking for a job", was the answer. The master was delighted to hear this, and promised the man a good job with good pay. But first of all he wanted to know whether the young man had the tool needed for making love. When he was told that he didn't, he was even more pleased, he had been afraid his daughter might come to some harm. So they went back together to the master's house, and the master began to give his new servant orders, assigning him various tasks. He seemed willing and hardworking. Thus the day and the evening passed, and when they had had their supper, they made ready to go off to bed. The master climbed in alongside his wife, and the servant alongside their only daughter, because there wasn't enough bedlinen in the house to make up another bed, and in any case there was no danger that the young man would be able to satisfy the daughter's desires.

During the night, the master began making love with his wife; he thought the youngsters were fast asleep by now. But the girl couldn't sleep, what with the warmth of the young stranger beside her, and the moans of her mother from the other bed; when she heard this she pulled the young man close to her and began to moan too. She asked him what on earth her father could be saying to her mother at this time of night, when the stars were shining. At first, the young man pretended he didn't know what the girl was making such a fuss about, but since he wasn't an only son from a house full of plaster saints, he eventually told her that her father was just 'brushing' her mother under the stars. As soon as she heard about this 'brushing', the girl wanted the boy to explain to her the why and wherefore of it. At first he hesitated, then he explained. And then he did a bit of brushing for himself.

Thus the night passed, until the sun brought morning again. The master led his people out into the fields, to cut the hay. But the boy seemed to be tired, and stayed in a corner sharpening his sickle, to the great annoyance of his master, who upbraided him for wasting his time in this way. Furious, the boy flung his sickle down into the hay and ran off with the whetstone still in his hand. At this point the girl spotted what was happening and, ignoring her father's rebukes, she ran after him, shouting: "Hey, give me back my brush, you thief! Give it back!" The boy reached a bridge over a deep riverbed, and there he met a priest who was just arriving from the other side. He flung the stone into the stream and ran off. When the girl arrived, she was in such haste that she didn't even notice the priest, but began tearing her clothes off to jump into the river and recover the whetstone, thinking that it was her brush that the boy had thrown away there. The priest looked at her in amazement from the bridge, and asked: "What are you looking for? She answered him from the water: "Oh, how wretched I am, what an unlucky girl! I'm trying to find my brush, which that man just threw into the water!" The priest wasn't without feelings, and he genuinely wanted to help the girl, so he too undressed and left his robes on the bridge, and went down into the water to help her in her search. But when the girl saw the tool that is used for love-making, she pulled the priest close to her, and as they grappled, he found himself underneath, then he started swimming, trying to get them out of the water. The girl hurried off back home and said to her father: "I don't understand how he managed to steal it, but the fact is that it's the priest who's got my brush". The father was infuriated by the whole affair, and leaped on his daughter, who—he was sure—was already prey to desire, and in an excess of rage he killed her.

When he climbed out of the water, the priest too went home, and soon he began to feel sharp pains inside him. He asked his neighbours whether it was the person who is underneath in the water, or the person on top, who becomes pregnant and bears children. The neighbours replied that it was the person below who gave birth. Then the priest was overcome with fear, because he remembered that he had been below when they were in the water. In order to find out more he sent his servant to the doctor, but he came back saying that the doctor was unable to make any judgment unless some urine was brought to him. The priest peed into a birchbark bowl, and the servant returned to the doctor to obtain the required information. However, while the servant was crossing a field he tripped up and spilled the contents of the bowl. He was horrified, and couldn't think what to do, when all of a sudden his glance lighted on a brindled cow, which was in the act of pissing right there in the ditch. Necessity is the mother of invention; he ran quick as a flash to the cow with his bowl, and held it under until it was full again. With the bowl refilled, he went cheerfully on his way to the doctor. When he had examined the brownish liquid in the bowl, the doctor said to the servant: "A brindled calf is what will be born here; I can tell that from the water!" The servant ran off home and told his master all that he had heard from the doctor.

The poor priest then felt overwhelmed with pains. He went straight out of his house and off into the woods, to wait till his pregnancy was over. After he had spent three whole days in the woods, he came to a house and asked if he could stay the night there. But he chose to go and sleep in the sauna, where he barred the door, took off his boots and left them beside the hearth, and went off to sleep. In the sauna, a brindled calf had already been put to stall, and when the priest woke up in the morning and saw it, he felt sure it was a creature of his own making and he fled in terror from the sauna, leaving his boots there. So when the people of the house came to invite him in to breakfast, they didn't find him. They believed that the calf must have eaten the priest, and they beat the poor creature so hard that in the midst of its mooing, it almost left its skin behind. Not far away there was a workman who was infuriated at the noise the calf was making. He was a stone-quarrier, and when he heard that it had eaten the priest he was so angry that he filled it up with gunpowder and blew it sky-high.

Chapter 8
Son versus Father

This story is still unpublished, and was collected in 1889 in Laihia, in western Finland, by the folklore expert Alexander Lindqvist. It was told to him verbally by a 60-year old comb-maker, Samuli Suurtalo. We can read it in comparison with other Finnish variants, also unpublished, and a Russian variant which has been published.

We shall indicate the Finnish variants as follows:

a) *The servant with no balls*: as told in 1880 at Tyrvaa by a 30-year-old tailor named Saxback;

b) *The priest gives birth*: as told in 1893 at Noormarkku, by the 22-year-old marksman, Frans Viktor Snaell;

c) *A tale without a title*: as told in 1896 at Sahalahti by a 71-year-old woman, Henrrika Erikintytär.

The Russian variant, which we shall refer to as 'R', is entitled *Le Peigne*, and was published for the first time in French in 1863, but with no details as to the name of the informer or the place where it was collected. The collector who wished to preserve his anonymity was in fact the well-known Russian folklorist, Aleksandr Afanassiev, who died in 1871. He would probably have collected the story some time earlier.

This Finnish tale is even more closely linked to the two medieval Aesopian fables than the Danish tale which we have just been examining. In fact, all the basic characters presented in the two fables are present here as well: the father-master, the daughter, the thief, the doctor, the chorus of local folk, and the animal-child. However, some of these characters are doubled because of the demands of narrative technique, and may appear two or more times. The father-master doubles as priest-master; the servant of the father as the servant of the priest, and as the quarryman who appears at the end. The animal-son

92

remains single, but although there is no increase in number, he certainly increases in size, for the tiny beetle is replaced by the monumental calf. Even the second animal in the Aesopian fable is replaced: instead of the dog, the cow is introduced, and this introduces a new element with respect to the other animal, because the cow gives birth to the calf, while the dog has nothing whatever in common with the beetle. In perfect symmetry with the cow, there also appears a new personage who was not present in the original Aesopian fables—the wife of the master and mother of the girl.

The identity of the characters, quite apart from their transformation, demands some specific explanation. There is no doubt that the priest is a duplicate of the father because of the narrative function which the two figures fulfil. If there were any doubt, this would be dispelled by variant (b), where the priest immediately shows all the natural requirements of a father, and replaces him right from the beginning. He is in fact the Lutheran pastor, whom the Reformation introduced into Finland from Sweden in the sixteenth century, and he duly appears already provided with wife and child. The priest is presented as master in all four of the tales, because he is always endowed with at least one servant. The identification of the servant of the father with the servant of the priest is obvious. But the servant in this story is the same character as the thief in the Aesopian fables. In fact in all these tales, the servant is commonly a thief; he is called such by the girl when he runs away, taking her 'brush' with him. But above all he is a thief in relation to his master, because he robs him of his working time by sharpening his sickle instead of getting on with the reaping. In the variants he is even more of a thief because—with the excuse that he needs to buy a brush—he manages to relieve the daughter of a nice little nest-egg.

Moreover, in variant (c) the girl in turn robs her father of the money, which she then passes on to the servant. The thief of the Aesopian fable is therefore reintroduced into the social context of the peasantry, so that he may be identified with the poorest fringe of the unemployed and vagrant, who regularly finished up as thieves.

The rich man, father of the girl in the second tale, corresponds to the thief in the first Aesopian fable. In the fable, two abstractions, the thief and the rich man, are brought into the concrete context of the social relationships prevailing in the Finnish countryside in the last century: the rich man is the small proprietor—i.e. the kulak, or landed peasant— while the thief is the servant who works for him on a daily basis—the day-labourer, in fact. To save the cost of lodging, he makes him sleep in the same bed as his daughter, "because" as we are told by variant (a) "he was a very miserly master indeed". As in the two Aesopian fables, avarice is closely associated with jealousy. Careful not to allow himself to be robbed by his servant in his work, he also controls his daughter's sexual behaviour, and in order to put a curb on it, he demands a guarantee of castration from the servant. (Variant (a), in fact, specifies that he was looking for "a servant with no balls"). The master fears his daughter's sexual independence, while the fable acknowledges that in fact this independence was endowed with a good deal of initiative. The girl's initiative finds a ready response in the servant's lust, for he had feigned impotence only with the intention of deceiving the father and taking advantage of his greed to get hold of the daughter in the same bed. In variant (a), the servant of a neighbour, having heard that the father-master is searching for an impotent servant, presents himself to him after having symbolically cut off his horse's tail; he says "Good day to you sir: here you see a horse with no tail and a servant with no balls!"

The girl's ingenuousness, moreover, is as false as the servant's impotence. From the beginning of the fable we realise that the two young people are really after the same thing, in defiance of the father's prohibition. The story reveals his indefensible claim to reserve for himself the sexual activity denied to the two young people—seeking to monopolise it, in the literal sense—in his relations with his wife, and in the symbolic sense in those with his daughter. In effect he claims the right to dispose of her sexuality at will, as was demanded by the renunciation of sex with her, which the incest taboo imposed on him. But the tale challenges the validity of this right, and recognises that the girl has every right to dispose of her own sexual nature. A free and voluntary sexual relationship thus springs up unequivocally between the two young people, with mutual desire as its only regulator. The fable is thus putting forward an alternative sexuality to the one based on violence and inequality which was in force throughout the whole of Christian Europe.

For this very reason it is presented as a transgression—some coincidence this—parallel to that of stealing from the master part of the working time due to him by contract. Indeed, the second transgression appears to be a direct consequence of the first: the servant doesn't work in the field during the day because he has been making love in bed all night! The symbolism of the sickle sharpened with the whetstone is ambivalent: it refers to the sexual activity of the night but also to the refusal to work during the day which follows it as a natural consequence. The sickle, in turn, suggests castration, which would favour work, but it also suggests its opposite—the sexuality which impedes it. The reintegration of the phallus is achieved at the expense of work, and in the variants, it is also involved in the obtaining of the brush—i.e. of the phallus eliminated by the father-master—through the intervention of the girl, who in variant (c) actually steals the money needed to buy it. The servant achieves compensation for the castration imposed on him by the father-master through a double theft: the theft of wealth and the theft of sexual privilege, to the detriment of the father-master, and in common accord with the daughter. The rich man, the thief and the daughter in the two medieval Aesopian fables are thus found face to face once again. And this time the point is even clearer because in the variants the servant often impregnates the girl, and the father sacks him as a punishment.

The father-master reacts against the two transgressions with fury and violence: he berates the servant for not working, and forces him to lose his job, while he actually kills the girl when he learns that she has experienced sex. However, the story was concerned first of all to introduce the new character, the priest, who is the protagonist of the second of the two parts into which the story is divided, just as the father was the protagonist of the first part. It introduces him first of all on a bridge, as he fulfils a narrative bridging function—linking both parts of the story, and representing the themes and personages of the first part in the second. On the bridge itself, the priest meets their servant running away, and immediately takes his place. He helps the girl to search for the whetstone which the servant has thrown in the river, and almost at once he has intercourse with her. The variants are more specific on this point: variant (a) says "when the priest succeeded in getting out of the water, the daughter wanted to sample the brushing again, and she put the priest underneath and herself on top". The other variants also insist on the upside-down copulation, engaged in on the girl's initiative, and always exclusively in her intercourse with the priest—never in that with the servant. The priest's imagined pregnancy is supposed in fact to have derived from this unaccustomed position. The parish gossips declare that it is the one who is underneath who becomes pregnant, and the priest believes them and thinks that he must, therefore, be pregnant. But this belief is based on an equivocation, which gives rise to a whole series of events. The gossips only mean, of course, that women only become pregnant if they lie underneath during intercourse. This was in fact the teaching of both the Church and medicine for centuries. As far as they were concerned there would not have been any doubt about the sex of the person who lay underneath; it is the priest himself who is responsible for the ambiguity. This is no mere chance; it is he who preaches the miracle of a male pregnancy to justify all the power-relationships existing in the family and in society. It is he who gives the supreme moral sanction to the power of the father, puts curbs on sexual behaviour, programmes castration and legitimises exploitation. The priest is the principal architect of the established order, and it is therefore on him that the story naturally causes the whole weight of its construction to fall. If the person who creates children has authority over them, and the father has authority over them because he has created them, it seems logical that this should apply to an even greater extent to those who preach this doctrine day after day: the priests who are, by definition, 'fathers' of their faithful flock. The children are objects, belonging to the father: they belong to him by divine dispensation, states Christian doctrine. Because of this, the story says, the father decides their sexual behaviour just as he decides the rest of their lives—even to the point of killing the daughter who dares to have sex without his consent. The jealousy and the assassination which follows it, are effectively linked to the incest taboo: the priest, the father par excellence, takes the place of the servant, and has sex with the girl, and thus he, as father by autonomasy, in effect commits incest with her. But this compensation granted to the father for the disobedience of his daughter serves only to expose the fact that the power of sexual control, recognised by society as the right of the father, is the counterpart of the renunciation of his own desire, imposed on him by the incest taboo.

This is what is revealed by the Russian version (R). This faithfully follows the narrative scheme of the Finnish fable, but it stops at the return of the daughter from her wetting in the river, and omits any reference to the priest's pregnancy. In compensation, however, it replaces the father's assassination of his daughter by an act of incest with her on his part. Here the father is also the priest-master, and when he sees his daughter arriving from the river, he "takes his papas' penis out of his drawers, shows it to his daughter from the window, and shouts to her: "Here, my daughter: here is your comb!" "Why yes, it really is mine", says the girl: "look what a red cap it has!" Turning to his wife, the papas despairs of the lost honour of his daughter. But the papessa exhorts him to find out for himself what has happened before coming to such a grave conclusion. The priest then lowers his drawers, and gives his daughter the 'comb'; while they are in action, the priest whinnies and shouts: "No, no, my daughter has not lost her honour..." The papessa says to him: "Little father—push the honour further into her!", and he replies "Never fear little mother; she will not let it go; I've pushed it a long way in!" The daughter is still young and does not know how to raise her legs by bending them together; "Bend them more, my daughter; bend them even more" cries the papessa. But the papas answers: "Ah, no little mother, she is already so rolled up that she's nothing more than a ball." This was how the priest's daughter got hold of her father's comb, and since that time the priest combs both of them—the mother and the daughter—he makes them a gift of his little doll, and since then he has spent most of his time fucking both of them".

The daughter's honour, then, is a pledge given to the father to compensate him for his renunciation. If the daughter loses it, if she takes back the pledge, then the father takes back his own rights. The taboo then ceases to operate, and even his own wife authorises him to commit incest. But society is based on the incest taboo, and cannot allow it to be so easily set aside, even in fairy stories. As a rule incest is replaced by a punishment which, in the Finnish tale, is carried to the extreme point of death, just in order to show the father's gratuitous cruelty. In the other Finnish variants, there is no trace of the assassination of the daughter—that legacy of a cruel ancient custom which even Roman law to some extent legalised. In variants (a) and (c), however, we find condemnation to death by beheading instead: in modern society, the execution of the death sentence is no longer the responsibility of the father, but of the public authority which represents him. Hence the authority which imposes the penalty changes, and the guilty person also changes, in the sense that here it is a man, and nothing at all is said about the crime which has merited the maximum penalty. The two variants only say that the priest in flight provides himself with good boots, removing them from a scaffold which he comes across along the road. They are taken from a condemned man lying there; the boots still have the legs of the condemned man in them. Those chopped-off legs, then, must give some weight to the notion that the calf had indeed eaten the priest, leaving only his legs.

We know that in the age in which the two variants were recounted (the last decades of the nineteenth century), the death penalty existed in Finland only for certain particularly serious crimes, such as treason and the attempt to assassinate the Czar; it was hardly ever carried out, and certainly not publicly, by the roadside. As Michel Foucault has shown, in the late eighteenth and early nineteenth centuries, punishment had ceased all over Europe to be a public spectacle, and this was especially true of the death penalty. Thus the two variants refer to the era of Swedish domination in the eighteenth or even earlier centuries, when the death penalty was common, when executions were held in public and were ubiquitous, and when the numerous crimes for which the death penalty was prescribed still included theft and incest. The scaffold with the decapitated man thus seems to remind us of the fact that the crimes were both punished with maximum severity. It seeks to remind us of this especially in relation to the priest, who in the story commits both crimes, though only in the symbolic form which characterises all that he does (the girl accuses him of the theft of her 'brush'). The priest, who condemns sexual activity, hands over the initiative to the girl at the opportune moment, and then has sex with her. In so doing, he not only avenges the father for the disobedience of his daughter, but also the servant and the girl, for the castration imposed on them by the father.

The coitus takes place either in the water or (in one of the variants) after they have emerged from the water, with an obvious parody of the evangelical symbolism. The servant throws the stone into the water, and it is in the water that the girl rediscovers her 'brush'. The rite of immersion-emersion is the very same as that which symbolises death and rebirth—only instead of the soul being involved, here it is the phallus. However the parodic deconsecration of the baptismal rite is carried to the furthest degree because the rebirth in the water is a birth from the father, and the child to which he gives birth is in effect the calf of the evangelical story of the miracle of the dropsy victim. The deconsecration has a sarcastic air: if the son is born of the father, the story says, then let him be born according to the rules. If there is to be a birth there must be coitus, and the one who produces the child must have been underneath when it took place. So the priest is underneath, but instead of a child, what comes forth is a calf! So, says the story, beware: in reality the calf is produced by the cow, just as the daughter is produced by her mother. To bear children, parents are needed: coitus between them, and gestation and parturition on the part of the mother. This is the natural process of generation; all the rest is confusion and embroglio. To arrive at this conclusion, the story makes use of a very ancient logical procedure, which was always held in great esteem—particularly by mathematicians—the method of reasoning per absurdum. The procedure is divided up as follows: the father produces the son just as the priest produces the calf; the priest produces a calf just as the calf eats a man. The polemical drive of the story can now reach its conclusion: the worker who appears in the finale fills the calf with gunpowder and blows it into the air. This pestilent calf, forced to jump out of its skin—in other words, to be reborn in parody form as a result of the blows it receives—he couldn't put up with it.

As we can easily see, the story does not seem to have been contaminated in any of its details by christian assimilation. It remains faithful to the scheme of resistance to christianity which was already finding expression in the folklore of the High Middle Ages with the motif of the pregnant man. The two medieval Aesopian fables are thus nothing other than the ecclesiastical transposition into folklore terms of this same motif. As Jacques le Goff remarked, the most important part of the ecclesiastical proceedings against folklore was precisely that of seizing its motifs and modifying their meaning and nature in a christian direction. However, this was not the only proceeding adopted by the Church: in order to beat the resistance of folklore, it also made use of other weapons.

At the little church of Hattula, a remote village in western Finland, one of the most original of all the representations of the Birth of Eve is to be found, painted by an unknown artist in the first years of the sixteenth century. In the centre-left of the image, Eve appears at the level of Adam's thigh, while he is sleeping, following the medieval scheme already widespread in Europe by the sixteenth century. However, the Eternal Father is not, as usual, beside the couple, but above them, in the sky, surrounded by a corona of clouds, and flanked by two winged angels. To the right of the couple, instead of the figure of God, there is a Siren or mermaid, with the breasts of a woman but the belly and tail of a fish. In the foreground are a number of animals: various fish in front of the mermaid, and in front of our primeval ancestors, a bear attacking a calf and a fox which has caught a chicken and is holding it between its teeth. Another fowl is shown perched in a shrub at the level of the bear's head. The animals fit perfectly into the European iconographical tradition of the birth of Eve, though this predatory element is not usually shown; however, the mermaid has never before been seen in the Garden of Eden. In European iconography, there appears at most the serpent with the woman's head— and that is found always in the scene of the temptation, never in that of the Birth of Eve. To allude to her function of seduction in Hattula, it was the Siren which was chosen, with her long hair and female graces corresponding exactly to those of Eve herself. The correspondence is intentional, and was meant to stress that this same Eve who was born— supplicating and obedient—from Adam's rib, would lead him into ruin with her powers of seduction.

According to the *Fiore di virtú*, the mermaid symbolised the vice of flattery, because with her sweet song, she induced seafarers to sleep at the most perilous moments of their voyage, the inevitable result being shipwreck. The *Fiore di virtú* is a fourteenth century Italian compilation which classifies and defines the vices and virtues in relation to their respective symbols, taken from the bestiaries. It is founded on the encyclopedias and most well-known moral tracts of the Middle Ages, and enjoyed great success all over Europe. It was translated into several languages. It reflected a culture which was widely diffused in ecclesiastical circles throughout Europe, and could very well be used to explain the late medieval iconography of a Finnish fresco. This is all the more likely as there is actually a man in it sleeping heavily while a woman emerges from his side.

The warning was clear, then: take care, sons of Adam, for the attractions of the daughters of Eve will cost you dearly. In conformity with the Biblical foundation which gave them their sanction, the warnings were obviously directed towards sexuality and generation; they had to do with the forbidden fruit of the tree of the knowledge of good and evil, and were a response to demands like those of the infantile world, as to how children are made. It could even be that the animals in the painting establish a link between knowledge, suspect because associated with seduction, and the folklore motif of the pregnant man. In fact, we find the calf and the fox, which appear as the animal/ children in the Finnish and Danish folk-tales, with the contrary attributes of prey and predator. The calf is in fact the prey of the bear, and the fox seizes a fowl. This in particular would seem to be meant to re-establish the truth of facts, as opposed to fables. Calves do not eat men in reality; they are eaten by bears, and it is certainly the fox which eats the chickens. The reference is to the daily life of the Finnish countryside, where hungry bears often attacked the cattle, and foxes wreaked havoc with the chickens. The fox who rejects christianity in the Danish fable is also mentioned in the *Fiore di virtú*, in the chapter where the mermaid or Siren appears. He appears in the role which the Aesopian fable gives him: after seducing the crow, he steals the piece of meat which he is holding in his beak. The fox tricks the chickens and then seizes them, in the same way as the Sirens do with men. Manifest falsehoods form part of the weaponry of seduction: priests giving birth to calves, or calves eating men. The fresco contraposes the evidence of facts tested by experience to the reasoning ad absurdum of the story.

The procedure followed by the ecclesiastics who provided the artist with his programme as he worked for them at Hattula is the usual one of passing off a reasoning *ad absurdum* as a realistic judgment. However, the peasants knew perfectly well that calves do not eat men, and there was certainly no need for priests to explain this to them. They didn't fall into the trap, and they answered that it is the wolf that eats men. According to variant (b) of the Finnish tale, the priest, in the course of his flight in the woods, sees "a pair of boots in a very fine state; he takes them and finds that the lower legs of a man are still in them. The wolf had eaten the man but had not succeeded in eating the legs that were inside the boots". In the same variant, the passage in which the calf 'eats the priest' is found once more. When the people cannot find the priest, and see the boots with legs inside them beside the calf, they say "this devil of a calf has eaten the man, and just didn't manage to eat the legs inside the boots!" The difference between realistic judgment and reasoning per absurdum is thus re-established with the maximum logical rigour. The clerical editors had greater difficulty in setting aside the first proposition that the reasoning *per absurdum* sought to deny—i.e. the proposition that the father 'makes' the sons, as Adam 'made' Eve, according to the iconographical scheme which the Hattula fresco put forward once again with intrepid boldness.

However, the fresco also stressed other issues which were considered even more persuasive. It called the attention of men to be on their guard against feminine seduction, the eternal incitement to sin. The attempt to divide men from women in order to try and load the principal weight of sin on to the latter is very ancient indeed, and runs like an easily recognisable red strand through the history of the Christian Church. Among the witnesses to it in Finland, there is a most eloquent iconographical document, which is preserved in the National Museum at Helsinki. It is an anonymous undated picture (Figure 12) which represents the Last Judgment. It comes from the Church of Keuruu, another village in western Finland, and it was given to the museum in 1824. Although it may seem to be conceived according to the stereotype of much more ancient west European art, it seems that it actually dates from the beginning of the nineteenth century. Its main interest lies in the division of sex assumed as a criterion for salvation. One can see at first glance that the Blessed are all men, while the Damned are all women. The only exception, and a very notable one, is the Madonna, who is seated in full view on the left, but at the expected distance from Christ in Judgment. Apart from the sexless angels, and a small group of three little boys who are looking on curiously from the right, the other Blessed all have long beards, which place their sexual identity beyond all doubt. If we look very carefully and scrupulously, we must admit that a doubt remains about certain beardless heads which are visible in the second rank in the first left-hand column, and in a few people at the back of the first rank. Among the beardless heads of youths and adults, it may just possibly be that there are a few women. But it is difficult to be certain, and there is no doubt at all about the Damned, whose breasts and buttocks are unmistakably female, and among whom there are no primary sexual characteristics at all which are unmistakably male.

However alluring the prize might seem to be, Finnish peasants nevertheless continued to allow themselves to be seduced by the Siren: she was, after all, a beautiful woman, at least in part. Incontrovertible proof of this is provided by the decisive fact that the narrators of the sixty-four different Finnish versions of the Pregnant Man story, preserved in the Folklore Archives in Helsinki, by far the most part were men, and of all ages. If the men of the people narrated the tale of the priest who gave birth to a calf, it means they must have approved of it. And they also approved of the specific element of female polemic which is undoubtedly endemic in the structure of the tale. Their approval was not a disinterested one; the Christian doctrine of the inequality of the sexes, closely interwoven with that of generational inequality, was exemplified in the relationship between serf and master. It pre-supposed a precise ideology of working relationships, and it

Figure 12 The Last Judgement.

clamped the conditions under which wealth was produced in an iron grip, together with those concerning the reproduction of the species. The Finnish fable resolutely attacked that doctrine and weakened its foundations. It boldly connected subordination with castration, and insubordination to the figure of the father/master with sexual freedom. The paradigm of creation as a theft of procreation thus lost all its meaning; creation and procreation returned to their natural equilibrium. God the Father was reduced to what he really was: the pure and simple mask of the priest: an amplified projection of the eternal father/master, the omnipotent ruler of all social relationships. It was useless for the Hattula fresco to send him back to the skies to regain a little of the prestige which he was evidently failing to preserve on earth.

But we must be very careful here: however interwoven they may be with real elements, fables remain fables, and never become photographic copies of reality. They combine with their reality the dreams and desires which find no place in it. In the specific case of our Finnish fable, it is clear that it put forward a possible solution to the conflicts of the sexes and the generations, as well as the conflicts of society. The reality of these relationships in the Finnish countryside evidently remained the customary one of all the other countries of western, Christian, Europe.

Chapter 9
Nobleman versus Serf

The path taken by the two Aesopian fables in medieval Europe was long, and by no means devoid of dramatic moments. While no trace remains of the English tradition, though there is evidence that it did exist, the French counterpart has been preserved. It was the work of Marie de France, a noblewoman whose origin was the French domains of King Henry II of England, and who lived in his court. The transposition of the two texts from their original monastic environment to the aristocratic one of the English court involved a drastic reappraisal of the polemic against folklore, and recourse to the threat of severe reprisals against those who transgressed against the christian ethic of the master. While the translation into ancient French seems fairly faithful to the Latin original, the introduction of a number of variants stresses the violent nature of the remodelling which has taken place. The first concerns the substitution of the figure of the thief by that of the simple peasant (the villein or serf). Hardly a major transformation. We remember, however, that to the proprietor the peasant had always appeared a thief because of his desire to appropriate to himself the fruits of the earth which belong to the lord who owns the land, and not to the peasant, who is confined merely to working on it.

The peasant's condition is thus closely linked to 'folie'—a word which carries two meanings—madness itself, and total and absolute stupidity, in both cases it implies the complete absence of reason. Serfs believe and hope in the absurdities of folklore myths because they are 'fols', i.e. completely incapable of reasoning. 'Folie' in the sense of ignorance and stupidity is the hallmark of the peasant population, in contrast to knowledge, aristocratic by nature, which is understood as wisdom, and revealed as power. This power to exploit, subject and even ridicule the peasant inspires, in the Middle Ages and later, a rather well-received literature: to be precise, a satire of the servile classes.

Chapter 10
Woman versus Woman

The translation of the second fable is likewise fairly faithful to the Latin text, which it modifies in only a few points, notably in the concluding moral of the story. After the doctor has diagnosed his pregnancy, the father calls his daughter and "by fair means and foul, forces her to confess the truth: she tells him about the spilling of the blood, and that the replacement was her own. The same thing happens to thieves and traitors who cling obstinately to their crimes: they sign their own condemnation, and when they least expect to be taken they are surprised and killed". This conclusion about sinners being surprised and killed is absent from the Latin version of the Aesopian fable; it is an addition by Marie de France, and requires an explanation.

In medieval England the death penalty was not so easily imposed as our tale might lead us to believe. It was certainly not imposed for the crime of fornication, which was the term used in those days for sexual relations between free individuals—i.e. those not married or bound by the vows of chastity. The *Tractatus de legibus et consuetudinibus regni Anglie*, attributed to the jurist Ranulph Glanvill who lived in much the same period at the court of Henry II, merely specifies that this crime had, for women, the effect of excluding them from any inheritances which they might have expected. Historians of English law also tell us that crimes of fornication were reserved for the ecclesiastical courts, which used to punish offenders by whipping in a public place, occasionally with prison, but never with death. The theologian Thomas of Chobham, who lived in a slightly later period, called attention to the gravity of the sin of fornication in principle, but in his *Summa confessorum* he introduced an increasing number of subtle distinctions divided up into a wide range of cases, and of carefully graded penances. The main concern of the church was basically that the manifest punishment of the sin should be followed by the natural reparation of matrimony. The theologian does not say a word about death.

The exaggerated extremism of Marie de France, therefore, can only come as something of a surprise. But in her fable there are two sins for which the girl deserves such severe punishment: the illicit sexual relations which have caused her pregnancy and the ruse to which she has recourse in order to hide her carelessness. The two sins are independent of each other, but in the end they turn out to be closely connected, since the discovery of the one automatically involves that of the other. The one is an echo of the other, as both seem to be motivated by the urge to be unfaithful, which is actually defined as a felony (felunie)—i.e. as a breach of the basic relationship of dependency which governed feudal society in all its aspects. It was only in such a context that the sin of fornication could become so serious as to evoke the threat of the death penalty. The ethic which Marie de France shows herself to adhere to wholeheartedly is, therefore, that of feudal society, which formed an alliance with the christian ethic and even surpassed it in fanaticism. We may find such a passive attitude even more astonishing in view of the fact that the person concerned is a woman, addressing herself to other women. We know very little of the *Ysopet* attributed to Marie de France, but one of the few things that is certain is the sex of the author: it is undoubtedly the work of a woman. Moreover, that woman was a member of the aristocracy, the highest class surrounding the king at court; she emerges from the silent anonymity which was habitually imposed on women and enters the Olympian heights of literature, until then the exclusive preserve of the clergy. The acquisition of a voice; the permission to speak, obviously meant that some sort of promotion had been awarded her—all the more exciting because it was so exceptional. Canetti has written some interesting pages on promotion as a disciplinary technique, a secret and insidious mechanism of power—and we would do well to pay close attention to it.

Chapter 11
Jew versus Jew

At a certain point in their progress, the two Aesopian fables part company and go their separate ways. The second, based on the confusion with the blood samples, is to be found, remodelled and amplified, in the Hebrew collection of Aesopian fables by Berechiah Ben Natronai Ha-Nakdan, who lived in Normandy and England in the latter part of the twelfth and early years of the thirteenth century. A copyist, translator and grammatician, Berechiah was also very interested in the natural sciences and medicine.

His main source was undoubtedly the popular French version of the fable rather than the text of the *Romulus* which he also knew; however, he freed this version from the feudal fanaticism of Marie de France. In the moralistic exhortation which ends the tale, the learned Jew left out the threat of death to thieves, swindlers and traitors associated according to Marie in the crime of infidelity (felunia) with the girl who involuntarily reveals to her father her illicit sexual relations. It is easy enough to see why: in Christian society, who was considered a more anti-social element than the Jew—anti-social par excellence and infidel by definition? Who more than the Jew suffered daily humiliations, and lived under the nightmare of the permanent threat of death? In 1188, on the occasion of the Third Crusade, a number of atrocious massacres of Jews took place in England. The same thing happened in southern France at the beginning of the next century, and then again in 1236 in both eastern France and England. The procedure is notorious: bands of assassins would confront the Jewish communities, demanding their instant conversion to Christianity. Those who refused, and they were the majority, were slaughtered there and then on the spot, without exceptions for women, children and the aged. The ecclesiastical hierarchy naturally did not approve, and they even intervened as a rule

107

on behalf of the Jews; they offered some help and protection, but with little success: the massacres took place even under the eyes of the bishops, in their own palaces where the Jews sometimes went to take refuge. The charity of the hierarchy was useless, and cannot be taken in any way to compensate for the heavy weight of responsibility which the Church must bear, having for centuries declared that the Jews were the principal enemies of Christ. Moreover, there was no lack of highly-placed churchmen who openly advocated persecution. Peter the Venerable, the Abbot of Cluny, is certainly one of the most eminent of the French clerics of the twelfth century—yet in 1146, on the occasion of the second Crusade, he wrote a letter to the King (ed. G. Constable, I: 327–330) boiling over with *odium theologicum*; it remains one of the most disturbing documents of medieval anti-semitism. "What use is it", he wrote, "pursuing and combatting the enemies of the christian faith in distant foreign lands, if the evil-natured and blasphemous Jews, far worse than the Saracens, can curse, scorn and defile Christ and all the sacraments near at hand and even in our midst?" "God", he allowed magnanimously, "certainly does not wish that they should be killed or completely eliminated, but that to their greater torment and shame they should be left, like the fratricide Cain, in a life worse than death". If a prelate with such high office wrote in this way to the king, it is small wonder that an obscure monk, a certain Rodolfo, wandered around in the Rhine valley during that same year, inciting the people to take up the cross to massacre the Jews. (Otto of Freisingen is one of the several chroniclers who record this episode). At the news of the chain of murders which the monk's preaching provoked, St Bernard of Clairvaux intervened energetically, making it clear that "the Jews should not be killed for their excessive crimes, but merely scattered". Even the saint, therefore, though he deplored the massacres, spoke of crime and punishment. In this climate of fierce intolerance, the fable spread of the homicidal ritual, in which the Jews were supposed to parody the passion of Christ by murdering a young Christian boy every now and again. The Jew who managed to get away from the recurring massacres could consider himself lucky, but this did not mean that he was out of danger, because anyone could accuse him of ritual massacre and send him to the stake without running any risk of recrimination.

So then, no threat of death in our fable, but alas this was the only concession made to the transgressors. It was a concession seriously compromised by the attitude taken by the doctor towards the girl's father, whom he held to be pregnant on the basis of his examination of the blood. In effect he advises him to cut his throat in order to eliminate both the guilty person and the unbearable scandal in one blow. His pregnancy, he tells him with horror, is intolerable. It can only be a punishment for your sins, which make you deserving of death. If a man is degraded to the point of becoming pregnant like a woman, he has merited, quite obviously, the maximum punishment. Death returns in the form of suicide, with which the Jewish religious spirit reacted in the face of Christian persecution. Often preceded by the extermination of a whole family, the suicide was intended to forestall the arrival of the assassins, unknowing emissaries of divine justice. The purpose of this was to placate the wrath of God with these sacrifices, as he had been offended by the sins of his Chosen People. Thus suicide became a sort of tragic ritual, a form of introverted violence, used by the Jews against themselves as it could not be enacted against christians. It was a desperate inverted violence which we are astonished and disconcerted to find imposed as a punishment for the presumed degradation of a man to the level of a woman.

The secular and rational veneer which seemed to exclude the intervention of the priest, or rabbi, therefore, is a poor disguise for the same old spiteful moralistic attitude. The Jewish doctor shows no less zeal in upholding the hierarchy of the sexes and the order on which it is based.

Chapter 12
King versus Queen

"Johans der Jansen Eninchel": John, the grandson of Jansen. This is what the author of the *Weltchronik*, a universal chronicle in verse composed in the years around 1280, calls himself in his work. Possibly of Slavic origin, Johann was a citizen of Vienna—a merchant, to be specific— and very well-off. He had a smattering of literary education, and was so fond of tales that he collected all kinds of them and wrote them up on himself. His chronicle is in fact nothing more than a rag-bag collection of anecdotes, in which anything and everything is to be found. Our merchant was not a man of great learning, and he had not acquired a knowledge of Latin—a somewhat serious limitation for a medieval writer. However, he made up for this by his friendship with the monks of a Viennese monastery who undertook the considerable task of translating into German for him everything appearing in Latin in the monastic library which seemed to be useful to his purpose. Not even the monks, however, seem to have been competent Latinists, and scholars have accused Johan of more than one misinterpretation with respect to his Latin sources. The monks must naturally bear at least some share of the responsibility for this. In his chronicle we find the story of Achilles and Deidamia, which has come from Latin among other sources. It is taken from the legend of Achilles on Skyros, as transmitted to the Middle Ages by the Latin scribes, and in particular by Statius. It is hard to establish whether he was the first to interpolate the theme of the pregnant man into the classical legend, but it seems certain that either he or his source knew the second Latin Aesopian fable, the one based on the confusion of the blood samples which made it possible to attribute the daughter's pregnancy to her father. By this stage the blood is replaced, in conformity with the progress of medicine, by the urine of the father and the girl. Deidamia, who has been made pregnant by

Achilles, is no longer merely a rich man but a king. The doctor reveals to him his monstrous pregnancy, diagnosed from the urine, and it implies certain death, because of the obvious inability of the male body to bring about the birth. It is at this point that we find for the first time reproaches aimed at the wife, because she has always insisted on being on top during intercourse. The queen attempts in vain to exculpate herself by saying that she only did it to please him; the king is inflexible in accusing her of diabolical violence, and he calms down only when he gets to know about the exchange of his daughter's urine for his own. At this point the story is interrupted, for unknown reasons, and omits the violent reprimand which the father usually inflicts on his daughter as a result of her illicit pregnancy.

Thus, the only new point with regard to the texts we have already considered concerns the king's reproach to the queen for having subverted the hierarchical order which ordains that the woman must remain underneath during coitus. Obviously this lying underneath is an effective sign and symbol of a condition of subjugation which is strictly concerned with the difference between the sexes. In comparison to this, the social position of the woman counts for nothing—and it is no accident that in this story it is the queen herself. Not even she, that is, the woman who as the king's wife ranks higher than any other woman, is allowed to take the place which belongs to man. Such a faculty, on the other hand, is clearly allowed to the man, for in the legend we find Achilles living on Skyros disguised as a woman, on his mother's orders; this is to escape the mortal fate which the Trojan War has in store for him. He is still disguised as a woman when he arrives on the fabled isle of the beautiful princess, sneaks into the king's castle and seduces his daughter. She, however, tells him that she has only one desire: to be a man and go off on some adventure like a wandering knight in search of fair ladies. Achilles replies that there is a God who can satisfy her desire: all she has to do is offer a prayer that he knows and practise a certain rite which he will teach her. It is not hard to guess what rite he is talking about. The princess finds herself cured of her desire to become a man, but also finds herself pregnant. Both mother and daughter are brought to their senses, and are led back to the natural order of things which demands that they should remain beneath and resign themselves to the position.

Thus man may take the place of woman, but only in disguise, while preserving intact his prerogatives of superiority and command—a serious change is involved if a man truly degenerates to the level of a woman, and effectively assumes the female role.

Chapter 13
Pope versus Emperor: The Medieval Legend of Nero's Pregnancy

In the *Chronicle of John*, Bishop of Nikiou, compiled in Egypt around 700, partly in Greek and partly in Coptic, which has only come down to us in the Ethiopian version, we read: "After the death of Claudius, the abominable Nero reigned in Rome; a pagan and an idolater. He compounded the series of his crimes by the vice of sodomy, and played the part of the woman in a marriage. When the Romans learned of this disgraceful act, they were unwilling to put up with his government any longer; it is well known that even the priests of the idols hurled maledictions against him, and the Elders of the people made up their mind to kill him. When he learned of the plot of the Elders, this criminal left his abode and hid himself, but he could not escape from the hand of Almighty God. In fact, how deeply his soul was sunk in misery, because as a result of the debauchery to which he had abandoned himself, in the feminine manner, his belly had swollen like that of a pregnant woman. He was deposed, and in his sad sickness he suffered terrible pains. Then he ordered doctors to come to him in the place where he was hiding, and to bring him some help. The doctors gathered round him, and thinking that he was bearing a child, they opened his belly to remove it. This was the sad manner of his death".

In contrast to all the other texts we have looked at up to now, this one is put forward as an historical source which was supposed to be recording real facts about events which had actually taken place. The ancient historical sources, beginning with Tacitus and Suetonius, provide a wealth of material on this matter, giving plenty of particulars

112

of Nero's faults and vices, by no means excluding the sexual ones. The unbridled lust, the incest with his mother followed by matricide, the public celebration of at least two homosexual marriages, are among the best-known and most colourful ingredients of his biography. Both Tacitus (XV. 37) and Suetonius (*Nero*: 29) record homosexual marriages in which he played the part of the bride, but without connecting them with a pregnancy, much less with his deposition and death. There is a reference in Suetonius (*Nero*: 21) to the pregnancy, but in a different context: it refers to the imperial amateur actor's dramatic repertoire. Among the various parts which Nero performed, he mentions that of Canacé, who gives birth on stage. The reference is certainly to a lost tragedy by Euripides—Aiolos—in which Canacé does in fact give birth in this context. The other dramatic roles (Oreste, Oedipus and Hercules) attributed by Suetonius to his histrionic hero are evidently chosen for malicious reasons, as they correspond precisely to his notorious faults and vices.

But to what vice did the role of Canacé correspond? According to an article by R.M. Frazer, the vice was, for an emperor, the quite serious one of wanting to sing on the stage at all costs—without having a voice suited to the task! This interpretation is taken from a passage in Plutarch (*Moralia*: 567F–568A) where the soul of Nero, in order to return to life, is forced to reincarnate itself in the body of an animal "which sings in the marshes and the swamps". The choice of the frog is meant as a reminder that Nero sang like a frog, and it must have been to his croaking that Suetonius was alluding too when he used the name Canacé, which in Greek referred, in fact, to the sound made by the frog. The connection between Nero and the frog must have been firmly rooted in the classical tradition, and the connection remained unbroken throughout the Middle Ages. It is more than likely that Suetonius wished to pour ridicule on the theatrical pretensions of the imperial buffoon. It is more likely still when we find that the allusion to the part of Canacé returns in the same terms, but with an even more obviously satirical intention, in a passage from Dio Cassius (62.10.2). The reference to Nero's pregnancy was, however, made by both historians only in terms of the theatrical fiction, and it is not found again, in similar or different form, in any other ancient source. Only in the Chronicle of the Bishop of Nikiou did it find an echo after so many centuries—and the echo serves only to exaggerate and distort the original. It moves away from the theatrical stage into historical reality, and inflates the whole thing to the point where pregnancy becomes the cause of the death of the hero. The reasons for this astonishing revival of the tale are to be sought in the centuries-old development of the Christian legend of Nero.

If the identification with the Beast of the Apocalypse of St John is correct, then the legend was abroad as early as the first century, while Nero himself was still alive. The pragmatic immoralism of the Roman Emperor who showed no indulgence to the new religious sect in fact offered Christian polemic a golden opportunity. The confrontation between the new power, purified and legitimised by the blood of Christ, and the old power, stained with every kind of vileness, was almost too easy: power which was not yet christianised was the work of Satan, and took on the demonic face of Nero. It lay, however, within the designs of Providence as a punishment for sin and as the indispensable precondition of the final victory of the Lamb, the "Lord of lords, and King of kings". Power would then belong to his followers ('These are they that are not defiled with women, for they are virgins", Rev.14.4), according to the usual sexophobic divide which always gave preference to castration. The identification of Nero with the Antichrist, who must return to prepare for the end of time and the advent of the Kingdom, derived, as an automatic consequence of this outlook, from the mysterious circumstances of his death, and persisted throughout the first centuries of the christian era, until the decision of Constantine to accept the cross removed its most important motivation. The most authoritative Christian writers, with Lactantius in the lead, then began to deny it. Nero redivivus would never come back to earth, of course; but his monstrous doings there must remain as a warning: the uncontrolled greed for power was what had led inevitably to his excesses of lust and cruelty. This is how St Augustine put it in his *De Civitate Dei* (V.19). The sexual vices of the detested Roman emperor thus came back into prominence and were once again and for centuries to come adduced as the christian limits of power. After Augustine, Orosius (*Historiarum*, VII.7) set out the compendium of these vices, not omitting the homosexual marriage in which Nero played the part of the wife, and for good measure adding an incest or two. From Augustine and Orosius, therefore, and on into the fifth century, a portrait of Nero as the perfect incarnation of power cursed by God was handed down to christian posterity—a power allowed by God for the punishment of sins.

To this portrait, the pregnancy attributed to him by the Bishop of Nikiou was added as a final touch. But what reason could there have been for this final touch? What relationship existed between power and pregnancy? The Bishop of Nikiou was a Greek writer, and according to a precise exegesis by Emile Benveniste: "the same notional relationship in Greek links the present kuein—'to be pregnant; to bear in one's own bosom', the noun kuma—'swelling (of the waves), surge'—on the one hand, and on the other hand kuros—'strength, sovereignty'; kurios—sovereign". From the initial meaning of 'to swell', Benveniste explains, there derives that of 'strength', 'strength of fullness, of swollenness, of growth and potency'. This same evolution is common to other Indo-European languages such as Iranian, and the Slavonic and Baltic tongues. In the latter, however, "this correspondence defines an adjective which has kept a very strong religious value in a different kind of belief: in Slavonic and Baltic, it belongs to the Christian vocabulary and means 'holy; sanctus'". The sacred is defined as a superabundant force, gifted with "a power of authority and effectiveness which has the capacity to grow, to increase, both in the neutral and in the transitive senses". These are Benveniste's conclusions. They enable us to understand that the Egyptian bishop had been able to derive the swollen belly and the pregnancy which he attributed to Nero from the conception of potency which he held because of his role as a priest, engaged in sacred functions. However, the pregnancy involved an inevitable feminine implication—unacceptable to a bishop if it were to be connected with a man. But Nero was not Adam, and in his case the pregnancy might be attributed to the negative factor of homosexuality. His swollen belly, mistaken by the doctors for a pregnancy, was in fact the consequence of the vice of sodomy, and cost him his dethronement and his life, as a punishment from God. From a factor of potency, therefore, pregnancy became converted into a reason for degradation and condemnation.

"The Lateran Palace was one of Nero's; its name derived either from the 'latus' or side of the northern area where it was sited, or from the huge frog (*lata rana*) which, so it was said, Nero had given birth to when he gave himself to a man; in this palace today is to be found the great Church of Rome". This gloss was an attempt to explain, by an etymology based on pure fantasy in the unmistakable style inaugurated by Isidore of Seville, the name by which the Roman Palace where the Popes resided was known all over medieval Europe. The fantastic etymology was recorded in the *Lexicon of Papias*, a Lombard grammarian of the eleventh century, but the modern editor of his Glossary, Georg Goetz, was able to establish that its origin in fact lay a lot earlier. It was based on a tradition found in Rome during the pontificate of Benedict III (855–858) by the learned Carolingian monk, Lupus de Ferrieres. The Christian legend of Nero's pregnancy had thus passed down to the ninth century from the east to the west, and had become naturalised in Rome. Indeed it was so much at home that it became closely associated with the Pontifical Palace, through an etymological explanation which revived the ancient connection of the raucous imperial songster with the frog.

The Christian tradition, however, had from the start, even in Nero's time, left out his frog-like singing qualities, in order to concentrate on another of his attributes, no less ancient and well-adapted. In the Revelation of St John (16: 13–14), the Beast, with which Nero as the incarnation of Satan was identified, actually vomited out at a certain moment an unclean spirit in the form of a frog, charged with calling together the kings of the earth for the war against God. The frog was associated with Nero because it was considered a diabolical animal, which was opposed to the installation of the Kingdom of God upon earth. And it was from the frog that they attempted to derive the name of the pontifical palace, in order to allude to the victory of Christ over the Evil One. In this etymological transposition of the legend of Nero, Christ triumphed over Satan, as his Vicar did over the Roman Emperor. In fact the gloss which was produced in Rome in the age of Pope Benedict III is easily explained in the context of the political tradition which had its most important expression in the most famous forgery of history—the so-called *Donation of Constantine*. The churchmen who compiled this document were intent on claiming for the Papacy the succession to the imperial dominion over Rome, Italy and the entire empire of the west. The Emperor Constantine was thus made to declare in this document that he conceded and consigned to Pope Sylvester, apart from the empire and the insignia of power, "the Lateran Palace, seat of our Empire, which surpasses and excels all the palaces of the world". The Palace, then, was the seat of power, and at the same time its most evident symbol.

In the course of the high Middle Ages, no Pope could declare himself to be such in all effects until he had taken up his throne there. It stood in an area of grandiose Roman ruins; in the open space before it stood the equestrian statue of Marcus Aurelius, later transferred to the Capitol, alongside the fragments (a head and a hand) of another huge ancient statue. There too was the bronze wolf which suckled Romulus and Remus, and the whole monumental complex at first sight represented the continuity of the ancient grandeur of Rome with that of the Pontifical city. In the most ancient plan of Rome, which dates from the beginning of the thirteenth century (Figure 13) the palace is shown in the foreground, and beside it stand the statue of Marcus Aurelius and the two fragments of the other. An inscription actually written on the palace notes that it represents the Palacium Neronis Lateranense. Needless to say, in historical reality Nero had very little to do with this palace, the ancient residence of the noble Roman family of the Plauti Laterani. But who better than Nero could represent the demonic power subjected by the triumph of the Church? Moreover, the gloss does not fail to refer to the homosexual birth of the frog, taking up from the Bishop of Nikiou the connection between male parturition and homosexuality. The ancient priestly equation between power and male

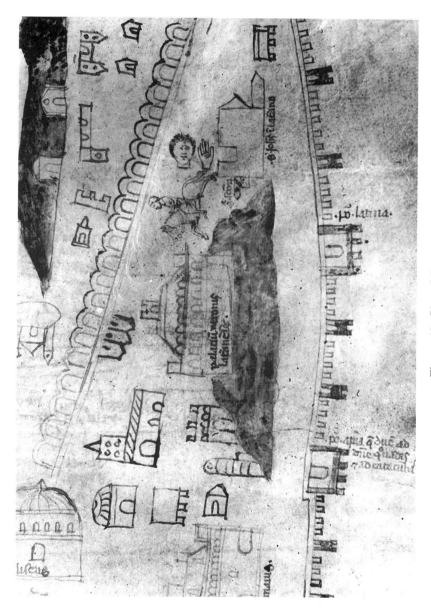

Figure 13 Plan of Rome.

117

pregnancy remained unaltered. The pejorative component, linked to homosexuality, could, however, prove to be compromising in the long run, because if the accursed power was based on homosexuality, the blessed power favoured castration, rather than heterosexual activity. In the *Graphia Aureae Urbis Romae*, a description of the city of Rome datable to about 1030, the gloss is repeated in its entirety, with the sole exception of the reference to homosexuality, which was censored then and never appeared again.

The legend of Nero's pregnancy was widespread in Europe throughout the Middle Ages. The detail of the frog which was borne by the Roman Emperor stirred the imagination of writers, and not only of historians or would-be historians. In the twelfth century it inspired one of the most bizarre episodes in the *Kaiserchronik*, the weighty anonymous compilation which at least two monks cobbled together in many thousands of verses in middle-high German. Nero's pregnancy was no longer the result of his homosexuality, but of his capriciousness. Nero wanted at all costs to give birth like a woman. His doctors, when summoned, were threatened with death unless they fulfilled his whim. So they gave him a potion to drink, and the frog which was born from it in his stomach came forth unexpectedly from his mouth, just as predicted in the Revelation of St John. Enriched by more and more fantastic and romanticised details, the legend passed, in the course of the thirteenth and fourteenth centuries, into the chronicles and poems of half of Europe. From Germany to England, from France to Italy, it was sometimes recounted in Latin, sometimes in the common tongues, within a fantastic and miraculous framework. But it was always the same old edifying tale of demonic power, now sanctified in more tangible form by the sacrifice of the martyrs. It is at this point that the legend of Nero's pregnancy meets up, in its fortunate progress through Europe, with that of the Roman martyrdom of the apostles Peter and Paul, characterised by the presence of another historical personage, the Samaritan messiah, Simon Magus. Mixed up with all the other details of the most ancient christian tradition, in this version of the legend which begins with the *Kaiserchronik*, a new element appears, which seems to us to be of the greatest importance. The birth of the frog here seems to be linked to the belief, recurring in the folklore of Europe but certainly much more ancient, that anyone who drinks water from a pond in which frog-spawn is present risks conceiving one of the creatures in his own stomach. There is an explicit reference to this belief in one of the latest versions of the legend of Nero's pregnancy, included in the novel *Gargantua*, by the sixteenth century German writer Johann Fischart. Here the doctors give Nero frog-spawn, and in this way make sure that a frog is born in his stomach. This detail makes it clear that the Christian legend of Nero had already come into contact with folklore by the twelfth century. Even more than this, returning to the *Kaiserchronik* we find Simon Magus competing with the two apostles to show his levitational capacities, climbing up on to the Irminsaeule, the column sacred to the religion of the ancient Germans. From there he launches himself into space and is sustained by devils. With the aid of Simon Magus and the ever-present devils, then, Nero is also linked in this fashion to the folklore which the Church was attacking specifically as a diabolical survival of the ancient religions. A second point of contact with folklore is provided by the *Weltchronik*, or universal chronicle, of our old friend the Viennese merchant, Johan, the grandson of Jansen. The legend of Nero is to be found there with all its usual ingredients, but Johan, as we already know, loved to mix and remix the most varied sources, and couldn't resist introducing some novelty into it. His story tells of the frog which is brought into the world by Nero, riding through Rome in a silver chariot studded with gold and precious stones, between two ranks of applauding people. It leaps into the Tiber from a bridge to join some of its companions who are awaiting it. The tale has an undeniably fantastic character, and must have delighted Gottfried Keller, because he took it up again in one of his short stories. Another detail takes us back again to folklore, and this time specifically to the theme of the pregnant man; this is the reference to the diagnosis of the pregnancy which the doctors give to Nero after examining his urine.

In the struggle which the Church conducted against folklore, the evil and vicious Roman emperor had to take the place of the priest as the polemical target of the folklore theme of the pregnant man. It was not the priest, but Nero, the devil incarnate, who was the representative of power—that is, of power which was cursed by God. In this view of things, the folklore theme could be harmonised with the Christian legend, to rob it of its true nature and deflect from it its original significance. However, in order to inflict this idea directly onto a people who were largely illiterate and certainly unlettered, special means were needed. There was a need for the intervention of verbal technicians, capable of communicating directly with the uneducated, and this meant first and foremost the hagiographers and preachers.

The *Legenda Aurea*, the 'Golden Legend' of the Dominican, Bl. Giacomo da Varazze (second half of the thirteenth century) is intended as a sort of 'summa' of folklore, christianised and transposed in hagiographical terms. It enjoyed enormous popular success in medieval times. The legend of the pregnant Nero was inserted into the life of St Peter, in a context which assimilated the Church's struggle against folklore into the struggle fought and won by the two Apostles Peter and

Paul against the false Messiah, Simon Magus. The birth of the frog from Nero's mouth concludes the edifying tale, though there is no reference to the etymology of the name of the Lateran Palace. Just as in the eleventh century, any mention of the connection between Nero's pregnancy and homosexuality was considered compromising, so in the second half of the thirteenth century, there was reluctance to mention any reference to the Papal Palace in this context. It was better that the palace should have nothing in common with Nero, being a symbol, as it was, of a continuity of power which in the eyes of ignorant people might appear all too significant. From the *Legenda Aurea* after undergoing some adaptations suited to the taste of the times, the story of Nero's frog passed into the *Alphabetum Narrationum* of Arnold de Liège, the great collection of exempla dating from the fourteenth century. In this same century it also found a place in the Low German collection entitled *Der Grosse Seelentrost* which was also translated into Swedish, and in the following century, it appears in the English and Catalan translations of the *Alphabetum Narrationum*. In all these versions of the exemplum of the pregnancy of Nero, no mention is ever made of the Lateran Palace. On the other hand two fourteenth century writers do continue to refer to it, but not without a certain embarrassment. The English monk, Ranulph Higden, took up the reference again from the thirteenth century chronicle of Martin von Troppau, but he deliberately distorts it: instead of the pontifical palace, he speaks of "a certain tower" in which Nero had the frog kept under guard. According to the notary of Liège, Jean des Preis known as Outremeuse, Nero gave birth to the frog in a great Roman palace which was called the Lateran. However, no-one who did not already know about it personally would have guessed that this was in fact the Pope's palace. These two writers, in any case, were writing for an educated public, and moreover the distribution of their manuscripts was very limited; it does not bear comparison with the wide popular appeal of the exemplum. Its considerable success also signifies that the story of Nero's frog rumbled on for centuries in the churches of Europe like a kind of counterpoint to the figurative litany of the birth of Eve. The exempla were in fact the most formidable arsenal of the preachers, and provided sensational corroborative evidence of the edifying cases which the scarifying preaching of the friars produced.

The preaching of the friars, however, didn't bring about the desired result; indeed it produced quite the contrary. According to the examples collected in various regions of Italy during the last century, Nero did enter into folklore, and the evidence suggests that it was preaching that put him there. He entered, and he remained for centuries, but only to give greater credence by his example to the proverb which says: The worst always comes later. An Umbrian version puts it this way: "A certain old woman met up with Nero; she said to him: 'May you be blessed and live a thousand years. The tyrant, well aware that he was hated by everyone, was astonished at this benevolence, and asked the old woman: 'How is it that while everyone is wishing for my death, you wish me a thousand years of life?' 'Because the worst always comes after!', replied the old wretch: 'I remember your grandfather, and he was pretty dreadful, and your father, and he was worse, and now I know you, and you're a real devil... what will become of us if anyone comes after you?'" Now we all know who Nero's successor was to be— the person who established himself in the Lateran Palace to continue the exercise of his power throughout the centuries. The Pope was thus paid back, for the anecdote was published in 1869, and up until 1861, Umbria had been part of the States of the Church, that same patrimony which the Emperor Constantine was supposed to have given to Pope Sylvester and all his successors, along with the Lateran Palace and the entire empire of the west.

Chapter 14
Excursus: Homosexuality and Male Pregnancy

The relation between the masculine fantasy of pregnancy and homosexuality, well-known to psychoanalysts, has also been confirmed by anthropologists. Freud established its existence in the seventh chapter of his clinical study *Man among the wolves*, and he went on to formulate his theory in a subsequent essay. Later on, Georges Devereux was to study it in specific detail. The conclusions of his investigation appeared in an article published in 1937. For Freud, the masculine fantasy of pregnancy is the mark of a regression to the infantile 'cloacal theory': the anus, confused with the vagina, is the seat of both sexual relations and pregnancy. The regression is accompanied by a tendency towards female identification. But under the pressure of the violent reprobation which this excites, this is repressed and transformed into a symptom. In *Man among the Wolves*, the fantasy of pregnancy, accompanied by recurrent intestinal disturbances, expressed the desire to renounce virility in order to obtain the father's love, and make him a present of a child. The Mohave Indians of North America, wrote Devereux, show a great tolerance towards homosexuality, and even have a special statute governing it which gives it an almost institutional status. Among so-called 'passive' homosexuals, the pregnancy fantasy is not the subject of any repression. It is freely expressed in a faithful imitation of pregnancy, which is resolved by a faecal delivery. From the clinical as from the ethographical viewpoints, the masculine fantasy of pregnancy and homosexuality coincide; the man identifies himself as closely as possible with the woman in both cases. As Sandor Ferenczi has said, 'passive' homosexuality is in fact the characteristic of the man

122

who feels himself to be feminine in contrast to other men, "not merely in the genital relationship but in all the circumstances of life."

Now in the documents which we have been studying up to this point, the identification is always momentary, and there is no fear of the social judgment which represses it. This characteristic comes to the man concerned from outside himself; it takes us back to the Freudian distinction between fixation and symbolic conduct. For Freud, fixation is based on the confusion between desire and reality, and in the more extreme cases it ends up in psychosis. Symbolic conduct, on the other hand, excludes any possibility of confusion with reality; in this case fiction knows itself to be such, and desire recognises that it is desire. The homosexual tries to make-believe that he is pregnant; the father-master feigns that he is so, and he knows, as everyone else does, that this is not and cannot be the case. Moreover, the fiction may be a necessary stage in development; it may favour the development of the libido. At the moment of passage from infancy to adolescence, the male child identifies with his father. The fiction of the father who gives birth to the child, the symbol of this identification, helps the child to grow, to become adult like his father. According to Theodor Reik, it is in this that the profound meaning of initiation rites really lies. But the symbolic function may be taken over to serve the purposes of power. Then the identification becomes a trap, and instead of growing, the child becomes a slave. There is no desire whatever in the symbolic pregnancy of the father-master to become identified with woman. It is only a matter of symbolically despoiling woman of her attribute of potency. The envy which female potency excites in the man transforms itself into dreams of expropriation, just as female envy of male potency is transformed into the need for castration. By reasoning in terms of power, both the sexes seek to steal from the other instead of valuing each other's creative faculties. And this is the case for the simple reason that here it is not really sexual power which is at stake, but social; that kind of potency, in other words, which is expressed in relationships involving domination, and makes control of the family and of society possible. The identification is thus clearly subject to a manipulative intention: it appears in order to expropriate, or else to accuse and denigrate. For this reason, the christian writers who took such great delight in the homosexuality of Nero, never dreamed of attributing it to Adam. And yet there was Adam, giving birth to Eve all over the churches of Europe.

Nor has folklore turned Adam into a homosexual. It attributed homosexuality to the priest, just as the priest had attributed it to Nero. In both cases, much play was made of the equivocal element, transferring the male pregnancy from the level of symbolic fiction to that of fixation, and the purpose was always to use the social judgment of disapproval of homosexuality to degrade and denigrate the powerful. However, with their usual ferocity, the priests pushed their tactic to the furthest extreme: Christian society punished homosexuality with death, and death overtook Nero as a divine punishment. Folklore, on the other hand, was more magnanimous to the priest; it almost always contented itself with punishing him with a few blows, and the reason was not homosexuality, and even less his arrogance. Usually it punished him with the simple humiliation which the general rejection of homosexuality involved. In the fables, the reaction to homosexuality usually sets off a mechanism of refusal-flight-rejection. Incapable of bearing the weight of the female identification, the priest refuses it, runs away or is separated in some other way from civil society until he is freed in some hidden fashion from his intolerable symbolic burden. The identification thus regains the transitory and instrumental nature which the symbolic fiction originally bestowed on it, and the priest can re-enter the ranks and take up his former functions again. Society has pardoned him, and reintegrated him fully into its order. Society has pardoned him, yes, but the fable has nevertheless unmasked him.

Section III

Chapter 15
The Monk's Sorrows: A German Verse Tale

It is in a German verse tale of the fourteenth century that the theme of the pregnant man reaches its most perfect expression. It is called *The Monk's sorrows*, and the author was an obscure poet of the name of Zwingäuer. Even though it is a rather longer text than the usual ones, it is worth reproducing it here because of its peculiar importance:

"Here is a really lovely story of how a monk became pregnant with a little child."

I would willingly tell you something which would delight you even more if I was actually present among you. But now listen to this story— it really is very curious—of the monk who became pregnant and what happened to him. Judge for yourselves whether it wasn't a real and true miracle.

A little boy was entrusted to a monk so that he could dedicate his life to God. The world was quite unknown to him when he was taken off to a monastery hidden in the woods... he was only seven years old. He learned how to write, and many many other things, and he was so well-taught that he could read everything written which came his way. The boy grew more in height than in girth, and when he was a lad, the abbot welcomed him into his own lodging.

One day, after Matins, he was sitting beside his bed and reading. And this was how he came to see written in a page of the little book the words "Love's chains". He asked himself what this could be, or why it should be that love should tie anyone in chains. At once he put down the book, and began to ponder, to try and understand what these 'chains of Love' might be. The monk went secretly to a servant whom he knew, who regularly accompanied the Abbot when he went off on horseback.

125

He considered this man to be trustworthy, so he asked him what this 'Love' might be, and where it could be found—among the young or the old—and whether it really had such great power as to be able to enchain people. The servant replied to him: "You haven't an idea of what you've just asked me. If you were ill, Love would cure you. He doesn't enchain people in any way; in fact anyone who receives his consolation is freed from all suffering. His house is well-furnished and well-stocked with good food and wine". The monk replied: "Very well, I want to go there, before the half year is out." The servant told him to ask the Abbot for a servant and a horse, with the excuse that his relations were in great trouble and he needed to go and help them. The Abbot accepted his request, and immediately gave him a servant and a horse, and moreover as much money as he needed. He himself was prudent enough to put aside about ten livres for his own needs.

He left as the servant had advised him. A servant rode before him and he followed behind, since he had never before left the monastery. The servant had already found this out. They came to a fine city, where the servant asked a woman who was neither too young nor too old if she could give them lodging. Her husband was away at sea on a long journey, and she had to look after the house. The servant ordered her to prepare an adequate meal, and he gave her the bag to look after. The woman welcomed them with open arms, and busied herself greatly in preparations, taking care to give the monk a room to himself so that she could look after him conveniently. An abundant meal arrived, cold and hot dishes, and excellent cooled wine. The monk said: "This seems to me, indeed, to be the court of Love in his majesty. Everything seems to me so good; if things were only like this in my monastery, how happy all the monks would be!"

The servant asked the mistress of the house: "Do you know of a girl who would suit my master, and who would do it with him for money? He could pay ten livres in exchange for a bit of love-making".

He was very insistent, this servant, and begged her to oblige the monk in person, assuring her that she would be well-rewarded. The woman said at once: "I've pawned my goods; if they're taken out of pawn, the young monk will get his consolation, and I'll do everything I should for him". So the servant said "That's a wise decision. You already have the monk's money in the sack in safe-keeping; take what is due to you; don't be hesitant. He is very fond of you already, and he is full of ardent desire." They agreed on six livres, which were paid on the spot. Thus the servant paid the price of love. The woman accepted his request; she put on her best clothes, and sat down beside the monk. She wasn't at a loss for honeyed words, and her eyes shone like the stars; her cheeks were rosy, and her neck as white as ermine. She had fine little fingers and smooth rounded arms; her height was just right. The monk found all this very pleasing, but he knew nothing about the rest of it all. The servant suggested that he should pay very careful attention to what the woman told him to do; he said "She'll show you—you'll find out that Love is yours: go to it with a will, because I've paid well for it already". The monk was delighted at what he heard, and said: "I'll arrange it so that Love comes with me to the monastery to add to the pleasure of the Abbot and the whole community, both young and old". The poor innocent really thought that the Abbot and the whole company of monks had grown up without Love and had made a great mistake.

The mistress of the house soon arrived and took the monk by the hand. Ah, how quickly she led him off to the room which had been prepared for him; and there was the bed, all ready. She led the monk straight to it. He didn't take off his habit, so the fair lady said to him: "Come: you're not in your monastery now; take your habit off." When the light was out, she didn't waste any more time, and lay down beside him. The poor fool lay there, as stiff as a ramrod. The woman removed his habit, and came closer to him; she drew him to her, hoping that something good would come her way, too, but he lay there as motionless as a tree trunk which had been felled to the ground, because he hadn't the remotest idea what he was supposed to do. Ever since his earliest childhood, he had been kept safely away from women. He knew a lot more about singing and reading than about love-making. Annoyed at finding that she had to take the initiative, the woman began scheming mischievously as to how she could make a fool of him. All at once she gave the monk a shove with her foot, and made him turn over against the wall. Then she moved close to him, straddled him, and began kneeing and kicking him. The monk felt his back and his chest hurting as if they were burning. It seemed to him that it was a pretty troublesome matter, this love-making with women, and he would willingly have fled; he didn't want to know any more about this Love, which he had chosen. But then the woman gave him such a violent blow that he dared not move. "Now you can stay there, you useless creature! But nothing will happen to you! This is a present to you from Lady Love; you went out looking for her, and there you are!". The monk was silent; he said nothing about the blows he had suffered, and stayed there quite still.

When midnight came, the woman returned to the attack. She began twisting and turning, stretched out her hand towards Love, as the serpent did in the Temptation; then she began beating the monk again. She made him suffer blow after blow; he would have preferred to be anywhere but there. He felt that Love had come a bit too close. How little he slept. She said "This is the other letter that Lady Love has sent you. Now you can really live a life of joy!" He was still silent, but he was thinking: "If I were back in my monastery now, and Lady Love was in front of my door, I certainly wouldn't put a foot outside!"

A little before dawn, the woman again started moaning that she had been cheated. She gave him another blow-by-blow lesson, and this was the third punishment he had to suffer. Then she saw the dawn was breaking, and she packed the monk off; he was only too pleased and hurried away without even bestowing a blessing. He called his servant furiously, and ordered him to bring the horses because he didn't want to stay one moment longer. The servant was terrified; he thought that the master of the house had probably arrived. Both of them were in a great rush; the monk raced along behind the servant. They rode swiftly along through the fields for more than three miles, and they only felt safe when they reached a green meadow where they dismounted.

The servant gazed at his master, who seemed to him to be ghastly white, with pallid cheeks. He asked him how things had gone with Love. The monk replied thoughtfully: "I couldn't boast, even if things had gone well, because God does not love boasters. I'll leave it to you to tell about it." The servant did not ask him any more. The monk was in great haste to return to his monastery. Later he said to the servant: "I have often heard tell that when two have been together, babies are born. Tell me now, on your honour: which of the two gives birth to the baby?" "I'll tell you how things really are", the servant replied: "It's the one who is underneath". "Oh poor me" the monk thought, for it was only now that he began to realise his misfortune. "Oh no: what can I do? I was the one who was underneath. Now I must bring a child into the world. My honour is lost—and if the Abbot finds out, how will I be able to live? I'll be expelled from the community. I would rather die than suffer their disdain."

About twelve weeks passed, and the monk began ailing, so badly had the woman beaten him about. His brothers asked him what was the matter; why had he become so thin? But he did not want to tell anyone that Love had done this to him, because he was convinced that he would have to give birth to a baby. After a certain time a serious complaint was presented to the Abbot by one of his peasants, and the pregnant monk happened to hear it. The man said: "I have to bring a complaint before you. The son of the widow in my village thrashed my cow, and caused it to abort its calf". "I shall be a good judge", replied the Abbot; "that man is so beholden to me that I can compel him to come to terms with you and compensate you for the calf, as he is obliged to do by the demands of justice." The pregnant monk had been listening intently to everything the peasant had said. He sent someone to the widow's son, whom he knew well, and told him to come to him secretly in order to hear what he had to tell him. The widow's son came to the monastery, where the monk welcomed him kindly and escorted him to his cell without anyone seeing. Now, just listen to what this monk said to him: "Today I heard someone complaining about you that you had thrashed a cow and made her abort her calf. I think I need the same kind of thrashing myself, because by ill-fortune I know that I have a child in my belly, and I'm afraid of being put to shame if I tell anyone about it". The widow's son replied "Oh heavens; how on earth did that happen to you? The prior seems to me to be too feeble, and the abbot's too old. Who was responsible for this miracle? If it was the brother-steward, he's got a nerve". The monk said "No, it wasn't him, either. None of the monks is to blame; none of them has ever had anything to do with my body. I had the child from a woman, with whom I made love". Then the widow's son said: "Master, I'd like to do anything you want, but only a very few of those people who wanted to put an end to their pregnancy have ever survived". But the monk answered: "I'm willing to risk it: don't hesitate—beat me hard, because I really need it. Don't worry about me dying; I sincerely absolve you of any sin you may commit against me. And to be quite certain that you'll do the job properly, I'll give you three whole livres". The widow's son cheered up greatly at this and didn't waste any more time. "Come tomorrow at daybreak to the little wood near the monastery, and I'll help you as much as I can before midday arrives". Said the monk: "I'll do as you say, and be sure I won't be late". The widow's son was a scoundrel. He prepared three oak rods for the monk's back, and brought them with him. The monk arrived early as he had said, and when he saw the servant, he gave him the three livres and admonished him: "Go on beating and don't stop; don't spare me and I'll reward you even more." The widow's son then ordered him: "Take your habit off". This was soon done; he now only had his shirt on. The man threw him to the ground like a cow, and gave him such a beating that if he'd had seven babies in his belly not one of them would have survived. The force of the blows broke his bones. Near at hand, hidden by the grass in a little dell, was a hare, which was so frightened at the noise of the beating that it didn't dare move. When the third oak rod was broken, the monk saw the hare sprinting away, and cried out: "Stop now, stop: I want to run after my son! If I can only catch him, I'll find a wet-nurse to raise him." The hare bounded off towards the woods, and the monk watched him going; he cried out desperately: "My son, my dearest son: how fast your legs carry you! Oh, what a sorrow for me; I would have made you a prince's runner, because you've covered so many miles in a few moments—or perhaps a cook, seeing you already have the spoons which are used to eat with!" Just think, this idiot was thinking of the hare's ears, which he had seen raised, of course. The monk wanted to follow him into the wood at all costs; he couldn't bear his sorrow any longer and was desperate to find his son. He ran like a mad dog, beating his breast a thousand times, wringing his hands in wretchedness—but he didn't find his son, and he tore his hair in sorrow.

An old monk who happened to be passing by on horseback noticed this and asked him: "What's the matter, that you're behaving in this way? Why are you so upset? Have you provoked our Lord's anger, by any chance?" He answered: "I've lost the son I was carrying in my belly: that's what has happened." The monk on horseback said to him: "God knows, I've never in my life seen a monk carrying a child in his belly". The young man went on: "I don't care now who knows about it, for better or for worse, as long as I get my son back; that's what is making me suffer". The old man then gave him a blow with a stick which made him fall to the ground in front of him. "You have gone mad and brought shame to the Order, and all the monks that belong to it" he said. "If I could only see my son just once, I wouldn't care about anything else which might happen to me". "In the name of God" the old monk exclaimed: "you want to hunt for a son in this wood?" So he tied his hands like a thief, and mocked him. "If other peoples' babies delight you so much, you'll soon gather what I think about it". And he at once began to beat him again, causing huge bruises. After that, he rode off, while the young monk ran beside him, tied with a cord. He was weeping warm tears as he thought of his son. When he was brought in to the monastery, all the monks saw, and crowded round. As soon as the Abbot came up, he asked him in a low voice: "Tell me my son, what happened?" He answered: "If you had seen my son, he would certainly have pleased you. I can't tell you anything else. If I could only get to him, I would have him baptised, and would beg you and the Prior and the Cellarer to act as his godfathers." All this seemed very strange indeed to the monks. They lifted up his undershirt and saw the signs of the beating, and they became convinced that he was possessed by the evil one.

The Abbot ordered that the Psalter be brought, with other sacred books, and set the monks about exorcising the devil with all their might, to free the monk from his heavy burden. They did as the Abbot ordered, passing over the monk reciting benedictions. But he began to rave in his great sorrow. He said "My son is still a pagan; if he had only been baptised, my sorrow would have passed". The Abbot then said: "Do you hear how the Devil mocks us! What crafty ways he uses. He cares nothing for our exorcism; he knows too many subtle tricks". They brought holy water and began to sprinkle him with it, arranging the stole around his neck. But everything they did, all their prayers and threats, were in vain. He went on repeating: "If only I had the son whom I carried in my belly for twelve weeks, how happy I would be!" Then the monks grew angry and became convinced that he really was mad. They shut him up angrily in the prison, where the poor devil remained for fifteen days and fifteen nights, and was given nothing but a little bread and water. He prayed constantly to God to send his son back to him, so that he could make him into a Christian.

On the fifteenth day, the monk told the Abbot the truth in the confessional—the whole story of Love and the servant and the woman who had beaten him and from whom he had had the child, and how he had lain underneath when they made love. He told the story from beginning to end. Then the Abbot ruled "Your misfortune comes to an end today. You must no longer be ashamed before me or before the prior. You must go to choir and sing and read, and go back to being the good son you were previously. And pray for me also. You are absolved from your sins; now turn your attention to life eternal".

This is the end of the story by Zwingäuer, who recounted the tale of the monk's sorrows. Now let us pray to the same God that on the Day of Judgment He will not deny us entry to the Kingdom of Heaven.

Chapter 16
Servants and Women versus the Monk-Master

This German saga of 544 verses (in rhyming distychs, following the pattern aa bb cc dd), is undated, but probably belongs to the beginning of the fourteenth century; it was not published however, until the nineteenth. The language is middle-high-German, i.e. the German that was spoken and written in central and southern Germany in the early medieval period. On the basis of the dialectical inflections in the text, Upper Franconia has been suggested as the specific area of origin—a region then dominated by the powerful bishopric of Bamberg, which shared the ownership of the land and the control of the serf population that worked on it with a number of rich abbeys.

The first and most obvious cultural reference in the story is to the tradition of the love lyric which had such wide currency in medieval Europe, and found its most perfect form in Germany in the poetry of the Minnesänger. The reference is quite clear: at the beginning of the poem, the young monk appears seated beside his bed, while he reads in a book the words "der minne bant" (the bond of love), which he is unable to explain for himself. The same words literally recur in a poem by Heinrich von Rugge (Des Minnesangs Frühling: 102.3) which sings of the pains of love's service. The quotation is specific, and introduces a reference point which remains constant throughout the first part of the work, devoted to the adventure of the monk in the city.

The servants and the woman who agrees to collaborate with them in the monk's amorous education, however, are persons of low rank and as such not in a position to introduce the young man to the code of courtly love, as socially elevated as it was intellectually sophisticated. The ideal of 'courtesy' originally took shape in the feudal France of the twelfth century, when it was the exclusive appange of the nobility. It was clearly contrasted with the 'villeiny' of all the other classes, all of them relegated to the same level as that of the peasantry. When the rapid development of the cities and towns aroused interminable discussions about nobility of birth as opposed to that of the heart, and allowed the upper classes of the towns to find their way into the life of courtesy, the peasants remained as always, confined to their rustic and servile condition. According to André Chapelain, the best-accredited medieval writer of treatises on courtly love, the privilege of reason could not be accorded to the peasants, whom he judged, therefore, to be capable only of animal and instinctive love, akin to that of donkeys and horses. The contrast between courtesy and villeiny conditioned the poet's choice, and gave a very obvious polemical value to his work: the role of masters of courtly love is conferred upon those who are radically removed from it—the peasant servants of the monastery, rustic, ignorant villeins by definition. In relation to this choice, the social position of the woman whom the poet chooses to be companion and collaborator of the servants in the monk's amorous education is also significant. Her position is presented clearly as being quite modest, because she offers both hospitality and sexual favours only in return for money. To the servant who leads the monk into the city then, is added a woman who was equally discriminated against by the courtly code. It is well-known, of course, that at the apex of that particular kind of social pyramid which the court of love represented, there stood the noble lady, dispensing all the virtues of love to her lovers from on high. The great mass of women of all other classes who did not have the good fortune to marry a great lord barely entered into the game; they had to content themselves with the merely animal and instinctive love which is accorded to all mortals. It was also accorded, of course, to the very knights who were most devoted to the ideals of courtly love, for they could not be denied the right to satisfy their baser instincts, and quite specifically by abusing the wives and daughters of the peasantry, as the somewhat over-inflated André Chapelain advised them to do. The ethic of courtesy, which prescribed good manners and respect for woman, made no provision for restraining the knights from doing violence to the peasant womenfolk.

In contrast to the servants and the women, the natural repositories of love of the vulgar kind, we find, instead of the knight or knight-aspirant, the monk. A relationship of social equivalence is created between these two figures of society, based on the existence of at least two common traits. Above all, there is the link both of them have with the two parallel power-systems (the Court and the Monastery), which permits their entry into the privileged sphere of those who do not work, but live off the labour of others. Then there is the same formal commitment to two exalted forms of spiritual love (the love of the Lady, and the love of God)—certainly differing from each other, but nevertheless given a common character by a single trait—sublimation. The association of the monk with courtly love instead of religious love conforms to a hidden intention of burlesque and mockery, which stresses the ambiguous relationship between courtly and sensual love. Half-way between the two opposing poles of the love of God and sensual love, courtly love contains traits of both, and is thus perfectly adapted to the equivocation. The servants play on this in order to attract the monk into the trap of sensual love, and bring out the erotic vanity of courtly love along with the specific social function it fulfils. By launching the monk into an initiation which is at once frankly and purely sexual, the woman supports totally the servants' plan. When she has discovered the monk's basic ineptitude, she again puts the courtly ideal to him in the form of a ferocious parody: the kicks, elbowings and shoves which she bestows on him so relentlessly are to be understood as the pains of love; the sufferings which the knight is bound to endure in order to gain the favour of the Lady, for which he so yearns. Real sufferings here, not imaginary ones; physical not spiritual blows, which belong to the hard reality counterpoised by the poet to the dream world of courtly love. The monk reacts to the woman's blows with bitterness. He must return as soon as possible to his former state, to that existence which insisted perforce on the distancing of the lover from the Beloved, as a precise and inescapable part of his existence. The monk laments that he has come too close to the Minne, which as Mittner notes, "originally signified thinking about the Beloved, or remembering her", and the ceremony of the letter, to which the woman has recourse when she is showering blows on the monk, actually presupposes the absence of the Lady, and the need to communicate with her at a distance. The same derisory intention, the same parody, can be seen in the concluding phrase with which the woman packs the monk off: "nu mugt ir wol mit vrouden leben" (now, indeed, you can live in joy). After receiving the full treatment in the form of blows and kicks, the woman of joy (the *vroude* of the Minnesänger) cannot be denied to you. This is the recognition which belongs to you according to the laws of courtesy.

The poet thus strikes at the heart of the paradox of courtly love which was based on an irreconcilable contradiction between desire and fulfilment. If the courtly ideal can only subsist as long as the fulfilment is excluded, then the celebration of a love free from all institutional chains which it exalts cannot be anything more than a fiction. It is an expedient; a mere verbal game in which adultery is placed in counterposition to marriage, considered to be absolutely incompatible with courtly love; adultery is thus the only way in which it can be realised. Adultery, however, is as desirable as it is unrealisable. We are faced with an impossible desire, capable of inspiring a vast literature, and providing the terms for a highly complicated notion while being impossible to realise. Thus the institution remains intact; the sacrament of marriage is not violated. In this way the courtly ethic is revealed as a mere 'spiritualistic' appendage to the christian notion of conjugal love— a concession to the gallantry of the court ceremonial, which could be perfectly integrated into the old value-system with a slight frisson of anti-conformism, all the more to be valued because it was innocuous. In the reality of Christian and feudal Europe, adultery continued to be severely punished as a grave anti-social crime, and marriage continued to be the institutional pillar guaranteeing dynastic continuity and the passing on of inheritance from one generation to the next.

As Erich Köhler has noted, love of 'the Lady', who is the wife of the feudal overlord, the effective head of the court, must necessarily remain unsatisfied, so that it can be converted and sublimated into service seen in terms of a recognition (valour and honour) which is deprived of erotic content and takes on the significance of a social sanction. The courtly ethic, centring as it does on renunciation, obedience and humility, is defined as a particular form of social relationship, an ideology for the existing order, and a powerful cement for the power-system. It is in this form that the poet battles with it, scraping off the courtly varnish with a real peasant roughness. Thus the *Minne* appeared with all the trappings of power: its attributes are strength (*Kraft*) and potency (*Meisterschaft*), riches (seen from the peasant's viewpoint as an unlimited faculty to eat and drink), happiness and even—a supreme attribute reserved to kings alone—the ability to cure diseases.

Thus the poet, in polemical mood, counterpoises '*Liebe*'—sensual sexual pleasure, to courtly love in the *Minne* which becomes the ideological meeting point of power relationships. Furthermore, he presents it in the form that was most infamous to the conscience of the time—venal love. The woman who agrees to lend herself to the monk's desires is no prostitute, but an 'honest dame', who prostitutes herself in a casual way, just to satisfy certain pressing financial needs. The Christian conscience judged such behaviour very severely, and feared it, as a grave attack on the existing order. By effectively destroying the distinction between an honest woman and a prostitute, it in fact removed the barrier of institutional control on sexual pleasure, and left the way clear for the spread of prostitution. But the poet goes further than this; he takes it for granted that the woman, apart from her pecuniary interest, has a specifically sexual one, as is proved by her violent reaction to the monk's impotence. A professional whore, only interested in the money and not at all in pleasure, would not have batted an eyelid, especially since the servant, a more than accommodating go-between, had already paid her well in advance.

Now certain catholic moralists such as Thomas of Chobham, mentioned by Jacques Le Goff, judged that it was impossible that a prostitute should derive enjoyment from her sexual relations with her clients; they were therefore even disposed to allow some justification for prostitution provided that it was presented as paid work, and thus equal to pure commercialisation of the body. The participation of the prostitute in the enjoyment, on the other hand, superimposed on the economic bond the diabolical arousal of sexual pleasure, freed from any aim of procreation. It would thus become a legitimate aim which men and even women might pursue in full freedom.

The defence of sexual pleasure in its most elementary form, therefore, did not merely overthrow the whole structure of the ethic of courtly love. It was also a full frontal challenge to the christian morality which had always attacked sexual behaviour as the greatest of sins. Just listen to the fury and the impressive battery of pseudo-scientific arguments with which the most famous German preacher of the Middle Ages, the Franciscan Berthold of Ratisbon, railed against sexual pleasure: "Medicine tells us that the greater the pleasure in the act, the more harm it does to the body. Even life itself is jeopardised. The philosopher tells us that coitus weakens more than the two bloodstreams. And Holy Writ declares that it harms the body, and also harms property, as the parable of the prodigal son tells us, for he loses all his riches. It harms the senses because it confuses and weakens the brain. In fact, according to the scientists, semen is pure blood, which descends from the brain and becomes pure white, so that those who give themselves up to unbridled lust become stupid. Moreover, it eats up the strength, and is pleasing to the devil, who uses it to trick and subject an infinite number of people".

In the Print Museum in Basel there is a drawing in Indian ink, signed by Urs Graf, and dated 1521, which takes up the popular reaction to the morality of the friars after several centuries (Figure 14). It is entitled Two women brawling with a monk. They are holding him, on his knees, between them. One of them is tearing at his forehead, and grasping him around the scapular, causing him to cry out in pain. He is trying in vain to defend himself with the closed missal in the leather cover. The other woman is pressing against his neck with her knee, holding his head with her hand while she beats him with a bunch of keys. In the background there is a chapel sketched in roughly. The two would seem to be 'women of ill repute'. A purse stuffed with money dangles from the belt of one of them—the fruit of carnal commerce, no doubt—and she has a

Figure 14 Urs Graf: Two Women brawling with a Monk.

knife to defend it. The other also has a mass of keys in her hand and may well be a hostess of sorts.

In the poet's representation, the woman of the people, discriminated against by the courtly ethic, challenges its power mystique with irreverent violence, kicks and elbow-jabs. The noblewomen who had the right to enter into the new code of 'courtesy' behaved very differently, for in certain ways they profited from it. For instance, they gained in regard due to the respect which the new code demanded towards them, and due to the social consideration which they were to come to enjoy in a society which until that time had treated them with a certain roughness and even violence. It goes without saying that the real role of the noblewoman did not correspond in any way to the ideal which the code assigned to 'the Lady'. However, the Lady, the real wife of the Lord, willingly assured him of her wholehearted collaboration in a power operation which was based on the mystification of her role, and on discrimination against all other women. The fact is that it did not seem too bad to her to be caught up in a liturgy of power in which one played a role of high prestige.

So far from contemptible, did it seem in fact, that she was induced to collaborate not only in the practice and spread of the new lifestyle, but also in the framing of its doctrine. The courtly movement of the twelfth century is characterised by a substantial female presence, and this is not exhausted simply in the assumption of the role of the adored Lady of the poets and the knights, even if this remains its most important element. There were many noblewomen, often, though not always, of the highest lineage, who gained distinction by way of the judgments they gave in the love-trials surrounding them, or even by their own poetic compositions. To name but a few we could cite Eleanor of Aquitaine, the daughter of Duke William X, Queen first of France and then of England, where she introduced the new aristocratic ways. Her writings are well-known, and are often quoted along with those of her daughter, Marie de Champagne by André, Marie's chaplain, who presents them as doctrinal foundations of the courtly tradition. Among the many female writings which had the force of norms, also cited by André, are those of Ermengarde, Viscountess of Narbonne, who also appears in the political chronicles of her time because of her capacity for settling disputes of a very different kind—with the sword if necessary, in defiance of her two husbands, who seem to have reigned but not governed. No less numerous are the poetesses, who like Marie de Ventadour, the Countess of Die, Castelloza, and many others, engaged in disputes with the troubadours, or wrote songs in their own name. The adhesion of women who enjoyed the privileges of nobility to the courtly compromise is an undeniable fact. So the limits of power functioned then, as always, like a watershed. Social inequality met with the inequality of the sexes, and prevailed over it, without eliminating it totally.

The courtly love celebrated by the Minnesänger is not the only literary reference in the text. Another tradition is there alongside it, which has not been forgotten by the critics; it concerns the element of the verse novella which deals with the theme of the amorous initiation of the young and innocent girl, Dulcifleure, the daughter of a king, who offers her love to a knight who in exchange gives her his *Sperber* (sparrowhawk). She owes her total inexperience in matters of love to the segregation imposed on her by the rigid education of the court. In our text, however, there is a change in the person of the victim: it is no longer the innocent daughter now, but the monk. Monk and daughter, however, have an element in common which makes the identification possible, and allows the substitution of the one by the other in the role of victim: they belong to the same age-group. Their youth renders them interchangeable, and their weakness and need for initiation bring them into opposition with the world of adults, old and powerful people who exercise authority over them. Sexual initiation is clearly the frontier between uninitiated youth and initiated old age. It goes without saying that the monks' sexual inclinations are accepted as a matter of course, without reference to the vows of chastity.

But the element of youth, which provides a common factor between the girl and the monk in the novella, and makes the latter a suitable victim, by no means exhausts his significance. The fact that he is a monk at all places him in a totally different position on the social chessboard. Belonging to a monastic community, in fact, makes him a participant in a well-constructed power-system, which operates on three distinct plains: the spiritual, the economic and the political: power is exercised over the soul, over the exploitation of the work-force made up of physical bodies, and over the body and soul together in the dominion of lordship. By virtue of his social condition, then, the monk himself sums up a remarkable quantity of power: he is at once priest, master and lord, and in the text he exercises all three forms of power: spiritual power when he assures the servant of absolution in advance for administering the beating, economic power by possessing enough money to pay for his amorous initiation and for the beating he demands in order to produce an abortion, and finally political power by his use of the faculty of command over the servants when he imposes his orders on them. The pivot of the narrative is thus the ambivalence of the figure of the monk, who is shown to us in a double role: both oppressor and oppressed. From this contradiction, the poet draws an argument which will erode the entire structure of power, and expose the nakedness of the innermost workings of oppression.

As we have seen, the monk was involved in a social relationship with the peasants who were bound to the monastery; a relationship which can be reduced to the basic *dominus-servus* status which ruled life in the countryside. Though it was mediated by a collective body (the monastic community), and was justified by reasons of religion, this was still the fundamental relationship. However, though the monks and the peasants are antagonists, they use the same linguistic code, that of feudal law which disciplines their relations with each other. When the peasants approach the monks, they regularly honour them with titles like 'Sir', and 'Master' (the German *Herr* which corresponds with the Latin *dominus*). The monk designates the peasants by the word 'serf' (*knecht*), and he appeals to their fidelity (*triuwe*) to save his honour (*ere*) which his presumed pregnancy threatens. The general picture of social relations which lies in the background is further evoked, in its judicial aspects, by the episode of the peasant who is beating his cow in order to make it abort its calf. The villein (*der Hofmann*) the proprietor of the cow, calls for justice and the Abbot to whom he appeals promises that the person responsible for the wrong shall be made to pay for it. And he adds: er ist mir so under tan/Daz ich in wol betwinge. (he is so subject to me that I can easily compel him). The two peasants who live and work on the monastic lands (and thus who work for the monk-masters) are also juridically dependent on them, by virtue of a relationship of personal subordination of a servile kind. The social and juridicial condition of these peasant-serfs with regard to their monk-masters is presented unequivocally; the former are obliged to obey the latter, who are possessed of the faculty to command them. The peasant-monk relationship is equal to that of the servant-master, and involves the same ineradicable antagonism. Following a very specific pattern of reprisal, it is this antagonism which in the text regulates the attitude of the peasants towards the monk.

The social antagonism between serf-peasant and monk-master is further complicated by the religious question. Popular resistance to christianisation is in fact far from ended in this epoch, in defiance of the very real ideological terrorism which the Church had been operating for centuries. We can find the most significant reflection of this in the preaching of the two mendicant orders, the Franciscans and the Dominicans, who from the thirteenth century onwards were engaged in a new and enormous enterprise of evangelisation of the cities and countryside of Christian Europe. The fact that things were not going too well for the German Church is made clear with some insistence by the Franciscan Berthold of Ratisbon. For him, Christianity in Germany was still largely a matter of upper-class behaviour, and in no way a popular religion. "You peasants, workmen and servants" he declared from the pulpit, "are well on the true road to sanctity because of the hard life you lead: but even so, hardly a single one of you succeeds in becoming a saint. Among persons in all the other conditions of life, on the other hand, many become so. Many princes and rulers, like the sainted kings, Oswald, Charles, Henry and Wenceslas. Many noblemen like Maurice and his legion. Many bishops, cardinals, popes and clergy—but almost no peasants or artisans. Why? because you are so completely lacking in devotion: you are like horses overcome with tiredness and exhaustion. Like them, you never pray; you are unfamiliar with God; you never go to Mass; you do not take Communion; you do not take part in any of the ceremonies of religion: not in prayers nor in anything else which brings one close to God. You should familiarise yourselves with God; be devout and pray willingly, not be like horses. You say: I can't pray much because of my master; because of my poverty, or my children. I answer: Oh, but you could. You do not wish it. For you would have found time for it long ago, if someone had offered you an egg for every Pater noster!''

The mechanism of peasant resistance, however, can only function when the monk finds himself declassed, degraded to the inferior level of woman, after his adventure in the town. It is the degradation from monk-master to monk-woman which makes him vulnerable to the reprisal of the peasants, because inasmuch as he is now 'woman', he is also subjected. The equivalence between social and sexual inequality is stressed by the use of the same adverb, beneath, to denote the position of the woman in coitus with respect to the man and that of the servant with respect to his master. As a point of passage from high to low, and a step downwards towards inferiority, the poet puts forward the factor of youth, as we have seen; it is this which makes the monk needful of initiation, and brings him into common rank with the woman. So, in this story the theme of the pregnant man is once again presented as the point at which three basic forms of equality merge: social, sexual and generational. Servants, women and young people are subjected in the same way. But, the poet goes on to argue, the degradation of the monk is purely instrumental; it makes the reprisal possible, but it is not the motive for it. The monk is beaten not as a monk-woman, but as a monk-master. Even so, it is true that the two forms of reprisal, the blows of the woman and the beating by the servant, recall the two most common forms of punishment which the right of correction allowed the husband and the master to inflict respectively on wife and servant. In the person of the monk, the reprisal is thus striking as the ethic which dominates the right of correction, and the religious motivation which christianity gives to it.

The hail of blows which induce the monk to believe that he has had an abortion ends the chapter of reprisals on a burlesque note, and opens a new and somewhat surprising one. Convinced that he has in fact aborted, the monk despairs for the loss of his son, and weeps because of his unexpected flight. Initially the credulity which makes him mistake the hare for his child provides the opportunity for a series of jokes and buffoonish tricks. The real fool is the monk: a man of faith by profession who believes in the pregnancy as if it were a miracle. But quite suddenly the identification with a woman becomes a serious matter: the sorrow of a mother for the loss of her child, which the monk imitates dramatically, introduces the theme of impossible maternity in a very different light from that in which it is seen by the Church. Then as now, the latter was concerned solely with denouncing sin, without taking any account of the reasons a woman might have had for aborting, or for the price in sorrow and pain which she pays.

The Franciscan Berthold of Ratisbon did not mince his words, and he habitually spoke very clearly to woman. For him, abortion was nothing other than pure and simple homicide, even if four different modes of carrying it out could be distinguished: sterilisation of the woman before conception, the killing of the still inanimate (or animate—it made no difference) foetus in the womb, and the killing or abandoning of the newly-born child. This last, the abandoning of the child, is the subject of such a violent tirade that it is worth recording it here: "No animal acts in this way: not even the crow, the most faithless of all creatures, abandons its child until the moment of its first flight. Every rational being, even the pagans, the Jews and the heretics, nurtures its offspring; even the non-rational animals—birds, pigs, even wild beasts and reptiles. If one could ask the animals whether they were prepared to nurture their young, even to the point of weariness, they would answer Yes!—birds, beasts and reptiles alike. Even some non-rational creatures bring up the young of others, like those who care for the young of the cuckoo; like the partridge, the mule, and even some wolves which have been known to suckle human offspring. No beast in this world is like an evil woman: O evil worse than any evil, the evil of woman!"

The poet's answer to the preacher's malevolent philippics is the same as the one which women have been giving to the church for centuries: you priests and friars always do the opposite of what you preach, and if you were women, you would do as we do, in defiance of all your most solemn declarations. Placed in the difficult situation of having to choose between abortion and illicit and dishonourable maternity (which was capable of costing him expulsion from the monastic community), the pregnant monk in fact opts inevitably for abortion, as the women of the world have always done in cases of this kind. To the self-motivated charity of those who show so much more concern for an unformed foetus than for an already existing child or adult, the poet counterpoises the simple and elementary truth that abortion is a painful necessity imposed on women with ferocious determination by so-called 'Christian' society. The same society which, while deaf to the pain and sorrow of the girl-mother compelled to give up her child, nevertheless feels itself offended in its philistine morality by the 'transgression', and demands only the satisfaction of exemplary punishment.

The mouthpiece of the offended christian conscience in the text is the oldest of the monk's confrères, who happens to run into him in the woods, and asks him the reason for such agitation. The pompous dialogue between the two monks, the old and the young, the one on horseback, exalted, authoritarian and violent, and the other on foot—beneath—overwhelmed by sorrow, but still not submissive, refusing in fact to abandon his attitude of defiance and insubordination—is among the best parts of the story. His contemptuous replies cost him a beating, so energetically administered that it makes him fall flat on his face on the ground. The old man was not joking—he carried a stick with him and knew how to use it with undeniable skill.

It is easy to understand why the story makes the monk who disputes with the young man an old confrère of simple character rather than one of his hierarchical superiors. The abbot will appear on the scene later, because what concerned the poet was first and foremost to show the conflict of age rooted in the father-son relationship, and the right of correction widely recognised as belonging to the father by Holy Scripture, and duly legitimised by the Church. St Thomas (Summa II.II.65.2) writes that "since the son is under the power of his father, and the slave under that of his master, the father and the master respectively have the right to beat their sons and their slaves with the aim of correcting and educating them". By thrashing the young monk, then, the old one is exercising a paternal right which belongs to him merely because of his age. However, an impediment to this right might derive from the term which he uses to the young man—unsinnik— 'mad'. If he were indeed mad, then no blame would attach, and no punishment would be justified. But things were not as simple as that. The attitude of medieval society towards mental illness has been little studied (the famous *Histoire de folie* by Michel Foucault begins at the close of the Middle Ages), and it remains fairly obscure. It is certain, however, that in fourteenth-century Germany, where our poem was written, the mad were imprisoned and whipped before being expelled from the towns and consigned to the devil. We are helped in our understanding of this behaviour by a text from St Thomas (I.II.10.3), which links the onset of madness to the "violence of anger or lust". If madness comes on "when the reason is totally overcome by passion", then it is a vice, and as such may justly be punished. There can be no doubt at all of what passion was involved in the case of the monk: was he not insisting that he was pregnant? And could he even have had thoughts of pregnancy without sexual relations? In fact, when the old man gets off his horse to tie the young man's hands, the text says that he tied them like those of a thief (*als einem diebe*)—probably alluding to another well-known christian teaching which closely associated theft with incontinence. This doctrine had been preached with habitual fervour by our friend Fra Berthold of Ratisbon. Servants, he said, "should be as faithful to their heavenly Lord as to their earthly one. To the latter they are to be faithful in work and in goods, in the sense that they rob him of nothing and are not idle in their labours. And to the heavenly Lord, they must be faithful in body, in the sense of keeping that body which he has given them chaste and pure". How astute this friar was, to be so aware already that working-time was the property of the master!

However, the most important episode of the story is that of the exorcisms. Mad or demon-possessed as he may have been, it is clear that the utterances of their confrère appeared nonsensical to the other monks, because they were in clear contradiction of the sex of the person who was making them. Monk or no monk, he was first and foremost a man who was talking like a woman—something quite inadmissible, which could not be placed in any category of normality, and must therefore be placed under the comforting headings of madness or demonic possession. To his astonished and increasingly infuriated listeners, the young monk was in fact confronting them with a situation in which the 'I' who is speaking is no longer himself but another. The very act of speech thus causes an identity crisis for the subject: "I am myself", the linguistic presupposition which constitutes man as a subject, seems to be destroyed, and to be transformed into "I am another". But the other, distinct from the person who is speaking, and yet the real subject of the speech, is here a woman. And this is the real scandal.

In his essay *Subjectivity in Language*, Emile Benveniste has noted that the subjectivity which constitutes itself in language does not in fact exclude the presence of the other; on the contrary, it necessarily implies it, since there can be no 'I' without 'you'. "The consciousness of one's self", writes Benveniste, "is possible only by contrast. I do not use 'I' if I am not relating to someone who, in my speech, will be 'you'. It is this condition of dialogue which constitutes the persona, since it implies reciprocally that 'I' become 'you' in the speech of whoever designates himself in turn as 'I'." The poet seeks to remind us that the first 'you' of mankind is woman, who in relation to him occupies the same position which the 'you' occupies in relation to the 'I' in language. "'I' supposes another person", continues Beneveniste, "who, while being completely external to myself, becomes my echo to whom I say 'you' and who says 'you' to me". The opposition between 'I' and 'you', then, does not imply exclusion of either of the two terms, but nor does it imply subordination of one to the other, and this is the most important point. For if, as Beneviste says, the 'I' who is speaking always has "a position of transcendence" purely by virtue of being the speaker, it is also true that this position is absolutely temporary and completely instrumental. The 'you' who is listening may listen and allow the 'I' to put itself forward as the subject of the speech, but only in as much as it then has in turn the faculty of becoming the 'I' and taking on the position of transcendence which that implies. The 'I' and the 'you' are therefore not merely complementary, in the sense that one cannot even be conceived without the other, but are also reversible, in the sense that one necessarily takes the place of the other in turn. Since this is the way that things are in language, it is clear that the poet deliberately breaks the identity of his subject: he is split into an 'I' spoken by a 'you'. He starts polemically from the given linguistic fact to make it clear that the reversibility of the 'I' and the 'you' implicit in language, does not govern the relation of man and woman as it should. Here, the transcendence of the 'I' who is speaking in relation to the 'you' who is listening is crystallised into a relationship of dominion, the product of pure and simple violence, which excludes all possibility of reversal, and reserves the faculty of speech exclusively to man, tying the woman, who is reduced to silence, to a permanent destiny of subordination. This, then, is why the man loses his identity and appears to be invaded by a woman who speaks within him. The mechanism of diabolical possession, of schizophrenic delirium and, in short, of the speech of the other, forms a perfect part of this logic: the poet puts his subject into an identity crisis in order to call in question the foundations of his confidence in his superiority. He suggests that the man-woman conflict can only be resolved in reciprocal and complementary terms. Man and woman are not equal; they are different. But the difference does not permit the subordination of the one to the other. There is therefore no question of high or low, above and below, which are mere inventions of the powerful in the service of the oppression which they exercise. A truth as old as the world, and yet ever-new, which will never be understood while it is still believed that there can be no co-existence without one in command and the other in obedience.

The monks react to this elementary truth with beatings, exorcisms and imprisonment. There is no longer any reciprocity between man and woman, because it would bring the whole system of exclusions on which the established order is built to ruin. Ruin indeed—because the principle of the reciprocity of the 'I' and the 'you' reduces all hierarchies of superiority and inferiority; all power of one over the other, to nothing. The monks' violent reaction, therefore, is meant to show in this story how closely the church and the power structure are interwoven, and how impossible it is for the latter to compromise on the subject of the natural inferiority of women to men. This issue is not an accessory to the doctrinal apparatus, but an essential part of it, and the poet was well-aware of that. In effect, the young monk puts the possibility of reconciliation between women and the church before the abbot, when he shows himself to be so concerned about the baptism of his son. It is no accident that he suggests to the abbot that he should act as Godfather, along with the prior and the victualler—the same three people whom the serf had previously mentioned as possibly responsible for the young monk's pregnancy, as if to say that the three superiors in the hierarchy, who are also its most crucial members, are best suited to guarantee the faith of this child of guilt, in that they themselves were guilty of a corresponding transgression. But as far as the abbot is concerned, there is no question of equating the two transgressions; the young monk's guilt is of quite a different order, because—as the old monk had already made clear in the wood—the mad claim to attribute to oneself the specific female faculty of pregnancy overturned all order, in shame and intolerable degradation. The assumption of female attributes implicit in the 'androgynous compromise' of the celibacy of the clergy could not be carried to the extreme point of pure identification with woman, which would annul the compromise and plunge the clergy into the shame of female inferiority. Instead, the recovery of virility requires a different assessment of the transgression, because while it may be true that this introduces an element of imbalance into the androgynous compromise, it is also true that it drives it back up to a higher plane— i.e. towards the peak of male potency. On the fundamental issue of the difference in the condition of men and women as a result of original sin, the doctrine of the Church is unequivocal. No reconciliation was possible while the young man persisted stubbornly in his absurd conviction that he had borne a son just as a woman would have done. His suggestion was to be regarded as a smart trick of the Evil One, who was in point of fact speaking within him in a woman's voice, and who, moreover, had always been closely associated in christian demonology with women. Things only changed when the young man decided to come to his senses, and confess his true sin: the escapade into the city was judged as a venal sin, easily pardonable and far removed from his claim to consider himself similar to a woman.

We may be permitted to ask at this point: who could have been the author of this verse-tale which demonstrates such a rare ability to understand the female point of view, and to link it with the peasants, young people and all other excluded and alienated folk? Towards the end of the text, in the last quatrain, a name appears: Zwingäuer. But all that scholars have been able to ascertain is that such a name appears with some frequency in southern Germany; nothing more. Certain technical details of his poem have led to the assumption that he was a wandering poet; it is probably the work of a minstrel, one of those Spielmänner who so easily aroused Fra Berthold to savage fury. He was a poet, therefore, who was used to telling the truth and taking risks. Anyone who has seen Tarkowsky's film on Andrea Rubliov will know that the mighty do not always laugh at the jokes of the jongleur; they can just as easily cut his tongue out if they find it too long. The poet was no ignoramus, as can be seen, if from nothing else, from his sure knowledge of the lyric poetry of the Minnesänger—however, 'Zwingäuer' seems to be closely linked to the popular and folklore traditions. His relations with the oral tradition must have been determinative, though it is not easy to be precise about the extent of his debt to them in all its particulars.

A yet unpublished fable, collected orally in 1931 from a carpenter in Gross Jerutten, a village in East Prussia, once again witnesses, at many centuries distance, the persistence in folklore of some of the elements directly related to our verse-tale. The fable is entitled *The Pregnant Pastor*, and this is the tale it tells: It was a little before Christmas, and at that season of the year the Pastor normally slaughtered a big fat pig. He ate and drank, and was in excellent spirits. As there wasn't a great deal to do in his parish, he became more and more gross: from day to day, the circumference of his belly grew larger and larger. "There must be something behind all this", the Pastor thought to himself, and though the people made fun of him, he became convinced that he was pregnant. Soon the Pastor's wife had had enough of his constant laments. "Our shepherd beat one of his pregnant ewes on the nose not long ago and it aborted", she told him. The thing seemed convincing enough to the clergyman; finally here was a piece of advice which was worth something. When the shepherd led his sheep back to pasture once again, the Pastor came to him with this proposal. "But Reverend, how can I give you a thump on the nose?" he asked. However, the Pastor gave him no rest and eventually he agreed: "All right then, if you must have it that way, come into these bushes, at least" said the old villein. The stick which the shepherd always carried with him was quite a fine specimen; he'd cut it many years earlier from an oak tree, and those who had felt its caress had no wish to feel it a second time. What happened in those bushes was quite a sight. The Pastor was on his knees in the grass, with his face looking upward to the sky, and there stood the shepherd in front of him, ready to administer the blow. But as soon as the blow was carefully aimed at his nose, a hare leaped out and went racing off. The Pastor, believe it or not, was sure that the fleeing animal was his son: he ran after him, shouting loudly:

> Dear son: Stop!!
> I want to give you a name
> You must be baptised,
> My son of this earth...

As we can see, despite the few transformations (the monk has become a protestant Pastor with a wife at his side in this story, in conformity with the requirements of the time and place) the tale corresponds perfectly, in slightly abbreviated form, to the central section of the verse-story (verses 287–394). There is, however, one new image, evidently taken from devout iconography, which ironically presents the

Pastor who is seeking an abortion, in the attitude of martyrdom, with his face turned towards the sky, while the shepherd with his stick raised is about to give his body a good beating. The Lutheran Reformation had largely done away with sacred images, but we know that they survived in many churches, and in East Prussia frescos and paintings certainly lingered on. In any case, the coincidence between the two texts is beyond dispute. On the other hand, it is difficult if not impossible with our present level of knowledge to establish the exact relationship between them. Does the tale derive from the verse-story, or does the verse-story depend on a folklore motif of which the Prussian variant collected in 1931 is a descendant? The verse-tale which is so much more ancient, certainly had a very wide currency in manuscripts (this is attested by three surviving codexes now in the public library of Königsberg). Perhaps it also enjoyed widespread oral diffusion, if it followed the route of popular poetry and was recited in the market-places of towns and cities. The existence of a text from the same period in Middle High German, The Pregnant Miller,—also anonymous and in verse—further complicates the problem, because this text is clearly linked with Zwingäuer's verse-tale, but to different parts of it, and with different transformations (the protagonist, for instance, is a rich miller, and no longer a cleric). As things stand, the only thing that can be said with certainty is that two medieval texts were derived from the same folklore soil, and it was very probably in that same soil that they continued to live and flourish until times not very far removed from our own.

That the motif of the pregnant man found its most complex and profound expression in German popular poetry is not a mere coincidence, if it is true that in medieval Germany, buzzing with subterranean anti-christian currents, it laid down deeper roots than anywhere else in Europe. "The transplanting into the German heart of a profoundly anti-German myth, that of Christianity", wrote Nietzsche, "was the real fatalité allemande."

Specialists equipped with the necessary linguistic and philological tools essential for its study have never given much thought to this masterpiece of popular literature. In Hans Fischer's book, which as far as I know is the most important recent monograph on the German popular poetry of the Middle Ages, only a few lines are devoted to our text, and they do not come anywhere near to giving it a proper critical reading. The few lines of Fischer are even further reduced—to a mere biographical mention—in the otherwise extremely valuable work of Gerhard Kopf. Some critical notice can be found in the item by H.F. Rosenfeld in the Verfasser lexicon of Stammler and Langosch (IV: Col. 1169–1172), which sums up all the available facts and the sparse bibliography existing (in all, a few pages in specialist reviews). Things are no better as far as the text itself is concerned, for it can only be read in the old annotated edition of 1850 (*sic*), edited by Friedrich Heinrich Von Hagen. The only recent initiative which is recorded in the country where philological pedantry is at its highest, is a translation into modern German by Ulrich Pretzel, which has maimed the text to such an extent that its original design is unrecognisable. The fate of oblivion, therefore, not, only affects the author, but the work itself in its attack on the powers that be, and their oppression.

Chapter 17
Town versus Country

"It is said that a group of jokers got together one day to play a trick on one of their friends. They went to him one after the other, and the first of them said, as soon as he arrived: 'My poor chap—whatever's the matter with you? You really don't look too good: it must be dropsy!'. The second arrived, and said the same thing. So the poor fellow replies: 'But in God's name what are you talking about? I'm in the best of health!' He runs off to look at himself in the mirror, but sees nothing unusual. But then more of the jokers arrive, and each of them says the same thing to him. The man begins to get quite anxious, and says to himself 'I'm not seeing myself as I really am; it's impossible that so many people could be wrong! It can't be'. He is seized by fear, and all of a sudden he becomes dropsical: the very same illness, of which he died a few days later. So you see—even the biggest lie will be believed as long as enough people repeat it... "

This passage is taken from a sermon which Fra Giordano of Pisa delivered in Florence in 1304. It refers to an *exemplum* well rooted in the Dominican tradition, which appears in two manuals of sermons for the use of the order—those of Humbert of Romans, and John Bromyard. In both manuals, the story of the fool, the victim of a joke played by a group of cheerful tricksters, is adopted as an example of facile credulity, so obviously absurd as to be senseless. We must indeed believe, the *exemplum* seems to be saying, but not everything and everyone. Only revealed truth, consecrated by christian doctrine, and accredited by God's ministers, deserves to be believed. All the rest, and above all heretical doctrines and folk-tales, should be rejected as the work of the devil. The simplicity of those who believe in any old thing thus passes rapidly into stupidity, and the stupid, as we read in the Bible (sufficient to consult the *Book of Proverbs*, 10.23 and 24.8–9) are

150

not only insensate but also vicious, and thus sinners worthy of exemplary punishment. Faithful to that doctrinal scheme, Fra Giordano gives it greater life and breadth, with an oratorical talent which deserves recognition. He carries it to the extreme limits which the *exemplum* permitted: by virtue of senseless belief, the fool ends by doubting himself and his own identity, and thus becomes deserving of the most severe punishment. It isn't enough that he actually becomes dropsical; he must also die. In this preacher's tale, we can thus easily find the ideological matrix and the basic mechanisms of all the later Florentine literature of the *beffa*—the hoax—though this was never to be pushed to the extreme limits of ferocity reached by the Dominican.

In Florence, as in Monreale, dropsy was connected with the motif of the pregnant man. In the popularist poem *La Buca di Montemorello*, by Stefano Finiguerri, known as Za, which dates from the beginning of the fifteenth century, the lack of skill of a certain doctor is sneered at with the jibe that he mistook dropsy for pregnancy. But even before Za, Boccaccio had already thought of this connection. Taking the preaching of Fra Giordano as his starting point, he changed the mechanism of the joke which lies at the heart of the tale of Calandrino's pregnancy, in the *Decameron* (IX.3). Here it is three painters, Bruno, Buffalmaco, and Nello, who make their assistant Calandrino believe that he is ill, in order to allow their doctor friend, Mastro Simone, to diagnose a mock pregnancy for him on the basis of an examination of his urine. The pregnancy element was discovered by the writer in the two Aesopic fables with which we are already familiar; in Italy they were to be found both in the original Latin and in the French translation by Marie de France, and they had even been vulgarised into Tuscan dialect more than once during the course of the fourteenth century. Boccaccio literally produces a sentence of one of these popular versions of the first fable, which is the phrase used by the doctor to inform Calandrino of his diagnosis of pregnancy ("You've no other illness than pregnancy"). In relation to the tradition of Marie de France, on whose version it depends, this Tuscan version (in which the peasant is the antagonist and not the thief of the Latin original) has a number of variations which stress its different location. The animal and the orifice of the man are changed: the beetle (*l'escharboz* of Marie de France) is changed into a scorpion or a cockroach; the orifice is no longer the anus but (perhaps in homage to the prudishly genteel transformation effected by the legend of the pregnant Nero) the mouth.

The people therefore seem less involved in the foolish credulity of the peasant: they appear to keep their distance and adopt an attitude of amazement which seems to turn sceptical. The villein does not feel any solidarity in his disgrace, but fears their mockery.

The doctor, for his part, does not contrast the scientific explanation with the superstitious credulity of ignorant folk. Instead he emphasises his complicity in isolating the credulous man, and making a fool of him. The orientation of the story has thus been changed, and points more towards a farcical situation, more suited to the environment of the town into which it has been transplanted. The climate of trickery, however, remains in suspense: laughter has not yet broken out, but seems to have become entangled in the skein of the original narrative, which did not contemplate it. In order for it to break out, it was necessary that there should be some reference to the preaching of the Dominican, which introduced the essentially 'country' theme of the pregnant man into the more urbane joke-story with its context in the city. The doctor was certainly to be its principal agent.

Present in all the versions of the Aesopic fables, the Doctor (as we have seen) does not confine himself to denying the presumed popular belief in the pregnancy of a man. He now associates himself with the practical jokers, and plays the card of medical science, with its power of life and death, to ensure the success of the joke. In Boccaccio's tale, it is therefore to the doctor that the task is assigned of bringing the story to a conclusion with a resounding laugh. The key position which the doctor always retains in the literary tradition of the pregnant man can also be found in the iconography of Calandrino. Thus in the woodcut which illustrates the story in the German edition of the *Decameron* published by Anton Sorg in Augsburg in 1492 (Figure 15), it is the diagnosis of pregnancy which occupies the stage. The doctor is announcing it solemnly to Calandrino, who is stretched out on the bed with his prominent belly emerging from the garment which lies open at the front. With his left hand the doctor is holding and raising up an ampulla filled with urine—the unmistakable sign of the objectivity of his diagnosis—while with his right hand, he accompanies his words with a gesture. The artist has made Calandrino an invalid, and as such at the doctor's mercy; there is no escape for him: he is at the mercy of the doctor, and must obey him and pay up. The fake lamentation of the three jokers, who appear at the foot of the bed alongside the wife who is genuinely thunderstruck, puts a seal on the complicity of the viewers, and underlines the reality of the power-relationships involved.

We owe to Carlo Muscetta two important critical observations about Calandrino, which will make a useful starting-point. The first is that the four stories dedicated to him in the Decameron form a single whole, and should be read as four acts of the same comedy. The second point clearly identifies Calandrino's social position as a typical representative of the "new folk", those new arrivals in the town who appear gauche and embarrassed, as they often do in the eyes of the established

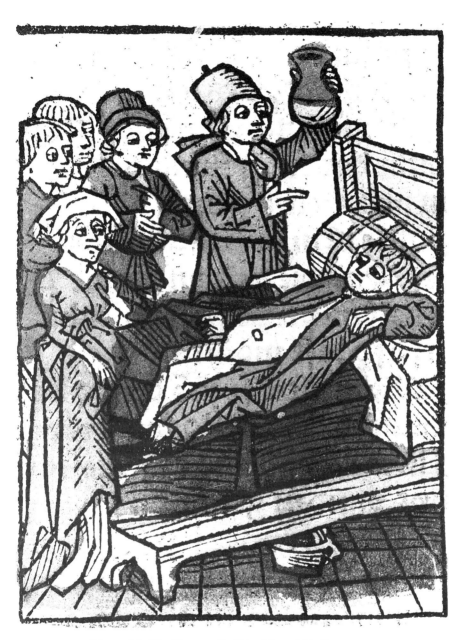

Figure 15 The Doctor tells Calandrino of his Pregnancy.

residents. From the country where he originated, Calandrino has brought to the town a more or less pre-packed ideological baggage. Muscetta provides us with the inventory: an atavistic hunger for land, the dream of getting rich quickly, envy of the mercantile astuteness of the citizens, and the ambition to mix with "elegant and sharp-minded intellectuals" such as the painters who play the joke on him. He seeks to adopt the artistic temperament, restless and imaginative, the polished speech and—why not?—the same erotic spirit of adventure, which produces undeniable success with women. As can be seen, the inventory has been very carefully composed, and almost everything is there. Almost everything, that is. For with all its significance, the most important thing is missing—Muscetta mentions it at the end and only fleetingly—the thing which makes the bumpkin inescapably vulnerable to his tormentors, and distinguishes him more than anything else as Calandrino and no other: his inimitable and incurable credulity. He is simple because he believes. But he doesn't just believe any old tall story; his credulity has a specific mark, which once again betrays his peasant origins: the readiness to listen to folklore tradition despite the fact that his urbanisation is supposed to be virtually complete and consolidated. All it needs is for these beliefs to be brought before him once again, and he accepts them blindly. In effect folklore beliefs, (or presumed beliefs) are the specific object of mockery in all four stories: the land of plenty and the heliotrope in the first (VIII: 3), the bewitching of bread and cheese in the second (VIII: 6), the pregnancy of the man in the third (IX: 3), and the amorous spell in the fourth (IX: 5). The fact that the comedy of Calandrino was built around an unquestionable anti-folklore purpose is an elementary one, which seems to have escaped the critics.

"A simple man of original (nuovo) charm" is how Boccaccio describes him in the first of the four stories, which also functions in some ways as a prologue to the comedy. The adjective 'original' (nuovo in Italian) has a semantic function in this introduction, covering various meanings, related to one another by a complex network of basic ideological importance. The 'nuovi', as we have seen, are the recent arrivals in the city, the 'unurbanised', whose 'original'—different, unaccustomed and thus strange—manners and habits startle the city folk. They are always ready to believe "any new thing"—i.e. any sort of oddity or tall story which touches on the marvellous and the out-of-the-ordinary. This series of meanings supposes the existence of a basic concept of the 'nuovo' which is never explicitly stated, though it constitutes the constant ideological background of the whole comedy. The 'nuovo', in that he is different, is extraneous to the old and the accepted; unwanted and unassimilated, he must simply be expelled, pushed back, or forced to return to the original condition of inferiority from which he has dared to escape.

Calandrino is thus the villein transformed; the 'parvenu'. His transfer to the city (no longer recent), the prestige which his activity as a painter confers on him (even though he is merely an assistant), the city ways and the affected speech, do not in fact save him from his peasant origins which reassert themselves at every move and in every word. In short he remains a man of 'coarse grain', and as such the inevitable butt of his mocking friends who are, on the contrary, we are assured, "men who were full of fun but also shrewd and intelligent". Thus we are once again back with satire used against the villein, though the contempt is now no longer expressed by nobles and priests, but by the city which has entered into the patrimony of both these classes by possessing, dominating and exploiting the countryside.

There are two reasons why the mockers are painters. The first refers us to the social rise of a category of artisans who were promoted to a higher rank than that of the most wealthy and most powerful citizens by virtue of the prestige conferred on them by their art. The second explains the social privileges of the artist in relation to all other manual workers, by the specific character of his work, the only work capable of perfectly imitating nature and making what is merely fictitious appear real. The hoaxes which the painters perpetrate at Calandrino's expense reflect the wonder at the paintings of Giotto, in which according to Boccaccio "one frequently finds that the visual sense of men is led into error, believing what is painted to be real". The hoaxes always point boldly to the confusion between reality and fiction—boldly, because they attribute connotations of reality to events which are literally impossible, such as the pregnancy of a man. And this is the point—the confusion between reality and fiction, Boccaccio is saying, is a joke rightly reserved for the educated public. The vulgar world of rude and ignorant manual workers, insensitive by nature to the divine artifice of make-believe, is only capable of mistaking it for reality. Amazement at the skill of the artist is thus closely associated with contempt for the rudeness of the ignorant, and is converted into an element of distinction and discrimination. Painters may now assume the garments of intellectuals with their roots in the city, exponents of the culture of its citizens which is in contrast with the lack of culture of the countryside and its inhabitants.

In the case of Calandrino there is a negative triumph for the vulnerable credulity of the villein, as a synonym for pure and simple stupidity. But, it may be argued, Calandrino is a fool because of his country origins; that is to say, cultural discrimination is a reflection only of the social discrimination emphasised by the Tuscan writer with uncompromising harshness, and without reserve or scruple. No scruple was permissible, in fact, if we consider the christian concept of foolishness, from which Boccaccio had drawn his model. Had the Dominican not preached at Florence that the stupid and the credulous should be punished? And what does the writer say, by the mouth of Buffalmacco, in the first of the four stories?, The mockery of Calandrino is perfectly acceptable, since we ourselves have been so stupid as to believe that such precious stones could be found in Mugnone. But the person who really believed in the magical virtue of the heliotrope was in fact Calandrino, who thus merited the just punishment for his stupidity in being hoaxed. Even so, the writer shows himself to be more magnanimous than the preacher, because at least he lets the victim of the hoax live, whereas the Dominican would have had him put to death. As an ignorant bumpkin, Calandrino must be mocked, offended and humiliated, but also stoned, robbed of his pig, his capons, his money and his food, and then manhandled, injured and scratched by his wife, to the accompaniment of the uncontrollable laughter of our critics of the Left—Marxists of the strictest observance—who continue imperturbably to cry "Masterpiece!" Mocked and castigated, because he desires the same things as the citizens and the lords have always had (money, power, prestige, culture and women), and which must be strictly denied to him, and to all clodpolls of his kind.

In this cruel game at Calandrino's expense, the sadistic painters make use of four accomplices, who always represent the institutions preordained by society for the maintenance of law and order: the tax collectors in the first story, the priest in the second, the doctor in the third, and the prostitute in the fourth. It will be worth our while to take a closer look at the prostitute, because she offers invaluable guidance for the better understanding of the male-female relationship as it is portrayed in these four stories. Nicolosa is introduced by Boccaccio without any frills for what she is: a girl tied to a pimp who hires her out like a mule. She serves the pleasure of the traditional figure of the "young bachelor who is in the habit of taking some girl to his home for a day or two for his pleasure and then sending her packing". And with these few words, the game of chance between men and women is played: an object of currency and exchange between the pimp and the customer; she maintains the one and brings solace to the other. But why should the whore collaborate with the gentlemen to the detriment of Calandrino, who when all is said and done is another poor, exploited outsider like herself?, It is here that the term 'nuovo' comes back into play; the woman joined in "more because Calandrino seemed to her to be a nuovo than for any other reason"; his attitudes seemed to her "bizarre". So to her too he is an outsider, and therefore to be laughed at. In this way the whore allows herself to be involved in the drama of the hoax, though obviously in a subordinate role, and always that of the executor of orders. The moral of the story is that among poor devils there is no solidarity; they are ready to run and do the bidding of their masters, and find themselves regularly lined up and armed against each other. It is the same moral that governs all the moves of the other female personage in the comedy—Tessa, the wife of Calandrino, for whom the writer appears to reserve especially favourable treatment. He presents her in the first story as "a beautiful and worthy woman", and we are soon to see what sort of worthiness he is talking about. Tessa goes for her husband and begins to hurl imprecations at him when he returns with the stones from the Mugnone, cancelling out the magic of the heliotrope which was supposed to render him invisible. According to the precise logic of violence which she follows, it was just that he should retaliate for the stoning which he had received during the return journey from the Mugnone by raining blows on her. The mechanism of violence is shown by the words used: 'discharge' and 'carry', which Boccaccio with his usual technique of verbal transference, applies to the stones rather than the stonings. When the jokers hear that Calandrino has treated his wife to a massive beating they get themselves out of the mess quite cynically, and put all the blame on him. Later on they will go so far as to pay him back for his blows at the crucial moment of his adventure with Nicolosa. Here too it is his wife who plays the role of the spectre at the feast, who bursts in with her great common sense and her clumsy clogs, to smash her husband's happy dreams brutally and bring him back to reality in the inevitable hail of blows given and received. The blows exchanged between husband and wife automatically place them in the same social sphere, in the inferior rank of the *minus habentes*. Wife or prostitute, the woman in this distribution of roles can at least strike a blow in turn, but only on condition that she agrees to collaborate with the gentlemen, and make herself an instrument of violence and suppression. However, the writer is generous with Tessa, even though it is at the expense of Calandrino: everything he takes from the one he gives to the other, so that in the end we arrive at the complete comic reversal of roles, and find the woman dressed as a man and the man as a woman. The game of give and take remains within the family, and inside its bosom nothing is lost. To the same degree as the man is diminished and degraded to femininity, so the woman is exalted and given the powers of the male, but with the result that the oaf is denied his virility, and the woman her femininity, and thus the condition of both of them is degraded.

A veritable wife-mistress in the story of the stolen pig, Tessa has so many cards to her advantage as opposed to her husband—and above all, her incredulity, her lack of readiness to believe. The husband is afraid of her, and knows that she is ready to "kick him out of the house", of

Figure 16   Gravelot: Calandrino's Abortion.

which she is clearly the effective boss. It is from her dowry that their little smallholding in the country comes; she controls the expenses and the management of the house—and when they make love, she always wants to be "on top". In this way the wife also takes over the management of her husband's sexual potency, if not the actual sexual potency itself (for Calandrino reproaches her for her bestial desires). The more potent she is, the more impotent he, and in the fourth novella he is again subjected to the potency of woman (though this time it is the prostitute who 'rides' him), and he ends up having no intercourse and being manhandled, and insulted with charges of impotence and homosexuality into the bargain. However, Tessa's potency remains ephemeral, and purely instrumental; it is a mere reflection of his impotence. The game of superior and inferior could not in fact be in the hands of the woman, for existing society required that she should be rigorously subjected to the man. If the writer urges her on to the high peak of male potency, it is only to make the dangers for the man emerge more clearly, and thus perfidiously reinforce the chains which bind her. Under the mannerist portrait of the "good wife and honest person" there lurks hidden the old and unmistakable christian misogyny, which breaks out in the first story, needless to say from the mouth of Calandrino himself: "Women make you lose your virtue in every single thing" he states desolately, at the end of his adventure with the stones of the Mugnone, for the magic of the stones disappears as soon as "that devil of an accursed woman appeared in front of me and saw me".

The author of the *Decameron* is the same man who wrote the Corbaccio—a faithful servant of his audience of Guelph merchants, well rooted in the Christian and civic ethic. If you open the *History of Italian Literature* by De Sanctis, at the Chapter on the *Decameron*, you will hear the word 'revolution' sing out from the first lines, with that same impetus which inspired the famous painting of Michele Cammarano in the Neapolitan Museum of Capodimonte, entitled 'The Charge of the Bersaglieri' "the comedy of Boccaccio is a revolution, where the whole edifice crumbles, and out of its ruins emerges the basis for a new one". A revolution made by the Bersaglieri for the benefit of their masters!

This then is the context in which the motif of the pregnant man found its place in Italy. In the background, the communes which enslaved and dominated the countryside; at the centre a mischievous adult literature, but one which was servile in its turn, and re-elaborates and enriches the ancient priestly traditions of Christian Europe, giving them the splendour of a formal dignity which the brave monks of another age had never dreamed of. The substance, however, is still the same as in those times: the polemic against folklore, women and peasants remains unchanged. The novelty resides in an uninhibited style—bold, but well-mannered—which allows the writer to bring the prostitute into the scene quite casually, and to talk about abortion. The doctor in the story—in return for a fee, of course—arranges for an abortion to be procured in order to calm the despairing Calandrino who believes himself to be pregnant. "Bourgeois realism", in fact, demands that the Tuscan writer should call a spade a spade. It is the end of the line for the stories of the beetle's return journey (now become a cockroach in the Italian version)—now it is a matter of a real abortion, brought on by the doctor by means of a "certain distilled drink, very good and pleasant to take". However, the joke is all too soon discovered: the priest can sleep soundly because if Calandrino's pregnancy is false, then obviously his abortion must be so as well. And what reason could there be to be scandalised about a false and even comic abortion? Does it not perhaps serve rather to ridicule the bumpkin who still dares to believe in the anti-christian tales of folklore?

In the Parisian edition of 1757–61, which presented the *Decameron* to a malicious, cosmopolitan public under a false London imprint, Gravelot commented on the farce of the fake abortion with a rather witty engraving (Figure 16). A little cherub is holding out a fuming bowl of abortion mixture to another cherub, who is languidly laid out in a curtained alcove. He takes it with one hand while he points with the other to his well-rounded belly, eloquent symbol of the presumed pregnancy. Another three Cupids, the same number as Boccaccio's jokers, are leaning over the top of the frame which encloses the tasteful scene, and watching it attentively, though without any sign of laughter. The earthy and witty figures of the story have been diluted in their eighteenth-century transposition, and converted into the charming little cherubs so favoured by Rococo taste. The subtle atmosphere of libertinism thus suggested accentuates the grotesque element in the situation: even so, the pregnancy remains false, and the abortion thus a parody.

Chapter 18
Excursus: Above and Below

The polemic about the 'above and below' positions, i.e. the positions of man and woman in sexual intercourse with reference to social relationships and the question of dominion between the sexes, has a very long history. Since it intervenes more than once, and insistently over a period of centuries, in the motif of the pregnant man, this may be the right moment to trace at least its main outlines.

The obligatory point of departure is Greco-Roman antiquity, in which the position of the woman on top of the man was clearly very common. It even represented, as Paul Veyne has stated recently, "the end of the end of love". Like the Romans, the Greeks used generally to describe it by the metaphor of the horse (*keles* in the latter case and *equus* in the former)

The contradiction between the position which the two partners assumed in intercourse and the opposite one which prevailed in all other social relationships is very clear, and could not escape the notice of historians. Ancient man, Veyne noted, preferred this position but had no intention, in using it, of surrendering his superiority over woman in any way, because even when he lay underneath he still made use of the woman. As master, the man was always active, and hence superior and admirable. The woman, who placed herself at his service, remained passive, and hence inferior and contemptible. As evidence of this he adduces a passage from Apuleius (II: 17), in which the woman who rides is the household servant, and her casual partner is the guest. Thus the contradiction seems to be resolved. But in fact, in this very passage from Apuleius, the service which the woman performs for the man turned him passive, and the initiative was always left to her.

The passivity of the man who allowed himself to be ridden is stressed too much by the literary texts and iconographical representations for us to assume that it can be cancelled out by references to social relationships. Activity in the woman is appreciated in the measure to which she shows ability in exercising it: Three Greek epigrams from the *Anthologia Palatina* (V.55: 202,203) leave us in no doubt, nor for that matter do the wall paintings of Pompei. In the *Book of Dreams* of the Greek writer Artemidoros (2nd century), we can read that for a women to be possessed is perfectly normal and advantageous, whatever may be the social position of the man. On the other hand, it would only be advantageous for him to be possessed by another man if the latter was a richer and older person. Allowing oneself to be possessed by a servant was the worst thing that could happen to a man, even if only in his dreams. The hierarchy of the sexes and that of society itself in relation to sex, could hardly be better defined. However, Artemidoros himself does not judge the *keles* to be despicable to the dignity of man, and he appreciates its not inconsiderable advantages, which according to him consisted, in the first place of enjoyment without effort—that is (note the coincidence) that very passivity considered degrading in any other circumstance. If the social judgment on male passivity was one of contempt, the first thing to explain is why the author, who had subscribed to such a judgment nevertheless admitted its contribution to the delights of sex with women.

In all the Greek witnesses which have come down to us, the *keles* seems to have been an apanage of the courtesans: for the Greeks, the Amazon of pleasure was, by definition, the prostitute—the only female figure to whom all societies based on masculine values have acknowledged the prerogative of sexual initiative. We thus enter into that sphere of sexual licence which ancient Greece regulated with the Adonian rituals, and defined by the myth of Adonis, the lover of Aphrodite. From Marcel Detienne's fine book *Les Jardins d'Adonis*, we know that sexuality inspired by female initiative was conceived entirely in terms of pleasure. Because of this it risked sliding easily into the realm of dissoluteness, and in any case, it contained the signs of sterility within itself. This kind of sexuality was therefore rigorously excluded from marriage, which did not have the aim of pleasure and was directed towards the purposes of procreation. Against the sterile gardens of Adonis which produced passivity within a few days, were contrasted the fruitful fields of Demeter, ploughed by the labour of man, with the harvest of crops in view. The ritual of Adonis was contrasted with that of Tesmophoris; his myth with that of Demeter, which assigned to women the role of modest wife and fruitful mother. Neither of the two rituals was exclusive of the other; they delimited two spheres of influence corresponding to two different social practices. The prostitute ensured the pleasure of the man, while the wife guaranteed him legitimate offspring and the continuity of his patrimony. But why was it that man had to allow to some women in the sphere of sexual pleasure that freedom of initiative which he denied to all of them in the social sphere?

The renunciation of the management of sexual pleasure, in fact, hid a deeply negative view of its social consequences. Sexual pleasure was perceived as something animal and savage—a disturbing and anti-social element which needed to be disciplined and restrained if the decay of the state and the dissolution of society were to be avoided. It must be disciplined, but it could not be eliminated, for the need which led to it was recognised as being irrepressible. The recurrent upsurge of the need for pleasure was opposed to the imperious demands of duty, without which the one could never discipline the other. The social fabric was constituted and held together by a division of tasks which assigned the management of power to the man, and that of pleasure to the woman. One of the pillars of society which emerged from this division of tasks was, therefore, the subordination of woman, representing the pleasure-principle, to man, who represented the power principle. The real Achilles heel of the Spartan political system, as Aristotle observed in *The Politics*, was the freedom granted to women. The Spartans thus fatally subjected themselves to female licence, and the consequence was the triumph of unbridled lust, and the ruin of the state. The woman must always remain submissive to the man, at all times and in all places, as in their social relationships. Above all she must remain so in marriage, the true institutional basis of the state—even to the point of denying sexual initiative to the spouse, whose role must be confined to the task of reproduction and the care of the domestic hearth. As far as pleasure was concerned, it was the prostitutes who must provide for it, along with other women such as slaves, whose social position exempted them from the duty of upholding the state. It was on their shoulders that the heavy burden must fall of performing a function which was judged to be anti-social by nature, and of absolving man from responsibility for it. Once again the social stigma is attached, and as always to the prostitutes themselves, never to their clients.

At this stage it is easy to comprehend that the division of tasks between men and women hid a deception. The true driving force in the sexual relationship remained the man, even when he was passive and immobile; even when the woman was portrayed as the only active partner. This choice, however, provided an opportunity for ensuring the indispensable female cooperation in this paradoxical dialectic between the sexual and the social. In effect the woman collaborated in the illusion that she too was somehow or other 'on top'; she gave in, then as always, to the fatal charm of power, and to the temptation to use it like a man, over men and over other women.

The split between marriage and sexual pleasure is then reproduced in Rome in all its essential ingredients. The *equus eroticus* symbolised extra-conjugal love, exactly as the *keles* did in Greece. Only in Rome, at a certain point it ceased to be clear exactly which women were to be considered appropriate for this liberty and which not. Towards the end of the Republic, and in the early days of the Empire, Roman matrons no longer accepted the old division of roles. The special conditions of the society in which they lived and the deep conflicts which disturbed and divided it favoured insubordination, and even a certain ascendancy of the female element, which has little parallel in the history of womankind. (The American feminist, Sarah B. Pomeroy, acknowledges this, and that says enough in itself). In this context we can understand the title of *equus Hectoreus* which was sometimes applied to the 'erotic horse' in Rome—not without causing serious scandal to right-minded people. To attribute to Hector the adoption of the controversial position in his relations with his wife Andromache meant admitting it into the marriage context, and setting aside an important barrier. Ovid, with a caution which he did not always show, denies it. In the *Ars Amandi*, (III: 78) he writes that Andromache was too tall to ride her husband. For Martial (XI: 104) on the other hand, the thing was obvious. It was a sign of the times which were changing—though not without provoking resistance and counterblows of one kind and another. With the *Lex Julia de Adulteris*, Augustus sought to put a check on the matrons by categorising adultery committed by women as a crime against the public interest, punishable even by death on the sentence of the paterfamilias. But he cannot have had a great deal of success with this law, since Juvenal, well over a century later reproved matrons (VI: 32) for, among many other things, having the insolence to challenge and even win prizes in the riding stakes. Before him, Seneca, the philosopher who was Nero's mentor, had thrown his weight in a very different direction. For him it was not a matter of merely deploring the sexual conduct of the matrons, but of all women, without distinction of rank or position. In a letter to Lucilius (95.21) he expresses his horror at the idea that women, born to be passive, dared to become active by mounting men. This demand he says is to be condemned as absolutely contrary to nature. A contemporary of Seneca, who had more than one point in common with him, but who died a martyr and certainly not by his own hand, expressed himself in the same way. At least it seems to be possible that the mention by St Paul (*Romans* I: 26) of the Gentile women who had "exchanged natural relations for those against nature" is a reference to the 'erotic horse'. He thus opens up the chapter of the sin against nature—the great barrier which morality began to erect against the spread and vogue of the need for pleasure.

Included in the general notion of the sin against nature, along with sodomy and onanism, the 'erotic horse' gallops through all the patristic writings, and thus through the hundreds of volumes of the two collections of Migne. From time to time it reappears through the centuries with its own particular physiognomy, adapted to the times; as far as I have been able to ascertain, it appears in Clement of Alexandria (*Protrepicus* II: 39.2), in St Jerome (P.L.24 226), in pseudo-Methodius (ed. Sackur, I. 61–62), who were writing respectively in the 2nd, 5th and 7th centuries. For christians, the only position admitted was the so-called normal one (woman below and man above). The 'erotic horse' must therefore disappear; and disappear it did, at least from the texts of the theologians, through almost the whole of the earlier medieval period.

It reappeared, however, in the 12th century, on the initiative of Peter the Glutton (a glutton for books, the authorities assure us), who in his *Historia Scholastica* (P.L.198.1081) once again takes issue with women who are so mad as to wish to ride. He refers back to the text of pseudo-Methodius, and thus re-establishes the continuity of the Christian tradition. From then onward, condemnation of the 'erotic horse' regains favour with the moralists. What had happened that was so important as to reawaken the interest of the theologians?, The answer has been provided by Noonan in his voluminous book on marriage and contraception: it was as a result of the Latin translation of the works of Avicenna that the ban returned to the centre stage. Indeed, the Arab doctor had confined himself to merely expressing a doubt as to whether the position of the woman above and the man below might not hamper or indeed impede the process of fertilisation. But Avicenna's doubt becomes a certainty for Albertus Magnus: if the woman is above, he argues in *De animalibus* (X.2.1), the womb is inverted and easily loses its contents. This was enough to give the go-ahead to the crusade against the 'erotic horse'; in the thirteenth century, the condemnation was repeated in the *Summa of Perrault* (III.II.3) and in the fourteenth century in that of the *Astesanus* (VIII.IX). It is only in the latter work, however, that we find the first reference to the preoccupation with anti-contraception. Previously the argument had centred on the traditional argument of the subversion of the natural hierarchy of the sexes; thus the polemic was substantially directed against the sexual initiative which antiquity had permitted to the women of the brothel, and all those other women who were available for extra-marital sex.

That the theologians were referring with their *mulier super virum* to a practice common in extraconjugal relationships is apparent from the miniatures which illustrate the *Decretum* of Gratian in many manuscripts. Every time they seek to represent cases of adultery and fornication, the woman regularly appears above the man. The same position can be seen in the fresco of the Palazzo della Ragione in Padua, dating from the first decades of the fifteenth century (the artist was Niccoló Miretto), which in the context of a huge astrological cycle illustrates the influence of Capricorn on mercenary love.

In the *Ballade de la Grosse Margot*, François Villon, celebrating bawdy-house love as usual, introduced the prostitute riding the man (in verses 1614–1618). Moreover Boccaccio himself found it perfectly natural that Nicolosa pretends to be making love to Calandrino while riding him. There was only cause for scandal if his wife, Tessa, demanded to do the same thing. And if the wife did it with her lover, the scandal went beyond all limits, and the shame inflicted on the husband must be punished by death. In the Novellino by Masuccio Salernitano (XXVIII), the adulteress surprised while riding her lover is speared with a lance together with him. So rooted was it in the medieval conscience, this distinction between the male and female initiatives in the sexual sphere, and hence in the more general social one, that it reappeared even in places quite beyond suspicion. The very code of courtly love which enjoyed such enormous success in the poetry of the twelfth and thirteenth centuries in France and Germany—what else was it but a sublimation of the old distinction and the ancient roles which man and woman played? In fact, courtly love, by its very nature adulterous, regularly placed the lady above and the knight below, though certainly not in sexual intercourse, in which it was rigorously forbidden, but in the complicated series of amorous precepts which served as symbol and substitute for that forbidden love.

The ecclesiastical ban, then, can hardly be said to have been very successful, and indeed all it succeeded in doing was reasserting the ancient distinction: sexual initiative for women only in the brothel and in extra-marital relations; subordination and passivity in marriage and in all other social relationships. A poor result from the point of view of catholic morality, and even more meagre if we consider that from the early Middle Ages, a powerful ally had entered the fray on the side of the priest—the doctor, using the fearful threat of damage to the health which could be caused by the erotic horseride. Damage, presumably, only to the health of the man, judged as morally the injured party thanks to the initiative of the woman. The fourteenth century doctor, Magnino da Milano, upholds it as something to cause fear and trembling in his *Regimen salutatis* (III.v).

The check suffered by the sexophobic campaign of christianity should not surprise us: here, the actual survival of sexual pleasure itself was in play, and however much the friars might strain their guts to thunder menaces and penances from the pulpit and the confessional, there was no way of convincing the people. Prostitution remained one of the pillars on which Christian society was built, as it had been for pagan society in the past. Adultery and fornication were the indispensable corollaries of sacramental marriage. But there was more than this. The need for sexual pleasure remained indestructible in those very people who strove so hard to proclaim its illegitimacy. The ghost of the woman riding the man robbed theologians, preachers and confessors and inquisitors of much sleep. Why is the number of witches so much higher than that of wizards? asked the two Dominicans, Heinrich Krämer and Jakob Sprenger in the *Malleus Maleficarum* (I.VI). The reply was obvious: because women are so much more carnal and lustful than men! What is the most insatiable thing: the thing that never says "Enough!"? "The mouth of the vulva". For this reason, the two worthy brothers concluded, we must speak of the heresy of witches, not of wizards. The connection between witchcraft and sexuality was thus perfectly established: witches are adulterers and fornicators and concubines: all those women, that is, who in the view of the most widespread opinion used always to ride on top in their coitus with men. But here we are faced with a new difficulty connected with the ancient theological doctrine of *incubus* and *succubus* devils, according to which the devils in their relations with witches must be above; i.e. they were *incubi*. But in order to obtain human sperm with which to fertilise the witches, they became *succubi* also and lay below, but for this they assumed female form. It would seem, then, that the witch didn't have much to do with the woman who rode on top. A woodcut which illustrates the *Layenspiegel* (Augsburg 1511), a manual of juridical procedure by the German jurist Ulrich Tengler, however, represents among other scenes of witchcraft one of coitus in which the witch is above and the devil below (Figure 17). How can this be? The most plausible explanation is that the devil had to be above when he wished to fertilise the witch, but below when he only wanted to excite her pleasure. The image of the witch who goes to the Sabbath riding a devil transformed into a he-goat, or simply riding on a broomstick, which appear as early as in the *Canon Episcopi* of the twelfth century, must obviously have evoked that of the woman who rode the man. This connection was perfectly depicted by more than one artist in different epochs.

A print by Parmigiano, rediscovered by Peter Webb in the British Museum, and dated at around 1530, represents a witch on the Sabbath, riding an enormous penis, which a winged devil is leading like a horse. The woman who sits astride it is wearing boots, and is carrying under

Figure 17 Scenes of the Life of Witches.

her arm, as if it were a lance, a spindle with a skein of wool wrapped round it. A fantastic animal rests its paw on her shoulder: a lioness with a goat's horn. A devil, evidently, and symbolising lust. Behind them a confused mass of female heads appear, sinister, menacing and dishevelled, and among them can be seen the head of a baby boy—the witches' favourite victim, supposedly—and that of an old man, evidently a wizard, who is wearing two spindles on his head in the form of horns. It was scarcely possible to state more clearly that it was overwhelming male desire which called forth the prostitute, and hence the witch her counterpart. But the analysis is carried even further, because spindles and spinning-wheels, traditional symbols of female domesticity, appeared frequently in the sixteenth century iconography of husband-beating wives, who seek to take the place of their spouses in command. The witch, Parmigiano seems to be saying, was not persecuted merely as the counterpart of the prostitute who rides on top of her man; inasmuch as she evokes the spectre of female insubordination, she is feared as a grave threat to the constituted order.

Goya dedicated one of the etchings of the *Caprichos* to the witch riding to the Sabbath on her broomstick, in 1799. However, there are two women here: one, who is old and ugly, supports a second young and beautiful, who rests her arm on the old woman's shoulder and covers her face (Figure 18). Two bodies, both naked, but with a single face, that of the old woman. There are two witches, but the title of the sketch is in the singular, and is ironically 'Linda Maestra'—fair mistress—signifying that the witch is the ghostly duplicate of the woman of pleasure. The whole tragedy of witch-hunts was thus summed up by two artists at a distance of centuries in a single image.

The basically sexophobic content of the witch hunt was moreover clearly perceivable in the tract literature on matrimony itself. As early as the beginning of the fourteenth century, the French Dominican Pierre de la Palude (*Quartum Sentent*, XXXI: 111) had associated the position of the man who allows himself to be ridden with the *succubus* devil. This reference was taken up again by his German confrère, Johannes Nider, in the next century (*De morali lepra*, Ch.16). The demonological terminology, *incubus* and *succubus*, appears to have become part of the regular vocabulary in the tract *De Sancto Matrimonio Sacramento* (IX.XVI.1), in which the Spanish Jesuit Tomas Sanchez places the seal of the Counter-Reformation at the end of the sixteenth century on the active condemnation of the 'erotic horse'. The only natural position, the theologian writes, is that of 'mulier succuba, vir autem incubus'. The opposite position is condemned as a mortal sin. "This way of proceeding is absolutely contrary to the order of nature, because it puts a barrier against the seed from the male ejaculation being received into

Figure 18   Linda Maestra.

the female vessel. Furthermore, it is not only the position of the persons which is inverted, but also their condition: it is in effect by the nature of things that the male acts and the female submits. The very fact of placing himself below renders the male passive, while the female in placing herself above becomes active. Who can refuse to acknowledge how much horror nature feels at such an overthrow?"

Mother Nature in this case was none other than the Holy Mother Church, and her admonitions could not always be followed. "The woman is always esteemed to have the upper hand and advantage over him who pays her court, for she is called his mistress, and he her servant" wrote the jurist Etienne Pasquier at the end of the fifteenth century. But what woman was he talking about? The courtier Brantôme, who knew the secrets of the closet better than anyone, was more precise. For him it was a matter of all ages, including those of the highest rank. He had no doubts even as to the nature of 'above': the old sublimated 'beneath' of courtly love had ceased to be an issue. Women no longer wished to hear mention of it; they wanted to be above in fact, and not just metaphorically, as several episodes in the Dames Galantes witness, with close attention to detail. The 'erotic horse' of the Greco-Roman tradition had regained the favour of the aristocracy, and the women went back to practising it regularly with their lovers, who did not seem to be troubled by the fact. "I always much prefer to play in reverse rather than to play piquet", we read in *Caquets de l'Accouchée*, an anonymous satirical compilation of the beginning of the seventeenth century. From then onwards, adultery in France was the only triumph which the aristocracy was allowed to celebrate under the rule of absolutism. The ancient solidarity of Church and State showed signs of breaking up, and toward the end of the seventeenth century, the King's mistress was officially installed in Court. The King set the example, and his sister-in-law, Liselotte von der Pfalz, was in the position to state wittily: "Conjugal love is no longer in fashion".

The century of gallantry, the eighteenth, basically cared little about the 'erotic horse'. To judge from the hesitations and tergiversations of St Alphonse Marie de Liguori (*Theologia moralis*, VI: 912), even the intransigence of the theologians had softened; with the result, as Piron noted, that:

> "Pious young beauties with down-looking eyes
> Are often the best at night-riding"

Certainly, doctors continued to go on reassuring people that it is the position least conducive to conception. The celebrated *Tableau de l'amour conjugal* however, preferred to jettison the traditional condemnation of the sitting position, and De Lignac's manual specified that while it was perhaps in conflict with marital dignity, it nevertheless provided greater pleasure. This was in fact a more or less explicit way of advising its adoption in extramarital relations. In short, as long as women were able to command in one way or another, little notice was taken of the fact that they also rode on top. Polemic at this time had a very different target: the woman who commands is much more worrying than the woman who rides on top!

However, adulterous love had unpredictable consequences, because the ladies were now no longer contented with riding; they also wanted to give the orders. In effect, according to Montesquieu (*Lettres persanes,* CVII), the king was "absolutely governed by his womenfolk, and like him were all those who counted for anything in the government of the state". St Simon confirmed, as Anka Muhlstein has pointed out, that in the last thirty years of the century of Louis XIV, France was in fact governed by Madame de Maintenon. The King's absolutism, by debasing men, had favoured women. Following the interval of the Regency, the situation reverted to more or less the same state of affairs in the reign of Louis XV, when the post which had been occupied by Mme de Maintenon was occupied by Madame de Pompadour; not even she governed 'in her own person', and she did not do so alone, but it should nevertheless be admitted that she was the effective ruler, and that her government was not all that different from that of the king and his ministers. The real discriminating element was thus provided by power, and not by the sex of the person who exercised it.

Without this premise it is impossible to understand the significance of the critique levelled by Rousseau at the female management of power. "French galanterie", he wrote in *La Nouvelle Héloïse* (II.xxi), "has given women a universal power which has no need of any tender sentiment to uphold it. Everything depends on them: nothing is done except by them and for them". But 'women', as in the previous citation from Montesquieu, refers to the ladies of high society, who have learned from men "to speak, act and think like them". They have done so without conquering their esteem, however, for it is "no less essential to French galanterie to despise women than to serve them".

Having fallen into this trap, man hid his contempt and prepared his revenge, while galanterie invaded Europe. In other countries, however, a mere simulacrum of the power of women was substituted for its reality, by means of different political conditions. In Italy, the Cicisbeo, the ladies' man, became fashionable: one who served the ladies without any hope of bedroom recompense. In Germany, where the fashion for the 'gallant' never caught on, 'Sturm und Drang' produced the similar phenomenon of the 'Machtweib', the woman who subjugates the man with the power of her beauty and her virile spirit. The reaction to the power of the ladies, whether real or feigned, promptly attached itself to the change that was about to come about in the political sphere. Rousseau's critique, though it did not depart from the distinction between ladies and women, did not keep to this distinction with the necessary rigour; instead it offered a general ideological weapon to the restoration of misogyny which the Revolution took it upon itself to develop and define.

The keynote of the female question came to the fore in the Convention, the Assembly of the Representatives of the French People, in November 1793. The conclusion was that women did not have "the moral and physical strength" necessary for the exercise of political rights, from which the Assembly therefore duly excluded them. Two years earlier, a young officer who was a passionate reader of Rousseau had gone to the root of the question by asking himself the question: "What then is love?" The reply was that it is "the sentiment of man's weakness; the sentiment of his impotence". It must therefore be condemned as "harmful to society", as well as to the "individual happiness of man". When this young officer, whose name was Bonaparte, became First Consul, he issued a proclamation against suicide for love: for Werther and Jacopo Ortis there was no longer to be any justification. And in 1804, by now Emperor of France, he sanctioned the Civil Code, which established (in Article 312): "the husband owes protection to his wife; the wife owes obedience to her husband".

An historical cycle was closing, then, but at the same time another was opening. "I have a real passion for obedience; nothing could make me so happy as seeing you command me". Thus wrote Wilhelm von Humboldt to his beloved—who was, however, no longer merely his lover but his wife. The seventeenth century of Liselotte von Pfalz had been completely overturned in the meantime and conjugal love was back in fashion, as never before.

Excluded once again from the government of society, the ladies could continue to command as long as they limited their activities in this sphere to their husbands. This new Gospel of Love had been proclaimed by Friedrich Schlegel in 1799 with the publication of his *Lucinda*. But what passed into history as Romantic Love was nothing other than the home made version of adulterous love. The woman in bed had to transform herself into the lover if she wished to satisfy her husband. In the second paragraph, dedicated to sexual relations, the 'erotic horse' thus makes a timely return to the scene. This was the price which had to be paid if sexuality was to be restored to the sacrament of marriage, and some meaning was to be given to its indispensable corollary: conjugal fidelity. The true price, however, was something else, and it was Madame de Staël who revealed it—not without a touch of cynicism—in her book on Germany: "They are right to exclude women from political and civil affairs; nothing is more contrary to their natural vocation... But if the destiny of women must consist in a constant act of devotion to conjugal love, the recompense for that devotion is the scrupulous fidelity of the man who is its object". The lines of the discussion were drawn, with his characteristic systematic rigour, by Hegel in his *Principles of Law*, where he specified (par.166) that the man "has his substantial real life in the State, in science, etc... while woman finds hers only in the family". By this definition, the philosopher returned the discussion of this idea from the ideal world where literature had transferred it, to its real dimension.

Romantic love in fact remained an ideal for schoolboys. In the concrete reality of family relations, things were quite different. The ladies of high society continued to ride with the same zeal as before— but it was their lovers and not their husbands whom they rode. As we can see from an amusing engraving by Thomas Rowlandson, dating from around 1815, and carrying the title 'The Husband's Departure'. The scene takes place in a harbourside tavern, where a feathered and bejewelled lady is riding a bewildered sailor, while with her free hand she waves to her husband out of the window as the ship on which he has embarked sails into the distance. The dog sitting at the feet of the couple reminds us of the fidelity which the woman is casting to the wind.

After the Revolution had settled accounts with the ladies, the erotic horseride came back into fashion, but it is no longer much talked about. In the nineteenth century proliferation of discourses on sex, its presence is difficult to discover. In order to trace clear signs of it, we must turn to unusual sources, like the erotic *ex libris* of the Belle Epoque, recently published by Eberhard and Phyllis Kronhausen, or to refer to the major investigation into erotic European literature which the Viennese review *Anthropophyteia*, directed by Friedrich S. Krauss, conducted in the first ten years of our century. The ancient ban thus recovered its strength. In 1870, in his little tract *De rebus venereis ad usum confessariorum*, the Vicar-general of the Archdiocese of Paris once again restated it.

The ban was still so strong in the twentieth century as to induce Havelock Ellis to demonstrate the absolute harmlessness of the 'erotic horseride' to the health. But the great sexologist descended into the fray in order 'to liberalise the bedchamber'. His struggle was in vain—his most formidable adversary, the ancient and unbeatable ally of the Church in his usual skilful fashion changed position by clever strategic moves, and was no longer to be found where Ellis looked for him. Already in 1923, Albert Moll, the favourite pupil of Krafft-Ebing, had in fact given a warning in a new and updated edition of *Psychopathia Sexualis*, that the *equus eroticus* should no longer be considered a cause, but rather a symptom, of sickness. The Englishman could gain no advantage from proclaiming his controversial position; for the German the *succubus* was a masochist, and he needed curing. By using the ancient Latin term, taken from demonological theology, he exposed his hand without intending to do so.

"It is said in Lower Britanny that when the woman lies above the man in coitus, the child she brings into the world will be a priest". This figurative popular sentiment is to be found under the entry 'Belek' (priest), in the *Glossaire cryptologique du Breto* published in 1884. The Latin term is also a sign of the times in this case—the same prudery which led the folklore expert to hide behind anonymity. However, the vulgar tongue sweeps away the entire thousand-year old discussion of 'above and below' with a few well-chosen words. It says: "If the priest is the guardian of the established order based on the inequality of the sexes, and every transgression provokes the punishment which it merits, then according to the law of retribution the woman who overturned the hierarchy of the sexes will have as her punishment the stigma of having produced the guardian of that very law." As proof of this, European folk-tales featuring the pregnant man often present the priest lying beneath in intercourse, and for that reason alone becoming convinced that he is pregnant.

PART III

Section I

Chapter 1
Peasant versus Monk

In African folklore, the motif of the pregnant man appears quite frequently. Denise Paulme devotes a lengthy chapter to it in her book, *La Mère dévorante*. In the African stories of the "male who gives birth", the leading personage is always the figure of the 'enfant malin'—the mischievous child who openly challenges the power of the father, or even more often that of the chief, and regularly wins, thanks to his astuteness. He challenges and he wins, but most importantly he unmasks the claim of the father to appropriate his son for himself with the excuse that he made him. For the child, the contest between the father and the mother for possession of the son has no biological foundation. According to nature, both the male and the female are essential. The complementary nature of the sexes is the only indispensable element for procreation. "A man", concludes Denise Paulme, "cannot bring a child into the world, but a woman alone cannot engender one". In the African fables, the 'enfant malin' usually says this in the first person. But the narrative scheme of the story of the "man who puts down" is sometimes transferred to animal stories, and in place of the 'enfant malin' we find the hare appearing. In the European fables of the pregnant man, the mischievous child never appears as a character in the story. The figure of the daughter appears, but only occasionally, and even then only in the fables of northern Europe, such as the Finnish one we have studied. But to judge from the second Latin Aesopic fable from the twelfth century, the figure of the daughter must have had a great influence on the medieval versions of the folklore myth of the pregnant man. The discourses of the African 'enfant malin' are only referred to indirectly in Europe, and often in such a reticent and self-censoring fashion that they are positively Sybilline. Africa, with all its misfortunes, at least had the good fortune to meet up late with the

179

benefit of Christian culturisation, with a few exceptions well-known to antiquity. The repercussions of this cultural invasion on the nature of power-relationships are thus not very strong, and are a far cry from the omnipresence of social control such as has been exercised by the Christian church in Europe ever since the middle ages.

In Europe, the place of the son, as we have seen, is at best taken by an animal—the beetle, the hare, the fox or the calf. The fable of the priest who believes that he has given birth to a calf is the most widespread, especially in northern and eastern Europe. In fact a great number of versions are recorded in Germany, the Scandinavian countries and the Baltic area, in Finland, Russia and Poland. Its most ancient version dates back to the beginning of the sixteenth century, and appears in a droll tale by the German humanist, Heinrich Bebel, which bears the title: *About a certain monk*. This is the text:

A certain friar who was also a cowherd spent the night during the begging season in the house of a peasant. He was forced by the poverty of the latter to sleep in the hayloft, on the straw. Not far from where he slept, the peasant had placed a newborn calf, because of the cold. The friar dreamed that he had given birth to it: waking suddenly he saw the calf and believed that it was true: he really had given birth. Seized by great fear, and not knowing what to do, he threw it into the pit, and rushed off in haste. The fact was discovered by the peasant who went to the friar's superiors to accuse him of the damage he had caused. The friar was forced to pay him compensation, and it became the talk of the town. This was an event that actually happened, or so at least I have been told.

The annotation which concludes the little tale clearly goes back to the original oral tradition, to which, Bebel declares, he adhered strictly. The son of a peasant himself, the German humanist in fact showed a great interest in the folklore traditions of his country. Despite the linguistic clothing (Latin) which they wear, and the humanistic framework into which they are fitted, his droll stories are considered to be genuine folklore texts.

The references in the droll stories collected and published by Bebel to the passage from the Gospel according to St Luke dedicated to the miracle of the healing of the dropsy victim are unequivocal. There, it was a matter of extracting a son or an ox from the pit into which they had fallen in order to save them. Here, on the other hand, it is a matter of throwing a calf into a pit in order to save the friar from the shame of having given birth to it. Son and ox, closely associated in the Biblical miracle, are here replaced by the calf which stands for them both, just as the friar represents Christ whose priestly ministry he continues. The metaphor of salvation, however, is sarcastically reversed in a parody; in order to save himself the friar sacrifices the calf by throwing it into the pit.

In the Finnish version of the folklore myth of the pregnant man, this parody of salvation reappears at a distance of many centuries, with an even more polemical intention. In this one, while the priest may think he has given birth to a calf, the people believe that the calf has eaten the priest. Thus the calf is taken for a diabolical creature; an incarnation of the devil, which must be exorcised by the intervention of another priest. This other priest arrives and begins the exorcism; in one version, things go as follows: "The calf was brought out, and the priest began to exorcise it, using the Bible. The calf cried out 'pook', and nuzzled against the priest as if it were searching for an udder. The priest took fright; he placed himself in front of the calf, walking backwards all the time, and continued to exorcise it with the Bible. In the end, the priest fell backwards into the old pit; the calf followed him, still lowing. The people took stones and filled up the pit, saying: 'It doesn't matter at all that the priest fell in as well; we've managed to free ourselves from the diabolical calf before it could eat us all up, since it obviously wanted to eat the priest too." As we see, the priest ends up in the pit with the calf, for the salvation of all the others. The story ends in this way because the calf, indifferent to the exorcism, is only looking for the cow's udder. Thus the calf in the Finnish folk-tale does what the enfant malin does in the African fables; he reminds us, as a calf may, that children are made by their mother, even though the father's cooperation is necessary. In Europe the shadow of the cow always fell in some way on the story of the priest who gave birth to the calf. Once, in that same sixteenth century in which the collection of droll stories by Bebel was published, we meet up with it in this rather bizarre form, which is worth re-telling here:

In Freiberg, a small city in Saxony at the foot of the iron-bearing mountains of the Erzgebirge, a strange phenomenon was observed in 1522. While a cow belonging to a certain peasant was being slaughtered, it was discovered that it was carrying in its belly a foetus that resembled a monk; it even had a tonsure and a cowl. No-one doubted this identification which the butchers swore to, and the story of the monk-calf spread throughout the whole of Germany. The portentous foetus was actually sent to Prague, where the court astrologer discovered in it the unmistakable signs of a divine condemnation of Lutheran polemic against the religious orders. Backed by an appropriate woodcut, an eloquent little tract was rushed through the press, to which Luther himself promptly replied. His *Deutung des Mönchkalbs zu Freyberg* (explanation of the monk-calf at Freiberg) was also provided with a woodcut, no less eloquent than the first, from the hand (or so it seems)

Figure 19 Lucas Cranach: The Calf-Monk.

of none other than Lucas Cranach himself (Figure 19). The dispute
raged, and various other learned men entered the arena. Meanwhile, in
Freiberg itself the popular muse got hold of the extraordinary event: for
years a satirical song was sung, and it must have had quite a sting,

because a clerical intervention in 1525 obtained its prohibition by the authorities. This popular song has not come down to us, but as far as we know the episode was linked to the fable of the monk who bore the calf, then current in Germany. The story of the monk-calf is in effect the simple reversal of the fable, and it says: it is not the monk who gave birth to the calf, but (rather more logically) the cow that gave birth to the monk!

Chapter 2
Artisan versus Peasant

A shoemaker, a Lutheran, and a monstrously prolific writer (something near 6000 titles, and always in his spare time at that) Hans Sachs was more than once attracted by the theme of the pregnant man. His main source was the Calandrino story, well-known in Germany in various translations, from which many of its components are derived. The only direct link with folklore sources, however, is traceable to the droll story *The peasant made pregnant by the mule*, which dates from 1559, and represents the last and most mature of the versions. The pregnancy of the mule, which takes the place of the calf; the escape of the hare in coincidence with the man's liberating defecation; the gesture of running after it with promises of maternal assistance and nutrition, the pride in having aborted/given birth to such a fast-moving animal are all clearly folklore motifs unknown to Boccaccio, and they occur regularly in the German versions of the motif. In the tale by the Meistersinger of Nuremberg, however, one element remains of the Boccaccian scheme: the fundamental counterpoising of the city and the country, inspired by an intractable contempt for the peasant. In contrast to the Calandrino story, however, the scene is set in the country, and three of the four characters who feature in it are country people: the peasant, his wife and the servant. Countrymen they are, and poor devils all of them, the peasant, rich only in the wind which enters his house through a thousand cracks, his wife, and the servant who depends on the peasant and shares his wretched fate. But the most wretched of the four is the last, the Jewish doctor, a veritable famine victim, on whose social standing the honest literary cobbler spends a good deal of effort. A Jew without art or parts, Isaac has lived by expedients off the backs of the peasants, as a fortune-teller and wizard, as occasion arises. Their legendary credulity sanctioned every kind of trickery. There is no need for any astonishment at this: "I've frigged the peasants and had them by the balls for years", says Isaac, winking at his public of town-dwellers. There was a certain amount of risk in such a trade; his predictions weren't always right, and sometimes the score would be settled at spear-point. This had happened more than once, and had induced him to change profession in order to win the greater security of the quack doctor, capable only of prescribing—as a remedy for all diseases—a deadly purgative which from time to time hastened some unfortunate into the next world. Nor was this surprising. Had not the preachers and theologians been saying it for centuries? Was it not confirmed by Papal Bulls and Conciliar Decrees? There was no doubt at all about it: Jewish medicine was directly inspired by the Devil, and Christians (with the sole exception of kings, popes, princes and prelates who derived a great deal of profit from them) must stay away from them. In fact it was well-known that every Jewish doctor had made a formal undertaking to assassinate a certain percentage of his unfortunate Christian patients (according to the University of Vienna it was at least one in ten). Luther too had recommended, in one of the anti-Semitic works of his old age, that Jewish doctors were not to be trusted. What could a poor shoemaker from Nuremberg do other than join in the chorus? And if the Jew—represented with undeniable realism as the pariah which he certainly was—sinned through cynicism, were the other three famine-victims, peasant, wife and serf, any better than him, even though they were Christians (and of the reformed faith, moreover)? The same elementary cynicism is shown by the serf, a real lout, of whom it's hard to say whether he is more stupid or ill-natured, and who hopes in the effectiveness of the purge to get rid of the peasant and take possession of his wife: "The blind", he asserts, "often find an iron horse". With the Jew he carries on a dialogue full of references to all the commonplaces of the city-dweller's satire of the countryman. The complicity of the public is so assured that it even constitutes a genuine means of communication between the two characters in the scene. The serf doesn't actually tell the doctor that he has replaced the peasant's urine with that of the mule; it's enough for him to tell his public in his absence, so that he can diagnose the man's unheard of equine pregnancy with sufficient pomp and ceremony. In this villainous game, which draws the whole circle of his adversaries around the poor peasant in complicity, the wife is obviously bound to be involved as well. In the end, Goethe declares that she will agree to leave her husband and go off with the serf, because the poor man has given birth to a thoroughbred colt. A lifeless character, without personality, a peasant woman sunk in domesticity, the woman has nothing to talk about except turnip soup and bran mash. It is not even remotely conceivable that her husband makes love to her any longer. When the servant exultantly announces the infamous news of his pregnancy, the peasant, faithful to the Boccaccian model, takes it out on his wife. "You old bag!", he cries. "You're to blame for this. If I succeed in getting rid of this mule, I'll break your head for you!" He doesn't say, however, what she has been guilty of, and without having read Bocccaccio's tale where the accusation is quite specific (Tessa always wanted to be on top in intercourse), no-one could understand what he is talking about. Genital sexuality is in fact ruthlessly excluded from the text. "In the Middle Ages", Brecht noted in his diary, "it seems that even in this camp, the only depository of culture was the clergy. The German nobility was incapable of enjoyment; the German bourgeoisie was puritan in ideals—which is to say obscene in reality. The German student did this or that after a good swill of beer—so much so that when he devoted himself to copulation, others would have found it hard to do anything but vomit in his place. It would have been salutary for the Germans to have their first comedy of love—their Mandragora, so to speak, in the form of a work dedicated to Luther and his Catherine, for instance". "How much beer there is in Protestant Christianity", Nietzsche pronounced, in turn. The only form of eroticism which appears in the farce of the Lutheran shoemaker is anal, closely linked to the peasant's defecations. Basically his greatest sin, and the one for which he has deserved the cruellest injury, his supposed pregnancy, lies in not wanting to control his sphincter, just like little children. His free and spontaneous defecation is the source of comedy as facile as it is gross, and it occupies the front of the stage throughout, in an orgy of farts and flatulence. "Is it possible to conceive of any form of Christian faith more spiritually rancid, poltroonish and paralysing than that of an average German protestant?" demanded Nietzsche. The Reformation then, reformed little, while on the other hand it brought sixteenth century Christianity, polluted by worldliness, back to its original principles: liberty and equality for all good Christians (Satan would deal with the rest), but only after death in the great Beyond. Here, in this life, everyone must remain in place, and all were obliged to respect the authority above them: wives of their husbands; children of their fathers, servants of their masters. On this point Luther—the foremost advocate of Christian liberty—left no room for doubt: "Baptism", he wrote, "does not free body and goods, but only the soul".

With Hans Sachs, the petit-bourgeois enters into history: Europe would come to recognise him. The verses of this 'genuine talent', and 'simple citizen' were quite enjoyed by Goethe, who brought them back into favour, adopting on occasions "their light rhythm and facile rhymes" (so he wrote in *Poetry and Truth*). And if they were pleasing to

Goethe, we can imagine the effect they had on Wagner. "In the rough art of our old popular poet Hans Sachs", he wrote, "germs of the highest Idealism were born". It was enough to see the marvellous construction which Goethe built on the so-called 'Knuttelvers', a knotty kind of verse, so-called with obvious reference to the Knuttel, the knobbly cudgel. Admiration for Sachs, of course, induced Wagner to adopt him as the protagonist of his music-drama, *The Meistersingers of Nuremberg*, in which he is supposed to represent the German popular soul. But Sachs equals Knuttelvers, and Knuttelvers is made with the club, it is as knotty as the cudgel itself. Where Sachs is, the cudgel can't be far away. And in fact, there it is: in the sixth scene of the second act, there appears in the stage-directions: "mit Knutteln bewaffnet, kommen von verschiedenen Seiten dazu" (armed with cudgels, they run in from various parts). This refers to the artisans of Nuremberg, awakened by the nocturnal fracas of the beating of Beckmesser (according to commentators, the Viennese music critic Eduard Hanslick is concealed beneath this character, for he was in habit of using his critical faculties and therefore—according to the Saxon musician—deserved to be beaten, at least on stage). So taking the national Knuttel in their hands, the worthy artisans beat each other about without any real notion of why. A true outburst of vitality: the healthy German people, Wagner insinuates, cannot do without the stick. And Nietzsche added: "The fact that the arrival of Wagner coincided with the arrival of the Reich is of deep significance: both these facts demonstrate the same idea—obedience and long legs. Never has there been better obedience; never has there been better command".

Chapter 3
Peasant versus Artisan

The Danish fable, *The Calf which ate Men,* was collected in Jutland and published by Tang Kristensen in 1890. Its protagonist is a shoemaker, but it reproduces in other respects the narrative scheme of the European fable of the cleric who gives birth to the calf, and it is certainly derived from it. This is proved by a German tale, *The Carter,* collected in Hesse and published in 1853 by Karl Weigand; it preserves the clearest traces of the phase of passage from one tradition to another. Here too the protagonist is an artisan—a carter in fact, who believes, just like the cobbler, that he has given birth to a calf when he finds himself next to it in the hayloft where he has spent the night. Subsequently, however, in the course of his flight for freedom, he takes refuge in a priory where he is taken on as a porter, and is forced to become a friar. In this guise he leaves the priory, and ends up in the court of a duke, and after a whole host of mishaps, he finds himself in the pulpit of the church, without a notion of what to preach about. He solves the problem by having recourse to Rabelaisian language and gestures (readers will remember the debate between Panurge and the Englishman at the Sorbonne), and this enables him, by sheer chance, to save the court from ruin when the platform on which the whole court is seated collapses.

Twice the fake friar revolves his hand slowly three times; then the third time he does so far more vigorously and at great speed, as if he is anxious to incite them to flight because of the nearness of a great danger. In fact, this is the way in which these gestures are interpreted, and "When the Duke saw him, he leaped off the platform and the court followed behind. They had hardly left the Church in great haste when the platform fell; if they had remained inside, they would all have died beneath the beams, planks and all the rest of it". A real miracle, then, which prevented a disaster of the kind which actually happened once in a church in Foligno, under the amused gaze of Luigi Pulci. There it was the Friar who, "jumped with feet together like a cat from the pulpit"— but after the disaster had taken place and the people were buried beneath the rubble. A rare event, comments Pulci shrewdly, that the trap should spring at the opening words of the preacher! But of course there had to be a difference between a real friar and a fictional one...

The two protagonists of this story recall a third artisan, the hero of another German version of the pregnant man motif. This is an old text, in Middle High German; it is anonymous and written in verse, and evidently of popular origin; it bears the title *The Pregnant Miller.* Judged by the critics to be chronologically quite close to the story of *The Monk's Pains* by Zwingäuer, it actually reproduces the same intrigue, differing from it only on one of two points. The triangle of master, servant and woman remains the same, but the master here is no longer a monk but a rich miller; the animal is a swallow, and the abortion induced by the blows of a stick is replaced by a false birth in a bowel discharge, brought on by a bellyful of honey which the woman, a part-time whore, has tempted him to eat. Old witches (*unhulden*) are present at the miller's 'accouchement', and they take great delight in the joke.

Another, as yet unpublished, German tale, *The Fable of the Tailor who gave birth to a Calf*, was collected in 1897 in a village of Franconia, and its main character is a tailor. The metamorphosis of the protagonist, who in these various versions becomes cobbler, carter and miller, requires explanation. In all four cases the story concerns a figure in society characterised by strong antagonism to the rural community. Artisans of the countryside, privileged somewhat by the division of labour, lived by exchanging goods and services with the peasants, and regularly made them pay more than the goods were worth. There is more to it than this, however. Whatever their economic condition— substantial and wealthy like the miller, or great poverty in the cases of the cobbler and carter—these artisans almost always had a dependent on whom they could unload the burden of their heaviest work, and their resentment at life's inequalities. In the case of the cobbler, the Danish fable specifies that his apprentice "didn't have an easy life". The whip danced merrily on the shoulders of someone who, moreover "suffered from hunger like a crow". He had to learn his trade from the master-cobbler, and according to all human and divine laws, he must therefore serve and obey him at the crack of a whip. So we can understand why he is the one who spills the urine of his master on the road, and takes cow's urine to the doctor in its place. It is clear that he is motivated by the same justifiable hostility to his master as causes the servant to play his trick on the miller.

In the second German fable, as yet unpublished, the antagonist of the tailor is a cowherd. He advises the man who is carrying the tailor's urine to the doctor to replace it with that of one of his cows. Peasants, serfs and apprentices are all natural antagonists of these artisans. The women, who appear in the story of the miller, are not present in the other tales. Their presence is felt, however, in the background, as the negative pole of a degrading condition which motivates the terror and the shame of the artisan for his supposed pregnancy. With the passing of the centuries, the motif of the pregnant man thus preserves intact all its social implications, and continues to attack the power of the links in the hierarchical chain which passes the desire to command from one rank to another. However wretchedly poor they may be, the artisans in these stories always have someone to take it out on. If they lack the apprentice-boy or the serf, there is always the woman, at least as a comforting point of comparison.

Chapter 4
Husband versus Wife: Bourgeois Morality

Troyes, an ancient city of Champagne, southeast of Paris, is the capital of the wool-making industry: stockings and underwear are made there in great quantities. This has been so for many centuries, as it was in the sixteenth, when the saddler Nicholas, (who called himself Nicole de Troyes), was born. The title referred to the city of his birth; he had in fact abandoned it for Tours, not a great distance away, at some time and for some reason which we do not know. A passionate reader of the *Decameron*, which in France as elsewhere existed in numerous translations and had a vast semi-educated readership, Master Nicole himself became a teller of tales. He also collected them—a large number in a big manuscript collection in his own hand which, with a certain naive pride, he entitled *Le Grand paragon des nouvelles nouvelles*, by which he meant the model or sounding-board for modern short stories. The short story, or 'Novella' in the French language the genre which spread and ramified throughout the following centuries was not, however, to have any chance of comparison with this 'model'; at least until the last century, and quite late on in it, when it finally emerged from the manuscript in which it had been preserved. Even then, the first version which appeared was far from complete.

Having been born at Troyes, Master Nicole places the interesting little story which he dedicates to the pregnant man there. He declared it to have come from the oral tradition, and said that it was told him by a certain Jehan du Bois, who is not otherwise identified. The pregnant man here is a wealthy merchant—"a young *galant*, very sure of himself", and happily married to a rich, beautiful young woman who is honest to the point of ingenuousness. As in all the houses of the well-off in that era, in this merchant's house there also lives another young woman, the domestic servant. She is the repressed and degraded double of the wife, and like her, is duly available for the sexual desires of her master. Husband and wife "love each other most wonderfully", but not all the man's *galanterie* can be satisfied in this love, so according to a well-worn convention (social rather than narrative in character) he seduces the maid and makes her pregnant. At this point the fourth indispensable character appears on the scene: the doctor, the cousin and friend of the merchant, whose task it is to get him out of the mess. Since the wife is in love with her husband, she justly insists on marital fidelity, and she can count on the support of her parents. The doctor doesn't hesitate for a moment: he knows exactly what must be done. All that is needed is for the man to lie in bed pretending illness, a pain in the gut or the kidneys, say, and send the wife with the usual sample of urine. He will then see to it that the husband is diagnosed as pregnant, and will put the blame on her; then he will suggest the remedy of a (purely functional) intercourse of the husband and the maid by which her master's unfortunate pregnancy will be transferred to her. The wife does not for one instance doubt the efficacy of this prescription, and they both struggle to overcome the fake resistance which the husband and the maid make great play of putting up. The two make love again, this time with her benediction, and the maid's genuine pregnancy is made fully justifiable. After she bears her child, the mistress of the house will find a good home for her, providing her with a dowry and marrying her off to some worthy fellow.

The comedy of the man's pregnancy can continue without impediment because the doctor shrewdly bases it on the indisputable authority of his medical science. He has no difficulty at all in stating *what* is involved: the principal question is the now all-too familiar one of 'above and below'. When the wife hears in astonishment from his lips of her husband's impossible pregnancy, the doctor puts the insinuating question to her: "When you made love, did it ever, by any chance, happen that you mounted on top of him? Come now; don't tell any lies, because this has much to do with his recovery!" "Oh dear, cousin", the woman answers in embarrassment; "To tell you the truth, it *has* happened—though only once, I swear it". "Upon my faith!", the doctor says triumphantly: "that's enough. I don't need to know anything else. He is unquestionably pregnant!"

By her compromising admission, the woman becomes entangled in the doctor's net. When the moment arises, he doesn't miss the chance to warn her: "No-one must know anything about this, because if they do, they'll say 'ah—here comes that woman who made her husband pregnant by mounting him!'. In this way he sought to frighten her with the veiled threat of public ridicule. To dare to overthrow the sexual hierarchy was, in fact, a sin for which one paid dearly. The social control over the conjugal order was guaranteed in France in those days by certain institutions, not least of which was the highly popular *Charivari*, a ceremony of punishment which involved the neighbours of the incriminated couple. Their task was to parade around the streets of the neighbourhood making a great din, with the banging of saucepans, a lot of shouting, and the singing of suggestive songs. The favourite targets were widows on their second marriages, adulterers and wives who beat their husbands. For this latter offence, there was also the *Asouade*: the beaten husband, or one of his neighbours impersonating him, rode around the area back-to-front on the donkey. He has to sit reversed in this way to symbolise the reversal of roles which the ceremony was intended to stigmatise and punish.

However, the doctor in the story is a man of science, not of the Church, and in order to explain to the bewildered wife how her husband can be cured of his pregnancy by making love to the maid, he reveals some biological arguments worthy of Ambroise Paré, the most famous French doctor of the sixteenth century. "It is essential that you find ways and means of talking to some young girl who is a virgin", explains this eloquent Aesclapius, "and that your husband goes to bed with her for a night or two. He will then put the seed which he has in his body into the girl".

This suggestion was perfectly in keeping with the medicine of the times, which explained generation as a mixture of the male seed with the female inside the uterus. "The male expels his seed outside his body, and the female inside hers", wrote Ambroise Paré in his treatise *On the generation of humankind*. However, if we imagine the two functions of the male and female inverted, then it is obvious that the female will expel outside and the male inside. "It is in the seed that the creative and formative virtue resides", continued Paré, though without specifying what seed he was talking about, the male alone or both the male and the female. An excusable omission for a sixteenth century doctor, when medicine represented virtually a solid front on the basis of the ancient Aristotelian thesis of the absolute pre-eminence of the male seed in generation. "From ancient times to the Renaissance", the biologist François Jacob has observed, "the knowledge of the living world changed very little. When Cardano, Fernel or Aldrovandi spoke of beings, they repeated roughly what Aristotle, Hippocrates and Galen had said." In the matter which we are considering, they continued to claim that the male seed had the faculty of "activating and giving form to the matter contained in the female". Whence comes the question: if the formative virtue lies in the male seed, which is the superior, then how can babies of the female sex, the inferior, be born of it? An authoritative colleague of Paré, Laurent Joubert, Chancellor of the Faculty of Medicine at Montpelier, and a Protestant into the bargain, had no doubts at all. His explanation of the problem is delightfully simple: the defect is entirely on the female side, which provides the matter required for the work of generation. A great artist who was also a real scientist, as it was still possible to be in those days, made short work of this nonsense with a simple observation: "The blacks in Ethiopia are not black because of the sun, because if a black man impregnates a black woman in Scythia, they will have a black baby, and if he impregnates a white woman, she will bear a child with a lighter skin. This shows that the seed of the mother has equal power in the embryo with that of the father". But then, as is well-known, Leonardo Da Vinci could not bear doctors.

It is clear on which side the doctor in our story stood: for him the seed which counted, and with which he was exclusively concerned, was obviously the male, and in the case in point, the seed of the female, as a result of being beneath her husband in the act of intercourse, acquired the characteristic of the male. Not everything, however, depended on the male seed, and this doctor was not such a fool as not to admit it. "Conception can never take place unless two seeds concur together at the same moment, and the womb is well-disposed", continued Ambroise Paré, with cautious neutrality. But this is where the whole thing fell apart, because the merchant obviously couldn't invent a womb for himself, so if he kept hold of the female 'seed' for too long, he was in big trouble. So then, it was necessary to restore it at once to someone who possessed a womb by the gift of nature. Why not, then, the wife herself? This objection has been foreseen by the Doctor, who immediately mentions that the girl must be a virgin. The requirement of virginity—clearly not to be hoped for in a married woman—was, on the other hand, usually assumed in the maid, whose domestic service required of her an enforced chastity. Naturally, it is she of whom the master first thinks, when he hastens to assure his cousin: "with the help of God, we shall overcome this problem, for I have a maid who, I believe, is a virgin". Who better, indeed, than this girl who shared the domestic chores with her mistress, and all the connected duties of obedience and fidelity, to come to his aid in this way? The sacrifice of her virginity, the ancient royal road to feminine perfection, was the necessary tribute she must pay to save her mistress. Only the sacrifice of the obedient virgin could redeem the mistress from the sin of having mounted her husband, and disobeyed the commandments of the Church. And with this consideration we have reached the central point of this story.

The saddler-storyteller of Troyes shows himself to be far more resourceful than we might have imagined. Though his grammar may have been a little lame, he was in compensation strong in theology, and had a sprinkling of knowledge of more than one of the profane sciences. So well did he know his theology, in fact, that he could allow himself a subtle parody which more than once has a whiff of highly blasphemous ridicule. The interview between the doctor and the mistress of the house is an important element in this as it reveals itself progressively as the narrative unfolds, though it begins merely in the realm of allusions. A second stage in the process is provided by the interview between mistress and maid. To the mistress' pressing request for a special and much-needed service which she does not yet specify, the young girl, duly instructed beforehand by her master, begins by replying with great caution: "Madam," she says, "I will do everything which is possible for love of you, saving my honour and yours". However, the concept of honour referred to here is not summed-up completely in her purely social acceptance of the proposal. The dishonourable action which is put before her is a mortal sin, and a sin for both of them, as the maid makes no bones about stating: "What, Madame: do you want me to do this dishonour to you? If another were to ask me such a thing, you—who are such a virtuous woman—should dissuade me with all your strength. Oh no... I swear I would rather be dead!" We are well aware that behind this eloquent tirade from the young girl, there is a very clear commandment of the Church. For confirmation it will be enough to refer to the *Somme des Péchez*, by the ropemaker from Lyons, Jean Benedicti, quoted by Jean-Louis Flandrin. In Article 45 it is stated: "those masters who do not care for the salvation of their servants and maids, and do not seek to correct their faults, allowing them to commit perjury, swear, blaspheme, fornicate, steal, and so on, themselves participate in their sins".

Even the husband declares to his wife that he would rather die than commit the breach of marital fidelity, to which he is bound by the sacrament of matrimony. And as the wife, the doctor and the husband throw the ball of this sin back and forth, with more than a touch of the grotesque, the real inner meaning of the story begins to unfold. To the threat of death ('You are so good and true that rather than exchange you for another, I would prefer to die'), the doctor replies with Jesuitical cunning; he appeals to the specific weight of the two sins, and the relative cases of conscience which they pose. "If you were to die in this state", he says, "you would be damned to hell for having caused your own death, since you know the remedy by which with God's grace you can cure yourself, but you refuse to take it". The merchant finally 'gives in' to his wife's insistence and his cousin's persuasion, but not before he has imposed on their consciences the sin he will commit in making love to the maid. The wife hastens to accept this, totally unaware that she has been the butt of the cruel trick by the two cronies.

The result of the cynical manipulation of catholic matrimonial theology is that the whole weight of the church's bans and the limits deriving from them is thrown onto the woman's shoulders. A brilliant operation, in fact; liberating man from the oppressive morality of sacramental marriage—and all carried out in the name of those very principles which it is actually meant to evade: the principle of the inequality of the sexes was surely the indestructible pillar of that morality. With an air of desecrating traditional catholic morality with a series of blasphemies and affronts, the two free-wheeling cousins do nothing but adapt it to their own tastes while even increasing its rigour. If the notion of superiors and inferiors exists within the actual framework of the moral law, how can it be applied equally to one and all? The Church itself, however intransigent it had always been in principle on the punishment of adultery, had always left the door open for a certain measure of more or less veiled and indirect flexibility as far as the husband was concerned. The theologian Benedicti gives some significant pointers in this direction: the undoubted superiority of man to woman he says, does allow a certain tolerance as far as men are concerned. To the wife "swollen with pride, with self-esteem, with her own beauty, her goods, her parentage", he admonishes that in refusing to obey "she resists the Divine judgement, which demands that she should be subject to her husband, more noble and more excellent than she, since he is the image of God, but she merely the image of man". Thus he advises her who is "possessed by jealousy and never ceases to reprove and torment her husband on the basis of some false notion she has about him" to look well to herself, because this is a matter of "a sickness of the Evil spirit". Woman's jealousy, then, was not of the same value as that of man, and could not be considered properly motivated by her husband's infidelity, but by the old familiar promptings of the devil, her age-old and faithful inspirer. But there is even more to it than this.

The story in fact seeks to put forward a new scale of values inspired by a quite unscrupulous vision of the nature of human and sexual relations. And the best of it is that the woman, the victim of this change, finds herself charged with the task of presenting the new morality which commercialises everything, and resolves all questions in terms of cash. Who but the woman is set to corrupt the maid, and convince her to adhere to the plot by promising her ten écus and the guarantee of a good marriage? We have to acknowledge that the saddler-storyteller knew his facts, though he cannot bear the sole responsibility for the undertaking of such a sophisticated operation.

Moving on down the Seine towards the sea after leaving Troyes and passing the formidable obstacle of metropolitan Paris, the traveller arrives at Rouen. Once a great emporium of French overseas trade, and today an industrial city of the first rank, Rouen in the sixteenth century was one of the richest and most populous cities in Normandy and indeed in France. An important court was held there—the Parlement of Normandy—which gave effect to the royal edicts, making them effective throughout the Province, in which it also functioned as the Supreme Court of Justice. A great host of lawyers thronged its halls, organised in a powerful corporation known as the *Basoche*. Through judicial practice this court began to impose a particular conception of life on civic society. It was a secular and civic view of the world, sharply opposed to the austere and grim view imposed by the Church; ebullient in spirit, it even had something of the pagan about it. In response to an ancient tradition which was impossible to suppress, the Church had to descend to at least one compromise with this spirit, and concede at least the break provided by Carnival; one cut of the cake from each year which could be as long or as short as the seasonal caprices of the Calendar allowed, but always destined, in any case, to end up in the mournful coffin of Lent. Death reigned over life, and waited for it as the Day of Ashes drew near. During the break, however, madness took hold of the market-place, perhaps in the vain allusion of exorcising death. Every possible entertainment was provided. As willing organisers of the festival, the lawyers of Rouen also came together in the *Compagnie des Conards*, one of the best known joyful fraternities of the sixteenth century; it laid on carnival spectacles, and in particular the procession of the carts, and it delighted in the performance of farces and comedies.

This whole environment is recalled for us in an anonymous farce of *The Pregnant Man*, found in a well-known manuscript collection of the sixteenth century, and only published in the last century. The city of Rouen is specifically mentioned in the opening verses, and there is a specifically judicial terminology which clearly refers to its authors and amateur actors. In the frontispiece of this farce (entitled *La farce joyeuse* in obvious reference to the ritual jollities of the Carnival), immediately after the title, *Le Médecin et le badin*, (the doctor and the buffoon) there appears a list of characters, four in all, in the following order: the Doctor; the Buffoon, the Wife and the Maid. It is the same quartet, of course, as in the tale of Master Nicole of Troyes, virtually unchanged, and mixed up in much the same intrigue. The social connotations of the characters also remain unchanged, though the role of the 'Buffoon' seems to hide behind its rather more strongly delineated characteristics, the comic role of the one who, according to Rabelais' apposite description, "played the part of the fool in a farce or comedy". As a synonym for fool or clodpoll, the word *badin* recurs frequently in the popular language of the sixteenth century. However, in its theatrical transposition the role of the buffoon sometimes takes on an ambivalence in which cunning and shrewdness are mingled with ingenuousness or stupidity. "The *badin* is not a real fool", a farce of the period tells us, and the *Recueil général des sotties* (III.60), states that they are neither foolish nor wise. One cannot, in fact, say either about the *badin* of our farce. However, he figures there as a well-off citizen with a wife well-endowed with worldly goods and domestic virtues. He is also (quite a coincidence?) the crony of the doctor.

The condition of the maid is even more clearly portrayed here, despite the fact that the character is in many ways tied to a theatrical convention, that of the saucy servant. There may well be a reference to sexual provocation even in her name—*Malaperte*, but to dispel any doubt, the farce opens with a canzonetta which is much more explicit:

> There once was a pretty little tomboy girl,
> Who wanted to learn love's games:
> One day on her own
> From Venus in her room,
> She learned a pretty trick or two...

The same cheeky mischievous tone characterises the seduction scene: almost immediately, however, a troublesome problem arises, and takes hold of things until finally it dominates the scene which follows.

The girl was afraid of becoming pregnant, and she asked her master for guarantees that her honour would be safeguarded. The vaudeville turns into melodrama, as soon as we learn that the dreaded event has become a reality. While the *badin* wavers between vanity and virile complacency for having made her pregnant on the one hand, and fear of the unpredictable reprisals by his wife, the girl despairs, and sets out the stages which her disgrace will take: dishonour is regularly followed by expulsion from the family—that is, sacking, which can only be avoided by a marriage arranged at the master's expense. Without this, the dishonoured girl must consider herself at the mercy of the sexual violence of anyone who comes along, and will very probably be destined for prostitution.

According to a study by Jacques Rossiaud, the French cities of the Renaissance were infested with gangs of young louts who roamed around virtually unpunished. They came from the best families and were organised in Confraternities (needless to say, these too were 'jolly'); they went in for the practice of rape with mindless frequency. This was not without the compliance of the civic authorities, who imposed only the condition that the violence should be visited exclusively on the most defenceless women, from the weakest and most alienated ranks of society. The women who were branded 'dishonest' by public reputation had little hope of mercy. If the girl was also a maid who had been dismissed, the rape was more often than not merely the preliminary to the brothel. As the girl in the farce constantly repeats, the step from *fille déshonorée* to *fille perdue* is very short indeed. Since this was the way things were, her hatred for her master who has made her pregnant can be seen as a true and realistic portrayal.

Crespinette, the wife of the *badin*, is rich on her own account, just like the wife of the merchant of Troyes. Like her she is ingenuous, and moreover, very devout. She goes off on a pilgrimage leaving her husband and the maid together, since she considers him to be above reproach. She comes back again and embraces them both happily, sure that they are equally glad to see her back; she brings little holy images for her husband and in moments of crisis she mechanically repeats pious phrases quite devoid of sense. Furthermore, she talks like a pious little novice, and hardly utters a sentence which does not include invocations of the Virgin, of Christ and the saints. Devout imprecation is, in fact, a constant characteristic of all the farces, and in contrast with the *novella*, this form tends to shift the polemical and anti-religious content from the doctrinal plane to a purely verbal one. The blasphemous effect is perhaps more external and superficial, but it is certainly more evident. "Faith which I owe to the Virgin, come here!" exclaims the *badin*, right in the middle of his amorous ecstasies; the appeal is in fact addressed to the maid. When he is feigning woe for his fake pregnancy, he calls to witness half a dozen saints (St Genevieve, St Blaise, St Roche, St Hubert, St Michael and St Tytenert), while his wife comforts him, and counsels him to bear all with resignation, recalling the pains suffered by Christ.

Again, the saints, the Madonna and God Himself, aid the Doctor in all the dialogues which he carries on with his crony's wife, with the sole intention of embroiling her in the game. Such insistence on the vocabulary of piety has obvious purposes of parody, as the openly blasphemous conclusion of the farce clearly demonstrates: "Don't forget to make love together diligently", Crespinette admonishes her husband and the maid, "while I go and pray God for you!"

The *badin*, therefore, can dismiss the audience with his final oath: "I pray Jesu to enable us by His grace to deceive the Evil One who is so full of lust". The contrast between the extra-marital sex and the catholic morality which prohibits it could hardly be more clearly expressed. On this point, the real ideological focus of the farce, the scene of the dialogue between the doctor and the *badin* is the definitive one: "A man seems to me to be stupid indeed if he allows his marriage to be broken up", the Doctor says sententiously when he hears the news that the maid is pregnant. But he immediately accepts the excuse put forward by the *badin* as sufficient justification "My wife was away on pilgrimage and I couldn't hold out any longer". There is no morality which can stand up in the face of the impelling sexual drive of the male, then: if the wife is away, the maid must provide.

Colmar and Freiburg, which today are separated by the Rhine frontier, were part of the same political and linguistic community in the sixteenth century, in that they both belonged to the Germanic Holy Roman Empire. The first is a great wine-marketing centre for the Alsace region, while the second is the heart of the Baden mining industry. Jörg Wickram, a German-language writer, was born and lived in Colmar, where he was librarian and secretary to the City Senate; however, it is in Freiburg that he sets his droll story of the pregnant man, which is included in his *Rollwagenbuchlein* (the little book on wheels). The intrigue is essentially the same as that of the story of the merchant of Troyes, and of the Rouen farce, with some minor variants of little significance. The pregnant man here is a rich senator of the city, married for fifteen years to a woman who has not succeeded in giving him an heir, and who has hurled the charge of sterility back in his face. To prove the contrary and to assure himself at least of some sort of progeny, he makes the chambermaid pregnant, and then finds himself in trouble with the city statutes which punish adultery with banishment from all city offices. The doctor finds the solution, and it is the one we are already familiar with: the baby is born, and the wife recognises him as her own. But how, she asks the doctor, can it be that the pregnancy has only lasted twenty weeks? Simple, explains the great medical trickster; "we must surely also take account of the previous twenty weeks of your husband's pregnancy!"

Jörg Wickram was no great story-teller, but his story had just as much popular success as the others. From Strasbourg, where the little travelling book was first printed in 1555, it journeyed on and turned up again far away in both space and time, and in three cardinal directions— north, east and south. In 1583 it found its way into a Frankfurt collection of droll tales, and later on it was translated into Dutch and printed in Amsterdam in a collection dated 1680. First of all, however, it arrived in Nuremberg, where in 1556 our indefatigable cobbler was whittling away at his knotty *Knittelvers*. Wickram was to Colmar what Sachs was to Nuremberg; both were *Meistersinger*, and long-standing friends. What one wrote the other read, and sometimes even re-wrote. Thus Sachs put Wickram's stories into verse, while obviously adding his own contribution to them as well. He presents us with no preamble, with the chambermaid already pregnant by her master. The latter has a lot to worry about, because in Constance, (the city to which Sachs transferred our tale on the wings of fantasy), the punishment prescribed for adultery was a great deal more serious than at Freiburg. Even though the two cities are not very far apart, the Alpine lake city of Constance was the seat of a Prince-Bishop, and the legislation on good conduct must therefore be far more severe. Sachs knew this, and he knew that the penalty for adultery in Constance was no less than death. From this fate his hero is naturally saved by the providential help of his friend the doctor, who convinces the wife to be kind and let her husband make love to the virgin, thus 'freeing himself' of his pregnancy.

As can be seen, the two German versions of our little tale differ from the French one on only one significant point: the anti-religious polemic which in the French version is so specific and so fierce seems to disappear here. The Christian morality of mutual marital fidelity is in fact transposed here from the religious plane to the juridical one. It is the civil law which punishes the adulterer as severely as the adulteress, and it is in relation to this same law that our two gallant heroes are so concerned to regain for the man that freedom for which woman alone must pay the price. The reasons for this difference are to be sought in the new situation brought on by the Protestant Reformation, which had a far greater effect in Germany than in France. For Protestants, marriage was no longer a sacrament, and the custody of marital morality could now safely be left in the hands of the state authorities. This did not involve any risk, because in Germany (as Marx was later to assert in *The Jewish Question*) the State "recognises Christianity as its foundation", and is "theological *ex professo*". It does not exist as a political state. In effect, the *Constitutio criminalis Bambergensis*, which provided the frame of reference for a variety of local legislative systems, provided in its Article 145 for punishments for the adulterer even more severe than for the adulteress—not excluding even decapitation if the denunciation were made by the wronged husband. If there was no wronged husband, on the other hand, and the adultery was committed by a married man with an unmarried woman—thus involving 'only' a wronged *wife*—matters changed, and the guilty person no longer incurred the death penalty. He could, however, be sentenced to banishment, the pillory or a whipping, and he was always branded with infamy and automatically barred from any public office he might hold. The initiative in making the denunciation was granted to the betrayed husband as well as to the betrayed wife, but in the absence of this, if the matter was one of public concern, the Magistrate's Office was obliged to intervene.

The *Constitutio criminalis Carolina* which followed the *Bambergensis* confirmed all its provisions in Article 120. The two major Imperial

Constitutions thus closely followed the prescriptions of catholic morality. "The Christian religion condemns adultery in both sexes with equal justice", we read in the *Decretum* of Gratian (II.XXXII.V.23). It is no coincidence, then that our friends Wickram and Sachs—who were both Protestants, transferred the action of their stories to two staunchly Catholic cities—Freiburg and Constance. By this move they intended to achieve two results simultaneously: to justify the supremacy of man over woman in questions of adultery, and to reject the old catholic acquiescence of the Imperial authorities towards the Church of Rome. The anti-religious polemic thus became anti-confessional, but it still pursued the basic objective of an adjustment of Christian sexual morality to the sexual demands of the male at the expense of the female.

In France, where the Reformation did not have the same degree of social or political force as in Germany, the same operation had to take a rather different route, particularly because the monarchy embarked at a certain point on the opposite road to that followed by the Empire. The first royal edict aimed at breaking the ecclesiastical monopoly even in matters of marriage dates to 1556. It provided that the juridical institutes could deal with the issue according to its own laws. Thus began a trend which should logically have led to the complete secularisation of marriage, viewed as a mere contract, and no longer as a sacrament. "The law considers marriage only as a civil contract" declared the French Constitution of 1791, the crowning point of this development (T.II.Article 7). We can discover what reservations there were as far as women were concerned in this development from a glance at the *Encyclopédie*, the real compendium of contemporary culture, compiled from a secular and 'progressive' standpoint, naturally. "At present", we read under the heading 'adultery', "in the majority of European countries, adultery is not considered a crime of public concern. Only the husband can accuse the wife; the Public Prosecutor may not, unless the affair has given rise to great scandal. Moreover, if the husband who infringes marital fidelity is as guilty as the wife, it is not permitted, even so, for the latter to accuse him, nor to pursue him for this crime".

It is worth mentioning here that the Marquis de Sade promised women quite a different freedom from that of accusing their husbands of adultery: "I wish that the law granted them the right to give themselves to as many men as they wish; I wish that they should be permitted the enjoyment of all sexes and all parts of their bodies just as men are, and under the clause allowing them the right to grant themselves to anyone who desires them, they should also have the freedom to enjoy for themselves all those whom they deem worthy of satisfaction." Towards the end of the eighteenth century, then, all the terms of secular morality are defined, even if only by implication. It is a secular morality, but no less arrogant and coercive than its predecessor, and it was to dominate the sexual life of Europe until very close to our own times. This 'civic' sexual morality, as Freud was to call it in his well-known essay of 1908, hinged on monogamous sexual behaviour, but was much more respectful of "the natural diversity of the two sexes", and therefore disposed to punish the transgressions of the man less seriously, and thus to admit, *de facto*, a double morality for men and women". The four sixteenth century literary versions of the motif of the pregnant man are thus in perfect harmony with this double morality. One might even say that they actually anticipate all its most essential elements. They overturn the folklore motif by presenting a rationalised version of it in which all the ridicule of credulity falls exclusively on the woman. The link between the pregnant man and the fool, which is present in all the earlier versions, is broken with here for the first time: the fool is no longer Calandrino, who believes himself pregnant, but his wife who believes that he is so. Boccaccio, then, created a whole European school, and as so often happens, the disciples have outstripped the master.

At this point we should ask ourselves, not just for philological reasons, about the relationships which exist between these texts. The only connection of dependency which we can establish for certain is in the tale by Sachs, which is derived from that of Wickram. We can, however, exclude direct links for any of the three other texts. Nothing exists to prove that Nicole was aware of the farce, or that the lawyers of Rouen had read his story. It seems even more unlikely that Wickram had any knowledge of either of the other texts. But the issue is complicated still further by the existence of a popular story of the fifteenth century, by the Italian humanist Ludovico Carbone, which provides us with an invaluable link in the chain connecting the *novella* about Calandrino's pregnancy to the four sixteenth century versions. The text is as follows:

"A Doctor of Law had been taken ill and the Doctor of Medicine asked to see his urine. As his young servant had spilled it in haste, she substituted her own for it. The doctor gave a laugh and said: 'This illness will have a happy outcome; our friend will be giving birth before long:' The maidservant, you see, was pregnant. The lawyer, very perturbed by this news, turned to his wife: 'I told you, wife; you always want to be on top. Now see what peril you've put me into—I'm going to have a child!'" As we can see, the master's desire for the maid has not yet become the mainspring of the action, and the link between the pregnant man and the fool remains intact. However, for the first time there are four characters in the story, and with the same social positions as they will have in the tales of the next century: the Doctor of Law and master of the house; his wife, the doctor and the maid.

A native of Cremona, Ludovico Carbone lived most of his life at Ferrara, as tutor to the Estense family and professor of rhetoric at the University. His collection of droll stories was published in 1900 for the first time, using the only surviving manuscript. They had no written diffusion, then, unlike the Troyes story and the Rouen farce, but the latter must depend on them to some extent. The question is, how? The most likely explanation is that all these texts in fact depend on the same oral tradition, to be found in the educated and semi-educated context of the cities of western Europe. That this is indeed so is confirmed by the fact noted by the Germanist of the nineteenth century, Heinrich Kurz, that our tale in the version recorded by Wickram was still being told in the eighteenth century—but as a real event which was supposed to have happened to a certain Michael Schüppach, famous for his miraculous cures and the talk of half of Europe. He even induced curious travellers like Goethe to go and seek him out without any need for his cures. It is a tale in transformation, then, at this stage; passing from city to city from the lips of a merchant to the ears of an artisan, from there to the mouth of a lawyer, and now ending up at the pen of some more or less dilettante writer who was capable of writing it down and preserving it at a particular moment of its circulation.

The fact that we can only know it today by reading it in well-defined versions which always have the particular stamp of a specific author should not mislead us: behind the story there is always a collective creativity, rooted in uneducated or semi-educated people, which entrusted itself above all to the medium of oral transmission. So far we have studied the particular literary versions of this creative tradition, closely linked to their specific historical contexts. On the basis of the Saussurian distinction between *word* and *language*, however, it is also possible to study its overall structure, as Bogatyrev and Jakobson proposed to do in the article already mentioned.

The sources of action are effectively the same in all our texts: a strong measure of aggressiveness towards his wife on the part of the husband; he resents her for demanding that he should be faithful to her. Extra-marital sex is considered an inalienable right of the male in all four cases, though for differing reasons. Neither the moral law nor that of the state can refuse to recognise it The hostility therefore originates with the wife and with Christian morality, and extends to the Imperial law which backs the woman in her claims by prohibiting and condemning adultery on the part of the man as well as that of the woman. This violent hostility is explained in terms of a precise historical situation which saw a strong revival of the religious spirit (the Reformation and

Counter-Reformation were already spreading throughout Europe), and in terms of the strong repressive counter-thrust of christian morality. The civic society of western Europe in its Renaissance flowering had codified a social practice which was in many ways to legitimise the privileges of man over woman. It had no intention of abandoning a single iota of it to the Christian threat which was once again making itself felt.

In Costnicz ein reicher purger pulet sein maid: In Constance, a rich citizen makes love to his maid. This is the verse with which Sachs' story begins. The pregnant man does not, therefore, have the specific social connotations he has in at least two of the other sixteenth century versions. A merchant in the *novella* of Nicole of Troyes, and a senator in the city of Wickram's story, in the Rouen farce he takes on the comic role of the *badin*, behind which, however, we can easily spot the figure of the rich citizen, identical with the protagonist of Sachs' story. The social designation varies between that of the man's profession (merchant) or his public responsibilities (senator), and the more general and abstract qualification of 'a rich citizen'.

The German term *Bürger* ('purger' is merely a sixteenth century phonetical variant), which we have translated literally as 'citizen', conveys a number of other meanings which may help us to give a more precise physiognomy to the person concerned and the text which deals with him. In the *Deutsches Wörterbuch* of the Brothers Grimm, under the entry *Bürger*, we read: originally an inhabitant of the castle, in contrast to one from the countryside", and examples are cited from texts in Middle High German, such as the *Nibelungenlied* and *Parzifal* (twelfth and thirteenth centuries) "Then inhabitants of the town, without relation to the castle, as opposed to the nobles and knights or to the peasantry and country folk". Numerous passages follow from Luther's translation of the Bible. And we have reached our destination; but it may be as well to go on a little, since we then find: "*Bürger Civis*, extended to all the subjects or legitimate component members of a country, kingdom or state, according to the idea of the *Civis Romanus*, which extended well beyond the walls of the city. The Roman expression was very soon translated by *Bürger*, which became current usage in this sense by the early sixteenth century". A quotation from the famous Lutheran translation of the Bible follows. As we see, the word *Bürger* employed by Sachs, had three distinct meanings by the early sixteenth century, when the Bible was translated: one was topographical and distinguished the inhabitants of the town from those of the country; one was social and showed the inhabitants of the city as a homogeneous group with a common status and in counterposition to the other groups, and the third was a political sense, recognising a juridical title and confirming rights to the exercise of power. The three meanings all recur regularly in our four sixteenth-century texts, of which Sachs' story represents a kind of unconscious compendium. The city and the social condition of its inhabitants are the essential basis of the narrative in all four variants, which allow discreet references to filter through here and there to the riches of the mercantile economy which lies behind the story. Only in one of the stories is the hero actually a merchant (the Troyes version), but the mentality of all four characters in all four variants is consistently mercantile. They live and breathe, in effect in the urban climate of an economy based on the exchange of goods and services, and all of them believe that they can exchange and turn virtually everything into coinage: sexual favours, honour, fidelity and virtue. The only explicit reference to the political organisation of the city is found in Wickram's story, in which the hero is a senator, and in which there is reference to the city statutes which punish adultery. The civic political framework always lies beneath the surface in the other texts, however, and the drama is closely linked with power and rights. The power of man over woman is translated into the power of husband over wife and master over maid. Each of these powers is exercised legitimately through the juridical order of the city and its statutes. The three meanings of *Bürger*, therefore, live side by side here, and they are closely associated in the person of the same character, who lives in the city, gets rich, and exercises rights. The rich semantic content of the word *Bürger* was effectively reflected in the historical situation in Germany and Europe in those times, when the 'bourgeois' was such by virtue of certain rights which derived from the fact that he belonged to a citizen community which admitted him to the exercise of a profession and economic activity, and allowed him to take part in public affairs. Along with this precise historical origin, the word has retained its semantic ambiguity in German, but has inevitably lost the strict link to the historical situation which it once possessed. With respect to his historic past, the *Bürger* or *bourgeois* of today suggests very varied connotations in economic, social and political terms. His morality, however, has remained unchanged, at least until the threshold of the most recent period, because what Freud called "civic sexual morality" is nothing other than "bourgeois morality", as our sixteenth century texts present it.

The first distinctive trait of that morality is very clearly its secular character: it no longer makes any reference to divine revelation, but entrusts itself to a code of autonomous values which contain their own justification. The autonomy of the will which makes laws for itself is the great Kantian discovery; a second Copernican revolution which restores man to the centre of the universe, just as the first one had done with the sun.

In the *Leçon d'éthique*, in the paragraph entitled "Of duties towards the body in relation to sexual impulses", we read the following: "Since sexuality is not an inclination which one being feels towards another as a human being, but an inclination towards sex itself, it represents a degradation of human nature, a motive for preferring one sex to the other, and for dishonouring it by procuring satisfaction of the impulse. The inclination which a man feels towards a woman does not concern her inasmuch as she is part of humanity, but inasmuch as she is *woman*; thus to a man the humanity of a woman is a matter of indifference, and only sex is here the object of the inclination." Thus sexual impulse puts humanity in danger of being reduced to the level of animality". Shameful and pernicious though it might seem, sex did not, however, cease to play its indispensable role in ensuring the survival of the species. Therefore it was necessary to come to terms with it, and for that purpose there was the ancient institution of marriage. "Marriage is a contract between two people, through which they reciprocally recognise the same rights, with the intention of entrusting their whole person to the other so as to acquire full rights over the person of the other" We are now in a position to understand how a *commercium sexuale* is possible without degrading humanity and infringing the laws of morality. Thus, "marriage constitutes the unique condition for giving way to one's sexual impulse". But doesn't this have a rather familiar ring? To an impertinent critic who reproached him with not having established "any new principle of morality, but merely a new formula", the philosopher replied irritatedly in the *Critique of Practical Reason*: "Who would pretend to introduce a new principle for all morality, and to be virtually the first to have discovered it? As if the world had been ignorant of what duty was before he came along, or as if it had been in universal error in this matter?" We shall understand more clearly what he meant if we pass on to the next paragraph of *Ethical Lessons*, dedicated to the *crimina carnis*, where we find spelled out everything— or virtually everything—which is to be found in christian sexual theology. Beginning with the postulate that "as far as sex is concerned, the aim of humanity is the preservation of the species without degrading one's person", Kant defines as *crimen carnis* every form of sexuality which departs from this intention—concubinage and adultery as well as onanism, homosexuality and bestiality. The three latter are *crimina carnis contra naturam*—"degrading human nature to a level lower than that of the animals and thus rendering man unworthy of humanity".

However, it was not only horror of sexuality and the untouchable principle of reciprocity which Kant—counted among the greatest champions of the secular liberal conscience of western Europe— inherited from christianity. He also inherited the radical *aporia* which is at the heart of this principle and eventually corrodes and destroys it. In his treatise on the *General Doctrine of Law*, after having repeated the conception of marriage as reciprocal possession ("the union of two persons of different sex for the mutual possession of their sexual faculties during the whole of their lives"), he asks himself the question: "whether there is a contradiction, as such, between the equality of those who marry and the law which says to the woman with regard to the man: "He shall be your master" (i.e he shall be the party who commands and she the party who obeys). The reply is unambiguous: "But this should not be considered as contrary to the natural equality of partners in marriage, because this dominion is founded only on the natural superiority of the faculty of men over that of women in the aim of procuring the common interest of the family, and the right of command which derives from it for the man. Since this dominion may be derived from the same duty of unity and equality with regard to the ultimate aim". Thus the exception in favour of the man which the rule of mutual respect had seemed ruthlessly to exclude, comes creeping back through the window after having been kicked out of the door. There never *can* be genuine reciprocity between servant and master, and neither can there be between men and women as long as one is considered superior to the other. Thus secular morality, in the long run, is bourgeois morality, and bourgeois morality is christian morality, thinly disguised and re-adjusted.

An anonymous German woodcut of the beginning of the seventeenth century presents an overall view in several scenes of bourgeois domestic life (Figure 20). The sequence begins with a man dressed in cloak and hat who is entering his house from outside. He comes forward in stately fashion with his hand raised in benediction—a gesture we easily recognise as identical with that of the Eternal Father which confers the seal of omnipotence on the figure of God in representations of the Birth of Eve. The man heads towards the centre of the picture, where the principal scene is taking place—the one which gives its title to the woodcut: *Domestic harmony ensured by the governance of the Husband.* Right in the foreground, a woman is kneeling with her elbows resting on a stool and her hands joined in a gesture of prayer. Her face, three-quarters turned, expresses shame and affliction; her eyes are lowered. The man has now taken off his cloak, but he is wearing the same hat and has the same facial traits as the other who is entering the house. It is thus clear that he is a duplicate of the same figure, and that he is meant to be the woman's husband. And in this quality, in fact, he has raised her skirt and is thrashing her backside with a birchrod. Husband and wife are arranged in a position which reminds us of the interrelation of the bodies of the men and women in the iconographical scheme of the

Figure 20 Domestic Harmony ensured by the Rule of the Husband.

Birth of Eve, as it became defined after the 'Christian euphemism' was introduced. Now however there is a change of position: the man is standing and the woman is kneeling before him. In the other man entering the house and giving a blessing we recognise the third member of the ancient trio, but this time with some updating: Adam has in fact woken up; he has stood up and clothed himself; he has put on his hat and taken up the rod of chastisement. He is now master in all effects; he has no longer any need of divine delegation. He can do very well without God, even to the point of directly taking His place in the supreme command. The morality which ensures domestic harmony is represented in the woodcut by the two scenes in the background: in one, we see the well-equipped kitchen with its plates and wooden implements, with the fire burning in the oven and the wife cooking meat on the spit, and offering her husband a piece. In the other, the couple are seated at the table enjoying a game of cards. Naturally, the children and the dog also come into this scene of domestic harmony. But they look warily at the rod, because they know that at the first opportunity, it will be their turn to feel its blows.

.

Chapter 5
Wife versus Husband

The theme of the pregnant man also recurs in the great oriental collection of tales known as *The Thousand and One Nights*: the *Tale of the Kadih who bore a child* is certainly derived from oral tradition, which appeared in written form at a later period; precisely when is difficult to establish. The conflict between the man and the woman takes place here in the context of the institution of marriage, and ranges the wife against her husband. The tale goes as follows:

Harun el-Rashid, the fabulous Abbasid Khalif of Baghdad, has installed as Kadih in Tripoli in Syria a man afflicted by incurable avarice. Compelled by Islamic custom, which takes a highly unfavourable view of bachelordom, he has to marry, but refuses to change his habits of avarice and frugality. He answers his wife's protests, when she is reduced to the extremes of hunger, by cutting off her nose and repudiating her; he also seizes the dowry which should in reality revert to her. The story is repeated with several other wives, until the infamy of his vicious practice even reaches Mosul. There a beautiful and enterprising young woman decides to avenge her sex. For this purpose she moves to Tripoli, dazzles the Kadih with her beauty, and allows him to marry her. As soon as she arrives in the miser's home, she finds out the secret hiding place of his treasure and she begins to extract sums from it in order to change the eating habits of the household. Instead of the meagre meals of dry biscuit and onions with which he used to starve his wives and his concubine slaves, succulent dishes now appear on the table, which the woman claims are provided by the generosity of her family. The miser accepts this as a valid explanation, and greedily gobbles up the food which his wife offers him, believing it to be free. The wife provides for his greed without stinting, even to the point of inviting other women from the neighbourhood to

211

join the feast too, and one in particular, a very poor woman with a number of children who is expecting yet another one soon. This neighbour's pregnancy provides her with the chance to play a clever trick on her husband at his own expense.

Having agreed things beforehand with the pregnant woman, she prepares a delicious plate of beans as the pregnancy approaches, and serves it to her husband with her usual generosity. He gobbles the beans up until he is near bursting-point, without thinking about the terrible indigestion which is inevitably going to follow. With his belly swollen and painful, he wakes up during the night, groaning and pleading desperately for help. This is exactly what his wife has been expecting: she massages his great paunch with a real midwife's skill, declaring in appropriate solemn tones that the birth of a child is imminent. Followed by the neighbour (who has in the meantime given birth), she reappears carrying a copper bowl and places it to receive the huge intestinal discharge which he is about to release. Then she presents him triumphantly with her neighbour's newly-born baby, which has been hidden in her sleeve. She ascribes the miracle of male parturition to the intervention of Divine Omnipotence, always so inscrutable to mortal eyes. The Kadih doesn't dare doubt, but he is immediately fearful for the consequences of such a serious event on his reputation. He feels a profound sense of shame, and in order to avoid the scandal which he is convinced is inevitable, he flees to Damascus, where he will lead a very dismal life of obscurity. Now unquestionably mistress of the situation, the woman of Mosul happily makes the best of her husband's treasure, distributing it in gifts to her neighbours, and not forgetting the ex-wives, who all recover their dowries. When the news of the flight of the Kadih and the generosities of his wife reach Baghdad, the Khalif summons her before him. He promises that she shall not be punished, insists on hearing the whole story of the deceit, and laughs his head off. Meanwhile the Kadih also arrives at the Khalif's court disguised as a beggar, and when his wife recognises him, he declares himself to be reformed, promises to change his ways, and asks to be restored to his roles as husband and judge. However, the woman doesn't trust his promises (the sons of Adam, she says, are not in the habit of changing their ways), and she insists on having it all in writing, with the Khalif's seal and guarantee. On these conditions she agrees to take her husband back. He will be transferred as judge to another town.

As we can see, the social background of this tale is closely tied to the condition of women in the Islamic East. It is particularly concerned with the judicial institutions, which do so much to sanction the inferiority and degradation of the condition of women, recognising the husband's right to repudiate his wife as and when he sees fit, even

without any real motive, simply by the fact of making public his wish to
do so. As a special mitigation of this, at least in economic terms, the
Koranic law retains the right of the repudiated wife to take back the
marital dowry, which her husband was obliged to provide in her favour,
paying it over at the moment of their marriage. "It is not just to take
back for yourself what you have given", the Koran declares (II: 229), to
husbands who repudiate their wives. And a famous fourteenth century
jurist, Halil Ibn Ishaq, recommended that a "consolatory gift" should
be awarded to repudiated women, in proportion to their husband's
wealth. But our miserly Kadih will hear nothing of such expensive
consolations. The very man appointed by the Khalif to see to it that the
laws are upheld, only the Kadih was recognised as a competent judge in
the sphere of family rights, which are those with which our story is
concerned. He was a magistrate who generally wore clerical robes, and
was chosen by the Khalif from among those doctors of the law with the
highest reputation for integrity of behaviour, to make judgements based
on Koranic law. The ideal target for feminine attacks on judicial
authority, the Kadih is presented from the outset as unmistakably a
miser. The whole tale is told in the anal register, which develops as it
goes along in a whole series of equivalents: avarice, frugality and
continence are all assimilated to the same class, and make up a single
feature, even though of course the frugality and the continence are in a
way also the *products* of avarice. In order to cut household expenses, the
Kadih contents himself with eating dry biscuits and onions, and with
limiting his harem to an ugly and charmless black slave (who looks like
a buffalo, says the narrative), who acts as both concubine and duenna.
Obviously continence was not much of a problem with such a woman.
This pattern of life, however, comes into conflict with the Kadih's social
position. A judge of his authority could not dedicate himself to celibacy
in defiance of the precepts of the Koran (XXIV: 32), which
recommended matrimony to all believers, and even more so to those
who were called upon to see to the observation of the law and to punish
its transgressors. When the court employees point out the incongruity of
his situation, the Kadih cannot deny that they are right. He therefore
seeks to integrate marriage into his old way of life: he accepts the need
to marry, but by starving his wife he leads her to the protests which
provide him with the judicial pretext for repudiating her and at the
same time keeping her dowry. Thus the scheme works out to the great
advantage of his avarice, which remains its basis and its mainspring.
Frugality and continence trail along in its wake.

But avarice, thrift and the hoarding of money lead us unmistakably
back to the pleasure of defecation. It is well-know that psycho-analytical
investigation has established a close connection between avarice and a

serious infantile difficulty in mastering the *incontinentia alvi*, and the fierce resistance sometimes put up by the suckling child which refuses to empty its bowel when the pot is produced because it derives an additional pleasure from defecation. This is confirmed by certain adults who admit that they also found pleasure during later childhood in withholding their faeces. "The original erotic interest in defecation", Freud remarks in his brief note *Character and anal eroticism*, "is destined to become exhausted when the child grows up, but just at that point there begins that interest in money which was lacking in infancy. In this way, the previous tendency which is on the way to losing its *raison d'être*, can easily be transferred to the new object which has just appeared." For this reason, "everywhere where the ancient modes of thought have been or have remained dominant—in ancient civilisations themselves, in myths, fables, superstitions, in unconscious thought, dreams and neuroses, money is always placed in close relation to excrement".

From the first series of avarice, frugality and continence, a second then emerges. Excrement and money appear as its primary elements, but Freud's investigations do not give us many clues as to the third element which goes to complete them. The Viennese doctor traces the path from money to excrement, but he goes no further, and indeed his research is incomplete at that point. The credit goes to Elvio Fachinelli for linking it to a paragraph in the first volume of *Das Kapital*, dedicated to *Treasurisation*, where a complex theoretical knot is untied in some splendid pages of exceptional force. Marx also pointed to an unequivocal mechanism of renunciation/compensation lying at the basis of avarice. But what may seem more surprising to us is the libidinous connotation he seeks to give to the renunciation. His choice of words is precise and carefully considered; he makes use of ecclesiastical language and the sternly prohibitionist terminology of christian morality. "The treasure-hoarder", he writes, "sacrifices his carnal pleasure for the gold fetish. No-one takes the command of the Gospel more seriously than he does!" However, the fetish to which he sacrifices his pleasure promises a generous reward. "What a wonderful thing is gold! He who possesses it is master of all he desires!" exclaims Christopher Columbus, according to Marx's quotation, and he continues "Everything, whether merchandise or not, is transformed into money. Everything becomes saleable or purchasable. Its circulation becomes the great social crucible to which everything rushes in order to be transformed into the crystal of wealth. Not even the bones of the saints resist this alchemy, let alone sacrosanct objects of greater delicacy—the *res sacrosanctae extra commercium hominum*". The choice of money as the object of compensation is explained with strict logic: by the mediation of money, in fact, "social power becomes the private power of the private individual". Beginning with money, Marx thus arrives at power, while Freud stopped at excrement (a point where too many of those who investigate the fate of civilisation find themselves blocked). The second series is now complete: faeces, money and power.

If attachment to money conceals an ambition for power, it is equally true that both of them act as compensations for the renunciation of libidinous instincts which is imposed by society. The basic situation, therefore, is that of the baby forced to make sacrifices to the demands of civilisation ("order and cleanliness are essential demands of society", Freud observes)—the sacrifice, of course, being his free and enjoyable defecations. This means that power sets itself up as civilisation by the general repression of eros. It is not, then, a mere apanage of a particular sphere of society, which can easily be isolated from it (the state or the ruling class)—as its impenitent devotees still seek to make us believe. On the contrary, it lies at the heart of society, intimately mingled with its deepest and most secret mechanisms. This is something that those who have felt the thorn of power penetrating their own flesh have always known.

The woman of Mosul reacts against the pattern of life which joins the authority of judge to that of husband and seals it all with avarice by forcing her husband to defecate. A torrential and salutary intestinal discharge frees the Kadih at one and the same moment of his faeces, his money and his power. The attack proceeds on the lines of a clever strategy which identifies the weak points of his defences one after the other, and exploits all the resources of domestic intimacy which feminine ingenuity can summon. The weapons available to the woman are really very modest, but they are insidious because they involve the domestic hearth: the kitchen is the place where the plot which will lead to the Kadih's downfall is brewed. The masterpiece of this strategy is the rigour with which she locks the man in the grip of anal eroticism, and thus provokes a forced expulsion of what has been held back.

Freud observed in his brief work *Infantile Sexual Theory* that the difficulty of recognising the existence of the vagina induces the child to restrict its view of birth to the anal region. "If the infant grows in the body of the mother and is then expelled from it, this can only happen through the sole available route, provided by the anal aperture. The baby must thus be evacuated like excrement, like faeces." Such a concept does not involve any kind of repulsion for the infant, constitutionally inclined towards coprophilia. In fact it seems quite natural to be born in the midst of excrement, quite devoid of any associations of disgust. "Cloacal theory, which remains valid for so many animals, was the most natural and likely to make sense to the small child. This being so, it was only logical that the male child should not accept the painful privilege of the female to bear children. If children are born through the anal passage then males can give birth just as well as females". "It all works out just as in a fairy story: you eat a certain thing and you then have a baby".

The woman of Mosul drives her husband back towards the past of his infantile beliefs, and she finally nails him there, defenceless. For though cloacal theory may be perfectly acceptable in an infant, it is far less so to an adult. There is total incompatibility between the cloacal theory of childhood and the civil conscience of the adult: to regress to the cloacal theory, in fact, means in the adult case an inevitable backsliding in relation to established values, consecrated by custom, into the ghetto of degradation and inferiority: that same ghetto in which society has imprisoned women since time immemorial. The female revenge, however, does not stop merely at retribution. It goes beyond that, to the roots of the question, revealing a perfect equation between the greater and the lesser, between deficiency and excess. Power is founded on dung, and it is sexual impotence which converts it into social power.

Chapter 6
The Chariot in the Parson's Belly: A French Tale

A parish priest who had been ill for some time decided to go and consult a village healer who lived in a place called Frise. As this woman diagnosed the nature of the illness by inspecting the urine, our Reverend friend duly filled a glass bottle with his; then he called his servant and said: "Catherine, here is a bottle of urine. You must take it and consult the woman of Frise; if she tells you to get some drug or other, call in and buy it when you are passing Albert the Chemist's". Clutching the bottle, the servant went off on the road to Frise. As she was passing through the last village, the poor woman caught her foot on a stone, and fell so badly that she broke the bottle. "Jesu, Maria! What am I to do? What will his Reverence say?"—and she was near to tearing her hair out in despair, but then she had an inspiration. She went into a house nearby and told her story to the good wife of the house—who chanced to be expecting a baby. "It would be a great kindness to me, Madame, if you could find me another bottle and pee in it. His Reverence will never know, and then he won't throw me out". "Nothing simpler; I'll do just as you say" replied the good wife. When it was done, the servant took the bottle, and soon arrived at the Wise Woman's house. "His Reverence has been ill for quite a time, and he's sent me to consult you. Here are twenty francs which he has sent you." The woman examined the bottle, "But this isn't a man's urine", she exclaimed. "What? Oh yes, indeed it is—and his Reverence the Vicar's, no less". "Impossible!" "But I tell you it *is*. Nothing could be truer." "Well, in that case, the Reverend gentleman is carrying a chariot in his

217

belly!" "A chariot! You're joking..." "No, not at all. But it'll be easy enough to cure him. When you pass by Albert the Chemist's, buy two sous' worth of this ointment that I'll write on this paper. When you get back to the Vicarage, tell his Reverence to rub all his lower parts with a piece of linen cloth, and he'll soon be better". So off went the servant and as she passed through the village she made sure to get the two sous' worth of ointment from the druggist. When she got home to the Vicarage, the Parson said to her: "Well, Catherine, what did the woman of Frise have to say?" "Oh don't ask me, your Reverence; she said such an extraordinary thing that I still don't know what she meant". "What sort of thing?" "That you have a chariot inside your belly!" "What? Impossible!" "No, indeed, that was what she said...and I bought two sous' worth of ointment at the druggists, which is supposed to chase that accursed chariot away. You must take a linen cloth and rub it all over your lower parts". The priest lifted up his cassock, unbuttoned his underpants, and began to apply the remedy. But then he turned round and said: "Catherine, you come and rub this grease onto me". "Oh! My heavens, your Reverence, I couldn't even think of such a thing!" "No, come along; don't be shy; anyway, it'll be far better done that way." So the servant did her duty as she was ordered, and began anointing her master's lower parts. All at once, the parson's member sprang up. "Ah, now, your Reverence" she cried; "didn't I tell you you had a chariot in your belly? And look, there you are, the prow is beginning to emerge!"

Chapter 7
Woman versus Doctor

This French fable was collected in the second half of the last century in Picardy, the northern province which borders on Normandy. The exact location was the countryside around the small town of Albert. In this version, as in many other unpublished versions of the tale of the pregnant man, the female healer of folk tradition appears in place of the doctor. This change of roles is of great significance; the healer behaves as a doctor, not as a healer; she undertakes the examination of the patient's urine without establishing any personal relationship with him, prescribes the cure by writing a prescription for the chemist and pockets the fee. No malign spirits, herbal remedies, spells or other paraphernalia of popular medicine. But even though she carries out the function of a doctor and reproduces the ritual acts of his profession, doctor she certainly is not. Her social position, her lack of education and the difference of sex all get in the way; we may be quite sure that there were no women doctors in the French countryside in that period. Woman and medicine were still far removed from each other; and could only be united in the remembrance of that old magical medicine which was already losing much of the credibility it had once possessed.

The presence of the healer, however, does not seem to be motivated by any sterile regret for a past lost beyond recovery. The woman takes back for herself that ancient role of high prestige, and she makes clear that she knows how to exercise it, and according to the modern procedures of scientific medicine. She thus reclaims a professional status which is legitimised by nature and history. But she goes beyond this, for from this reconquered position she goes on to unmask the arrogance of the medical profession, and the perfidy of the person who gives him his orders. Thus we find the woman and the priest face to face in conflict once again. However, the healer does not actually say that the priest is

219

pregnant—which in the other versions is the usual diagnosis (real or pretended) of the doctor. Instead she pulls out of the hat this tale of the cart, which according to her, the parson is carrying in his belly. The cart, widely used all over the French countryside, is a perfect symbol of the association of male and female organs, with its sleeve or prow. According to the healer, then, the real disease of which the parson needs to be cured is *androgyny*, which forces him to live with his domestic servant in the unnatural cohabitation demanded by the vows of chastity. There can only be one cure: the love which, with the help of the woman's prescription, the erection of his member makes evident between the priest and the maid. This is the only relationship which, because of its genuine character, is capable of cancelling the androgynous state and the servitude of the woman which hides behind it.

But the healer's story of the cart in the priest's belly reveals another important card in her game. She also implies that the man falls easily into the trap of believing himself pregnant because he is impelled in that direction by his anxiety to keep the woman subject to his control. Diagnosis of male pregnancy, therefore, is a matter for men, for doctors, not for women. This is the reason why in this story, where the woman healer has taken the place of the doctor, the examination does not reveal a pregnancy but the androgyny of the man and the domination-relationship which underlies it.

The male desire to control the female faculty of procreation is so strong that it flourishes even in places where it would be least suspected: in that same field of academic medicine whose scientific credentials are guaranteed by the stern refusal of all mythological claims. A very instructive chapter in the history of scientific attempts to give body to the fantasy of the Pregnant Man has recently been provided by Pierre Darmon in his book *The Myth of Procreation in the Baroque age*. The chapter concerns the eighteenth century exclusively, and it can hardly fail to astonish us with the fertility of the baroque imagination, which finds its place even in the century of Enlightenment. Amply backed up by reports and certificates proving the veracity of the facts and the assertions, the surgical interventions and the autopsies and dissections, the debate centres around a variety of cases which occurred during the century, in which obscure but courageous doctors took part alongside the flower of professional celebrity, such as the anatomist Pierre Dionis and the surgeon Jean-Louis Petit, both luminaries of a number of academies of medicine. It goes without saying that despite the ingenuity of many of the scientific arguments, they do not in fact succeed in proving the assumptions!

The culmination of such comico-heroic attempts was not reached until 1804, the momentous year of the proclamation of the Code Napoleon. On 12th July Stendhal, then only twenty but already knowledgeable in the ways of the world, recorded in his diary: "According to the *Journal de Paris*, it is possible that a man may bring forth a child and that both of them may survive. The event took place in Holland". The Dutch case was in fact already old news; it dated back more than fifty years and the Paris journal had recorded it as an important precedent on the occasion of another case which had taken place just at that time in Verneuil, a town in Normandy not far from Paris. Dr Jean-François Verdier Heurtin dedicated a learned dissertation to this case. However, the pregnant lad of Verneuil died of his pregnancy, while the Dutchman of fifty years earlier had borne a living male child and remained in good health himself. What more could any man ask?

A few decades earlier even Diderot had allowed himself to be carried away by the dream of the pregnant man. In his *Eléments de la Physiologie*, a great compendium of notes and material from a huge variety of sources, he reproduced a summarised report of one of these cases from a Gazette. He made no comment, and we do not know to what extent he saw clearly what would later be apparent to the naturalist Geoffroy Sainte-Hilaire, that the case involved a hermaphrodite possessed of female generative organs in more or less complete form. An amusing detail, which may not be purely a matter of chance is that Diderot's pregnant man is a soldier, but the one mentioned by Sainte-Hilaire is a monk—and a flesh-and-blood monk, not the usual fictional one of the folklore tradition. This surprising link between reality and fantasy had been demonstrated as far back as the fifteenth century in connection with another monk, in a poem by Jean Molinet:

> I have seen, all joking aside,
> a young monk living who had both,
> male and female organs.
> He conceived within himself,
> by himself a real child,
> engendered it and gave it birth,
> just as other women do
> without any borrowed help.

Chapter 8
Excursus: Woman as Castrator

Between Montivilliers and Fécamp, buried away in a deep valley which runs down to the sea, Tournevent, a village of a few houses, seems to bend to the force of the winds, as its name implies. We are on the Norman coast, beaten by the "hard and salty sea breeze which corrodes and burns like fire, and dries up and destroys like the frosts of winter". It is in such places, dear to Maupassant's childhood and the favourite setting for his stories, that he sets the tale of 'Toine' which bears the name of its main character.

Antoine Mâchelbé, the village café-owner, is famous throughout the surrounding district for his corpulence, as well as for his joviality and his exceptional drinking capacities. Huge and fat, he "ate and drank like ten normal people", and there was no quantity of food and drink which could satisfy him. He would have been capable of drinking up the sea, joked the habitués of his café. His wife was as tall as he, but in contrast skinny and scrawny. She spent all her time breeding chickens, and fattening them up for the pleasure of the village gourmands, her devoted customers. She was as quarrelsome and discontented as her husband was jovial and good-natured. They had been married for thirty years but they had no children: the drama of sterility yoked them to the same cart. For him, naturally, it was his wife's fault; in their daily rows he let this be known without any shadow of doubt, and their rows were the talk of the village. "My plank", he calls her, with obvious cruel reference to her physical appearance; *planche* is in fact a metaphor for flat, and is only used for a woman who is 'as flat as a plank', meaning that she has no breasts and is thus no good for lovemaking or for bearing children.

Naturally the wife is of the opposite opinion, and regularly calls her husband a *faignant* do-nothing) or a *propre à rien* (good-for-nothing). According to Butler, author of studies on popular parlance in the works of Maupassant, *faignant* is "the worst epithet known to the Norman speech". Coupled with *propre à rien* it expresses the highest degree of contempt; the good-for-nothing wastrel is the man who is no man, the man who lacks virility, in other words, the impotent. The game of exchange of insults between the man and the woman, impotence for sterility, goes beyond the normal bounds of cruelty in this tale, which makes it clear right from the start that it is a kind of figurative castration-drama. The wife who accuses her husband of impotence is in reality the one who is responsible for it; the actual agent of castration. Her portrait as the female castrator is drawn by the writer with meticulous care, though he does it by suggestion and implication, without ever stating it specifically; it is no less forceful a portrait for that.

The woman's appearance is sketched as soon as she is first presented: "She was a tall peasant woman who walked with great loping strides; her head, crowning a skinny, flat body, was that of an infuriated tawny owl". Rage is her dominant psychological trait, in fact; from the time of her marriage she has done nothing but quarrel with her husband. "Irritated with the whole world, she took it out above all on Toine. She detested him for his cheerfulness, his reputation as a good-natured fellow, his health and his fatness". She cursed him more than anything else for his voracity, his constant filling of his gut without ever being satisfied, which made him seem like a pig. This woman who passed her whole time fattening chickens, never ceased likening her husband to a pig. Chickens and pigs, as we all know, are stock animals which it is customary to castrate in order to render them fatter and more strongly flavoured. So the woman who fattens the chickens with so much enthusiasm, is the same one who fattens up her husband by making his food for him. the human-animal parallel is clear: the fattening of the man, like that of the chickens and pigs, reminds us of the castration which is its cause. The method is the classic one of metonymy: cause is suggested by effect, so castration is indicated by fatness. The body of the man is thus presented as a container, a recipient enclosing a void which it is impossible to fill, in that it is produced by an irreparable lack.

But while the husband is likened to the chickens and pigs, the wife resembles animals which are even less likeable, and of a completely different nature: a stilt-walker as far as her legs are concerned, a tawny owl in the face and a barn-own in the eyes (later on he will say of her that she 'fixed one with her owl's gaze'). In the first case the analogy refers only to the length of her legs, but in the second two cases it has far greater significance of a specifically psychological kind. This is confirmed by the *Grand dictionnaire universel du XIX siècle*—the Larousse Encyclopedia of Maupassant's time—where under the item *chat-huant* we find that these rapacious birds of prey are perfectly equipped for night-hunting; they have large heads with enormous eyes and dilated pupils, with very sharp claws and a powerful beak capable of inflicting deep wounds. Their general physiognomy is described as 'hideous', and it is said that they are used figuratively to describe a person who has 'an ugly face or a fierce and savage character'. The barn own is described as having very similar characteristics. To illustrate its figurative significance, however, the dictionary refers to an actual character in the *Mysteries of Paris*, by Eugène Sue. He is referred to as "one of those really repulsive types of the hideous world conjured up by the great novelist...one feels a desire to stamp out this bird of ill-omen, which torments for pleasure...and yet one realises that the owl has been copied in real life...the word *chouette* has passed into popular parlance to describe a woman who combines in herself some of the worst features of Eugène Sue's fictional character."

The zoological and figurative reference-points of Maupassant's analogy, then, were already well-established in the literary field as well as in popular language. The animal couple of breeding-stock/beast of prey is thus in complete accord with the human couple: the man is the prey and the woman the predator, with a deliberate and pointed inversion of the roles sanctioned by tradition, which regularly portrays the man as the consumer and the woman as the consumed. Here, the man represents weakness, passivity and submission, while the woman represents violence, activity and authority. Her power of castration announces itself in the form of a threat, which is in fact a threat of death: "You wait! You just wait, and we'll see what happens! Yes—we'll see—he'll burst like a sack of grain, that great bladder!" It was with these words that the furious old woman used to conclude every quarrel with her husband. And the threat was even more explicit when we consider that the word *crever* which she uses ("ça crevera comme un sac à grain") means to crack as well as to burst. But as if that were not enough, the writer feels the need to introduce death itself in support of the threat, giving it maternal characteristics like those of the woman who breeds, fattens and coddles the man like a child. "Death", he writes, "amused itself by fattening him [Toine], by rendering him monstrous and absurd, by colouring him red and blue; by swelling him and giving him the appearance of superhuman health. And the deformities which it inflicts on all beings become laughable in him, comical and diverting instead of being sinister and harmful." And to avoid any possibility of doubt in his intention of identifying death portrayed as a nursing mother and wife of Toine, he repeats the sinister threat once again: "Let's wait and see, let's just wait and see..." repeats mother Toine: "We'll see what happens".

And the threat begins to become a reality; Toine is struck by a sudden and unforeseen paralysis which reduces him to immobility. The mother-son relationship comes to the fore, and is carried to extremes, as with a mother and her baby. Paralysed in his bed, Toine is cared for by his wife exactly as if he were an infant of a few months old. "Look at him"—the woman shrieks: "look at the great do-nothing, who needs to be fed and washed and cleaned out just like a pig!" Like a pig, because the grotesque element in the situation lies precisely in the substitution of the baby for the castrated man; the wife-mother, in her sterility, is unable to have any son other than her husband, dethroned and reduced to impotence by castration. In his new situation, Toine doesn't lose heart; he is still cheerful even if it has to be "a different kind of cheerfulness, more timid and humble, with all the fears a little baby experiences before its mother". She is not content with having him completely at her mercy; she must continue to treat him badly. However, in compensation he has the sympathy of others, who don't desert him. His wife, who has taken over the running of the café, remains excluded just as before, because the customers soon learn to desert her for the back room where her husband lies waiting for them, unable to move from his bed, but always ready for a laugh and a joke. His former friends begin to visit him again; they keep him company with interminable card-games which drive her into paroxysms of rage. It is at this point that the element of farce enters the story; her excursions into the back room to interrupt the game and drive the friends out annoy them more and more, until the most enterprising of them decides to take revenge on her. He proposes to the woman, who continues to reproach her husband with being a 'good-for-nothing', that she should render him productive by using his natural warmth to hatch the chickens' eggs and thus replenish her beloved chicken-farm with extra supplies of chicks. The first experiment takes place a little later, with ten eggs which the wife arranges under the armpit of the reluctant paralytic. At first he refuses, and it is only the threat, put into effect immediately, that she will not give him any more to eat, that overcomes his resistance. He resigns himself to hatching, though with a very ill will, and on the first attempt he allows himself to be easily distracted from his task; a false movement and five of the ten eggs are reduced to an omelette. The punishment is immediate and vicious; trembling with rage the wife beats him furiously. He is forced to carry out the hatching more carefully, avoiding any movement, because "the old woman ferociously deprived him of his food every time he broke an egg". Thus reduced to the most complete passivity, the man ends up by immersing himself totally in the purely animal function of hatching. He feels himself to be a chicken in all respects, and as such he is in obvious competition with the real chickens which are at the same time hatching another ten eggs in the henhouse. "The old woman went from her chickens to her husband, and from her husband to the chickens in a state of possession; obsessed with her fear for the chicks which were hatching in the bed and in the coop". She could scarcely even distinguish any longer between the man and the chickens.

In effect, this reduction of the man to the level of the animal is carried to the point of reversing the terms of the analogy; it is no longer the man who is like the animal, but the animal which is like the man. The two terms of the metaphor exchange roles, and the position of the man who hatches the eggs comes to resemble that of a pregnant woman about to give birth. When it is revealed that the chicken has only hatched seven eggs, because three have gone bad, Toine is seized by "all the anguish of a woman when she is about to become a mother". But what an explosion of joy on the day when his eggs come to hatch; while the old woman plunges her hand into the bed to take out the chicks "with the careful movements of a midwife", Toine is swollen with pride at this "singular paternity", and talks exultingly of a "splendid baptismal ceremony". He even wants to keep the tenth chick in his bed, "overwhelmed with tenderness for this tiny being to which he had given life". But the old harridan does not allow this; she has understood too late that she has lost, irrevocably, and that her husband has triumphed. The whole village rushes to his bedside and makes it plain to her that he is being given credit for the fertility which is still denied to her.

This is the way the facts are presented. But in this vicious game between the husband and wife and the social group to which they both belong, where does the writer, Maupassant himself, come in? A first clue is offered by his choice of language: the text of the tale is arranged on two strictly hierarchical linguistic planes. One is that of standard French, the other that of dialect—the now largely Frenchified Norman *patois* which, in order to regain its power, resorts to the use of popular parlance. The standard French forms the upper floor, on which the narrative-descriptive part takes place; the indirect description of events. The dialect and the popular language which sustains it on the other hand are reserved for dialogue and direct representation. This is a strict distinction, and only very rarely does it bow to the temptation to bring dialect into the narrative text in standard French. The instances where it does occur are without exception quotations, duly provided with inverted commas and serving only an ornamental function. The 'noble' subject is the writer, the ignoble objects are the peasants. The contrast is even more obvious on the linguistic plane, because as Butler has already observed, dialect and popular language in Maupassant preserve their original poverty, which reproduces spoken dialogue in all its immediacy. These same peasants, who speak in a rough and elementary dialect, are *described* in a literary language clearly follow the ideological aim of distancing and placing the primitive and comic world of the peasants far below the level of the writer and his public. A primitive world, and thus a natural one; natural and therefore animal. Of course the peasants are not actually animals, they merely resemble them: Toine is like the chickens and the pigs, his wife like the birds of prey; the author of the joke, Prosper Horslaville, is like a ferret or a fox. (And there is an interesting exception there because Maupassant excluded from his bestiary any animal with even the slightest touch of nobility. There are no turtle doves or peacocks; only chickens and owls can be used in any analogy with the peasantry.)

A second element of judgement emerges from the atmosphere of warm sympathy which surrounds the hero in the text; the victim of castration. There is a complete reversal of the tradition which poured profound contempt on the husband dethroned and dominated by his wife. Maupassant takes no account at all of this tradition, and presents Toine to us as being at all times in perfect harmony with his village, of which in the end he becomes the veritable hero. As victim of castration but not of mockery, Toine is virtually rehabilitated by his misfortune, and it is only his wife who remains buried away in the ghetto of her long-standing alienation.

It is clear enough, then, where Maupassant stands: he is for the town, not the country; for the man and not the woman, and in the final analysis, he is on the side of his own bourgeois reading public.

It is there that he finds the woman-castrator, in the same social milieu as Sigmund Freud would find her not long after. Already present in various of his mature writings, the castrating woman really takes centre stage in the 1924 article *The Twilight of the Oedipus Complex*: "When the child (of male sex) has turned his interest towards his own genital organs, he often displays this interest by playing frequently with them by hand, and he is then forced to come up against the fact that adults do not approve of this conduct. More or less clearly, with greater or lesser brutality, the threat arises that they seek to take away from him this part which has come to have such great value for him. More often than not the threat of castration comes from women; they often seek to reinforce their authority by appealing to his father or to the doctor who—as they assure him—will carry out the punishment".

The woman who threatens castration is obviously the mother, who, within the intimacy of family life, becomes the deadly instrument of the establishment order as far as castration is concerned, with the authoritative support of medical science. For as Freud himself notes, it is the doctor who condemns infant masturbation, and advises the mother to repress it with great severity in the name of the child's health: sexuality is not only sinful, but it is also harmful. It must therefore be suppressed from infancy, even in its first infantile manifestations, i.e. masturbation, which medicine proclaims to be an undoubted cause of madness. The incredible story of the association between masturbation and madness was recently recounted by Thomas Szaaz, in a chapter of his book *The Manipulators of Madness*. Here it suffices to stress that the pseudo-scientific notion of masturbation leading to madness is correctly identified there as a mere appearance in a new guise of the ancient christian prohibition of any form of sexuality ('The supposition about masturbation is merely the traditional Christian ethic translated into the language of modern medicine'). Thus we come to see that the first victim of Christian castration, the woman who carries within her the deepest wounds of sexual repression, becomes its most insidious agent in bourgeois society, with the complicity of the medical profession. The theory of the thorn, expounded by Canetti in *Mass and Power*, thus receives another disturbing confirmation. "The power of the mother over her child during the first stages of its existence is absolute, not only because the life of the child depends on that of the mother, but also because the mother experiences the strongest possible need to exercise that power constantly". The child, in effect, helps her "to bear a little of the weight of the ancient orders from which every civilised being suffers". It is of this figure of the mother-castrator that Maupassant is speaking: the bourgeois writer exorcises the ghost which haunts his public by projecting it (according to a well-known literary device) into a different and distant world—the rough and 'natural' world of the peasantry.

But at this point we may well ask: did the Norman writer have any direct knowledge of the theme of the Pregnant Man in its dual tradition—that of folklore and that of literature? In all probability he knew both, in versions which were quite close to the text of his own tale. *Toine* was published for the first time in the magazine *Gil Blas* on 6th January 1885. Two years earlier, in 1883, had appeared the first volume of the great collection of folklore texts, *Kryptádia*, which contains the French translation of the Russian fable collected in his day by Afanassiev, *The husband on the eggs*:

Once upon a time there was a mujik and his wife; the mujik was lazy, but his wife was hard-working. She cultivated the land while her husband just leaned on the stove. One day when she had gone to work in the fields, the mujik, who stayed behind in the house to look after the place and tend the chickens, didn't bother to do anything at all, and the crows came and took all the chicks. A little brooding hen in the courtyard managed to escape and came squawking for his help, but what did he care? It didn't matter to him. The peasant's wife came back home and said to him: "Where are the chicks?" "Well, wife—I've been so unlucky. I went to sleep, and the crows came and took the lot"— "Ah, what a blow! Now, you son of a bitch, you sit on the eggs yourself and hatch the chicks out". The following day she went off to the fields, while the mujik, to keep the eggs from the crow, settled in the loft, took his drawers down, and crouched over the eggs. But the woman was no fool; she borrowed a cloak and a shako from a soldier on leave, disguised herself and when she got to the house, she shouted at the top of her voice: "Hey there, boss, where are you?" The mujik dashed out of the loft and fell to the ground along with the eggs. "So what are you doing?" "Soldier, little father, I'm guarding the house". "Don't you have a wife?" "Oh, I do, but she's working in the fields". "And why are you staying at home, then?" "I'm hatching the chickens". "Ah, you son of a bitch" And the soldier thrashed him with all his might with a whip, saying: "You shouldn't be staying at home hatching chicks, you should be working on the land, tilling the soil!" "I will, little father; I'll work, I swear to God, I'll work". "You're lying, you villain!" And the woman beat him again, and again. Then she lifted up her leg and said: "Look here, son of a bitch, I was in a battle, and I received this wound. What do you think—will it heal or not?" The mujik looked at his wife's c..., and said "It will heal, little father!" The woman went out, put her woman's clothes back on and returned to the house. The mujik was sitting there, sighing and groaning. "What are you groaning about?" "A soldier came here and beat me hard with a whip". "Why did he do that?" "He ordered me to work". "You should have been doing that a long time ago! It's a pity I wasn't at home, I would have begged him to whip you harder". "The one good thing is that he'll die soon". "Why so?" "He's been in a battle, and he got it right between the thighs...he showed me his wound, and he said "Will it get better?", and I told him, yes it'll heal, but it's all red and he'd put moss all round it!" Ever since that time the mujik has started to work hard, and he goes off to labour while his wife looks after the house.

The resemblances between these two texts are close, but in fact, the differences are more interesting and we should examine them more closely. Both the Russian fable and Maupassant's story are dedicated to the castration anxiety and the conjugal relations which result from it. However, the fable presents a diametrically opposed version to that of the short story. While in the latter, the woman is the implacable agent of castration, in the former she undergoes its devastating effects, reacts decisively and finally frees her husband from the anxiety which paralyses him. The mujik takes refuge in the passivity of the female role to defend himself from the danger of castration to which he is convinced the male role exposes him. But the woman does not in fact accept the male role which her husband forces her to adopt; she rebels and brings the situation back to its natural state. First she obliges her husband to hatch the eggs, in the hope that this punishment will induce him to react in a virile way. Then, when she sees that he accepts even this with his usual passivity, she resorts to more energetic means. She dresses as a soldier—i.e. assumes the guise of the most forceful of men—then she makes clear to her husband the absurd inversion of roles which is dominating their common life, and finally she attacks him with a whip, forcing a promise out of him that he will immediately reassume his masculine role.

The use of the whip calls up a ghost which haunted the pages of the illustrated magazines of the Belle Epoque in vignettes, finding a place even in that Chamber of Horrors, Krafft-Ebing's *Psychopathia Sexualis*. The image is that of the Russian peasant's wife who could not live without constant whippings from her husband. But the mujik does not react to the whipping like Krafft-Ebing's masochist; he does not enjoy the beating at all, and sits there groaning; to such an extent that his wife takes pity on him, and changes to the opposite approach. Now she shows him her sex, presenting it to him as a wound received in battle, and asks him if it will get better. The mujik looks at his wife's fanny and says: "It will heal, little father". In other words he has recognised his wife, and his reply has the effect of a confirmation of his previous promise, which his later declaration further reinforces: the soldier will die means that the wife will no longer need to put his uniform on to whip her husband again. She will not need to because he will return to his work in the fields, as the fable states in its conclusion.

Freud says in the work which we have already mentioned, that the maternal menace of castration achieves the desired result with the child only after he has been able to see the female genitalia, which act as a confirmation. They look to him like a wound inflicted by the mutilation of the penis. The woman in our fable shows her husband her 'wound', to take him back to the origins of his fear, but the intention is apotropaic. We know that in the context of magic, the exhibition of the vulva had the aim of exorcism. Freud mentions the passage from Rabelais in this connection (IV.47), in which the wife of the peasant puts the devil which is plaguing him to flight by showing him her vulva and presenting it as a wound. Rabelais' story has certainly a folklore origin, and it helps us to understand that the wife in the fable by showing her vulva is seeking to free her husband from the devil—i.e. from the illness which possessed him and forced him into passivity. However, her gesture has another significance; equally undeniably it is an offer of sex. The wife is seeking to tell her husband that for the man, the only way to save his penis from the threat of castration is by giving it a home in the vulva, as Freud puts it. But this is also the only way for the woman (again according to Freud) to regain the phallus which she believes she has lost as a result of maternal castration. Thus the fable shows that it has a basically therapeutic intention: the wife frees her husband from castration anxiety, because she too suffers from this anxiety, and in curing him she cures herself.

The fable of the man who hatched the eggs remains true to this 'anti-castration' intention in two French versions collected in Picardy at the end of the last century. The first, *La femme couveuse*s published in 1884 in the second volume of the same collection known as *Kryptádia* says:

A grocery woman once had a duck. She took a dozen eggs, put them in a basket without worrying, and put the duck on them to hatch them out. Everything was fine until one morning she came and found the duck dead on the eggs which were still warm. "What a misfortune!" she cried: "Another day and the ducklings would have been born. If I sit on them instead of the duck, that will be a good idea!" And she lifted up her skirts and crouched over the eggs. An hour later, one of her neighbours came in. "Good morning, good woman. Give me a pound of sugar". "Good morning neighbour. I fear I can't serve you; my duck died, and I am hatching the eggs in its place. I can't move from here". "Don't worry about that; I'll sit on them for a few minutes in your place". The man slipped down his drawers, crouched down and covered them with his shirt. The grocery woman prepared the sugar he had asked for, then, as she passed her hand under the man's shirt to see whether the eggs were well-warmed, she seized the man's member and exclaimed: "My God! It can't be duck's eggs I've been sitting on to hatch; they are hatched already—I'm holding one by the neck; they must surely be goslings!"

The second version of the fable reaches the same conclusion. Here too the woman triumphantly grabs the penis of the man who is hatching the eggs, thus contradicting the passivity which the position normally would imply.

It is very likely that Maupassant had read the Russian fable, or at least the first French version. But while he may have read it, he read it in his own way, or rather with the eyes of his bourgeois readers, and not without a glance backward to Boccaccio, who had something to teach him as well. The scheme of the trick which is present in *Toine* is missing from the Russian version, and it sends us back to the tale of

Calandrino. The *Decameron* was well-known to French readers of the last century, and it cannot be ruled out that a writer like Maupassant was aware of it. As a matter of fact, when a Paris publisher revived the idea of a collection of short stories entitled *Nouveau Decameron* 1884, planning ten volumes, Maupassant was among the writers who supported the initiative with greatest enthusiasm, contributing ten stories, one for each volume-day. This collaboration certainly seems to suggest a sort of ideal affinity with the father of European narration, whose attitude towards christianity, moreover, he strongly shared. It is now an accepted critical opinion, from the most traditionalist such as P. Cogny to the most modern and even over-presumptuous or technicist, such as Greymas, that behind the apparent atheism of the kind which was deemed suitable for fashionable writers of the de-christianised France of the Third Republic, there continued to lurk the old Christian mythology.

"Devoid of his own ideas and of judgment", Alberto Savinio astutely remarked, "Maupassant makes his own the notion of the rehabilitated prostitute, as he makes his own the hypocrisy of the priests, the sky devoid of God, all the ideas which nourished the 'neo-enlightened' France of those days". It was the simplest formula for becoming a writer and being sold on railway stations, and for seeing one's books rolling off the fast and generous presses of the great publishing houses, and finding a place on the shelves of the book-trolleys which did the rounds of the great stations". It is clear that the bourgeois readership which guaranteed the writer his astonishing success had as much Christianity in its head as Maupassant could produce with his pen. Perhaps the *Decameron*, the great short-story collection of the Christian middle ages, was not included in the Index of prohibited books and condemned by the Church of the Counter-Reformation to constant new purged and repurged editions?

Versions of the Story of The Pregnant Man in Order of Appearance

PART I

1. Iconographical representations of the birth of Eve not reproduced in this book can be found in the works of : J. KIRCHENER: *Die Darstellung des ersten Menschenpaares*, Stuttgart, 1903, and L. RÖHRICH: *Adam und Eva. Das erste Menschenpaar in Volkskunst und Volksdichtung*, Stuttgart 1968, and in articles by R. KEKULÉ: *Über die Darstellung der Erschaffung der Eva, in Jahrbuch des Kaiserlichen Deutschen Archäologischen Instituts*, V (1890), pp.186–209, and by R. ZAPPERI: *Potere politico e cultura figurativa: la rappresentazione della nascita di Eva, in Storia dell'Arte italiana*, X, Turin, 1981, pp.377–442.

2. All the documents concerning the Pregnant Man of Monreale were collected by Giuseppe PITRÉ in his volume of Sicilian tales, *Fiabe novelle e racconti popolari siciliani*, IV, Palermo, 1875, pp.143–144.

3. The original texts in Sicilian and Tuscan dialects of the two stories, *Le cafard* and *Le prêtre enceint* were published by Pitré in his collections *Fiabe e leggende popolari siciliane*, Palermo, 1888, pp.297–299, and *Novelle popolari toscane*, I, Palermo, 1885, pp.326–328.

PART II

1. For the Latin text of the Aesopic fables, *Le voleur et l'escarbot* and *Le médecin, le riche et la fille*, I have based my version on the latest edition by B.C. PERRY: *Aesopica. A series of texts relating to Aesop or ascribed to him or closely connected with the literary tradition that bears his name*, Urbana, 1952, pp.671 and 682.

5. The story *How the fox received his name* was translated from the Danish version found in A. CHRISTENSEN: *Dumme Folk. Danske skaemte aventyr i international belysning*, Copenhagen, 1941, pp.31–32.

6. The references to the German and Finnish stories of the pregnant protestant pastor are given below. The French translation of the Russian story *The tale of a priest who gave birth to a calf* was published in *Kryptádia: Recueil de documents pour servir à l'étude des traditions populaires*, I. Heilbronn, 1883, pp.101–105.

7. The Finnish text of the story called *The master who went looking for a servant*, still unpublished, is preserved in Helsinki in the Finnish Folklore Archives: Suomalaisen Kirjallisuuden Seura, ms Lindqvist a 100.

8. The three Finnish variants, also unpublished, *The servant without balls, the priest's accouchement*, and *a story without a title*, are also preserved in the same Archives, ms Ojansuna 13; ms. V K 9, Eklöf 2; ms V K 115, no 163. The French translation of the Russian tale *La peigne* was published in the collection *Kryptádia* mentioned above, I, pp.142–147.

9. For the text of *L'Ysopet* by Marie de France, I have used the critical edition of Karl WARNKE: *Die Fabeln der Marie de France*, Halle, 1898, pp.138–141 and 142–144.

11. The English translation of the Hebrew version of the first Aesopic fable *(A sick man, his daughter, a physician)* can be found in *Fables of a Jewish Aesop*, New York and London 1967, pp.147–149, translation by Moses HADAS.

12. There is a good edition of the Weltchronik by Ph. STRAUCH, *Monumenta Germaniae Historica*, and Jansen Enikels Werke in *Deutsche Chroniken III*, Hanover and Leipzig, 1900, pp.274–286.

13. The Chronicle of John, Bishop of Nikium, was translated into French by H. ZOTENBURG (Paris, 1893, p.290). The Gloss of PAPIAS is to be found in *Corpus Glossatorum Latinorum*, edited by G. GOETZ, V Leipzig 1894, p.655; I, Leipzig 1923, pp.182, 386, 389. The *Graphia Aurea Urbis Romae* is in P.E. SCHRAMM, H. de BOOR: *Die Deutsche Literatur, Mittelalter, Texte und Zeugnisse*, II, Munich 1970, pp.938–942. For the text of the story *Gargantua* by Johann FISCHART, reference should be made to the edition of A. ALSLEBEN, Halle, 1886, pp.350–351. The legend of Nero is found on pp.448–455 of the edition of JANSEN's *Weltchronik* cited above. Gottfried KELLER took it up again in his novella, entitled *Regine: Sämtliche Werke*, edited J. FRÄNKEL, XI, Bern and Leipzig, 1934, pp.93–96. For the *Golden Legend* of Jacques de VORAGINE, see the French translation by T. de WYZEWA, Paris 1902, pp.314–321. The collections in which the exemplum of Nero pregnant appears are

indicated in the work of F.C. TUBACH: *Index exemplorum. A Handbook of Medieval Religious Tales, FF Communications* No. 204, Helsinki, 1969, p. 53, no 645. For Higden, see *Polychronicon Ranulphi Higden Monachi Cestrensis,* edited J. HAWSON, IV, Lumby, 1872, pages 394–398. For Jean d'Outremeuse, see Jean des PREIS di d'OUTREMEUSE, *Chronique,* ed. A. BORGNET, I, Brussels 1864, pp.458, 469–471.

15. The text in Middle High German of the verse tale *The Monk's Pains* by ZWINGÄUER can only be found in the ancient edition of Friedrich Heinrich von der HAGEN, *Gesamtabenteuer,* II Stuttgart and Tübingen, 1880, pp.53–69. The translation into modern German by Ulrich PRETZEL (*Deutsche Erzählungen des Mittelalters,* Munich 1971, pp.206–214) is defective. The German story entitled *The Pregnant Pastor* is still unpublished, and is preserved in the German Folklore Archives at Marburg an der Lahn (Zentralarchiv der Volkserzählungen: M. 537). The original text in Middle-High German of the verse tale *The Pregnant Miller* was published by A. von KELLER: *Erzählung aus altdeutschen Handschriften,* Stuttgart, 1853, pp.463–470. Hanns FISCHER has provided a good translation into modern German: *Schwankerzählung des Deutschen Mittelalters,* Munich 1967, pp.115–120.

17. There is no modern edition of the sermon of GIORDANO DI PISA. I have therefore had to take my text from the ancient edition: *Prediche del Beato Fra Giordano da Rivalto,* Florence, 1739, p.200. For the original text of the BOCCACCIO novella, we now have the critical edition of Aldo ROSSI: *Il Decameron,* Bologna, 1977, pp.481–483. There are several editions of Tuscan translations of the two Aesopic fables: *Volgarizzamento delle favole di Esopo. Testo riccardiano inedito,* ed. Luigi RIGOLI, Florence, 1818, pp.78–79 and 106–107; *Favole di Esopo in volgare. Testo di lingua inedito dal codice palatino,* Lucca, 1864, pp.83–84; *Il volgarizzamento delle favole di Galfredo dette di Esopo,* edited G. GHIVIZZANI, II, Bologna 1866, pp.191–193 and 231–233; *Libro di novelle antiche tratte da diversi testi del buon secolo della lingua,* Fratelli ZAMBRINI, Bologna 1868, pp.90–91.

PART III

1. The droll story by BEBEL entitled: *Of a Certain Monk* was translated initially in the critical edition of G. BEBERMEYER: *Heinrich Bebels Facetien,* II, Leipzig, 1931, p.99. The Finnish tale is the variant (b), *L'accouchement du prêtre,* of section 8 of the second part.

2. The texts which Hans SACHS took from the Boccaccio Novella can be found in the edition of A. von KELLER and E. GOETZ:

Werke, V, Tübingen, 1870, pp.126–128; *ibid.* XXI, 1892, pp.62–75 (the farce: *Le paysan enceint du poulain.*)

3. The Danish tale entitled *The Man-eating Calf* is reproduced in the collection by CHRISTENSEN mentioned above, pp.29–31. The German tale entitled *The Carter* has been published by Karl WEIGAND in *Zeitschrift für die Deutsche Mythologie*, I (1853), pp.36–46. The verse tale *Le meunier enceint* has already been mentioned in no. 16 of Part II. The tale *Le conte du tailleur qui a eu un veau* is preserved in the German Folklore Archives (Zentralarchiv der deutschen Volkserzählung), no. 157, 495.

4. The novella by Nicholas of Troyes was published for the first time by Emile Mabille in 1869. There is now a critical edition by Krystine KASPRZYK: *Le grand parangon des nouvelles nouvelles*, Paris 1970, pp.40–48. For the farce, *Le médecin et le badin*, it is necessary to consult the old edition by LEROUX DE LINCY and François MICHEL: *Recueil de farces, moralités et sermons joyeux*, II, Paris, 1837, pp.1–30. For Jörg Wickram's droll story, reference should be made to the critical edition of Johannes BOLTE, *Rollwagenbüchlin*, Tubingen, 1903, pp.11–13. This refers in turn to the collection *Kurzweilige und lächerliche Geschichten*, Frankfurt, 1583, p.530, and to the Dutch translation which is to be found in *Groot klugtboeck*, Amsterdam, 1680. p.147. The tale by Hans SACHS was published by E. GOETZ and K. DRESCHER: *Sämtliche Fabeln und Schwänke*, VI, Halle, 1913, pp.230–232; that of Ludovico Carbone is found in the edition of A. SALZA: *Facezie*, Livorno, 1900, pp.62–63.

15. According to Victor CHAUVIN: *Bibliographie des ouvrages arabes*, V, Liège and Leipzig, 1901, p.184, the Arabic story *(Le Cadi avare)* can be found in the French translation of the *Thousand and One Nights* by Edouard GAUTTIER (VII, Paris 1823, pp.393 ff) but it has been impossible for me to confirm this. I have based my version on the English translation *The story of the Kazi who bore a Babe* by Richard F. BURTON, *Supplemental Nights to the Book of the Thousand Nights and a Night*, IV, Benares, 1887, pp.169–185.

16. The Picard tale, *Le chariot dans le ventre du curé*, is to be found in the previously mentioned collection *Kryptádia*, II, Heilbronn, 1884, pp.123–126.

18. I have read MAUPASSANT's Novella, *Toine*, which gives its title to the collection, in the 1886 edition. The Russian tale of the *Husband hatching the eggs* is found in the collection *Kryptádia*, mentioned previously, I, pp.55–57, as are the French stories entitled *La femme couveuse* (II pp.155–156), and *Couveuse* (X, Paris 1907, pp.22–25).

Select Bibliography

PART I

1. Georges DUBY: *Le chevalier, la femme et le prêtre. Le marriage dans le France féodale*, Paris, 1981; Edmund R. LEACH: *Genesis as Myth*, London 1962; Claude LEVI-STRAUSS: *Les structures élémentaires de la parenté*, Paris 1947; Theodor REIK: *The Creation of Woman*, New York 1960; J.A. BARNES: *Genetrix: Genitor: Nature: Culture?* in J. GOODY: *The Character of Kingship*, London 1973, pp.61–73.
2. R. SCHENDA: *Folklore e letteratura popolare: Italia–Germania–Francia* (Italian translation, Rome 1986, pp.279–287)
4. Vladimir PROPP: *Morphologie du conte*, French translation Paris 1970.

PART II

1. E. JONES: Essays in Applied Psychoanalysis, II; *Essays in Folklore, Anthropology and Religion*, London 1951.
2. Claude LEVI-STRAUSS: *Structure et dialectique in Anthropologie structurale*, Paris 1958; Georges DUMEZIL: *Les dieux des Germains*, Paris 1959; Folke STRÖM: *Loki. Ein mythologisches Problem*, Göteborg 1956.
4. Georges DUBY: *Les trois ordres ou l'imagination du féodalisme*, Paris 1978; Evelyn PATLAGEAN: L'histoire de la femme deguisée en moine et l'évolution de la sainteté féminine a Byzance, in *Studi medievali*, 3rd series, Vol XVII (1976), pages 597–623.
6. Petr BOGATYREV & Roman JAKOBSON: Le folklore, forme spécifique de la création, in R. JAKOBSON: *Questions de poétique*, French translation, Paris 1973, pp.59–72; Jacques LE GOFF: Culture ecclésiastique et culture folklorique au Moyen Age: Saint Marcel de

Paris et le Dragon, in *Pour un autre Moyen Age. Temps, travail et culture en Occident: 18 essais,* Paris 1977, pp.236–279.

8. Michel FOUCAULT: *Surveiller et punir. Naissance de la prison,* Paris 1975; Jacque Le GOFF: Culture cléricale et traditions folkloriques dans la civilisation mérovingienne, in *Pour un autre Moyen Age,* op. cit. pp.223–235.

13. R.M. FRAZER: *Nero the Singing Admiral in Arethusa,* 4 (1971), pp.215–218; Emile BENVENISTE: *Le vocabulaire des institutions indo-européens,* Paris 1969.

14. Sigmund FREUD: über Triebumsetzungen insbesondere der Analerotik in *Studienausgabe* VII; *Zwang, Paranoia und Perversion,* Frankfurt am Main, 1973, pp.125–131; Georges DEVEREUX: Institutionalised Homosexuality of the Mohave Indians, in *Human Biology,* IX (1937), pp.498–527; Sandor FERENCZI: Zur Nosologie der männlichen Homosexualität (Homoerotik), in *Bausteine zur Psychoanalyse,* I, Bern, 1964; Theodore REIK: *Ritual in Psychoanalytical Studies,* New York 1946.

16. Ladislao MITTNER: *Storia della letteratura tedesca,* I, Turin 1977; Erich KOHLER: *Trobadorlyrik und höfischer Roman,* Berlin 1962; Jacques Le GOFF: Métiers licites et métiers illicites dans l'Occident mediéval, in *Pour un autre Moyen Age,* op. cit. pp.91–107; Emile BENVENISTE: De la subjectivité dans le langage, in *Problèmes de linguistique générale,* Paris, 1966, pp.258–266; Hanns FISCHER: *Studien zur deutschen Märendichtung,* Tübingen 1968; Gerhard KÖPF: *Märendichtung,* Stuttgart, 1978; H.F. ROSENFELD: Der Zwingäuer, in *Die deutsche Literatur des Mitelalters. Verfasserlexikon,* published Karl LANGOSCH, IV, Berlin, 1953, columns 1169–1171.

17. Carlo MUSCETTA: Giovanni Boccaccio, in *La letteratura italiana. Storia e testi. Il trecento,* II, Bari, 1971.

18. Paul VEYNE: La famille et l'amour sous le Haut Empire romain, in *Les jardins d'Adonis. La mythologie des aromates en Grèce,* Paris, 1972; Sarah B. POMEROY: *Goddesses, whores, wives and slaves,* New York, 1975; J.-T. NOONAN: *Contraception: A History of the Treatment of Catholic Theologians and Canonists,* Cambridge, Mass. 1965. Peter WEBB: *The erotic arts,* London 1975; Anka MUHLSTEIN: *La femme Soleil. Les femmes et le pouvoir. Une relecture de Saint-Simon,* Paris 1976.

PART III

1. Denise PAULME: *Le mère dévorante. Essai sur la morphologie des contes africains,* Paris 1976.

6. François JACOB: *La logique du vivant. Une histoire de l'hérédité,*

Paris 1976; Jean-Louis FLANDRIN: *Familles. Parenté, maison, sexualité dans l'ancienne société*, Paris, 1976; Jacques ROSSIAUD: Prostitution, jeunesse et société dans les villages du Sud-Est au XV siècle, in *Annales* XXXI (1976), pp.289–325; Sigmund FREUD: Die Kulturelle sexualmoral und die moderne Nervosität, in *Studienausgabe*, IX, pp.13 ff.

7. Sigmund FREUD: Charakter und Analerotik, in *Studienausgabe* VII, pp.25 ff.; Elvio FACHINELLI: *Il bambino dalle uova d'oro*, Milan 1974; Sigmund FREUD: über infantile Sexualtheorien in *Studienausgabe* V, pp.171 ff.

9. Pierre DARMON: *Le myth de la procréation à l'âge baroque*, Paris 1977.

12. A.S.G. BUTLER: *Les parlers dialectaux et populaires dans l'oeuvre de Guy de Maupassant*, Geneva–Paris, 1962; Sigmund FREUD: Der Untergang des Ödipuskomplexes, in *Studienausgabe*, V, pp.244 ff.; Thoms SZAAZ: *The Manufacture of Madness*, New York 1970; P. COGNY: *Maupassant. L'homme sans Dieu*, Brussels, 1968; A.-J. GREIMAS: *Maupassant.* La sémiotique du texte: exercises pratiques, Paris 1976; Alberto SAVINIO: Maupassant et l'autro, Milan 1960; Elias CANETTI: *Masse und Macht*, Hamburg 1960.

Index